Could It Be I'm Falling in **LOVE?**

Eleanor Prescott worked in PR for ten years. She lives in Kent with her husband, son and daughter. *Could It Be I'm Falling in Love?* is her second novel.

You can visit Eleanor at www.eleanorprescott.com and follow her on Twitter @eleanorprescott.

Also by Eleanor Prescott

Alice Brown's Lessons in the Curious Art of Dating

Could it be I'm Falling in Love?

Eleanor Prescott

Quercus

First published in Great Britain in 2013 by

Quercus
55 Baker Street
7th Floor, South Block
London
W1U 8EW

A CIP catalogue record for this book is available
from the British Library

ISBN 978 0 85738 717 2 (PB)
ISBN 978 0 85738 718 9 (EBOOK)

10 9 8 7 6 5 4 3 2 1

Typeset by Ellipsis Digital Limited, Glasgow
Printed and bound in Great Britain by
Clays Ltd, St Ives plc

'It's awful to be famous and then not famous.'

ELTON JOHN

To Gerran and Carrie

ROXY

In the blue-lit nightclub toilet, Roxy peered into the mirror. Several Roxys squinted back. She was a mojito or two drunker than she'd thought. The checklist was going to be tricky tonight. She closed one eye to blot out the extra Roxys. She needed to concentrate – this was important stuff . . .

HAIR. Hah! She didn't need twenty-twenty to know her hair rocked; it was blonder than vanilla ice cream! She clumsily teased the ends with her fingers – missed – and ended up teasing an earring.

MAKE-UP. Tricky – but she could definitely spot some lippy in there. That was one of the benefits of scarlet: maximum beer-goggle visibility. She leant closer to spot anything else.

'Bollocks!'

Her nose bounced painfully off the glass.

Blinking back the pain, she rooted in her handbag for her eyeliner and expertly applied an extra layer. 'Ifinn doubt . . .' she advised the empty loos. She was proud she'd worn make-up every day since she was eleven. She might be too drunk to walk in a straight line, but she wasn't too drunk to draw one.

TEETH. She bared them. Dazzling – just as her dentist had promised.

TAN. She was *loving* this new Winter Clementine! Although – was it her imagination, or was the blue light tingeing her ever so slightly green?

TITS. Well, she could see two, so she wasn't *that* drunk! She delved into her dress, rummaged for a grip and then hoisted her breasts upwards. She plumped them up like St Tropez cushions.

'An' last but not leasss . . .' She bent over and looked up her own skirt. This was always the trickiest bit of the checklist, particularly in heels with a skinful. Many a time she'd wobbled, headbutted porcelain and given her forehead a shiner. But, it was worth it. The mags were *desperate* for cellulite. The newsstands were crammed with pictures of knickers wedged into celebrity bottoms. Last week's *Heat* had had four pages on celebrity waxing under the headline 'Private Stars Go Pubic', and the week before they'd done a montage of famous buttocks, complete with pimples arrowed in pink. It was all very funny, but it had turned getting in and out of a taxi into a minefield. Photographers used to be grateful if you stopped and smiled . . . now they lay on the pavement to get a shot of your arse. Roxy had no problem with her arse being in the papers – but only with apricot airbrushing. A pap-shot definitely didn't qualify.

At last, the checklist was over. Dizzily, Roxy straightened up. She grinned. She looked hot. Hotter than hot – she was Viagra in a mini-dress! She could see her work diary filling itself up already.

She grabbed her iPhone, squinted at the screen, and started tapping.

2.09am @foxyroxy
Fuckme – I ROCKK!! New dresss seriusly fierce. #ROXYSAYS: mustn passany mirrors or I might try2pull me sellf!

She slung her phone back in her bag, pushed through the door of the ladies and strutted unsteadily towards the front door of the club. This would be child's play. OK, so the world had partied itself stupid last night, but the smart girl-about-town partied cleverer. Today was 1st January – officially the deadest night in the celebrity calendar. And if you wanted to shine, you had to make sure you wouldn't be eclipsed. Only amateurs partied large on a Saturday; the big guns waited for Sundays and Bank Holidays.

Just before she stepped outside, she quickly slapped on her sunglasses. She never went anywhere without shades – especially at night. Everyone knew wearing shades out of a nightclub was imperative. In the dark, the flash of the cameras was blinding. It was impossible to breeze past the banks of paparazzi with your cool intact. Instead, the imprint of their flashes seared your retinas so you couldn't see straight, let alone walk straight. Even if you'd stuck to water all night – which, admittedly, in all her years of clubbing, Roxy never had, so this bit of her theory was untested – the paps' flashes still made you look like a bleary-eyed alky. Roxy was a rock 'n' roll kind of gal, but she fancied herself more as a young

Debbie Harry than a wasted Courtney Love. Sexy rebellion was employable. One-drink-from-wipeout was not.

'Evening, lads!' She greeted the waiting paparazzi, and paused dramatically in the doorway for their shots. A collection of miserable-looking blokes, clasping Burger King coffee cups, were chain-smoking in the cold night. They all wore dark-coloured puffa jackets, their cameras on stand-by around their necks.

Photographers always looked grumpy. Must come with spending your life hanging out on street corners, waiting for the beautiful people to finish having fun, Roxy reckoned. She liked to be one of the lads with the paps. It wasn't good to be untouchable. Nobody liked a celeb who was stuck up their own arse.

'Slow night?' She sashayed towards them. 'Cheer up! This'll help pay the mortgage!'

She thought she heard someone snigger, but ignored it. It was tougher than it looked – smiling seductively whilst simultaneously rolling your hips, thrusting back your shoulders, dangling your arms three inches from your body *and* sucking in your tummy with more force than the Hadron Collider. Roxy ignored the freezing cold (good for the nipples) and worked it for the cameras. This was what she'd come out for. She vamped everything up to eleven and channelled maximum cool sexy fun.

Damn, these glasses are good, she thought as she strutted past the final photographer. They were so dark she could hardly see the flashes at all!

And then her stilettos scraped to a halt as it hit her.

She couldn't see any flashes because *there were no flashes*.

She quickly span around. No one was looking. All she could see was a row of backs-of-heads as the photographers kept up their surveillance of the club door. There should have been a throng of activity behind her as everyone rushed to their laptops to edit her photos and wire them out to the picture desks. But the night was oddly silent.

Roxy stared in disbelief. She'd just worked the pavement like a stripper, in a dress short enough for the top shelf!

'Anyone got any sweeteners?' one of the photographers asked. 'The wife reckons I need to lose a few pounds.'

'Here.' Someone tossed him a packet of Canderel.

'Cheers, mate.'

He took one and slowly stirred it into his coffee. And then there was silence. Roxy was incredulous. Had they even *seen* her? Should she go back and do her exit again?

'Who was the wino in the glasses?' she suddenly heard someone ask. She quickly scanned the group to see who it was, and whether he was important. He was spotty and looked about sixteen; *an apprentice*, Roxy thought with horror.

'Her? Oh, just Roxy Squires,' somebody answered gruffly.

'*Who?*'

'Before your time, mate. She used to be a TV presenter, years back. Not worth firing a few rounds for now, though. She'll only clog up your hard drive when you're trying to send through shots of a real celeb.'

The apprentice nodded sagely. He thought for a moment.

'What a muppet, wearing sunglasses at night!' he sniggered. 'Desperate, innit?'

Silently, Roxy slipped off her shades. Suddenly she felt ridiculous in her tiny pink dress. And very, very cold. A gust of wind whipped a discarded burger wrapper against her ankle. What was she *doing*? she thought with a lucidity that sliced through the fug of the mojitos. She was coatless and freezing at two in the morning, on a scuzzy London street in sub-zero temperatures, seventy-four miles and a ninety-quid cab ride away from her bed. She had an overwhelming longing for her PJs. Luckily, she spotted a cab and hastily staggered towards it.

As she threw herself into the car, a roar went up and the steps to the nightclub burst into illuminated life. Photographers darted backwards and forwards and the night was filled with the echo of a woman's name as they all shouted for her attention. The street lit up with a hundred flashes, casting long, eerie shadows over buildings. A 'real celeb' was leaving the club.

On the dark side of the street, Roxy shivered.

It was time for a new strategy.

WOODY

The water hit the window with a splat.

Up his ladder, Woody hunched against the elements and rubbed his sponge against the pane, pushing soapy suds into each of the corners. The glass squeaked as he cleaned. He pulled his wiper from his tool belt and swept the suds away. And then he saw her.

She was a classic: satin robe and fluffy, high-heeled slippers; robe held fully open. No underwear, just an immaculately trimmed Brazilian and the best breasts money could buy.

His wiper squeaked to a halt.

She eyeballed him defiantly.

Behind the tenuous security of the windowpane, Woody held his breath and concentrated on keeping his eyes locked on hers. But, even through the blur of peripheral vision, he still couldn't help noticing how her nipples stood aggressively to attention, how her yoga-honed body was sculpture-perfect and how her StairMastered thighs were strong enough to crack walnuts – or any other kind of nut she fancied cracking.

The problem was, she fancied cracking his.

A gust of wind blew a leaf on to Woody's cheek with a slap. But he couldn't move. He knew the drill.

Slowly, her eyes fixed on his, she dropped her robe to the floor and rotated, making sure he got the full three-sixty. A framed photo of her husband and kids on the bedside table swam into view over her shoulder.

Woody knew her type; his round was littered with them. She was the kind of woman who saw shopping as a hunter-gatherer contest, and hired legal teams to get her kids into the right school. She probably hadn't heard the word 'no' in a decade.

Her slow pirouette completed, she locked her eyes back on Woody, daring him to take her; defying him not to.

It always made Woody feel weird when clients did this. He'd never been sure of the etiquette. There wasn't exactly a handbook he could refer to. Was it more polite not to look, or to look? Was it rude to pretend he hadn't noticed? Was it wrong to give a thumbs-up? After all, with a body like that, she'd gone to a lot of effort.

When he'd first moved to Lavender Heath and started window cleaning, hoping for a quiet, simple life, Barry – whose round he'd taken over – had warned him about flashing clients.

'Bold as brass they are, and bloody lovely. They spend all their time in the gym and the hairdresser's, making themselves look perfect, but hubby's too busy at the office to notice. Bored, they are. Not enough appreciation. There's not much good stuff about being a window cleaner: no pension or paid holidays. But at least you get the odd glimpse of muff. Not often, mind; a couple of times a year, if you're lucky. And if you're *really* lucky, they'll follow through on it too. Ask 'em if they want you to clean on the inside. If they say yes, you're on for a full sponge and shammy . . . Mind, I expect you had a lot of that in your old job!'

'Sorry?'

'Tits out; pussy on a plate.'

'Er . . . I suppose so.'

Barry had nodded sagely. 'Clever boy. Well, play your cards right and window cleaning'll keep you in pretty views and extra-marital for life. Although it'll mostly give you chapped hands.'

Woody figured he'd given her long enough.

He snapped back into action. He beamed his best vintage smile, wiped away the last smudge of soap and slowly backed down the ladder, whistling loudly. He'd take his time cleaning the ground-floor windows. That'd give her the chance to get the message and put her clothes back on before he knocked on the front door (definitely not the back) for his money and a chat. It was best to talk, he'd learnt. Otherwise embarrassment set in. Or resentment.

Far from being flashed at once or twice a year, as Barry had promised, Woody was confronted by open robes and geometrically precise bikini lines every month. He always respectfully declined. Some women got angry when he didn't bounce off his ladder and on to their Egyptian-cotton sheets.

Some were actually offended – despite the fact that Woody could look down from his ladder on to their top-of-the-range family four-by-fours, or that their nannies were just returning from the school run. But most were just mortified to be turned down. Many couldn't look him in the eye once they'd wriggled back into their clothes and would immediately set about removing themselves from his round. He couldn't have that. He wanted to keep his clients, and he wanted to keep them happy. He just didn't want to keep them *that* happy.

A quick chat was what was needed. And within ten minutes of the advance.

Woody finished off the French doors before stowing away his wiper and knocking on the front door.

She took a full two minutes to answer; fully dressed, arms folded, eyes locked firmly into the middle distance.

'I'll get your money,' she said frostily, turning away from the door. She returned, and thrust a twenty-pound note in his direction. The servant–master relationship restored, Woody thanked her and let her push the door to.

Just before it closed he said, 'Mrs Barrington-Stanley, I'm deeply flattered, you know . . . And more than a little bit tempted.'

The door froze, neither open nor closed. She was completely shielded behind it.

Woody spoke into the gap. 'It's just that . . . well, I can't. I've given that kind of thing up.'

There was a pause.

'What do you mean?' the door asked uncertainly. 'Are you saying you've given up *sex*?'

'Yep; gone cold turkey – I've given up women. Well, the extra women, I mean.'

'But you can't. You're Woody; you're *The Woodeniser*! The papers said . . .' the door wobbled. 'Oh my God! You said you've given up *women*. I don't believe it! You're . . . Are you telling me you're *gay*?'

Woody rubbed his head. They always seemed to jump to this conclusion.

'But what about all those girlfriends?' the door asked. 'The models? The actresses? Are you telling me they were all . . . what does my daughter call them . . . ? *Beards*?' There was a gasp. 'Oh my God! *Was Petra Klitova a beard?*'

Woody laughed. 'They were all real girlfriends, Mrs Barrington-Stanley. I'm not gay.'

The door opened and she moved into the gap, confused.

'I don't get it. If you're not gay, what's wrong with me? I thought . . . I mean . . . Don't you go for everyone?'

Woody smiled gently. 'There's absolutely nothing wrong with you, Mrs Barrington-Stanley. You're a very beautiful woman. But, well, I've got a girlfriend, you see, and she's lovely. I know what you must have read in the papers, but I've reformed. Not that it's been easy, especially when such temptation's put in my way.'

She visibly softened and leant against the door frame.

'Has it been terribly hard for you?' she asked, concerned. 'Were you one of those sex addicts?'

Woody tried to hide his smile.

'Every day's a test,' he said solemnly. 'Do you want me to do the conservatory and outbuildings as well next time?'

Woody scooped up his ladder and crunched down the long gravel driveway, relieved to get away. He caught sight of a dumpy, middle-aged figure in a duffle coat, scuttling along the pavement. She was clutching a packet of biscuits and a half-eaten bag of crisps.

'Hey, Sue!' he called out.

She jumped, looked up and reddened. She shoved her crisps into her pocket and quickly ran her hand through her hair.

Woody put down his ladder and jogged over.

'You still up for tonight?'

Her blush deepened but she nodded uncertainly. Little bits of crisp wobbled in her hair.

'Don't worry – you'll be great!' he reassured her.

'It's just that, I haven't . . . *you know* . . . for so long.'

'Hey!' He put a consoling arm around her. 'You'll feel great afterwards. Liberated!' He gave her shoulders an encouraging squeeze. 'OK?'

She nodded tightly, looking sick.

'Eight thirty, then – my place?' He pulled away and jogged back to his ladder. He heard the rustle of a crisp packet as Sue watched him go.

ROXY

Was she dead?

Roxy forced one eye to crack open. Daylight surged in, stinging like Chanel N° 5. Quickly, she crunched her eye shut, but it was too late; her senses had woken and, right on cue, her head started banging like an East End nightclub.

Roxy pushed her hand out from under the duvet, crabbed it over to her bedside table and groped for her phone. She found it under last night's knickers. Blearily, she forced out a tweet.

2.30pm @foxyroxy
Bleurgh. Am living proof 2much Veuve=nextday inability to use legs. Head banging. Feet broken. Tongue transplanted while sleeping.

She dropped the phone and groaned. Why hadn't she left herself a pint of water, like any sane person who'd been out on the lash? She wasn't dehydrated – she was *incinerated*. Even her eyelashes were dry! She felt like she'd slept in the tumble dryer. Her blood seemed to have evaporated and she was sure the only stuff left in her veins was forty per cent proof.

Tentatively she placed her hand over her eyes and tried to remember if she had any paracetamol. She resisted the urge to phone for an ambulance (the stomach pumps on *Holby* made her icky). But the Fire Brigade? If cats up trees were emergencies, then why not booze-poisoned blondes? Half a dozen burly firemen in her bedroom were bound to make her feel better. But she didn't ring. She knew the help she needed, and it wasn't from professional beefcake. When faced with adversity, whatever its nature, there was only one thing to do . . . It was time to consult the golden triangle.

Over the years, Roxy had made it her mission to be at the forefront of every cultural zeitgeist and passing trendy fad. She'd had a boho summer, a Dukan diet month and had even flirted with Kabbalah. But one of her lengthier fads had been yoga. Every week for eighteen months she'd forced herself to a Notting Hill class, enslaved by the promise of biceps like Madonna and the tantalising hope that this might be the week she inadvertently placed her mat next to an off-duty TV producer on the lookout for a hot new face to present their next programme. It hadn't worked. By the end of it all she was still Roxy-shaped, and hadn't downward dogged with a single TV exec. All of the standing on one leg had been a complete waste of effort, and if she'd had to endure the instructor urging her one more time to imagine a green triangle, with herself floating in it, weightless, worriless and free, she'd have rolled up her mat and forced him to eat it.

The only green triangle she could ever picture was a giant, seductive Quality Street, and her compulsion to leg it out of the studio and into the nearest confectionery counter was almost intolerable. So she'd substituted the instructor's green triangle for a golden one. And, rather than filling it with herself and her worries, she'd stocked it with a triumvirate of women – three sexy, sassy role models she could call upon whenever she needed help to kick the arse of her problems or bitch-slap away her self-doubt. Sod *Charlie's Angels* – these gorgeous ladies were Roxy's Angels: her oracle of lip-glossed cool.

Summoning every ounce of will in her body, Roxy zoned out her hangover and visualised the golden triangle. Immediately, her throbbing head eased and she was greeted by the pouts of her friends.

Mossy was there, of course, spanning the triangle's bottom left corner like the main stage at Glastonbury festival. With her rock 'n' roll style and God-given ability to make a hangover look sexy, Mossy's place within the triangle was assured. After all, she *had* single-handedly granted women licence to party *and* not give a stuff if their hair needed washing whilst they did it. If Roxy ever needed an outfit – or inspiration to turn any-old-night into a blinder – Mossy was always on hand.

In the bottom right corner was Debbie Harry – circa 1979, and 'Heart Of Glass'. This was when Debs was at the peak of her perfection and cooler than any other human alive! She was the ultimate frontwoman, combining sex, attitude and a perpetual expression of 'so what?'. Roxy might only have been one at the time (although technically she hadn't been born, her showbiz birth year being fluid), but she was sure there couldn't have been a person on the planet who didn't fancy getting dirty with Harry.

And finally – perched at the pinnacle of the triangle – was Hurley.

Some people thought Elizabeth II was the Queen of Great Britain, but Roxy reckoned it was Liz. OK, so she was a bit posh and 'dad-totty', but nobody rocked a white jean quite like Liz Hurley! She'd tried her immaculately manicured hand at everything from acting to modelling, from pig-rearing to celebrity best-friending Pamela Anderson – and made a fragrant success of it all. She'd been a constant high-glamour presence on red carpets for – well – *ever* and, via the power of Estée Lauder alone, had single-handedly halted the aging process. This wasn't to say that Liz's life had always been easy (the call girl, the DNA test, the embarrassment of nabbing a bloke called Shane . . .) but Queen Liz never lost her cool – or her make-up bag – in a crisis.

All this was reason alone for Roxy to love Liz Hurley more than anyone she'd never actually met . . . but it didn't even touch upon the *main* reason why Hurley was the closest thing planet earth had to a goddess: Liz's undeniable genius for lexicon.

Of all the new words to have been accepted into the Oxford English Dictionary – *sexting, jeggings, mankini* – Liz's redefinition of 'civilian' trumped them all. Roxy was a call-a-spade-a-spade kind of girl, and political correctness bored her arse off. So when Liz had split the world into 'celebs' and 'civilians', Roxy had fallen in love. Who cared that the public was outraged . . . Liz had spoken the truth! Celebrities looked better, dressed better and got paid better than civilians. They ate in better restaurants, never had problems hailing cabs and *always* shagged the best-looking person at the party. They weren't ordinary people – they were super people, leading luckier, prettier lives.

'Civilians' instantly catapulted Liz to the top of Roxy's lust list and granted her residency at the peak of the golden triangle. Roxy had always been a lover of mantras, with a catchphrase for every occasion (*If at first you don't succeed . . . Where there's a will there's a way . . . Fame costs . . .*). But if all her other mantras failed, there was one she could always fall back on – the single most important piece of wisdom to live her life by. When Roxy needed answers, she always asked herself this: *What would Liz do?*

So, from beneath the heat of her duvet, Roxy pondered:

What would Liz do if she had a hangover so stonking her brain had begun to dribble out of her ears?

And then the answer hit her. It was obvious, really. Liz would hydrate, hydrate, hydrate. And then she'd do a seventy-two hour cabbage-soup detox, ensuring that the blinds were kept down and her public kept waiting, right up until the moment she was restored to full red-carpet fabulousness and ready to face the cameras again.

Well, that was that, then – decided.

Groaning like a woman of one hundred and three, Roxy

rolled out of bed and on to all fours. The movement made her head pound and her eyes pulsate in their sockets. She took a deep breath. If she crawled really slowly, she could inch down the stairs, into the kitchen and over to the tap in twenty-five minutes. If only that extra thumping in her head would stop. Speaking of which – why had it just got louder? And why were there more bangs than usual? Had her heart begun to echo? Or was it . . . ? Surely not! Oh, bollocking bollocks – *rock off!* Someone was knocking on her door! That wasn't on, that wasn't on at all. Didn't they know what bloody time it was?

SUE

Keys in hand, Sue scuttled up the driveway and threw herself into her hallway. She slammed her front door behind her and then leant against it, her heart palpitating in her chest.

Why had she said yes to tonight? The very thought made her throat go tight.

It wasn't Woody's fault – well, not exactly. He meant well. But would it *really* make her feel better? *That* part of her – the sexy part – was gone. Dead. Buried. Kaput. Wrapped up like fish-and-chip paper and thrown in the bin. Dragging it into the light wouldn't be healing – it would be humiliating!

Tea; that was what she needed. A nice cup of ginseng and a biscuit. She hurried into the kitchen.

Some people turn to alcohol in moments of crisis, but Sue had always preferred tea and biscuits. Over the years she'd discovered that there was a flavour of tea and variety of biscuit for every problem in life. Making a perfect tea–biscuit match was like alchemy – a science – and Sue was a dedicated student. For instance, a trip to the supermarket never seemed as daunting after a vitalising pot of Lapsang Souchong and a

Garibaldi. The prospect of a phone call to a utility helpdesk was eased by a pre-emptive cup of lavender and a ginger snap. And the trauma of having to scuttle past the photographers who sometimes camped at the end of her driveway, by the gate to that Hollywood actor's house, could only be soothed by a calming Earl Grey and some shortbread. But tonight . . . ? That required something special: a large pot of ginseng and the most powerful pinnacle of the biscuiting world – a packet of Marks & Spencer's Extremely Chocolatey Dark Chocolate Rounds.

Still wearing her coat, she flicked on the kettle, opened the biscuit tin and started to power-eat.

As she hastily shoved a second biscuit into her mouth, she remembered that Woody had asked her to bring some old photos. God knew why. It would only add insult to injury, but she couldn't let him down. She might as well bring her scrapbook, although the idea made her throat close even tighter. She had to swallow really hard to get the biscuit down.

Sue had a strange relationship with her scrapbook. It was like a sore she couldn't stop scratching. She still looked at it every day. It was her daily dose of self-flagellation: an ongoing self-administered torture to remind her of the embarrassment and shame, and that nasty feeling of something precious being taken from her, which still wouldn't go away. Over the years the scrapbook had made her feel many negative things, but nowadays, if she was being honest, what it made her feel most was *fat*.

The kettle came to the boil. She poured the water on to the tea leaves and reached for another biscuit. As she munched, she miserably looked down at her middle, crushed against the kitchen cabinet. Although hidden under loose black layers, she could still feel her tummy splodging over the rim of her knickers like a huge rubber ring of flab. A flashback of her perfectly-proportioned former figure swam before her. Why had she ever thought she needed to lose weight? She must have been mad! She'd lived on a self-imposed diet of black coffee, cigarettes and Ryvita, but there'd been nothing of her. And, as everyone from the milkman to her mother had seen, her curves had been in all the right places.

Sue eyed the remnants of the Extremely Chocolatey Dark Chocolate Rounds, their crumbs spread across her copy of *The Times*. She couldn't believe she'd finished the packet so quickly – her tea wasn't yet brewed!

Tonight was going to be terrible.

It wasn't *just* having to reveal all the intimate things she'd spent so many years trying to hide. It was that inevitable moment when Woody would look up from the scrapbook and see her as she was now, and that brief glimmer of marvel would die. She didn't need to be a psychologist to read his face. There'd be a split second and then he'd force his expression back to normal, and Sue would want to slink home, never to set foot out of her front door again.

And that wasn't even the worst bit. The worst bit was doing it in front of Cressida.

Sue's heart beat even faster and her armpits started to prickle. She threw off her coat and flapped at her dress, trying to put air in its folds.

Oh, Woody – why did you have to be so nice? She'd just begun to enjoy their Thursday evenings. But then he'd brought Cressida, with her stiff upper lip. Sue had felt her disapproval and heard her barely-audible tuts, and Thursdays with Woody had never been the same.

And now there was *this*.

Sue suddenly realised she was pacing her kitchen. She needed to calm down and breathe, otherwise she might not make the meeting at all – and then what would Woody think? She fixed her eyes beyond the biscuit crumbs, to *The Times* underneath. The crossword was peeking out. She loved crosswords; they were one of the few things she was actually good at. It didn't matter what you looked like doing crosswords. And if you had your paper delivered, you didn't even have to leave the house! She exhaled deeply and tried to block out her panic. Twelve across: *Noun. Acclivity, incline (8).* Something, something, *A*, something, something, *E*, something, something.

ROXY

'Bloody hell! What are *you* doing here?'

Roxy clung to her front door, goggle-eyed.

The man on her doorstep laughed, rubbed his head and looked embarrassed.

'I always come now. Every other Thursday, between one and three. It's just you're normally still in bed.'

'That's not what I meant, and you know it!' Roxy took a deep breath. She'd never had a hangover so bad she'd hallucinated! She blinked hard. But when she opened her eyes he was still there. 'Jeez, I used to *love* you,' she blurted. 'I mean, really *love* you. I had a fight with my best mate on the school bus over who was going to marry you first.'

She looked him up and down and tried to take in the vision of her wildest teenage yearning standing on her doorstep with a bucket. And then a thought struck her: *wasn't absinthe supposed to be mind-altering?* She should never have done all those shots.

'Are you seriously telling me *you're* my window cleaner?'

'Yep! Have been for the last three years. Thanks for leaving the money in the plant pot, by the way.'

'I didn't . . . I mean . . . *Woody's Windows* . . . I never put two and two together. I might have to go and sit down – put my head between my knees. You can't be a window cleaner – you're—'

'Woody. But we've all got to eat.'

'Well, come in then.' Roxy staggered dizzily along the hallway to the kitchen. She motioned wordlessly towards the kettle. Through the double fog of hangover and shock, a clear thought popped into her head . . . Woody – the man who'd adorned her teenage bedroom walls – was standing in her kitchen . . . and she hadn't brushed her teeth! She probably reeked of booze, was no doubt sporting last night's mascara somewhere next to her nose, and she hadn't even got a bra on! The one and only time a certified love god knocked on her door, and she had to go and answer it with saggy Wonder Woman pyjamas and tramp's breath. Liz would be appalled. Liz would've made him wait outside until she'd at least powdered, spritzed and gargled; but it was too late now.

'Cuppa?' she tried to sound casual and keep her breath short.

'Got any herbal?'

'Tea?'

'What did you think I meant?'

'I dunno . . . Something a bit more rock 'n' roll?'

'I'd fall off my ladder!' Woody laughed.

Roxy forgot about the kettle and gawped. Even after all these years, he was still totally and utterly gorgeous. In fact, he seemed to have done a Gazza Barlow and got even more gorgeous than before! *How old must he be now?* she wondered. *Thirty-six?* He was certainly more rugged than she remembered – although, thinking about it, he'd barely been out of school when he'd hit the big time. Woody had always been bronzed, but now he had one of those natural all-weather tans you couldn't get from a bottle. And his body looked good: a real man's body – strong from doing real work, rather than just working out. He was still blond, but his hair was darker, scruffier – less gelled. Actually, she clocked with surprise, it looked gell-*less*. In fact, there seemed to be a complete lack of any hair product at all. She hastily ran her eyes over his body. He'd lost his signature white vest, but that wasn't a bad thing. And his chest was still . . . mmmm; his chest was *good*. Despite the fact that it was January 2nd and probably minus a hundred degrees, he was only wearing an old, fraying sweater, and his legs . . . *His legs!* . . . were in battered cargo shorts. If it had been August and Cornwall, she'd have reckoned he was about to go surfing. But it was January and Lavender Heath, and he was about to shammy her bathroom window.

Woody cleared his throat. Roxy snapped her mouth shut with a clunk.

Luckily, Woody didn't notice – or pretended not to. There was a pause, and then he filled up the kettle himself, picked a couple of dirty mugs from her washing-up pile and started rinsing them out.

'What happened?' Roxy croaked. 'I mean, how the hell . . . ? I know you dropped out of the public eye, but . . .'

Woody rubbed his head again.

'Ahh, you still do that cute thing with your hair!' she exclaimed fondly. And then she cringed. 'Bollocks! Did I just say that out loud?'

Woody laughed. It was such a familiar gesture.

'I do that,' she said in a rush. 'Put my foot in it. It's my thing – my "unique selling point" . . .' She petered off, aware she was wittering.

Her mum had always said she'd been cursed with the Squires motormouth. When she'd first started working in telly, people had been enchanted by her bluntness. She wasn't rude – she just didn't fanny about. Her producers had lapped it up, and she was hailed as a breath of fresh air. In a stiff, media-trained world, where anyone even fractionally famous made it their mission to talk in 'PR' speak (i.e. never actually *say* anything at all), Roxy was the antithesis. She couldn't shut up! Opinions literally spilled out. If she slipped up live on air, she'd make a joke of it, take a trip down a conversational tangent and lead the programme into edgy new territory. If she was interviewing a hot, male heart-throb, she'd come straight out and tell him he was hot, and then recount a rude dream she'd had about him. It was a cute thing to do – or at least it had been. It was beginning to get a bit embarrassing in real life.

'Look, do you mind if I just fill up my bucket?' Woody broke the silence and gestured towards the sink. 'I'll come back for the tea in a mo.'

Roxy nodded at the space where he'd been. A few moments later, his ladder appeared at the window. She held her breath as she watched his calves climb upwards. And then all that was left was his whistling. Roxy breathed out. And then a massive surge of excitement bubbled up inside her. *Woody* was her window cleaner! *Gorgeous, sexy, hottest-pop-star-of-his-generation Woody!* Endorphins obliterated her hangover, and she raced into her bedroom for her make-up.

'So, how come you're always in bed when I'm around?' Woody asked as she handed him a mug of tea. She wished she had biscuits to offer, but she hadn't bought any for years. Not since before she was famous. She hadn't eaten a carbohydrate for a decade. Drunk them, yes. But actually put one in her mouth and chewed? No chance. Everyone knew telly added ten pounds.

'Late nights. Busy. Work,' she blustered vaguely.

'What are you presenting these days?'

She tried to distract him with her breasts (the Wonder Woman pyjamas had been jettisoned for a mini and vest. Sod that it was totally freezing, *he* was as hot as hell!).

'There's tons of stuff in the can,' she declared airily. 'Anyway, I want to know about *you*! You were on top of the world a few years back, and then you just disappeared. And now you're here . . . cleaning windows. Hard times, then?'

'Hard?' Woody laughed. 'No! Different. Better, really. The old life was never really me.'

'But your old life was perfect. *You* were perfect. You were a star!'

'Don't get me wrong; I'm not ungrateful. I know I was lucky.

But I was just a boy back then. And, let's face it, I couldn't spend the rest of my life doing daft photo shoots and miming on *Top Of The Pops*.'

'You couldn't?'

'Besides, I was sick of either being locked away in a recording studio, or stuck in an airport lounge. And if I'd had to wear one more white vest . . . No, this is much better.'

'What, being stuck up a ladder for a living?'

'Yeah, why not? I'm my own boss. I keep my own hours; I work outside in beautiful countryside. What's not to like?'

'What's *to* like,' Roxy mumbled. Woody might be sex on a stick, with eyes so blue she wanted to drag him into her bedroom and ravish him until he was concussed, but he obviously needed a pep talk. And if there was one thing she was totally ace at, it was motivational speaking. She did it to herself every day. Nobody knew the 'fame costs' speech better than she did. If you wanted to be famous, you had to work at it – hard; every minute of every single day.

'Woody,' she commanded with as much authority as her hangover would grant her, 'you're only a couple of years older than me. You're in your prime – not ready to fade into oblivion like some *nobody*! You need to put down that sponge and get your pop-star arse back out there. Forget the windows – make another record! People loved you; they'll be queueing round the block to buy it! Get back on the party circuit, do a few chat shows, speak to the tabloids. Ditch the tatty-sweater-and-wet-shorts look and treat yourself to a new stylist. And maybe a bit of Botox while you're at it. Don't get me wrong; you look great, but everyone's got hi-def tellies these days, so why risk it? And you need to give your agent a serious rollicking; shove a rocket up his arse! I can't believe he's left you up a ladder all these years. He's been criminally negligent, if you ask me . . .'

Suddenly she noticed Woody smiling.

'You *have* still got an agent, haven't you?' she asked in alarm. 'You'll never get back without one! I've got a copy of *Spotlight* if you want to look a few up.' She rummaged in the pile of celebrity mags on her table. She always kept her agents directory close to hand. She read it like other people read the Bible.

'Thanks.' Woody held up his hands. 'But I'm happy as I am. I don't want to go back.'

'What do you mean, you don't want to go back? Everyone wants to be famous!'

'My life's good. My *simple* life's good. I don't want to go to clubs and premieres and parties. Been there, done that – and only just lived to tell the tale. Besides, I've got to get up at the crack of dawn for my round.'

There was a long pause. Roxy looked incredulous. And then she pursed her lips, blew a raspberry and burst into laughter.

'OK, I get it! This is a wind-up, right? Come on – where are the secret cameras? I can't believe I fell for it! My teenage pin-up knocks on my door and pretends to be my window cleaner! I'll kill whoever it was who set me up. Who're you filming this for? E4? MTV? You could've warned me; I wasn't even wearing any bronzer!'

Woody looked at her strangely. There was a long pause. And then he stretched across the kitchen table, looped a pen out

of the pile of magazines and wrote something on the back of
OK!

'Roxy, are you busy tonight?'

'Eh?'

'I'd like you to come over to my place.'

Roxy looked around her kitchen. No secret cameramen had
emerged from her cupboards; no producers had bounded down
her hall. She looked down at the magazine that Woody had
slid towards her. She tried not to gasp. He'd written an address
– just a few roads away, in Lavender Heath. She knew the road;
it was a residential street. And, unless she was very much
mistaken, Woody had just asked her out!

'There are some people I'd like you to meet,' she vaguely
heard him say. But his words were drowned out by her internal
screech. ROCKING HELL! WOODY HAD JUST ASKED HER OUT!
And he'd given her his address. If only the girls on the school
bus could see her now.

Woody was talking, but she was too hyped to listen.

'You'll need to be open-minded.'

She nodded dumbly, wondering which of her killer outfits
weren't bundled into balls on her bedroom floor. What time
did the dry cleaner's close? Or what about her dress from last
night? As long as she hadn't dribbled mojito on it, it might
just be OK. And there was no way he'd resist her in that!

She suddenly noticed Woody was smiling at her oddly. It
was the same kind of smile her mum did when she asked if
Roxy was eating enough. But she didn't pay much notice. She
was too busy wondering how long Woody had known where

she lived. He must have recognised her from her TV shows; or maybe he'd been a fan of her lads' mag shoots. Whatever, he must have waited and waited for his big chance, when he finally found her awake.

She giggled out loud. Woody looked surprised and stopped talking. She nodded, as though agreeing to what he'd just said. Woody wanted her, she realised with glee. The gorgeous pop star she'd fancied when she was fifteen! Woody . . . and her; they were going to be an item! More than an item: a power couple. Together they'd be the pop star and the TV presenter; the UK's Brangelina; the new generation Posh 'n' Becks. And with only six weeks 'til Valentine's, it was perfect! That'd give them a couple of weeks to get to know each other before inviting *OK!* magazine to share the story of how they'd fallen in love. And of course, all the daytime shows would want them. And the sex . . . the sex would be AWESOME: eye-popping, lash-curling stuff! After all, the papers hadn't called him 'The Woodeniser' for nothing. As soon as he'd gone, she was going to email all her contacts – tip off the producers and talent bookers that she was about to become VERY HOT STUFF. She suddenly wondered if she had any of Woody's old hits on her iPod. She should download some, re-learn the lyrics, so she could drop them into the convo later. Yeah, that'd be cute.

'See you later, then; eight thirty,' he was heading for the door.

'Eight thirty,' she echoed excitedly, having heard precisely nothing else of what he'd just said. 'Your place,' she added with a wink. She'd already decided she was going to give out. Chances like this didn't land in your lap often, and besides – it wasn't like she was being easy – *she'd fancied him for almost twenty years!* She wondered if the local beautician's could fit her in for an emergency Hollywood.

Woody paused on the doorstep and looked at her strangely.

Roxy beamed manically, hoping she'd not said any of that stuff out loud. A moment passed. And then he gave an odd little smile, and left. Almost sick with excitement, she closed the door behind him.

To: Roxy Squires

From: *I'm A Celebrity Get Me Out Of Here* production office

Dear Ms Squires,

Thank you for your recent correspondence.

Please note that we only consider requests to be an *I'm A Celebrity Get Me Out Of Here* contestant via registered talent agents.

For a full list of agents, please consult the *Spotlight* directory.

SIMON

It was hot under his wig and the nylon costume wasn't helping. Beneath the high-collared cloak and thigh boots, Simon was beginning to sweat. That was the problem with man-made fibres: no absorption. He needed to be careful. If he carried on perspiring at this rate, his eyebrows might slide off.

'Oh, no there isn't!' he bellowed wickedly at the sea of faces before him.

'Oh, yes there is!' they yelled back, their pre-pubescent voices several octaves higher than his. Simon evil-eyed the audience, making sure his gaze lingered on the mouthier seven-year-olds.

'Oh, no there isn't!' He struck an exaggerated pose, which was the cue for the crocodile to finally get one up on the Demon King and sneak up to bite him on the bottom. But the crocodile wasn't on the ball. It missed its cue and the audience fell about laughing.

'OH, NO THERE ISN'T!' Simon repeated knowingly, sticking his bottom out even further to show *he* knew *they* knew there'd been a fluff. There was nothing a panto audience liked more than a cock-up. Simon often wondered why they ever bothered with scripts. No matter how many crap jokes the writer shoehorned in, the kids always laughed loudest when the lines were forgotten. Or when someone accidentally fell over. Or, best of all, when someone forgot their lines, fell over and swore. In fact, unscripted X-rated profanities were panto comedy gold. And then there was always the bring-the-house-down comedy chestnut of the flying—

'Arghhhhh!' Simon yelped, as pain suddenly bit – not via a crocodile on his backside, but in a sharp smack on his temple. Only years of steely professionalism stopped him from letting rip with the F-word. He saw the blue and white wrapper of a mini-Bounty at his feet. He remembered throwing it into the audience a few minutes earlier. Some bugger with a strong throwing arm must have caught it. Not one of the seven-year-olds; one of the sullen-faced teens, who sat crossed-armed and sneering, right up until the moment an unexpected opportunity to inflict pain and humiliation landed in their laps in the form of an individually wrapped mini chocolate bar. Teenagers were a panto actor's worst nightmare. And teenagers armed with confectionery were even worse.

Why did it have to be a mini-Bounty? Simon pondered wistfully. Airborne, the mini-Bounty was surprisingly painful; it was something to do with the coconut. A mini-Crunchie would have been better. Or if it *had* to be a mini-Bounty, why couldn't it have landed a bit lower? At least then the blow would have been cushioned by his nylon eyebrows. His forehead throbbed angrily.

'Right, you 'orrible lot,' he improvised, shaking a fist. 'If I find out which one of you scallywags threw that, I'm going to get Demon Dave 'ere to pull off your pretty little fingers so I can wear 'em as earrings!'

He pointed towards Demon Dave, who was leaning unthreateningly against a piece of painted scenery. Some demonic henchman he was proving to be.

Am I cursed? Simon wondered as he watched the audience scramble to find things to throw at him. Year after year it was the same. Despite pleading with his agent to find him a proper role – a quality BBC drama – he found himself stuck yet again in the career-desert of panto. He was RADA trained, for heaven's sake! He'd trodden the boards, done the Bard! He'd spent eight years playing the most hated villain on the UK's leading soap. He had man-on-the-street recognition and a tabloid nickname. Yet here he was – *a thespian* – reduced to earning his living in a spit-flecked beard, playing a sitting-duck target for teens.

'Ffff—!' Simon had forgotten the crocodile. He jumped, inwardly cursing the surprisingly painful jaw action of gloss-painted papier-mâché. As his backside smarted, he was only dimly aware of the arm lifting above the audience, stage right. He heard Demon Dave improvise them back to the script. And then, as if in slow motion, he saw another confectionery missile hurtle through the air towards him, spinning like a Wimbledon ace. Out of the corner of his eye, he noted the heavier-than-normal shape – the whirr of yellows, purples and reds. With a flash he recognised the brand, and several thoughts crashed through his head at once: how the supermarkets were stocking

Easter chocolate earlier and earlier; how he must buy one for Linda when next in Waitrose; and how some bugger must have brought this to the theatre especially, and that this was taking the joke too far. And then, with a thud, it hit him – closer to his groin than a speeding Creme Egg should ever comfortably get.

Two hours later, Simon was nearing Lavender Heath. He'd wiped off his make-up, peeled off his eyebrows and washed his beard, leaving it to drip-dry on a makeshift line over the sink. He'd climbed gratefully into his car and driven home through the dark country roads, lulling himself back to normality with the gentle babble of Radio Four. With each mile he put between himself and the theatre, his spirits rose. And by the time he'd reached the village, the ruts of his frown had finally levelled. He was looking forward to the evening ahead.

The one good thing about panto – other than that working in panto was better than not working at all – was the early finish. Not like real theatre. The panto audience was in bed by eight thirty, so he could be showered and home by nine. And tonight he felt boyish with excitement. The twins were sleeping at friends' houses and he and Linda could languish in the blissful rarity of a few hours of privacy, curled up on the sofa with a bottle of wine. They might even get to do that thing married couples allegedly did. Simon stepped down on the accelerator and offered up thanks to the sleepover gods.

Sleepovers were the only saving grace of having children.

God knew there was nothing else. Palming your kids off on some other poor bugger was the only meagre relief from having two savage-tongued fifteen-year-olds in the house. The twins were a blur of attitude and acne, and Simon felt battered by their constant barrage of disdainful looks and savage put-downs. How had it all gone so wrong? They were cute when they were five – they'd loved him! But five had morphed into fifteen, and he'd morphed from Dad into Whipping Boy. And cuddles? The only physical contact he got from Euan and Scarlet now was when they mugged him for his wallet.

'Hang on in there,' Linda encouraged. 'Another three years and they'll have buggered off to university. They'll appreciate us when they've gone.'

Simon was doubtful.

But . . . tonight wasn't about the twins – it was about forgetting them.

Simon sighed contentedly as he drove down Lavender Heath High Street. He took a right at the Dog and Duck pub, and smiled at the immaculately trimmed hedges. He loved living here.

He'd almost kissed the estate agent who'd shown them the house. He'd just left the soap and had had his fill of trendy north London. OK, so it had delis from every corner of the globe, but he was fed up with living so near to other people. He was sick of hearing his name shouted in the street – or rather, Nick's name, because the great British public seemed to have trouble realising that the character he played in the soap wasn't actually *real*. And he was sick, sick, sick of the tabloids. They knew his every movement. It was bad enough opening the paper to be confronted with a picture of himself putting out the rubbish, but it was off-the-scale infuriating when *they* called him Nick too. It was as though he, *Simon*, no longer existed. The real him had been turned into someone unreal – and a complete bastard, at that. It was like a nightmarish version of mistaken identity, and it had slowly but surely driven him mad.

Lavender Heath had been the antidote. For a start it was a full hour's drive from London. And, unlike London's dirty streets, it was postcard pretty: a chocolate-box village in immaculate countryside. The estate agent promised it was a private village, where everybody respected each other's boundaries. Why else would so many rich and famous people live there? It was no coincidence that its properties came with long, winding driveways, obscuring their owners from prying eyes. Besides, who else could afford its huge rustic homes? Not the rustics. The estate agent had barely finished showing them the house before Simon had put in an offer.

Simon pulled into his own long, winding driveway, unlocked his obscured front door and soaked up the rare, peaceful silence.

Feeling relaxed at last, he stooped to pick up a business card from the mat. As he straightened up, he caught a glimpse of himself in the hall mirror. He was less keen on mirrors these days. There seemed to be some kind of conspiracy; the man who squinted back couldn't possibly *be* him. *That* man looked every one of his thirty-nine years: his hair was thinner and his nose was much bonier than his own. It was like a cartoonist's version of himself.

'You've got an intelligent face,' Linda would reassure him, and she'd ruffle her fingers through his hair.

'Sod intelligent – is it a romantic face?' he'd neurotically cross-examine her. 'Is it a Richard Curtis rom-com leading-man kind of face?'

Simon leant closer to the mirror. Sure enough, he could already see the purpling of a small bruise on his forehead. *Bloody mini-Bounties*, he thought dryly. Thank Christ his velvet pantaloons had cushioned the Creme Egg.

Out of the corner of his eye he could see the red button of the answerphone flashing. He pressed it and Linda's voice filled the hall.

'Simon, love, it's me. Look, sorry, but something's come up at work. I know the twins are out and it's supposed to be our night, but this is really important. Sorry, sweetheart. I'll be on the last train home. Don't wait up. Love you!'

Simon's shoulders slumped and he dropped his car keys into the key dish with a clank. He tried not to feel hard done by, but he felt a pang of longing for his wife. It wasn't just the sex. He wanted to breathe in the smell of her conditioner as they cuddled up watching TV, to spoon gently behind her as they drifted off to sleep.

Idly, he looked at the business card. It had a picture of a ladder and a bucket. He turned it over. There was a message scrawled on the back.

All right, Si? Tonight, my place. 8.30pm, or whatever time you knock off from scaring kids. Woody.

And then . . .

PS . . . Your bay window's looking a bit skanky. Want me to fit you in Monday?

Simon sighed and pictured the bottle of red he and Linda were supposed to be drinking. Then he pocketed the card, picked up his car keys and headed out.

ROXY

Roxy had the nagging feeling she looked like a hooker.

Normally looking like a hooker wouldn't bother her; you couldn't so much as interrupt a paparazzo's fag unless you were dressed like a tenner-a-trick slut. But, tottering past the manicured lawns and sculpted topiary of Lavender Heath, the hooker look made her feel twitchy.

The problem – she decided – was her coat. She wasn't big on coats. It was her job to be out there and be seen. Hiding her wares wasn't an option – even if the weather was arctic. A few years back she'd never noticed the temperature, warmed as she was by waves of heat from the photographers' flash bulbs. But, lately she'd begun to get cold; and last night she'd been positively freezing. Woody's place was on the opposite side of the village, a full seven minutes' walk away. So she'd rummaged in the back of her wardrobe to find something suitably 'coaty'. What did one wear when popping round to one's friendly neighbourhood pop star for small talk and internet-movie-worthy sex? She could only find a trench coat. It was so thin she needen't have bothered. And it was so short she looked naked underneath. If Lavender Heath had been gauche enough to have nets, she was one hundred per cent sure they'd be twitching.

It hadn't always been this way, she lamented as she clip-clopped past a hedge trimmed into the shape of a swan. She could still remember the minimal maintenance of her first years of fame. Back then her every night out had made it into the papers, even just beers and a gig with mates, in nothing more raunchy than combats. She'd loved the just-got-out-of-bed look. Sometimes she yearned for her old collection of tight T-shirts, combat trousers and dance-all-night trainers. It had been her look – part of the new breed of fun-loving, hard-drinking blondes on TV.

But then the next breed of girl had arrived, and everyone wanted clean-living types with bodies that could bend into the lotus position; the kind whose beauty secrets were an early night with a bottle of triple-purified water (Roxy had once listed hers as gargling with Red Bull and an al fresco shag in stiff wind). And so Roxy had had to work her wardrobe harder and smaller. The only thing that had stayed big was her mouth.

Roxy finally arrived at Woody's house, hurried up the drive (surprisingly short, she semi-registered) and knocked on his front door. Despite the cold night, she felt a hot wave of panic. She couldn't be nervous – she'd been hanging out with celebs her whole life. But still, it'd been a while since she'd met anyone like Woody, and she was glad she was wearing her most indecent dress. Everyone knew Woody had red blood in his veins and Roxy was determined to work every inch of her model-skinny curves. There had to be some payback for living off egg whites and edamame beans.

Hearing footsteps approaching behind the door, she gave her hair a final tease and fixed on her best ask-me-I-might smile. And then . . .

'Bloody hell!' she unwittingly blurted.

There were no two ways about it – she was staring at a vision of total bonkability. She stood stock-still and gawped. Woody's feet were bare and he was wearing old, battered jeans and a soft checked shirt that looked at least a hundred years old. His skin glowed with health and she noticed how his fore-arms were manfully strong, how his eyes ended in laughter lines and how his hair was shower-damp at the neck. He'd clearly lost his hairbrush since his pop-star days – *and* his iron, *and* his stylist – but somehow the lived-in look suited him. He looked as hot as hell. She had an urge to lean over and lick him.

'Hey, Rox. Thanks for coming over. Did you find it OK?'

She tried to ignore the butterflies moshing in her stomach. If Woody could play it cool, so could she. Hell, he might be the former favourite teen pin-up in bedrooms across the land, but she was a lads' mag favourite and the best-selling calendar of 2000* (*internet sales only). It was time to take the bull by the horns.

'Now, look,' she told him sassily, 'I know you're Woody and women throw themselves into your lap, but don't think you can get away with this. Normally I'd make you take me some-where nut-crackingly expensive, but I've decided to make an exception because, *obviously*, it's more practical – me coming over to your place – because, *let's face it*, we're not exactly Joe and Joella Normal. We can't just nip out for a few getting-to-know-you tequilas – the tabloids'd go nuts. But, just because I'm here, doesn't mean you're not going to have to put in the legwork later. I know the magazines make out I'm, like, the most promiscuous woman in the country, but it's not true. OK, so I did those photo shoots, and that calendar, and the 'Rox Does Cocks' problem column, but hey –' she stood back and did her best Steve Coogan – 'I'm no slag; tits first!'

She waited for Woody to laugh, but he looked kind of dumb-struck.

'It's a *joke*!' she stressed. 'You know – the old Pauline Calf sketch . . . ? Anyway, what I mean is, I'm *not* the kind of girl the papers say I am. Not that I'm saying I'm *not* promiscuous,' she added quickly, remembering the clean pants in her handbag. 'What I mean is, I *can* be promiscuous, if the situation requires. But I'm not easy – *oh no!* I'm no groupie doormat – despite that stuff I told you about fighting on the school bus. So . . .' She eyed him with what she hoped was just the right amount of allure. 'Is that clear?'

For a moment Woody looked stunned. There was a long pause – too long for Roxy, who liked every second filled. She was suddenly seized with the fear. Had her motormouth blown it? Had she been uncool? If there was one thing guaranteed to make a celeb run a mile, it was the prospect of someone uncool. It was their greatest fear (even greater than nostril collapse) that other people's uncoolness would taint them.

That's why they hung out in private members' bars and VIP enclosures – so the great, ordinary masses couldn't infect them with their uncoolness. And Roxy seriously needed Woody to think she was cool.

She held her breath. And then to her surprise he rubbed his head and smiled.

'Perfectly,' he bowed politely. 'I've got it. No doormat; tits first! But Rox, I think you've got the wrong end of the sti–'

'Yeah, great place, by the way,' Roxy chattered in relief. She made a show of looking around. Suddenly she noticed how small Woody's hall was. By Lavender Heath standards it was positively poky. She could see the prospect of an MTV *Cribs* episode receding into the distance. 'Actually, I'll be honest, Woods – titchy drive, disappointing hallway. And, I'm not knocking your interior designer –' she pointed at his coffee-coloured walls – 'but isn't this all a bit Homebase? I thought pop stars were supposed to have mansions. I expected mirrored ceilings, bowls of Viagra in every room, a separate wing for your Ferraris . . .'

'You're going to be very disappointed!' Woody laughed.

'Oh, I doubt that,' Roxy replied huskily, eyeballing his chest.

Woody took a tiny step backwards.

'Like I said, Rox, I think you're a bit confused. Tonight isn't a . . . Look, maybe I should just take your coat. I'll get you a drink in a minute, but first,' he propelled her gently towards a door just behind him, 'let me introduce you to everyone.'

'Everyone?' Roxy echoed in surprise. But the question died

in her mouth. The door had swung open and a roomful of people were grinning right at her.

'Here she is! Come in! We've just been hearing about you!' Bottoms shuffled up and a gap appeared on the sofa.

'But I thought it was just going to be us?' she protested from behind a clenched smile. 'Like, a date?'

But Woody didn't hear. He put his hand on her shoulder and introduced them.

'Roxy, this is Simon, Terence, Sue, Cressida and Holly. Everyone, this is Roxy Squires.'

Confused, Roxy felt the voltage as Woody's hand touched her skin. Her nipples pogoed to attention, but her stilettos dug into the floor. Who were these people? *What* had they just been hearing about her? And what the hell were they doing on her date? She took a breath . . . She couldn't stomp out – she'd miss her chance to shag Woody's arse off. And 'everyone' was bound to leave soon. They were probably just his staff and Woody was one of those trendy employers who invited them for a drink before they knocked off. Yes, that had to be it!

Reluctantly, she manoeuvred into the gap on the sofa.

'Macaroon?' the man next to her thrust a plate of biscuits under her nose. Even though he was smiling, there was something vaguely sinister about him. His nose was ever so bony. 'Home-made!' he encouraged, with a grin.

Dumbly she shook her head. The sofa was uncomfortably low. It pushed her knees higher than her bottom and her mini-dress even further up her legs. Opposite, a middle-aged bloke with a paunchy tummy politely averted his gaze.

She looked around. Everyone was smiling inquisitively and everyone looked faintly familiar, like faces from a dream. Or rather, a nightmare – the kind of nightmare where you think you're on a date with Adonis, but you're actually at some weird family gathering, and the family name is Addams.

She shot another look at the paunchy middle-aged man. He reminded her of someone. She briefly tried to place him. He was probably one of her old, pervy uncles. They all looked the same and she always blanked them out. And hadn't her mum said one of them was local?

Next to Pervy Uncle was a dumpy, mumsy woman, on the verge of a panic attack. Her eyes were locked on the macaroons.

Next to Dumpy Mum was Spinster Aunt: sensible shoes; old-fashioned make-up; probably born with a rod up her arse. Definitely not someone to get stuck next to.

Sitting demurely next to Spinster Aunt was a bland blonde in a pastel round-neck. *Smug Cousin*, Roxy decided. She'd probably been indoors studying for her next piano grade while Roxy had been out climbing trees and showing the boys her knickers. Another one to be avoided.

She wasn't sure who the macaroon-wielding weirdo on her left was. The black sheep of the family, probably. Maybe he was Pervy Uncle's son. Actually, the more she looked at him, the more she was sure she'd seen him before. Probably loitering in the park, or on *Crimewatch*.

Who the hell are these people? she wondered. And then a thought struck her. Surely they couldn't be . . . ? *No!* Woody was a pop star! OK, so he was a pop-star-turned-window-cleaner and seemed to have stuck all the trappings of wealth and fame into storage, but he *was* a pop star, nevertheless. Didn't pop stars hang out with supermodels and Formula One drivers? They certainly didn't hang out with this lot. Surely they couldn't be Woody's . . . *friends*? Roxy began to panic. Where were Woody's *celebrity* friends? *OK!* magazine would never shell out for wedding shots if the congregation was made up of this lot.

She accepted a large glass of wine from Woody and watched unhappily as he sat between Smug Cousin and Spinster Aunt. She tried not to frown – not good for the wrinkles. Besides, she liked to think she was a lager-half-full kind of girl. OK, so the night wasn't going as planned, but winning Woody would be like scoring the double rollover – career and love life sorted in one scoop. And Roxy wasn't the type to wimp out at a hurdle. Hurdles were there to be jumped over. Why else did she wear such high heels? She took a big slug of wine and sat back.

'All I'm saying,' Spinster Aunt declared frostily, in a voice that sounded uncomfortably familiar, 'is that a good man's career was ruined – and his family nearly destroyed.'

Dumpy Mum was looking red-faced.

'Well, that was hardly Sue's fault,' Pervy Uncle jumped to her defence.

'Let's not pretend she didn't play her part,' said Spinster Aunt.

'I never meant . . .' Dumpy Mum began forlornly.

'She was *nineteen*, Cressida!' reasoned Pervy Uncle. 'Just a child – innocent in the ways of the world.'

'Innocent? I don't think Deirdre Hunt would put it like that, Terence – do you?' Spinster Aunt Cressida replied tartly.

'Sue was just as much a victim as Deirdre Hunt. If you want to blame anyone, blame him – blame Hunt, blame the papers, God knows, they deserve it!'

There were grunts of agreement from the room.

'You can't help who you fall in love with,' Macaroon Man offered helpfully. 'Sue was obviously deeply in love.'

'And she's had to live with the fallout for years!' said Pervy Uncle Terence. 'The Hunts had each other. She had no one.'

'Not even a career,' added Smug Cousin. Roxy looked at her in surprise. It wasn't the kind of support she'd have expected from goody-two-shoes.

'I did get married, once . . .' Dumpy Mum Sue said quietly, her eyes fixed in her lap. 'To Jeff. It didn't last. He wanted Suzi, but I just wanted to be Sue. I wanted to put all the Suzi stuff behind me.'

'See?' Terence insisted. 'The Hunts weren't the only ones to have their marriage ruined!'

'They didn't split up. They're still together,' whispered Sue.

'Hunt was a good man,' Spinster Aunt Cressida said plainly. 'He had a lot to give this country – he was passionate . . .'

Macaroon Man stifled a laugh.

'He had a great career in politics ahead of him,' Cressida increased her volume, drowning out Macaroon Man's dissent.

'And it was all ruined by her!' She glared at Sue. Sue was visibly shaking.

'Politicians aren't allowed to make mistakes,' intervened Woody. 'If a pop star has a fling, it's not a problem. But if a politician has one, the papers punish him – and whoever it was he was seeing. It doesn't matter to the papers that the politician might be in an unhappy marriage, or that the woman he had the affair with may or may not be the love of his life.'

'Loads of MPs have affairs,' said Smug Cousin kindly.

'Well, don't they say power's the greatest aphrodisiac?' Woody smiled.

There was an awkward silence as everyone looked at Cressida. Roxy looked too. She was beginning to recognise Spinster Aunt. All the talk about power was stirring her memory.

Macaroon Man cleared his throat.

'So, you never managed to get your career back on track, Sue?' he asked.

Dumpy Mum shook her head sadly.

'I went to castings, but everyone just whispered and stared. They said I was too sleazy for the modelling jobs I went for. I couldn't even get catalogue work any more.'

'Yes, well, we all have our cross to bear,' Cressida said sharply. 'And yours came with a rich husband and a house in Lavender Heath. And it was thirty years ago, for heaven's sake. Isn't it time you stopped feeling sorry for yourself?'

'You don't know what it's like to know everyone's seen you naked,' Sue protested tearfully. 'People I've never met know things, *private things*, about me. It's not like I *sold* the pictures. I didn't choose to expose myself, like a . . . a page three girl! For years I couldn't even buy a loaf of bread without someone leering, or shouting that horrible name the tabloids called me.'

'Hah! I know what *that's* like.' Macaroon Man said ruefully. Roxy peered at him in surprise. Now she came to think about it, he did look *very* familiar.

'Bloody tabloids,' Pervy Uncle Terence added venomously.

'I had dreams.' Sue's voice had gone wobbly. 'I was going to branch out – get into acting. But instead I got labelled as her: as Suzi. Every schoolboy in the land knew me as . . . well . . . as, *you know* . . .'

Despite herself, Roxy was fascinated.

'Couldn't you just work with it? Play it to your advantage with a kiss-and-tell, or a sexy underwear campaign?' she asked.

'She's not that kind of lady!' Pervy Uncle retorted.

'Yes, well, you just need to retrain,' Cressida said simply. 'Do something useful with your life. The past is past. We, of all people, should know that.' She looked around the room meaningfully. Roxy noticed the atmosphere suddenly change. Everyone looked at their laps, or started contemplating Woody's walls.

A moment passed. Roxy put down her wine glass.

'What do you mean . . . "we of all people"?' she asked.

She looked at Woody. He smiled at her in the same way her teachers used to when they wanted her to work something out.

She looked at the others, her eyes travelling from face to

face. Now she thought about it, maybe they *all* looked familiar. The more she clocked Pervy Uncle, the more she felt sure she'd seen him before. He definitely wasn't one of her actual uncles, yet she had a weird feeling he'd been in her house – in her living room. And Macaroon Man was looking more familiar with every glance. Maybe she'd met him, drunk, at a party. Christ – they'd probably snogged!

Sue didn't ring any bells, but she'd obviously been famous once – she'd shown them the scrapbook to prove it.

And Spinster Aunt: she had that *voice*. Roxy was sure she'd heard it before. She remembered the lecturing tone.

Roxy looked at Smug Cousin. She didn't recognise her at all, but maybe she was too bland for Roxy's radar.

And then there was Woody. Well, she definitely knew who he was. *Everyone* knew who he was.

'Are you . . . ?' Her heart suddenly quickened. 'Are you all . . . *famous*, or something?'

Her question hung in the air. Her skin tingled with excitement. Could they *really* be celebrities? Could all these *ordinary* famous people have been plodding around Lavender Heath under her nose?

'Not exactly,' Macaroon Man replied.

They all swapped glances. Roxy looked at Woody wildly.

'No, we're not famous,' he smiled. 'We're has-beens!'

'Hanging on to the fact that we *used* to be,' Sue added.

'I couldda been a contender!' Macaroon Man joked limply.

Roxy's mouth fell open. Slowly she looked from person to person and a series of pennies began to drop.

'I *know* you!' she jabbed her finger at Macaroon Man. 'You're Sick Nick!'

'No, I'm Simon Drennan,' he corrected. 'I'm an actor who used to play the morally flawed character, Nick Fletcher, in the television soap opera *Down Town*.'

'You were in *Downton*?' Roxy looked at him, impressed. Now she thought about it, she could see him in a bow tie. He hadn't been one of the posh lot, but she was sure he'd been one of the servants.

'Not *Downton Abbey*,' Terence sniggered, enjoying the moment. 'Simon was in *Down Town*. Not quite the same thing.'

'And you're . . .' Roxy's finger moved to Pervy Uncle. 'You're that weatherman off the telly. The one who made everyone bankrupt.'

'Say hello to Tornado Terry,' Simon smirked, enjoying a swift revenge.

'A simple Terence would suffice,' Terence said stiffly.

'And you . . .' Roxy's finger swivelled round to Sue. 'I didn't get it at first, but you used to be Sug—'

'*Don't say it!*' Sue's hands flew up to her face.

'And you're . . .' Roxy lingered over Spinster Aunt, hoping someone would jump in and explain.

'Cressida Cunningham,' Spinster Aunt told her crisply. 'Former Member of Parliament for Biddington Borders, and Secretary of State for Work and Pensions.'

'Bloody hell!' Roxy exclaimed.

'Of course, you already know Woody,' Simon cut in. 'Our very own used-to-be chart-topping heart-throb and former runner-up for Rear Of The Year.'

'I still can't believe I got pipped to the post for that one,' Woody laughed. 'I should've demanded a recount.'

'And . . .' Roxy's eyes settled on Smug Cousin. She looked like a total civilian. Roxy decided to take a punt. 'I'm sorry – I don't do telly choirs.'

Smug Cousin looked up in surprise. 'Oh no, I'm not on television; I'm Holly Childs.' Roxy looked blank. 'The romantic novelist? I used to be a best-seller, when I was younger. Really young, actually. But my parents always tried to keep me out of the limelight. I didn't do any publicity. Anyway, I've given it all up now. Writing, I mean.'

'Holly was a teenage prodigy,' said Simon. 'She wrote three best-sellers before she was sixteen. One was even made into a film – *Puppy Love*.'

'What, the Austin Jones movie? The one where he was a vet?' Roxy blurted.

Holly nodded with a blush.

'But that movie was massive,' Roxy marvelled, looking at Holly with new eyes. 'I didn't realise it was written by a teenager. Why don't you write any more?'

Holly looked awkward.

'It was only ever supposed to be a bit of fun before I went to university. Besides, Mum and Dad . . .' She gave a funny little shrug.

'So there you have it,' grinned Woody. 'Welcome to our circle of used-to-bes! I thought you might find us of help.'

But Roxy was still looking at Holly. Maybe she wasn't so

bland, after all. She was young and thin and blonde – and she had a gap between her teeth like Madonna! All she needed was a sexy makeover and they could hit the town together – Roxy and her writer bezzie mate. It was about time she got herself some gravitas. Maybe she could get herself some glasses – work the intellectual look.

'Yeah, come on – join us.' Simon gave a mock rallying-call. 'We're a flock of failures!'

Or maybe there was something she could do with Simon, Roxy wondered. The more you looked at him, the less you noticed his nose. Besides, wasn't the ordinary look 'in'? It was certainly doing the business for O'Dowd. And didn't that Gandy bloke have a big hooter? Maybe she could phone her TV contacts, suggest a drama this time – some kind of buddy vehicle with her and Simon as cops.

'They say that everyone's famous for fifteen minutes.' Holly was talking. 'The problem is that those fifteen minutes are dazzling. And when they're over, real life just seems grey.'

'Fame's an insatiable mistress.' Terence's voice drifted over. 'She takes you to the highest summit and then hangs you out to dry.'

'It's tough,' somebody deadpanned.

'It's an adjustment,' another voice added kindly.

'I'm worried about you, Rox.' Woody tried to get her attention. But Roxy's mind was already elsewhere . . . flitting somewhere between his bedroom and a new plan. 'You're sleeping late, partying hard. Are you sure you're not chasing something that's already gone?'

'A young, fit woman like you . . .' Cressida's voice was muffled, as though under water. 'There are plenty of jobs you could do . . . It's what you do when the cameras *aren't* rolling that really matters in life.'

Suddenly Roxy noticed that everyone was studying her closely. The whole room seemed to be waiting for her to reply. She looked from person to person, barely able to contain her new excitement.

'Absorockinlutely!' she erupted in glee. *This* was what she needed – what she'd been looking for! This group of minor celebs and fame-recluses was her salvation – her revitalisation – her rebirth into the world. This was her big ticket back, the reason she kept subscribing to *Spotlight*, the mission she hadn't even realised she'd been seeking. Cressida was right, what you did when the cameras weren't rolling really *did* matter! And this lot had got it all wrong. It wasn't *them* who could help her – it was *her* who could help *them*. And by pushing them back into the spotlight, she'd be pushing herself back too. They'd *all* be winners! Her heart raced and her eyes sparkled.

She, Roxy Squires, was going to make them all famous again.

SUE

Sue lay in bed and bleakly tried to calculate the best tea–
biscuit combination for a mood-boost. Redwood and diges-
tives? Earl Grey and a Viennese whirl? Or maybe builders' tea?
Yes, that was probably the way to go. Builders' tea with toast
and marmite. Even *she* knew you shouldn't have biscuits for
breakfast.

But she didn't get out of bed and boil the kettle. Instead,
she burrowed deeper beneath her duvet and surrendered to
her maudlin mood. It wasn't her fault – it was all the raking-
up-the-past from last night. She suddenly remembered a game
she played as a little girl: If you were an animal what would
you be? Her friends had jostled to be the first to bag 'pony'.
But the young Suzi had never wanted to be a horse, or a kitten,
or a bunny . . . She wanted to be a swan. Swans were graceful.
Swans were a perfect snow-white. Her friends had called her
silly; who wanted to swim in circles in a dirty, smelly pond?
But Suzi was not dissuaded. And beneath fifteen togs of
feather, Sue knew Suzi had been right. Didn't swans mate for
life? And wasn't that what she'd done when she'd fallen for

Hunt? Yes, she'd married Jeff . . . but, looking back, was it really *love* she'd felt for her husband? Or relief at the armour he'd provided? A ring . . . An arm . . . A presence to deflect the attention . . .

Sue couldn't help herself . . . she let herself meander down memory lane . . .

Hunt.

Hunt.

Everyone called him that. His name was Rupert, but nobody used it – not even his wife, he'd laughed. He'd been an energetic backbencher, not quite in cabinet, older than she was – an ancient forty-two. But Suzi hadn't noticed his grey temples, or the lines at the corners of his eyes. When he'd turned his charm upon her over drinks at a magazine party, a nineteen-year-old Suzi (only a year out of the suburbs) had felt herself teeter and fall. She wasn't supposed to fancy older men; she definitely wasn't supposed to fancy politicians; and she absolutely definitely wasn't supposed to fancy married politicians. In fact, she wasn't supposed to be at the party at all. A friend – a fellow model – had talked her into coming. They were going out dancing, but popped in for a laugh. Having no invitation wasn't a problem for two young, pretty faces in short skirts, and they were soon sipping free drinks and hobnobbing with London's luminati. Suzi had chatted to a photographer, an actor and a multi-millionaire entrepreneur, but when Hunt had smiled at her across the room – before striding over to introduce himself and shake her hand – something in her molecules altered. She liked to think she'd put up some resistance, that she'd struggled with her morals before freefalling into love with an older, married man. But the truth was, from that very first electrifying handshake, she was smitten: hopelessly bedazzled by his elegance, worldliness and smile.

But, eight months and one cabinet promotion later, scandal broke.

Sue curled her duvet more tightly around her. She didn't like remembering what had happened next.

The minute the affair hit the papers she became public property. One morning she'd been Suzi, an under-the-radar model; a pretty, penniless thing you might have seen running down the pavement for a bus . . . But the next day she was *her* – the nickname Hunt had given her. Thanks to a break-in and a chatty, tipsy friend, suddenly the whole world knew the very personal details of what had passed between them: the dates they'd been on, the intimacies they'd whispered, the moments of lovemaking they'd shared. Every little aspect was reported, distorted and made to sound dirty . . . A sleazy bonk for him and, for her, a scheming piece of sluttism to boost a fledgling career. Nobody thought for a moment that what she and Hunt had was love.

Of course, Hunt scarpered. He retreated back to his constituency and his wife. They met the press together with matching stiff upper lips. His arm around his wife, he apologised for his 'serious error of judgement'. He lost his job, but kept his family – and the eighteenth-century manor house with wisteria around the door. A few months later he re-emerged to work in business – before emerging again, years later, beaming from the pages of *Hello*.

But Suzi didn't have a place to run to – no private country house with blossom by the door. Her friends thought it a hoot; Suzi was the hottest girl in town – they could go dancing wherever they wanted now. But it wasn't funny for Suzi. Her heart had been broken but she had no privacy to cry. She had rent to pay, castings to attend, a life to try to get on with. She ran the gauntlet of public transport alone.

But, of course, life wasn't how it had been. Her every move was trailed by a pack of hungry cameras; her castings inter-rupted by journalists on the scent. Now she was invited to every kind of party, but parties weren't any fun. Because once her private life was public, the public felt free to judge. Normal rules of politeness went out of the window. People she'd never met, never spoken to, would stand nearby and appraise her. Because she'd been in the papers, her feelings, it seemed, were fair game. They forgot she could still see and hear – or ignored the fact that she could.

Men would lurk close by, making suggestive comments before mentally removing her clothes. They didn't have to imagine much; they were already well acquainted with her naked body thanks to the photos stolen from Hunt's constituency safe (the only place Deirdre wouldn't find them). A few drinks later and the lecherous approaches would start.

The women looked at her differently, too. To them she was something dangerous – a home-wrecker, a husband-stealer, a purveyor of dark sexual tricks. And so they would collect behind their wine glasses, making sure their judgements could be heard. Suzi was fatter/scrawnier/tartier than in pictures. Her face was hard, her bust overrated and her motives despicably selfish. Not once did anyone consider that Hunt may have been her 'one'.

Suzi was suddenly famous in a way she'd never wanted to be. More than famous . . . a fascination. Was she *really* that beautiful? Had she *really* bewitched the straight-laced politician into a frenzy of sexual madness? Were her . . . *you knows* . . . really as good as *that* name? Everybody wanted to drink where she drank – to say they'd been at the same party. Men wanted to be with her, not for friendship or romance, but to boast about the conquest and parade her to their friends. Jeff was just the same. He was only different because he hung around longer. The thrill of displaying her at the races didn't wear off until they'd married. But he didn't want *her* – he wanted Suzi. He wanted to bask in Suzi's notoriety, to let the world know *he* was the one who got to fondle those famous assets, to slip between those famous thighs. And when the thrill had passed and Jeff had disappeared with the next image-boosting arm-accessory, Sue decided it was time for Suzi to disappear too. Without Jeff, she didn't have to go out. She'd already given up on modelling, and she definitely didn't want to go dancing with her friends. She wasn't even sure she had friends any more. Scandal seemed to have melted them away, replacing them with party-going acquaintances – gossip-fuelled fun-types who whisked you up, whirled you around and cosied up for 'one for the album'. But then they'd spin off to find the next hot thing, blabbing to the press on the way. Sue had had enough of the press. She'd had enough of everyone. She just wanted to shut her door.

And so she did.

Sue sighed and released her grip on the duvet. She shook herself and sat up. Sweet Fennel – that would do it. Reaching for her dressing gown, she set off to make some tea.

To: Roxy Squires

From: *Dancing On Ice* production office

Thank you for your application to be a *Dancing On Ice* celebrity skater.

Whilst we thank you for your interest in our show, we would like to take this opportunity to remind you that only the most colourful, entertaining and newsworthy celebrities are selected as contestants . . .

ROXY

Roxy woke with a snap.

Normally it took her hours to become fully conscious. She'd doze luxuriantly until hunger (or the need for Alka-Seltzer) eventually forced her to rise. But this morning was different. At 10.30am her eyes opened and stayed open. It was her earliest morning in years.

She grabbed her phone from the bedside table and dialled Tish's number. God, Tish would scream her head off to hear Woody was her window cleaner. And when she'd finished, she could help Roxy plot his seduction. Tish was always good for tips on a man-harvest. Or she always used to be. As Tish's phone started ringing, Roxy had a sudden, crippling fear. She quickly flipped through her memory log of Tish's shags. *Christ, Woody had better not be one of them!* But then she sighed in relief. Of course Tish hadn't bonked Woody! Of all the men in the world (most of whom, it seemed, had hurled themselves at Tish's feet at one time or another), Roxy would definitely remember him. Besides, Woody had already disappeared off the scene by the time she and Tish rocked up.

Tish's phone was still ringing. Frowning, Roxy hung up. Honestly – what was the point of having a best friend who never picked up when she called? But she couldn't stay mardy for long. Not now she knew Woody was just a few streets away. How was it possible she'd never noticed? Had she been walking around with her eyes shut and libido off? Grinning, she flung on her leopard-print dressing gown and hurtled down the stairs.

Automatically, she headed for the doormat. She couldn't function before reading the tabs. She picked up her copy of the *Daily Post* and flicked past the news stories straight to the Nicola Blunt page, stopping expertly at its infamous masthead silhouette. Greedily, Roxy's eyes drank in the stories of celebs behaving badly. She *loved* the Nicola Blunt page! It was catty, cutting and compulsive – all the best celebs were there. Roxy was forever calling the number at the bottom of the page, leaving anonymous messages about herself under the guise of being 'a friend'. She'd never made it into the page, though. Not yet, anyway. *But all that was about to change*, Roxy thought with glee. OK, so last night hadn't quite gone to plan – but next time it would. Nicola Blunt might be able to resist Roxy Squires alone, but Roxy and Woody together . . . ?

Roxy giggled out loud. She didn't know what was better . . . getting back in the papers, or horizontal with Woody? It was as if Christmas and her birthday had decided to come at once. Laughing, she hugged her dressing gown around her and raced back upstairs to shower.

WOODY

From the top of his ladder, Woody eyed the black Aston Martin. It had been sitting in Cedar Crescent, engine running, for at least ten minutes now. He was sure it was the same Aston Martin he'd seen earlier, loitering in Peach Street – and yesterday, in Cherry Blossom Drive. Not that an Aston Martin in Lavender Heath was unusual; every road had at least one, but this one always parked the same: a foot from the kerb, engine running, its wheel pointing out.

He watched its reflection in Mrs Henderson's window and then doused the pane in suds. His mind wandered back to Roxy. He'd been worried about last night's meeting and reckoned it'd be fifty-fifty as to whether the group would accept her. Famous people weren't like normal people – they saw themselves as a super-selective club. The moment fame struck, life adopted a door policy; membership was not open to all. Terence and the gang may only have been *slightly* famous, but they could still act like divas. Not that Woody minded – he'd been a right pillock himself.

But, luckily, Woody thought as he wrung out his shammy,

Roxy *had* been accepted. He remembered Roxy from the period after his own stint of fame. He'd wasted the last few years of the nineties, glued to late-night telly, wondering whether to curse or thank the hot new acts who'd replaced him centre stage. For months he'd hardly smiled at anything – with the exception of Roxy Squires. She had presented all the music shows back then. She'd interviewed all the bands in her special, bonkers style. Hell, if he'd held on to his record contract, she'd probably have interviewed him too. But he'd been too sick of the game by then – he'd just wanted to get out. He was sick of being the guy who'd forgotten how to smile for a family photograph without giving the camera his best side. He couldn't remember having a conversation that wasn't a career-enhancing schmooze. He'd even got bored with the shagging – the women came and went so quickly he barely learnt their names. He had suddenly realised that he was embarrassed by the man that he'd become. And so he'd decided to take his pop-star millions and supermodel girlfriend and leg it. So what if he was sued for six figures over the abandoned tour? And, yes, his supermodel girlfriend hadn't been so super once the parties all dried up – but normality hadn't disappointed him. It had just taken getting used to.

That was why he'd set up the group. After years of lazing about, he'd finally got a job. And, when he discovered he had used-to-be-famous clients, he decided he'd been a selfish arse for too long. It wasn't a cure for cancer but, in his own small way, he hoped he was doing some good. These days half the world wanted to be famous, but nobody thought about what came next . . . *after* you were famous – when the work dried up and the cameras went away. You might only be twenty-three, but life suddenly felt like it was finished. What could you do next? Fame was fun, but it turned into a millstone. When the whole world knew you, could you *really* work in a shop? An office? A bank? Would you even make it through the interview without being smirked at by the boss, or pressed for an autograph by a pink-faced woman from HR? Fame didn't open doors – it closed them. It stopped you moving on.

Woody tipped back the potted bay tree and collected the wages Mrs Henderson had left for him. The thing was, the group wasn't going quite as well as he'd planned. He was happy with his new life and wanted the others to be too. He wanted to stop Terence and Simon being bitter, to stop Sue worrying about the past, to teach Holly the trick of confidence and get Cressida to relax enough to make friends. He wanted to tell them that being not-famous wasn't failure, just a chance to do something new. But it wasn't exactly working. Terence was as angry as ever and Holly still wouldn't say boo to a goose.

He shouldered his ladder and headed off to the next set of dirty windows. Maybe he'd bitten off more than he could chew? he thought grimly. After all, who was he to meddle in other people's lives? *Smash Hits* covers were hardly qualifications.

He could see the group needed a bit of a shake-up – that was why he'd invited Roxy. Not that she could fix their psyches – but she might just make them laugh. When Woody thought about Roxy, he thought of a joyous Nike up the jacksy of life.

Of course, she had her own career crisis to deal with now, but she couldn't quite see it yet. And whilst she was figuring everything out maybe she could get the group to have fun. After all, she'd unknowingly helped him through *his* doldrums . . . Yes, Woody smiled – Roxy Squires was *exactly* what the group needed. And she might not know it yet, but the group was *exactly* what she needed too.

10.51am @FoxyRoxy

Wow! Liz Hurley right (as ever!). Lust IS good for the skin! My mug's GLOWING! Cheeks like an air-brushed baby – nips like champagne corks!

To: Roxy Squires

From: *Celebrity MasterChef* production office

Dear Miss Spires,

Thank you for your recent email(s) requesting consideration as a contestant on the forthcoming series of *Celebrity MasterChef*.

Thank you also for your admission that you can 'bollocks-up boiling an egg'.

As per our replies of 3rd October, 8th November and 10th December, we regret that we will not be offering you an appearance on the show.

SUE

Sue had plumped for Assam and Bourbons in the end. She placed her tea and biscuits on the kitchen table, opened her computer and readied herself for a surge of endorphins. But these endorphins weren't the kind that came from tea. These were technological endorphins, sparked into life by the reading of her emails. Or rather, her email, because her inbox only ever had one.

Sue's inbox was a bleak little corner of cyberspace. She'd become so invisible she'd never made it on to any spam lists. But her sole, weekly email brought a special kind of joy. The email was Holly's minutes and it turned up – without fail – just before eleven every Friday morning.

Sue *loved* Holly's minutes. She loved them just as much as her *Times* crossword and her weekly gossip magazines. Every Friday she'd pull out the biscuits and prepare. Holly was so punctual – Sue could boil her kettle at 10.55 in anticipation of the ping of her inbox at 10.59. She'd then lose herself in Holly's perfectly recalled, minutely detailed account of the previous evening's chat. *Bliss!*

Sue was about to devour this week's email when the door-bell rang. She jumped. It couldn't be Woody; he'd be busy on his round. And she'd already seen the postman stride past the end of her drive. She didn't get spur-of-the-moment callers, unless they were well-meaning old ladies from the church, offering her the path to salvation – but even they didn't come round very often. They didn't want her soul *that* badly.

The bell rang again.

She scraped her chair back and scuttled to the door. Neon-bright colours moved behind its mottled glass.

'Jesus, Sue – I'm freezing my norks off out here!'

Sue opened the door.

Standing on her doorstep – her breath steaming into clouds in the cold, January air – was a woman dressed for the beach. Or was it the Alps? Whichever, Sue was gripped with admir-ation. She'd never dressed like that – not even when she was Suzi. The woman didn't have a coat, but was wearing a pink sparkly T-shirt and a tiny miniskirt the colour of summer seas. Her legs were brown and bare. Her only conces-sions to the elements were a pair of enormous fluffy boots, a matching fluffy gillet, a Day-Glo muff and a woolly hat with dangly bobbles. The whole thing was topped off with two peroxide plaits, a slash of lipgloss and a pair of mirror shades.

Roxy.

'Sorry. I, uh . . . I'm on my way out. To the shops. To buy some . . . socks.' Instinctively she gripped the door.

To her surprise, Roxy looked disappointed. Sue felt a stab

of shame at her lie. But she wasn't used to visitors and, besides, how had Roxy known where she lived?

'No probs.' Roxy grinned. 'Can't stand between a woman and her retail therapy. So, anyway, I thought you might like this.'

Something shot out from the depths of Roxy's Day-Glo muff. Sue peered at it uncertainly.

'It won't bite!' Roxy laughed. 'It's a DVD, a fitness DVD. *My* fitness DVD, actually.' She shook the box. And sure enough, there on the cover, was a Lycra-clad Roxy. But this Roxy looked different to the Roxy on her doorstep; she was younger, curvier, less blonde. A pale-blue gem glinted in her tummy button.

'Oh . . .' Sue exclaimed, not quite knowing what to say.

'You've probably sussed I'm a no-bullshit kind of girl, so, straight up − if this DVD was bollocks, I'd say so. But it's not. I got shed loads of letters from women saying they'd lost whole dress sizes doing it. Now, I know what you're thinking . . .'

Sue looked at her, bewildered. She barely knew what she was thinking herself! She could see her frightened reflection in Roxy's mirrored sunglasses. She tried to relax her grip on the front door.

'. . . you didn't have me down as a fitness fanatic. And you're right, I'm not. Don't get me wrong − I love all the kit. In the run-up to Christmas you'd have to chisel me out of my gym clobber − not that I actually go to the gym − it's just to give the paps the chance to get me for all the 'Celebs' New Year Shape Up' articles for January. But you probably don't read those kinds of magazines . . .'

'Oh, but I *love* those kinds of magazines!' Sue gushed. She tried to remember if she'd ever seen Roxy in them. She'd have to check her back issues.

'Honestly, though –' Roxy stepped a little closer – 'I don't know my arse from my elbow about aerobics, but every Tom, Dick and Harry was putting out a fitness DVD back then, and a production company made me an offer. Never look a gift horse in the mouth – that's what I say! Anyway, don't let the fact that it's *my* DVD put you off. There's a real instructor doing the workout with me and she really knows her onions.'

There was a pause. Sue took the DVD. For a moment she thought Roxy was going to offer to sign it.

'So, great meeting last night.' Roxy suddenly changed the subject. 'Woody's very, um . . . *inclusive*.'

Sue felt a surge of relief. She hadn't got a clue about fitness DVDs and onions, but Woody's meetings were something she *did* know about.

'Woody's wonderful,' she told her. 'The heart and soul of the village.'

Roxy's sunglasses pumped up and down enthusiastically. 'Yeah, he seems very . . . caring.'

'Oh, yes, yes he is! He's always there to help. He's so giving – not just to me. He's giving with all of us.'

'And what girl doesn't love a giver?' Roxy replied – an eyebrow shooting up above the sunglasses. Sue paused, confused. Had she said something funny? But then Roxy swooped even closer, invading her personal space.

'But I'll be honest, Sue; I was expecting the evening to be a bit more – you know – *one–to–one*.'

Sue blinked. Roxy was studying her expression. Sue knew she was being prodded, but she didn't know what for.

'He's very community-minded,' she mumbled. 'None of us would know each other if it wasn't for him. We were practically neighbours, but had never even spoken.'

'Uh huh.'

'He's always trying to get us to socialise.'

'With him?'

'As a group, of course! He says we've all moped on our own too long; that it's not good for our . . .' She stopped. Roxy was looking peculiar, like she was just about to burst.

'Oh, bugger it.' Roxy exhaled loudly and propped her sunglasses on her head. 'Sod the soft soap. Come on, Sue – you know what I'm getting at!'

'I . . .' Sue didn't have the teeniest, foggiest idea.

'Why didn't Woody make a move on me?' Roxy demanded. 'I mean, Woody's *Woody*, right? And, you've got to admit, I pulled out all the stops with that dress.'

'Oh, yes! You looked wonderf—'

'*Foxy Roxy*, the papers call me! You don't get a nickname like that if you're a minger.'

'No, of course n—'

'He's supposed to be *The Woodeniser*, for Christ's sake! Four hundred quid, that dress cost. It's so bloody tight, it makes my eyes water. One sneeze and I'd be done for indecent exposure. I didn't bloody breathe out from the moment I left my house.'

'It's just that . . . well, the group . . . we . . .'

'You know – he's known where I live for ages. He invited me round to his place the very first chance he got. The tabloids said he and Petra split up yonks ago, so I just don't get it. He's obviously *interested*! I thought we were up for some . . . you know . . . *fun!*'

Sue balked. She wasn't *that* out of touch. She knew what Roxy had been after last night. Nobody wore a dress *that* short without being on the lookout for some how's-your-father.

'But,' Sue tried to explain, 'I expect he has *that* kind of fun with . . .'

'With . . . ?'

'Well, with Jennifer, of course!'

'Jennifer?' Roxy froze.

'Yes, Jennifer: Woody's girlfriend! Surely you saw all the photos? He's got one on every shelf.'

And suddenly, like a soufflé that had been removed from the oven too early, Roxy deflated. Her sunglasses dropped back on to her nose.

'No,' she muttered flatly. 'I must've missed them.'

Sue instantly felt bad. Roxy was looking depressed. Surely she'd known about Jennifer? *Everyone* knew about Jennifer! 'She's gorgeous,' she added awkwardly, probably making things worse. 'And very dedicated to her job.'

Sue was just wondering what to say next when there was a ruckus from the street. Three vans pulled up and a dozen men in anoraks clambered out, noisily clattering stepladders and tripods behind them.

'Bloody hell – paps!' Roxy snapped back to life. She hunched her shoulders to shield her from the street. 'What the hell are they doing here?'

Sue frowned and retreated further behind her door. 'He must be in the papers again,' she whispered. 'They only come when there's a story.'

'What story? Who's in the papers?'

'Thingamabob – *the actor*.' It always made Sue nervous when the paparazzi arrived. She wished she'd planted one of those really tall hedges that people complained about. She frowned. 'But I thought he'd given up acting. My magazine said he was turning his back on it all, that he hated show business and was retiring to count his money and grow a beard.'

'*Austin Jones?*' Roxy snorted loudly. 'What? Austin Jones lives *here?*'

Sue cowered in case the photographers heard and looked over.

'Sometimes,' she whispered. 'You never see him, though. It's such a big place he's got.'

'I can't believe it!' Roxy marvelled loudly, staring openly at the photographers as they assembled their kits and staked their claim on the pavement. '*Austin Jones lives in Lavender Heath.* Christ; I need to put more slap on.' She looked back at Sue sharply. 'For work. Publicity shots – new show I'm in.'

'You're working? I just thought . . . what with Woody bringing you to the—'

'I'm busy, busy, busy, me – phone never stops ringing!' Roxy turned, and then, just as she was hurrying away, she stopped. 'Hey, Sue; you ever thought about getting a fringe?'

Sue's mouth fell open.

'Just a soft one, sweeping to the side? And wearing your hair up at the back? . . . You've got great cheekbones. A fringe would show them off, give your face some drama.'

And then she was gone.

Sue slowly closed the door. In a daze, she carried the DVD into the lounge and placed it next to the television. She drifted to the mirror above the fireplace and looked numbly at her reflection. A doughy woman stared back – dull skinned and heavy haired. Roxy couldn't be right. Surely a fringe couldn't change *that* much . . .

. . . Could it?

With stiff hands, she tried to scoop her hair up and imagine.

To: Roxy Squires
From: BBC Three, New Programming Department

Dear Ms Squires,

Thank you for your recent email outlining some new programme ideas for BBC3.

Whilst we enjoyed your ideas, we're afraid they're not in keeping with our remit for freshness and innovation. Perhaps you might consider pitching them to a channel with an older demographic . . . Watch, perhaps? Vintage TV? Or even Yesterday . . . ?

ROXY

'Bollocks!'

It had been a tough day and Roxy was trackie-bottomed up. Sprawled on her sofa with the TV remote, her inner thighs ached.

The day had started well enough. OK, so she hadn't woken wrapped in the muscly arms and satin sheets of the former hottest pop star on the planet, but the night hadn't been a complete disaster. Victory was a matter of time. Woody might have been trying to hide it in front of the others, but she was as Sure as ladies' deodorant he was desperate to jump her bones.

But then Sue had dropped the clanger.

Roxy wasn't the kind of girl who stole another woman's man. She'd long since decided that if she was going to have sleepless nights it would be because she was clubbing, not racked with guilt over nabbing someone else's boyfriend. She didn't believe in God, but she did believe in karma and it was a well-known fact that, if you did bad stuff, karma got its own back and bit you on the arse. If you nicked another girl's bloke, karma got a different girl – *an even hotter girl* – to nick him back off you. It was just simpler all round to stick to the blokes who were free.

But with Woody . . .

Arghh! With Woody it was going to be a hard rule to follow.

Roxy hadn't fancied anyone for ages, but now she had the chance to get it on with the biggest crush of her life, fate had got a cob on and shoved him out of reach. It wasn't fair – she was sure Woody wanted her. Attraction was usually mutual, and her nips had been so busy perking they were pretty close to knackered. She and Woody would make a perfect couple. They were from the same world, a million miles from Lavender Heath. Theirs was a world of backstage passes, front-page exclusives and open-sesame red velvet ropes. Whatever the saintly Jennifer did for a living (which was obviously something boring, else Roxy would've read about her in the papers), it couldn't begin to come close.

'Bollocks!' Roxy shouted her verdict at each passing channel. And that was another thing that was annoying her. There was so much shit on TV – *and she wasn't presenting it!* Her finger paused over the remote as she watched a few seconds of the latest celebrity stunt show. Presenting this stuff was as easy as breathing – she could do it a million times better than the leggy bit of fluff pouting into camera. Besides, she *knew* the producer of this show; she'd worked with him, years back. They'd partied together – shared a few lines in the gents at Madame Jojo's. Sharing powder in a nightclub toilet was the media equivalent of a blood brothers' cut; she should have presented *all* his programmes after that. But he wouldn't even take her calls now.

Roxy tossed the remote away. There was only one thing for it . . . she needed to get pissed.

She eased herself off the sofa, limped into the kitchen and opened the fridge. Six pints of milk and a fat-free yoghurt stared back. Damn – she could've sworn she had a bottle of white. Undeterred, she pulled on a poncho, picked up her iPod and headed out to the offy.

Stuffing in her headphones, Roxy hit shuffle. And Blondie's 'Rip Her to Shreds' immediately filled her ears. She hit forward. Debbie's girl-on-girl anger was replaced by familiar sticky-sweet chimes.

'Argh!'

Roxy crushed her thumbs into her iPod. That was the last thing she wanted to hear – Woody crooning about falling in love. She'd never have bought his back catalogue if she'd known he was girlfriended-up. She'd a mind to demand her money back.

Stiffly, she walked in silence, rueing her day of bad luck. God, her legs hurt. She hadn't exercised in yonks. But when the photographers had turned up this morning the opportunity had been too good to miss. There were paps – *real, live paps* – in her village. She didn't have to schlep all the way to London to throw herself in front of a lens – there were a dozen, two dozen, a minute from her house! She'd hurtled back home and prepared an outfit.

Or rather, several outfits.

For her first spurious trip to the farmers'-market store (Lavender Heath was too posh for a common corner shop) she'd worn the classic off-duty LA-celeb look of jeans, white T-shirt, sloppy scarf and shades. But that hadn't even raised a glance from the paps who were intently studying the ornate iron gates at the end of Austin Jones' drive. So next she'd tried some vintage boho, before channelling VB in something tailored and torturously tight. The stakes were then upped with some fashion-forward Cheryl, before assets were maxed à la *Hollyoaks*-starlet. Finally, Roxy went the whole hog with some full-on Lady Gaga. Six unwanted pints of milk later, and still nothing! Eventually she'd dug out her roller skates. Normally she didn't resort to these until summer, when she'd take a trip to London and spend a day skating around St James' Park in microscopic knickers and a short, floaty skirt. That had worked several years in a row. Seven years back, she'd even made page three of the *Mail*! But even the combination of roller boots and a Lycra all-in-one (and then later – desperately later – roller boots, microscopic knickers and the short, floaty skirt) had failed to dent Austin's paps. Eventually, when she'd skated eight whole loops of the village and her thighs had been on the point of collapse, she'd given up, gone home and sat on a radiator to thaw out.

'BOLLOCKS!'

The offy was shut.

What was it with today? Was the whole world conspiring against her? Was a bit of Pinot oblivion really too much to ask? In desperation, she turned to the pub. Maybe they did

take-outs. She shoved the Dog and Duck door and stomped up
to the bar.

'Hey, Rox – over here!'

Roxy froze. She quickly tried to remember what she was
wearing and when she'd last glossed. Because, if she wasn't
mistaken, that voice had belonged to . . .

'It's me! Woody!'

She turned, and there he was, sitting at the bar in jeans,
an old Ramones T-shirt and a twinkly-eyed grin. He rubbed
his head and his T-shirt stretched gorgeously across his chest.

To her horror, Roxy felt herself blush. She could've kicked
herself. Jennifer or no Jennifer, she *knew* Woody lived in the
village . . . She should never have set foot out her front door
without the checklist and a killer outfit. But she'd just slobbed
into their local in trackies! Everyone knew trackies sagged at
the back and made your arse look humungous. Woody might
look gorgeous in the dressed-down, crumpled-up look, but she
looked like a bag lady! She groped in her pocket for a pair of
sunglasses to hide behind. But her pockets were empty.

'Hi.' She tried to look casual.

'Hi!' a female voice replied. Roxy froze again. She hadn't
seen Holly, scrubbed and perfect, perched on the bar stool
next to Woody. Roxy's mood plummeted further. Why was
Woody with Holly? Where were the rest of the gang? Sue
said he tried to get them to go out together. If there were any
one-to-one pub trips going on, why wasn't Woody doing them
with her? Everyone knew drinking was her all-time favourite
hobby.

'Would you like to join us?' Holly put down her orange juice and smiled.

'Yeah, come on, Rox.' Woody drummed the bar top. 'What are you drinking? I insist.'

Roxy allowed him to usher her on to a stool. The poncho got wedged under her bum, yanking the neckline tight over her throat.

'Cosmopolitan, please,' she grunted hoarsely, surreptitiously freeing herself from knitted strangulation. If she couldn't look sophisticated, she might as well drink sophisticated.

Woody laughed. 'I'm not sure that's in Dave's repertoire.'

'I could do you a gin and tonic with an umbrella in it?' the landlord offered gruffly.

Roxy nodded. Woody was tantalisingly close. She was within dribbling distance of his honey-dipped biceps. His eyes sparkled in the light of the pub, golden flecks of stubble glinted on his jaw and his lips were deliciously moist from his pint. She could even smell him – and *Christ, he smelt good!* His aroma of clean clothes and pure, solid man was total heavenly torture. She suddenly pictured them lying together, limbs entangled after a long, hard session; her steeped head-to-sparkly-toenails in his special Woody sex smell. She almost groaned out loud. He was so gorgeous, so close – *and so bloody taken.* She took a large gulp of G and T.

'You know,' Holly mused, 'I always thought our local would be more upmarket.'

'What, fiddly cocktails and a door policy?' Woody laughed. 'No call for that kind of thing around here.'

'But what about all the local celebs?' Holly reasoned. 'Surely they want something more than John Smith's?'

'Lavender Heath's not like that,' he replied. 'Most people are just like us. They move here to get away from London life. They just want a bit of normality: walking the dog in their wellies, that kind of thing. They don't want Cristal and blinis from their local. More like home-made pie and real ale. Eh, Rox?'

'Mega . . .' Roxy muttered glumly, rousing herself from her secret inspection of Woody's thighs. She'd barely stepped into the Dog and Duck before. There didn't seem any point when London was just an hour's cab ride away.

'That makes sense.' Holly thought for a moment, before shuddering. 'London . . . What a horrible place!'

Despite her gloom, Roxy peered at Holly. OK, so she was never going to make the *Vogue* cover, but Roxy could see that, despite the confines of her all-pastel wardrobe, she'd obviously made an effort tonight. She was wearing a pretty cream blouse, a pale pink cardigan and dainty, ladylike shoes. As she asked Woody about the local celebrities, and which ones the group should try to help, Roxy couldn't help but wonder what she'd look like with her hair bleached and teamed with smoky eyes. Holly wasn't the kind of girl Roxy had much in common with; she'd never been one of life's do-gooders, preferred magazines to books and only wore pastels ironically. But that didn't mean she couldn't do something *for* her. If Holly could just knock out another best-seller, Roxy was sure she could make her a star. For a start, she'd be great for all those 'before' and 'after' magazine makeovers. And didn't private members' bars like the Groucho love getting literary bigwigs on their list?

'I mean, it's great that Roxy's joined us,' she heard Holly add quickly, checking nervously that she hadn't caused offence, 'but I'm sure we can do more . . . *help* more.' She studied the bar before suddenly turning to Woody in excitement. 'Hey, what about Dwayne Blowers? You know . . . the footballer? I heard he lives near here, and he's had such troubles recently. You must know him, Woody. Get *him* to come to a meeting!'

'Dwayne Blowers . . . ?' Woody tipped his head back in thought, and Roxy lost herself imagining how good it would feel to nuzzle into his neck. He dropped his head back down and looked directly at her. Roxy blushed again and minutely inspected her cocktail umbrella. 'No – he's not on my round.'

'But what about Jennifer?' Holly persisted. 'Maybe she knows him?'

Roxy started at the mention of her rival.

'Jennifer?' Woody looked surprised.

'Yes, what does she do again? Maybe she's come across him?'

'She hasn't. Look, if I bump into him and get chatting, I'll ask him. But if not, let's just give the man some space.'

Holly submissively agreed.

'Austin!' Roxy suddenly blurted. Woody and Holly looked in surprise. It was practically the first word she'd uttered since arriving. She shrugged. 'If you want to help someone, help Austin Jones.'

'Oooo, great idea.' Holly jumped at the prospect. But Woody's face had turned dark. Roxy felt a scrummy thrill at seeing this new side of Woody. Mean, moody Woody – she hadn't known it existed. And *Christ*, it was giving her the horn!

'No.' He frowned.

'Why not?'

'Austin doesn't do anything he doesn't want to.'

Holly laughed. 'Clearly. He's just turned his back on making movies. Such a shame.'

'Total shame,' Roxy agreed. Although he'd never been her cup of tea (he wasn't in a band), Austin Jones was undeniably hot and it was a crime against gorgeousness to deny womankind the chance of an ogle. Roxy's mood brightened. She'd only suggested him to get Woody's attention, but now she thought about it, Austin was an excellent idea. He was famously handsome . . . and cosmically famous. Woody may already be taken . . . but wasn't the best therapy retail? And God knew she could do with some window-shopping . . .

'Trust me; Austin wouldn't be interested,' Woody told them.

'In me?' Roxy's motormouth piped up.

Woody looked at her sharply. 'In the group. He's not the kind.'

'What do you mean?' Holly asked, puzzled.

Woody paused.

Suddenly it seemed like the most important thing in the world that Roxy should get him to change his mind. 'Look, do you, or do you not clean his windows?' she demanded.

He nodded.

'And aren't you two already mates?'

'Not exactly . . .'

'Come off it, you used to hang out!'

'I used to see him at parties, we weren't exactly what you'd call close.'

'Oh, rock off! It's not like he's going to have forgotten you. Ask him. Let *him* decide if he wants to meet up.'

'Yes, ask him,' Holly agreed, almost falling off her seat with excitement.

But Woody wasn't convinced.

'He's just retired, in his *thirties*!' Holly added earnestly. '*And* he threw something nasty at the paparazzi this afternoon. He's clearly got things he needs to get off his chest—'

'His taut, manly chest.' Roxy grinned.

'And surely that's the whole point of the group: sharing our experiences with fellow fame survivors; offering a hand of friendship in their moments of crisis?'

'I wonder if he waxes . . .' Roxy mused.

'He's not going to want to meet us,' Woody warned.

'But you're Woody!' Roxy cried. 'If anyone can persuade him, it's you!'

Woody looked at the two women. He seemed to be wrestling with something. Roxy fixed him with her flirtiest look, mentally bending him to her will.

'OK,' he conceded in exasperation. 'I'll ask.'

'Rock and roll!' Roxy beamed. Round one may have gone to Jennifer, but round two was definitely hers. Woody had changed his mind. So she didn't fancy Austin – but she still had her fame protégés to think about. Maybe Austin could call up his movie-star pals, pull a few favours for the group. Yes, Austin Jones could be useful – very useful indeed!

Woody's pocket suddenly vibrated.

'Want me to get that?' she flirted on reflex.

Woody laughed and whipped out his phone. Roxy sneaked a peek at the screen.

'Hey, baby! How's it going?'

He motioned that he was going outside. Roxy watched him leave, her good mood already deflating. God, he had a good bum. Delicious – like it was sculpted from marzipan. But then she grimaced. His bum – just like marzipan – was off limits.

And then Roxy and Holly were alone at the bar. Roxy fought the terrible feeling that had sunk to the bottom of her gut. The phone had made Woody look happy: happier than he'd been at the meeting; happier than he'd been in her kitchen. In fact, happier than she'd seen him before. And she didn't need to be Vorders to work out why.

The name on the phone had been JJ.

Bollocks.

Round three went to Jennifer – and she wasn't even there!

Roxy watched Holly pick a bit of fluff off her cardie. She drained her G and T in one gulp.

2.45am @foxyroxy

Teeeny bitt drunk, but so wha? iPod shuffle given paws for
though.t. Think iss important we learn lessons from rock . . .

2.51am @foxyroxy

Sting rekons ifyou love someone set themfree. Dolly begs pleas
dontakemyman. Kelis says her milkshake brings allthe boys 2
the yard . . .

2.56am @foxyroxy

#ROXYSAYS: Whatkindofwomun pinches las MarcJacobs
skinnyknit jumper outof nother womanshoppngbasket anyway?
You jus don doit.Thanyou+gnight

SIMON

Simon grabbed a basket and swept into Waitrose. He felt trai-
torous even thinking it, but maybe it was time he got a new
agent.

Actually, he didn't know why he'd stuck with Barrington
so long. The only decent job he'd ever got him had been *Down
Town*, and that was fifteen years ago. And since he'd left, they'd
never agreed on which direction his career should be taking.
They'd argued and debated for so long, the only direction
they'd gone in was backwards. How else had Simon gone from
prime time to panto? His career – like his relationship with
his agent – was one of diminishing returns.

But Simon was nothing if not loyal. Besides, agents gener-
ally scared him. He'd met a couple a few years back, over
drinks at parties. They'd stuffed their sentences with a
rundown of their A-list clients – breathing from the diaphragm
to cram in the maximum number of thesps – before looking
right through Simon towards someone more *credibly* famous.
Simon was, after all, only a soap star – and everyone knew
soap stars couldn't act.

So Simon had stuck with the devil he knew. Twice a week, after dropping the kids at school, he phoned Barrington from his people carrier in Waitrose car park. There wasn't any reason to call, just a vague hope he might eventually irritate Barrington into finding him a decent job. He rarely got to actually speak to him, inevitably being intercepted by a minion and informed that Barrington was 'on the other line'. But this morning he'd struck lucky. Somehow the kids had shambled out of bed, through the tricky terrains of showers and breakfasts, and into the back of the people carrier early – well, on time – and Simon had pulled into Waitrose car park a full seven minutes ahead of schedule. Barrington was caught off guard. He forgot to call-screen and Simon had got straight through.

'Well, there is *something* we could put you forward for,' Barrington offered doubtfully as he rummaged through his papers to what sounded suspiciously like the bottom of the pile. 'It's TV – a young audience. Another villain. They want someone scary.'

'I don't want scary,' Simon reminded him for the eight-hundredth time. 'I want to move away from Nick.'

'Mmmm,' Barrington mused, his mind already elsewhere. 'There's not much around; quiet time, darling. Everyone's re-covering from Christmas.'

'But you said it was quiet *before* Christmas and that every-thing goes manic in January!' Simon protested. And then he sighed. 'OK, tell me about the villain. Which channel's it for?' He held his breath and prayed the next words out of Barrington's mouth would be 'BBC1'.

'A very prestigious channel!'

'Which channel?'

'A BBC channel.'

Simon's tummy began to tingle.

'*Which* BBC channel?'

'CBeebies.'

'Oh.' His tummy stilled with a thud. He groped for some equanimity. 'CBeebies isn't *so* bad. I mean, if it's good enough for Jacobi with all that *Night Garden* stuff, right?' And then he remembered . . . hadn't some big names read the CBeebies bedtime stories? Yes, he was sure Kenneth Branagh had done one. And Bonneville. Maybe even Mirren! He imagined the name of Drennan joining the line-up of thesps.

'It's a non-speaking role,' Barrington continued in a rush. 'A fabulous opportunity to showcase your mime and movement skills. The auditions are next week.'

'Next week, no problem,' Simon agreed automatically. And then his ears caught up. 'Hang on . . . Are you saying, I need to audition for CBeebies? For a *non-speaking* role? But I used to scare fourteen million people a week!'

Surely he hadn't got it so wrong, Simon thought bleakly as he dropped line-caught cod, pine nuts and organic pesto into his basket. Every actor had their moments of self-doubt, but at his core he'd always believed he had talent. And it wasn't just vanity; there was evidence. He'd received two commendations at RADA *and* he'd recieved warm reviews for the plays he'd been in, in the brief gap between drama school and the soap. 'One to watch,' is how *The Stage* had described him. He'd been steadily working his way up the ladder of support roles towards the ultimate prize of a lead. But then fate had intervened and suddenly treading the boards for four hundred people wasn't so important. He was destined for bigger things.

Simon contemplated a bag of muesli. Sometimes he wondered if *Down Town* had been such a good thing after all. It was supposed to have been his springboard. When Barrington had told him he'd passed his – was it seventh? – audition for the role of Nick Fletcher, he and Linda had been beside themselves with excitement. His stage work had barely kept them in mortgage payments and nappies, but soap wages meant Linda could take proper time off from her legal training to look after the baby twins. Life had suddenly rocketed upwards.

For the first year, Nick Fletcher had lurked in the background, propping up the bar and contributing a few lines whilst the producers decided if Simon could cut the mustard. Then, slowly, he started getting storylines. Bit by bit, Nick got creepier. He struck up friendships with young girls; he offered to help them with their school projects, lent them money, gave them lifts in his car. And then he'd begun to sniff. Not so as the girls could see him, but when they turned their backs he'd sensuously inhale their hair. He was 'making the nation's skin creep', the producers announced gleefully. And once the papers dubbed him 'Sick Nick' and he got heckled by the public on his days off, the producers knew they were on to a big thing. The storylines came thick and fast: the begging from his wife to start a family; his inexplicable refusal;

his wife trying to leave him; Nick beating her in reply; his cruel treatment of his Alzheimer's-suffering mother; Nick using her illness to steal her savings and torture her by continually breaking the news of her husband's death – even though he'd died decades ago. And then, finally, his predatory pursuit of his best friend's teenage daughter: frightening off her young boyfriend, surprising her at the school gates, touching her too often, too intimately.

But eventually – as all soap villains do – Nick went too far. His wife packed her bags and fled; his mother kicked the bucket. Suddenly there was nothing left to curtail his behaviour. At his mother's wake he laced the teenage girl's drink before using his grief to coerce her back to the graveyard and force himself evilly upon her. But she fought back, using the last remains of her intoxicated strength to strike him with the designer handbag his own money had bought her. She knocked him so hard that he fell into his mother's open grave, smashing his head on the coffin. The last the world saw of Sick Nick, he was glassy-eyed and spread-eagled – sprawled dead across his mother's coffin in a deathly parody of an embrace.

It had been Simon's choice for Nick to die. He'd wanted to leave unequivocally; with no escape route back, should his post-*Down Town* career fail. He was hot, Barrington had promised him. At thirty-two years old, the time was right and the world was his oyster. Sick Nick was the trampoline that would ping him out of the small screen and on to the big. Barrington had a plan: a lead in a quality BBC drama, before a career of chilling baddies, unhinged criminals and evil-genius psychopaths. He was going to be the British Christopher Walken, the new Dennis Hopper, the scariest Bond villain ever.

But whilst Simon agreed with the scale of Barrington's plans, he disagreed with their direction. He'd always felt cursed by his naturally maudlin expression; the nose that had stopped him getting girlfriends until – mercifully – Linda had come along. He knew his features were what had made Nick seem so haunted, but he wanted the world to see him differently. Playing a sicko was depressing. Besides, he was fed up with being heckled as a 'kiddy-fiddling pervert' whenever he was out with the twins.

What Simon *really* wanted was a romantic lead. He wanted comedy and feel-good, heart-warming fluff. He didn't want housewives spurning him as he waited at the school gates, discreetly turning their daughters away. He wanted house-wives to *love* him, to literally *fall in love* with him up on the screen. Sod being the nation's pariah – he wanted to be its sweetheart, like Firth striding out of the lake, or Grant bumbling at the weddings, or Austin bloody Jones being cute with puppies. What he really, *really* wanted was a Richard Curtis rom-com.

'A Richard Curtis rom-com?' Barrington had laughed. 'Really, Simon; the audience would never swallow it. And besides, playing a psycho didn't do Anthony Hopkins any harm!'

'But I want to be the good guy,' Simon had protested bleakly. 'I want to get the girl, and I don't want her to be underage.'

'Trust me, sweetie,' Barrington had soothed.

And so here he was, clinging to the craggy rock face of thirty-nine, peering into the career abyss of forty . . . the lush nirvana of a Richard Curtis rom-com as far away as the moon.

Trying not to feel depressed, Simon shuffled up to the checkout. Peering into his basket, he counted how many of the five a day tonight's meal would provide. The home-cooked delivery of the family's nutrition had recently become his obsession – far nicer to think about than his so-called career. Five a day was something he *could* deliver. If he couldn't bring home the bacon, he could at least cook it.

His mission was given added importance because the twins couldn't be relied upon to eat healthily in school, despite Simon and Linda scraping together the exorbitant fees for them to attend a plush private school. Their previous school's canteen had been far better, but Scarlet had insisted on leaving, the state school playground apparently too unforgiving for the kids of 'Sick Nick'.

'But I stopped playing Nick seven years ago! Your classmates would've been too young to watch!'

'Once a sicko, always a sicko,' Scarlet had countered smartly.

He'd reluctantly acquiesced, although the suspicion remained that the switch was motivated more by the new school's funky lilac uniform than her classmates' inability to distinguish fiction from fact.

Simon handed his basket to the checkout girl and pulled out his wallet. A fountain of loose coins cascaded out of his pocket, rolling across the supermarket floor. Simon bent down to retrieve them. A pound coin had rolled behind the swollen ankles of an old woman queueing behind him.

'I beg your pardon,' he apologised politely as he reached for his coin.

Despite her age, the old woman nimbly threw herself backwards.

'Keep your hands to yourself!' she scolded loudly as she placed her foot squarely over his pound. 'I know *exactly* where they've been, thank you. You should be ashamed of yourself.'

'Isn't he supposed to be dead?' her friend piped up.

'They're all the same, these sexual predators,' the old woman announced to the shop floor. 'They see a woman and they just can't help themselves.'

Simon sagged in exhausted frustration. He should have listened to Linda; she'd told him to get their groceries online. He'd lost count of how many times he'd been hassled in supermarkets. He felt himself shake with embarrassed indignation.

'I'm Simon Drennan, the actor,' he projected with as much dignity as he could muster on all fours on the floor. 'I used to play a character in the soap opera, *Down Town*. I am *not* Nick Fletcher, the fictional, morally-flawed villain. I'm a law-abiding, happily married, *real* person who just wants to buy his family's dinner.'

'Did he say *Downton*?' someone cooed from a few aisles along. 'Oooo, I *love* Captain Crawley! Is it him?'

'*Down Town*,' somebody replied, disappointed. 'It's just that paedo who was mean to his mother.'

Meanwhile the old woman stared suspiciously down at Simon before reluctantly sucking her cheeks.

'Keep your hair on,' she muttered gracelessly, her foot still covering his pound. 'I was only saying.'

Slowly, Simon stood up. The whole of Waitrose seemed to be staring in judgement. He threw a couple of twenty-pound notes at the checkout girl, grabbed his groceries and fled.

This would never have happened if he'd done a Richard Curtis movie, he thought as he bolted out of the supermarket and towards the safety of the people carrier. He bet Firth and Grant never got hassled in supermarkets. Not this kind of hassle, anyway. They probably just got ushered to the front of the queue where the till girl let them have their groceries for free, if they'd only agree to accept the bit of scrap receipt on which she'd scrawled her phone number and vital statistics.

'Bloody Barrington,' he cursed as he thrust his car into first and accelerated out of the car park with a skid. He'd probably never even emailed Richard Curtis his CV! Well, Simon had had enough. He was going straight home to find his old copy of *Spotlight* and ring all the agents he could find. Straight after he'd baked a fresh loaf of sourdough bread and tried out that new recipe for seafood chowder, that was. Mussels were in season and he didn't want to miss his window. But after that, there'd be no stopping him . . .

10.45am @foxyroxy

Just binned fave trackie bottoms. Hurt, but had to be done. Trackies = dangerously addictive gateway drug disguised as comfort . . .

10.46am @foxyroxy

1 minute you're sat watching TV, feeling comfy – next, you're pushing trolley round Lidl with no foundation + split ends

10.47am @foxyroxy

Plus they add 20lbs + give bumslide down to knees.
#ROXYSAYS: Chuck out your trackies – keep your arse at your arse!

ROXY

When she was little, there were many things Roxy imagined her grown-up self doing – parachuting out of an aeroplane, vogueing with Madonna, posing for Mario Testino . . . Spending a Thursday night at the home of a former government minister wasn't one of them. But here she was, perched on the over-stuffed chesterfield sofa of the former Secretary of State for Work and Pensions, doing her best to blank out a plate of Simon's home-made mini cheesecakes, and concentrate instead on the self-pitying grumbles of a former TV weatherman.

'One wrong forecast and I lost everything,' Terence moaned. 'My job, my income, my status . . .'

'Yeah, but, be honest,' Simon interrupted dryly. 'It wasn't just *one* wrong forecast.'

'It wasn't just the tornado?' Roxy asked in surprise, the mini cheesecakes suddenly forgotten. She read the papers religiously – well, the showbiz pages – but this was news to her.

'Let's see . . .' Simon made a show of remembering. 'Well, there was the small matter of him failing to forecast the UK's heaviest-ever hail storm . . . the one that caved in the roof of that school bus.'

'Nobody could have predicted that!' Terence protested. 'Besides, the children didn't complain.'

'The children were treated for shock.'

'What about the London floods?' Cressida piped up. 'Sunshine, you told us. We had to evacuate Parliament. The Lords was slopping with wigs.'

'And then there was the thunderstorm at the Royal Wedding,' added Holly. 'They'd never have used the open-top carriage if you'd said it would rain. Who knew white went so see-through?'

'And let's not forget the Telford Tornado!' cried Simon. 'Or the fact that you personally bankrupted thousands. People lost their life savings thanks to you!'

'I never said my forecast for a white Christmas was one hundred per cent accurate.'

'We could bet our houses on it, you said.'

'It's not my fault we're a nation of gamblers!'

'Four hundred families became homeless!'

'But I lost things too: My job, my reputation, my wife . . .'

'Your wife left you because you lost your *job*?' Sue looked shocked.

'The best years of my life I gave her. *And* my employer. And neither stood by me when the shit hit the fan.'

'Oh, Terence.'

'But your employer wouldn't have been able to stand by you after that,' Woody reasoned. 'Even the continuity announcer introduced you as Tornado.'

'He'd always had it in for me. It wasn't my fault the viewers never got to see him.'

'And you're sure your wife didn't leave you because of your enormous persecution complex and complete inability to move on?' Simon smirked.

'Yes, well,' Cressida interjected. 'Stiff upper lip, and all that.'

'It's all right for you, Cressida,' Terence said indignantly. 'Politicians have respect. I'm just a joke! My career's now nothing more than a Trivial Pursuit answer.'

'Yeah?' Roxy was impressed. 'What colour?'

Terence looked awkward. 'Pink.'

Everyone winced.

'I'm a meteorologist! I should be bloody green!'

'I think you've been treated very unfairly.' Sue touched Terence's arm and he momentarily calmed. 'Everyone knows how changeable the British weather is. They hardly ever get it right.'

'They get it a lot more right without Terence,' Simon muttered.

'Look, everyone.' Woody stepped in before Terence could rant again. 'We're not here to score points! What we *did* doesn't matter; it's what we're *going to do* that counts. We need to work out what we're good at now.' He looked around encouragingly. 'Any ideas?'

Silence.

'Simon's good at cooking,' Holly offered.

'Oh, great!' Simon snorted. 'Forget the BAFTAs – my future's fairy cakes!'

'Anything else?' Woody tried again.

More silence. They all inspected their laps. All of them, that was, except Roxy, who was inspecting Woody instead. It was weird seeing Woody be normal. She kept waiting for him to burst into lip-synch, or rip off his shirt and reveal a vest. But instead he kept banging on about self-help. She wanted his body, not his advice. And besides, she didn't need to think of an alternative career because she *still had a career* – she was still totally famous!

Mind, she couldn't help feeling sorry for the gang. They were obviously suffering from some kind of mental status-shift delay. It must be crap to have fame and then lose it, but they only had themselves to blame. Staying famous was easier than ever – *had they learnt nothing from Madonna, for rock's sake?* No scandal was bad enough to career-kill. Unless you were Gary Glitter or James Blunt – although, for the life of her, Roxy couldn't work out what poor Blunty had done to make everyone hate him, other than sell a gazillion records and snog loads of models. But other than being a paedophile or James Blunt, it seemed you could get away with anything . . . drugs, booze, adultery, sex-addiction, shoplifting, hitting attendants in toilets, waving your willy at policemen in toilets – even getting engaged to Darren Day, if you were sorry about it later. A Piers Morgan interview could get you back on track in a week – and bigger than ever before. Mud no longer stuck, it just gave you extra traction for getting up the ladder.

Satisfied with her assessment, Roxy's eye wandered over to the mini cheesecakes again. They'd done several circuits of the room and were now sitting on a nest of tables, right under her nose. She could've cursed Simon for bringing them. Was she the only person here career-minded enough to diet? She leant forward, about to edge them away, but suddenly found herself frozen. She hadn't been this close to a cheesecake in years. They looked at her enticingly. Despite a lifetime of training to remove herself from the scene of calorific temptation – it was the fight or flight principle, only with saturated fat – Roxy's mouth suddenly watered. She'd forgotten the alluring texture of cheesecakes: solid, yet soft, their creamy flesh inviting – luring you to sin. Of all cakes, the cheesecake was the most seductive: a femme fatale of puddings, beguiling even the most devout dieter into a ruinous state of cellulite.

'Any news on Austin Jones?' she blurted in panic, breaking the silence of the room. She wrestled her eyes over to Woody, but then realised she'd just swapped one form of temptation for another. She tried not to think badly about Jennifer. It wasn't her fault she'd found Woody first.

Everyone looked up, grateful for the diversion.

'Yes, contacting Austin was Roxy's idea,' Holly excitedly announced. 'And a brilliant one, too! I mean, can we think of anyone who needs our support *more*?'

'Austin Jones?' Simon looked strange. 'Are we sure that's a good idea?'

'We're not,' Woody agreed, dark and broody once again.

Cressida looked confused.

'I don't understand. Why wouldn't it be a good idea?'

Simon faltered. 'Well, he's just . . . you know . . . *Austin Jones.* Way out of our league – even yours, Woods – no offence.'

Woody's jaw clenched ever so slightly.

'I mean, we're just a bunch of soap stars and weathermen. We've had fame, but nothing like him. He's *world* famous.'

'He's hardly Mandela,' Cressida scoffed.

'Yeah, what's the problem, Si?' hectored Terence. 'Worried he'll make you look little-league?'

Roxy was gobsmacked. Woody and Simon were looking so grave! 'Come on, you lot, anyone would think that you don't want to rub shoulders with a mega-star. Austin rocks!'

'Is *on* the rocks!' Terence snorted.

'The poor man,' Sue piped up sympathetically. 'The photographers are giving him such a terrible time. It's awful, being under siege in your own home – unable to set foot outdoors without a dozen people taking your photo. So lonely. We can all relate to that.'

Everyone thought for a moment. Even Simon conceded the point.

'So, it's agreed?' Holly paused her pen over her notebook. Everyone but Simon and Woody nodded. 'Well, it's going in the minutes as an official action point: *Woody to approach Austin.*'

Roxy let out a whoop. And then she watched Simon pack away the cheesecakes, his face as pale as their toppings.

To: Roxy Squires
From: Channel Five, Talent Department

Dear Roxie,

Thank you for your email, suggesting yourself as a Five on-screen presenter.

As you can imagine, we get inundated with showreels from aspiring presenters, and I'm afraid we have no requirements for on-screen talent at this time.

Best of luck with your search for employment.

To: Roxy Squires
From: Channel Five, Talent Department

Dear Roxie,

Yes, we are aware of your substantial back catalogue. But we *still* have no requirements for on-screen talent at this time.

Best of luck with your search for employment.

To: Roxy Squires

From: Channel Five, Talent Department

Dear Roxy,

Thank you for your email congratulating us on the 'Gang Of Five', the five new faces of Five, launched on-air this week.

We at Five have an on-going commitment to unearthing dynamic, new presenting talent – as well as celebrating the nation's favourite, established presenters. Why not follow our new line-up of hosts on Twitter (@gangofFive), or vote for them at the forthcoming TV WOW awards? The gang would be grateful for your support!

We have attached their signed photo as thanks!

ROXY

Somewhere in the most affluent enclave of St John's Wood, an elaborate front door swung open and a beautiful woman with Green & Black's hair swore in surprise.

'Roxanne Squires; I don't bloody believe it! I know you said you'd be here for lunch, but in your world that usually means six!'

'Bloody cheek.' Roxy rolled her eyes.

And then the woman launched herself through the doorway and threw her arms around her friend.

'Good to see you, you old tart!' Tish hugged her tightly. 'How are you? Still flying the flag for all us lushes?'

'Someone's got to keep the faith.'

'Too right,' the brunette nodded earnestly. 'Don't be a sell-out, like the rest of us. I'm telling you – all this domestic harmony bollocks is overrated. I'd stick my kids on eBay for a big night out on the tiles.'

Roxy raised an eyebrow. 'There's nothing stopping you, Tish. I brought my make-up bag; we can go out tonight, if you like?'

'Party like it's 1997?'

'Party like it's 1997!'

Tish paused for a moment, misty eyed. Roxy gave her a nudge.

'Come on, Tish; you know you want to. It'll be just like the good old days. Let's trowel on some lippy and crack open a bottle of Jack. Guy can babysit.'

Tish sighed wistfully. 'And back in the real world . . . cup of peppermint tea?'

'If I have to . . .' Roxy grimaced.

'Sorry, Rox.' Tish ushered her through the front door. 'It's a booze-free, caffeine-free, fun-free house these days. You know how it is.'

'Yeah – I know how it is,' Roxy mumbled as she followed her friend into the kitchen. It was true; she *did* know how it was . . . but what she couldn't get her head around was *why*. Tish was her oldest friend and partner in crime from when they'd first moved to London and discovered the neon-lit playground of Soho's late bars. For seven super-short years they'd shared more laughs, big nights out and debilitating hangovers than most people got through in a lifetime, and Roxy still felt winded by the speed with which their fun had suddenly died. The kids bit she got. *Of course* when Tish had kids they were going to have to call a halt to the wild all-nighters; but it was the born-again purity that stumped her. OK, so Tish had always liked a drink, but it wasn't like she'd been an alcoholic. So what was with the teetotalling? And where was the harm in a full-strength tea, for rock's sake? Roxy blamed Guy, Tish's minted but tedious husband. It was like he'd won the girlfriend jackpot, defying the odds to miraculously bag himself the coolest girl at the party. But, bit by bit, Guy had sucked out all of Tish's fun bits. The Tish that was left *talked* like the old Tish and *moved* like the old Tish, but she wasn't the old Tish. She didn't look right. New Tish was immaculate in neat black pedal pushers and black ballet pumps (not heels or trainers . . . *ballet pumps!*), and her hair was salon-immaculate – no longer back-combed, dip-dyed or tied into ironic bunches. Whereas old Tish worked like a demon, partied like a warrior and had a weakness for bass players in broom cupboards, new Tish worshipped at the altars of pilates, school runs and early nights. It was as though Roxy's best friend had married Professor Higgins and not some city bloke with cuff links and jowls.

'Organic oatcake?' Tish proffered a plate of roughage. 'Gluten free!'

'No, ta.' Roxy waved the oatcakes away. It wasn't hard. They looked as tempting as herpes. 'So where are Seraphina and Rufus?' she tried to ask brightly. She ignored how uncomfortably the names sat on her tongue. She still couldn't believe Tish had such terribly named kids. She'd always sworn she'd never have children but had promised that if she *did* accidentally pop a few out, she'd call them something inappropriate, like Randy, Fanny or Butch.

'At school, silly.' Tish laughed. 'Big places – lots of books, remember? Although you probably never made it further than the bike sheds!'

'Where I was too busy smoking fags with you.'

'Too busy showing the boys our knickers, more like.'

'That was essential vocational training. I seem to remember we both made a career out of showing boys our pants.'

'Shhh!' Tish hushed her, despite the house being empty. 'We don't talk about that any more.'

'Guy's rewritten history, has he? Handily forgotten his old subscription to *FHM*?'

'Let's just put it this way – he's blocked the kids' access to YouTube. Doesn't want them stumbling across any of Mummy's old TV shows by mistake.'

'It was alternative youth telly, not late night baps and flaps! And you were a brilliant presenter. You interviewed the Beastie Boys and Oasis – you were voted the coolest woman on TV, Guy should be proud of you!'

'He is, he is,' Tish mollified. 'He just doesn't like me going on about it, that's all.' She looked sad for a moment. Roxy felt bad. OK, so Guy wouldn't have been *her* choice, but she didn't want to slag off her best mate's man. As she looked at her friend, she suddenly wondered if Tish missed her old life. Of course, *she* always wished they could go back to the good old days, but did Tish ever wish that too? Did she ever wonder what might have been when she turned on the telly? Tish had always been the most talented of their group, the one the stars preferred to be interviewed by. She'd made everything she presented look easy.

'Have you seen any of the others lately?' Roxy asked. 'Any of the old gang?'

'Course!' Tish grinned, her mood instantly cheering. 'Last weekend. Gabriella's sixth . . . You know, Genna's youngest?

Genna hired Cirque du Soleil for the party. Hey, why weren't you there?'

Roxy hesitated. She didn't like to say her invitation had got lost in the post. These days a party invitation stating 'plus one' usually referred to an under five. Roxy was a party veteran of many years standing, but this new breed of party was beyond her. Of all the clubs she'd ever belonged to, the kindergarten club had the toughest membership code.

'I was working.' She settled on bluster.

'Ah!' Tish marvelled brightly. 'Ever the committed career girl! So how's life in the media rat race?'

'Oh, you know . . .' Roxy fudged. She didn't want to lie – Tish was her best friend. But she didn't exactly want to tell the truth, either . . . especially not whilst she was sitting in Tish's 100k kitchen in her two-million-pound house, whilst her eminently successful husband was being chauffeured from power-meeting to power-meeting and her pompously-named children were writing Latin verse in their six-grand-a-term school. Besides, what was the point in telling the truth? The next big job was just around the corner. Everything could be different next week. It was only a temporary blip in her work-flow.

Tish nodded enthusiastically. 'God, I really admire how you've kept working,' she gushed. 'I just didn't have the energy. But you . . . You've got more staying power than the Duracell bunny. I don't think any of us lot have set foot in a nightclub since 2005, but you just keep on going. And you're looking amazing, Rox – still the same Foxy Roxy. Not like me; I'm such a frump these days. You know, I look back and I can't believe some of the outfits we used to go out in. Do you remember that award ceremony we went to handcuffed together?'

Roxy laughed. 'And that night at the Met Bar dressed as nuns?'

Tish squealed with delight. 'I laughed so hard I think I actually wet myself. It was the first time in years we'd worn anything that covered our midriffs.'

'Apart from that rubber catsuit.' Roxy grinned. 'Remember . . . ? The one you wore for that beer ad? The director fancied you so much he let you keep it.'

'Now, that's a part of the past that Guy doesn't mind revisiting.'

'I'll bet he doesn't.'

'Anyway, never mind all that bollocks.' Tish swept her past away with a swish of a tastefully-manicured hand. She suddenly looked mischievous. 'Let's cut the starter and skip to the sausage, shall we? So, Roxanne, are you getting any pork?'

Roxy squirmed, and tried not to imagine Woody in the buff. 'There *is* someone,' she said slowly, 'but it's complicated.'

'Don't be daft – since when are men complicated?' Tish scoffed. 'They're as intricate as tights!'

'It's Woody.'

'Woody?' Tish was momentarily silenced. 'What *the* Woody? Woody, *The Woodeniser*? *Woodypecker*? The scrummy pop star with the cute hair and Rear-of-the-Year arse?'

'Runner-up,' Roxy corrected her flatly. 'His arse was runner-up.'

'Whatever. You do mean *Woody*? The one who was top of the charts for five years and every woman in the country was desperate to bonk?'

'Yes. *That* Woody.'

'Bloody hell, Rox!' Tish exclaimed, impressed. And then she thought for a moment. 'Didn't we have a fight over him on the school bus?'

Roxy nodded.

'Did you win?'

Roxy nodded again.

Tish looked thoughtful. 'Is he still hot?'

'Scorching.'

'So what's the problem? A hot guy like him, a cool girl like you . . . Sounds like a slam dunk!'

'He's taken, Tish,' Roxy said glumly.

'What? Married?'

'Not sure.'

'Kids?'

'Don't think so.'

'So he's not *taken* taken then!'

Roxy frowned. 'No, Tish, he's taken; he's very, very taken. He's got this amazing, wonderful girlfriend called Jennifer, who's the closest thing to a living saint. She's a workaholic genius; queen of the boardroom, or something. Everyone thinks she's amazing and beautiful, and he's obviously completely in love with her—'

'But not in love with her enough to marry her,' Tish interrupted dryly. 'Don't worry about it, Roxster. If he's not taken her up the aisle, he's fair game. Besides, he obviously fancies you.'

'I didn't say that.'

'You didn't have to. Of course he's fancies you, you're sex on legs! Really, Rox . . . you need to bitch up. Girlfriend, schmirlfriend. I don't know what you're doing wasting time on my sofa. You should be over at his place, working your assets.'

'But how can you say that?' Roxy protested. 'You're married – you've got a family! And besides, I thought we were all about girl power? Didn't you always say never to shit on a sister's doorstep?'

'Yeah, well, I was young and idealistic back then,' Tish conceded. 'And probably drunk. And, honestly, you should see how some of our so-called sisters act when it comes to getting their little darlings into the right schools. It's every bitch for herself.' Tish stopped and sighed. 'Look, Rox, it's all very well being Mrs Moral, but get real . . . *this is Woody we're talking about!* You doodled his name on every pencil case you ever had. If you don't give it a whirl, you'll regret it for the rest of your life.'

Roxy sighed. That bit was certainly true.

'So you're saying I should just go for it?' She frowned. 'That I should just forget about Jennifer, and go all out for Woody?'

'Like a merciless, heat-seeking missile.'

Roxy picked up her tea. Tish's plan sounded good, and God knew she was tempted. But something was holding her back. And it wasn't just shock at Tish's standards.

'No,' she said quietly. 'It's not right.'

Tish looked at her strangely. 'Yeah, well, you're probably too busy for a boyfriend anyway,' she conceded. 'I mean, you're married to your job, right?'

Roxy searched her friend's face for a trace of mockery.

'Leaf salad OK?' Tish got up and headed for the fridge. 'Tomatoes are a bugger to work off, and my nutritionist reckons cucumber gives you crow's feet.'

'Leaf salad sounds fine,' Roxy mumbled hollowly as she looked at her unfamiliar best friend. Suddenly Woody seemed further from reach than ever.

WOODY

The morning was frosty and beautiful. All he could hear was the blood pounding in his ears and the beat of his feet on the pavement. It was Woody's favourite time of the day and he was nearing the end of his run.

Throughout his twenties, Woody had barely set foot into the clean air of a morning – unless he'd been booked on to breakfast TV, and even then he'd never breathed actual air, being bundled straight from a hotel lobby into the air-con of a chauffeur-driven car. It was only when his career was over that he rediscovered the beauty of mornings, and he suddenly realised just how many crisp, clean sunrises he'd missed. Almost three thousand, he reckoned – slept through, unnoticed or ignored. Three thousand chances to get up before the rest of the world and run through the empty streets whilst everything was untouched by the day. An early-morning jog had been one of the unexpected joys of his post pop-star life. And now, five times a week, he kicked the day off with a run, a shower and a home-cooked sausage sandwich.

He loved Lavender Heath. It was different to the other places he'd lived in: Notting Hill, Chelsea Wharf . . . He'd even had the obligatory rock-star country pad for a while – a vast, cavernous manor with a helipad. Someone had sold it for him whilst he'd been wallowing on his couch in London. They'd done him a favour. By the time he'd come to, he knew he needed to get out of the city – and moving into a manor wasn't exactly the new start he was after. Something modest was what he wanted now. He'd wandered, clueless, into the nearest estate agent's. The woman who'd brought him to Lavender Heath couldn't have been mortal, he decided. She must have been some kind of superhuman estate agent, normal on the outside, but blessed with the superpower to divine her client's perfect pad. The small but attractive house she'd found him was perfect. *Lavender Heath* was perfect.

Woody sped past Roxy's house, its curtains drawn; the place – like its owner – still asleep. He smiled as he saw her neon-pink door, defiant amongst Lavender Heath's Farrow-and-Ball tones. And then, a few minutes later, he rounded the corner to Bramble Lane and jogged up his drive.

Breakfasted, showered and ready to go, Woody picked up his ladder and made the short walk over to Cressida's to start the day's round. He liked Cressida. She wasn't most people's cup of tea but Woody always found something admirable about her. If there was one thing you could rely on, it was for her never to soft-soap. Cressida was more likely to bang heads than group hug. But she was sharp, positive and one of life's doers . . . and that was the heart of the problem. Cressida needed a purpose – something that wasn't just politics. But her whole life had been party political, and now nothing was left in its place.

Cressida's house was characteristically practical. If she'd fiddled her expenses, she might be living in one of Lavender Heath's roomier piles. Instead, Cressida's small home was conveniently close to the station and shops, and boasted a garden of low-maintenance shrubs, two modest bedrooms and a study. It may not have had the elaborate prettiness of its neighbours, but it was sensible and fashion-resistant.

'Good morning,' Cressida greeted him crisply as she opened her front door and stood stiffly aside so he could head into her kitchen to fill his bucket. Cressida Cunningham was a woman of routines, and Woody knew this one. He wouldn't get coffee until the cleaning was completed – and even then he'd end up making their drinks himself. But he didn't mind. It wasn't that Cressida was lazy – it was just that drink-making wasn't in her remit. It was what other people did.

'I can't get my blasted television to work,' she grumbled later, as Woody spooned out the Gold Blend. There were no fancy coffee machines in Cressida's kitchen. 'I fail to see why everything had to go digital. I was perfectly happy with five channels and one remote. Now I've got a blasted remote control for everything – and not one of the stupid things works!'

That was another thing Cressida wasn't so good at – modern life.

'Here; let me take a look,' Woody offered. She was constantly having trouble with her appliances, from her BlackBerry to her burglar alarm. She obviously had a brain the size of a planet – her walls were lined with photos of her with world leaders, and her bookshelves stuffed with hardbacks on economics – but simple, everyday gadgets had her foxed.

'Of course, when I was working I never had to bother with any of this.' Cressida waved her hand at the collection of remotes littering her table. 'I was too busy to waste time grappling with appliances or placing phone calls. My assistants did all that for me.'

'You didn't make phone calls?' Woody snorted.

'I didn't dial the numbers; my secretary did. I just picked up the phone and whomever I wanted to speak to would be waiting. Of course, I dial the numbers *now* – or at least I try. But phones have become so complicated. Half of them don't even have buttons!'

For a brief moment Cressida looked smaller than normal. But then she rallied herself.

'Still, Westminster is a strange little bubble to live in, and there's no point harping on about the past.' She straightened her shoulders. 'Onwards and upwards. He who hesitates *stagnates*.'

'Exactly!' Woody grinned. He pressed a few buttons and Sky News filled the screen.

'How did you do that?' She was amazed. 'Well, thank you, Woody. I don't know what I'd do without you. In fact, I was thinking, maybe I should get myself one of those gimps.'

Woody choked. 'Come again?'

'You know; *gimps*!' she fixed him with one of her looks that rendered the recipient in no doubt of her assessment of their intellectual capabilities. 'I read about them in the *Daily Mail*. If one wants one's house cleaned or garden tended, it's simple to find someone for the job. But what I really need is one of those IT gimps who do all the technological stuff, like flittering your spam and setting your video.'

'Oh, right!' Woody laughed in relief. He rubbed his head. 'But maybe don't say that to anyone else, Cress.'

'About my video?'

'You actually still have one of those?'

'Of course.'

'No, I mean that you're after a gimp.'

'Why ever not?' Cressida tsked. 'I can't tell you the hassle I have when the clocks go back. So many blasted things to reset. No, bring me a gimp, that's what I say. And maybe he could sort out my thermostat whilst he's at it. Now, how's that coffee coming along? And go easy on the milk this time; the last cup you made me was awful – I never knew coffee could be anaemic.'

Woody touched his imaginary cap. 'Yes, ma'am.'

'And less of the cheek, young man. Window cleaners are two-a-penny,' Cressida scolded, a twinkle playing about her eyes. 'And not half as useful as a gimp!'

To: Roxy Squires

From: MTV

Hey Foxy Roxy!

Cheers for getting in touch. Sorry, but we don't need new presenters at the mo. Well, we do, but we've got the blonde thing covered (unless your dad's a rock star? Joke!!!). Anyway, about your idea that we pimp your ride . . . we're not really doing that any more. Ditto your suggestion about your crib. Oh, and your idea that we follow you for a fly-on-the-wall series . . . we're not sure our viewers know who you are! You could try VH1, tho . . . They're about to start shooting *Celebs Our 'Rents Used 2 Fancy* . . .

Laters!

ROXY

Roxy sighed; they just weren't getting it.

'Look,' she informed the room bluntly. 'All this attention is very flattering, but you're barking up the wrong bush!'

Sitting in a circle in Simon's living room, six sets of eyes looked at her kindly.

'You've just got to let go,' said Holly. 'Trust us; we're trying to help.'

'But that's my point,' Roxy stressed. 'It's not me who needs helping. I'm not the help*ee* – I'm the help*errr*.'

'You don't need to keep up the act, Rox.'

'What act?' she cried. 'The only reason I come to these meetings is to sort you guys out. And to check out the . . .'

'Check out the what?' Holly frowned.

Roxy resisted the urge to say 'view'. Instead, she mumbled, 'Nothing,' and avoided looking at Woody.

'Classic denial,' Holly declared sadly. 'It's a textbook case of the career having stalled but the brain refusing to notice.'

'My career hasn't stalled! It's in top gear, thank you very much – firing like a rocket.'

Terence snorted. 'Pull the other one! You've not been on telly in ages.'

'I bloody have! I'm on telly all the time; late-night, cutting-edge stuff.'

'I can't believe I'm saying this,' said Simon, 'but Terry *does* have a point. I've not seen any of your shows in a while, either. *And* I've got two teenagers in the house.'

'Christ, who are you people? The *Radio* bloody *Times*? I'm telling you guys, I'm busy, busy, busy. Chock-a-block – no room at the inn.' Roxy took a deep breath and tried to calm down. 'Look, the reason I'm here is for *you*. You're all up shit creek without a teaspoon. But – don't worry – I've got a rockin' big spade. I'm going to U-turn your fortunes, reboot your careers and frogmarch you up the fame freeway.'

'Who is she, again?' Cressida asked suddenly. 'I know she used to be famous, but other than that I haven't the foggiest.'

'She was a television presenter,' Holly explained.

'A very funny and talented television presenter . . .' added Simon, before ruining it all by adding, 'In her time.'

Roxy was about to correct him, but Woody started speaking. 'Our Roxy was the real deal,' he said fondly. 'Edgy; subversive; funny. She was part of a girl gang who shook up youth telly.'

For a moment, Roxy basked in the glow of his praise.

'I still don't recognise her from Adam,' Cressida grumbled.

'She was one of those TV ladettes,' said Holly. 'Remember? The girls who acted like boys.'

'From the nineties,' helped Simon. 'One of the originals the papers went nuts for.'

Cressida tutted. 'Well, I certainly remember *them*; they were a disgrace!'

'They were brilliant!' Simon cried. 'A breath of fresh air. Feminism had got so po-faced. Roxy and her friends really kicked it up the jacksy.'

'Didn't they just binge drink and hang around in their knickers?'

'Well, there was that as well,' he conceded.

'Are you the one with the tattoo of the nun on your bottom?' Sue suddenly piped up from the corner.

'And a bottle of HP on my hip!' Roxy grinned.

Holly tapped her pen against the gap in her teeth.

'Didn't you go AWOL at Glastonbury?' she remembered. 'You were supposed to be live on TV!'

'Can't you drink a pint in five seconds?'

'And burp the national anthem?'

'Were you the one who punched that lecherous footballer?'

'And snogged that Hollywood film star on TV for a bet?'

'Did you go on *Newsnight* and flash your whatsits at Paxman?'

'Oh, Lord!' Cressida exclaimed suddenly. 'Were you the young lady who pinched the Prime Minister's bottom?'

'Yes, it was me; all me!' Roxy beamed proudly.

'Christ!' Terence snorted. 'It's no bloody wonder you're not working!'

Roxy stamped her foot. 'I *am* bloody working! That's what I've been trying to tell you. I'm working my arse off; fully booked 'til next soddin' Christmas!'

She suddenly noticed Woody looking right at her. 'We know

your schedule's busy, Rox,' he said with a sad smile, 'but do us a favour, eh? Make sure you come to our meetings. I think it's really important you're here.'

And suddenly Roxy's heart seemed to stop.

Was Woody asking for help?

Had he heard what she'd said about the fame freeway, and this was his way of asking her to step on the gas? Was *this* why he wanted her at the meetings . . . not to jump her bones, but to enlist her expertise?

She looked into his eyes and felt her skin go all tingly. Sex with former pop gods aside, there was nothing Roxy loved more than a goal . . . and Woody had just rolled the ball right up to the penalty spot. Everything was clear now; this had been his plan all along! They'd revitalise the group together! She and Woody would be equals; a team . . . standing shoulder-to-shoulder, singing from the same hymn sheet, sharing the same cheese and pickle sandwich.

'All right, Woodster,' she said lightly, her heart finally restarting. 'You're on!'

SIMON

Simon was so surprised, he nearly caught his finger in the whisk attachment of his Kenwood. His mobile was ringing and the name 'Barrington' flashed on the display.

'Simon, darling!' his agent greeted him with uncharacteristic enthusiasm. 'I've got a gig for you.'

Simon stared at the ingredients littered across the kitchen surface. 'A gig?' he echoed numbly and wiped his hands on his pinny.

'Decent bucks, leading role, TV.'

'What's the catch?' Simon quickly threw up his guard. Barrington never offered him a job without being badgered for it first. This one had to be a stinker.

'No audition necessary, sweetie; they're shooting next month – asked specifically for you.'

Simon breathed from the diaphragm and summoned his best BAFTA-worthy authoritative tone. '*Barrington!*'

'It's an ad,' the agent admitted lightly.

'An ad?' Simon swallowed hard. 'Well, that's not so bad.' He tried to be positive. 'I mean, if it's OK for Clooney . . . Linda practically climbs into the screen when his coffee ads are on. And doesn't Ewan McGregor do beer ads in Japan?' Actually, the more Simon thought about it, the better it seemed. Some adverts were really filmic. His mind began to race. Maybe his ad would be for Guinness, or Stella Artois, or a sports car . . . an *Italian* sports car! He suddenly imagined himself speeding along in a soft-top down the zigzag roads of the Amalfi. Could Barrington *just this once* have pulled it off? 'What for?' he blurted excitedly.

'There'll be hours of airtime, darling – and I mean *hours*! They're planning a long transmission window on all the major channels. You'll be on every daytime ad break for weeks. It's just what you've always wanted: Simon Drennan – housewives' favourite.'

'What's it *for*, Barrington?'

'Something vital. Something needed.'

'What's it FOR?'

'Insurance.'

With a pop, the Amalfi imploded before him; not the vibrant thump of a champagne cork, more the listless fart of a bottle of flat cola.

'*Funeral* insurance,' Barrington continued buoyantly. 'They've got a fabulous idea, inspired by your soap death. "Legendary," the client called your spread-eagle. So it's not just any old ad, it's a tailor-made campaign. You won't even need to be in character – just yourself. You know the kind of thing . . . "When I died the first time, I didn't know what'd hit me. But when I do it for real, I'll be smiling, because this time I'll die safe in the knowledge that my loved ones won't be left scrabbling in the dirt." You get the gist.'

'You want me to endorse funeral insurance?'

'It's on TV.'

'But it's not even acting—'

'You'll be the new face of funeral planning!'

'– it's just flogging a product.'

'Think of it as diversifying your CV; opening yourself up to a new audience.'

'But it's a sales job. It's practically bloody retail!'

'It's fabulous money . . .'

And then, like an out-of-body experience Simon heard himself ask something terrible.

'How fabulous?'

And then he put down the phone and rang Linda.

'It's not so bad, love,' she said encouragingly. 'George Clooney does ads.'

'Not funeral insurance ads; not filmed in an office in Basingstoke. I'm telling you, Linda, this is the end of the road. It's right down there with opening supermarkets.'

'Oh, sweetheart.'

'Fuck! I'm over!' Simon slid down the kitchen cabinet, his pinny ballooning in his lap. 'My career is actually over.'

'Oh, honey – if you don't want to do the ad, just say no. It's not like we need the money. My salary more than covers us, and your panto money is brilliant . . .'

'For six months a year,' Simon muttered.

'What I mean is, we're not exactly going to starve. And Nick

Fletcher paid off the mortgage – remember?' Linda sighed. 'Simon, love, don't do anything you're not happy with. Look, why don't you tell Barrington to stuff his crummy advert? In fact, tell Barrington to stuff everything. You're too good for him. He shouldn't be sending you adverts – he should be sending you dramas.'

'Rom-coms,' Simon automatically corrected.

'That's the spirit. Why don't you get back on the phone *right now* and tell Barrington where he can stick his crappy funeral insurance? He's a waste of space, that man. I ought to sue him for professional incompetence.'

'You're a defence lawyer.'

'Well I'll sue him for indefensible conduct.'

Simon put down the phone, hauled himself up and straightened his apron. He switched the Kenwood back on and bleakly watched the ingredients spin in the bowl. Maybe Linda was right. Maybe he shouldn't just roll over and accept his lot. Maybe he *did* deserve better. He spooned some cream cheese into the mixture and wondered whether to add more vanilla. He'd ring Barrington later and give him a piece of his mind; tell him he was better than CBeebies and ads, that he was a former soap-opera superstar who just happened to be momentarily resting in panto on his way to bigger and better. Yes, Barrington had better take cover because he, Simon Drennan, would give him what-for. He just needed to prepare himself first: do some breathing exercises; get in the zone.

ROXY

Roxy bundled down the stairs and flicked the kettle on.

According to legend, Mossy once said, 'Nothing tastes as good as skinny feels.' And, although Roxy reckoned skinny actually tasted hard (not to mention miserable, empty and a little bit tinny in your mouth), she had to commend Mossy on her single-mindedness. Lately she'd been so lost in lusting after Woody that she'd forgotten to focus. She needed to remember what was what. At heart, she was a career girl – and her heart shouldn't get in the way. Woody was already taken, and besides, Roxy already had a Significant Other – *work*. And there was no ride like the fame ride (despite all the Woody kiss-and-tells).

No, Roxy vowed in her Spice Girls nightshirt as she reached for her 'girl power' mug, there would be no more thinking about Woody – other than in a professional partnership sense. There would be no more watching his old videos on YouTube, no more obsessing about his sex smell and no more peeks at his marzipan bum. She and Woody were on a mission – joint mentors for the group. Yep, that was it, she thought as the kettle boiled itself off. Her days of perving Woody were over.

Really.

No, seriously – she *had* to be strict.

With a new sense of purpose, she briskly brewed up a cuppa and rummaged in her drawer for a straw. She then sat at the kitchen table, checked the time on her iPhone and slapped on a quick Veet moustache. As she waited for her tea to cool and her tash to dissolve, she opened *OK!* and set to work.

How *does* a former weatherman get back on TV if he's too discredited to forecast? she wondered as she flicked through the pages of creosote-dipped stars. Well, there was always the long route back: the yawnsome process of paying dues and starting again from scratch. Sure, Terry could open a few shopping centres, or crack jokes as an after-dinner speaker . . . It would take decades, but someone, somewhere was bound to eventually offer him a comeback.

But Roxy wasn't interested in the long game. She'd always been more of a grab-'em-by-the-balls kind of girl. She didn't want to *mildly* impress the group – she wanted shock and awe! The media didn't 'do' patient people, and Terry and the gang had waited long enough. She and Woody were going to get them fast, spectacular results – to catapult them back to fame like Usain Bolt on rocket fuel. She was going to relight their spotlights, even if she had to blow a fuse to do it!

She took a determined sip of tea from her straw and counted down the minutes 'til she could scrape off her tash. It was time Roxy Squires got cracking.

SUE

Sue was about to speak when a little old lady beat her to it.

'Do you have my puzzles magazine, dear? And could you help me find *Take A Break*? I've left my glasses at home and I can't see for toffee without them.'

The newsagent came round from the other side of the counter, bypassed Sue and – chatting extra loudly – helped the old lady hobble back to the magazines.

Sue did her best to look cross, but nobody noticed. All she wanted was her *Times* so she could do the crossword. It wasn't even as if she needed to pay. She settled her bill monthly, by cheque, in the post. The plan had been to be in and out and back to her kitchen as quickly as possible. She'd only left home out of necessity; the paper boy hadn't shown up that morning and, when she'd phoned to find out his whereabouts, she'd been told he was in bed, sick, and would she mind popping in to pick up her *Times* herself, seeing as she was only a couple of minutes away? Actually, she did mind; she minded very much. Not that she didn't feel sorry for the poor paper boy, but 'popping in' meant an unscheduled trip to the shops, and if she'd known *that* was on the cards she'd have prepared early with deep breathing and a pot of green tea. But, of course, she couldn't actually say any of this because it wouldn't be nice – and besides, the newsagent had already put down the phone.

'Oh, blow me down, it was there all the time!' exclaimed the little old lady as the newsagent pressed a brightly-coloured magazine into her hands.

Sue tried to breathe deeply. If she didn't get served in the next ten seconds, she'd have to abandon her *Times* and bolt out of the shop. And she really didn't want to do that – partly because she'd look like one of those rude London-types who thought they were too important to wait for little old ladies, but more importantly because that would mean she'd have no crossword for today, and that would only leave the cleaning and ironing to keep her occupied, which would barely see her beyond two o'clock . . . *and then what would she do?* But the newsagent was still trapped by the chatty old lady, so Sue was left marooned at the counter, mustering all her will to anchor her feet to the floor and stop herself breaking into a sweat.

'Any chance of some service?' a deep voice boomed from behind her, making Sue jump.

The newsagent ditched the old lady and hurried back.

Sue turned to look at the voice. She couldn't believe it had been so easy to get the newsagent's attention. She wished she'd had the chutzpah to do it. The voice belonged to a builder, holding a Mars bar and *The Sun*. He must be one of the men working on the hole in Blackberry Lane, Sue decided. And then, completely oblivious to the fact that she'd been queueing before him, the builder reached across her and dropped his money on to the counter.

'Have a good day!' The newsagent smiled sunnily.

The builder nodded, turned to leave and accidentally bumped into Sue, knocking her right off her axis.

Quick as a flash, he reached out and steadied her. His hand firmly clasped her elbow. 'Sorry, love, didn't see you there.' He smiled – held her arm just a fraction too long – and then strode on out of the shop.

Feeling more than a little bit flustered, Sue showed her *Times* to the newsagent (whose smile wasn't quite as warm for her) and scuttled up the road towards home. Her heart was racing, but then again, it always raced. She was perpetually anxious, even at home on her own. Some things never changed – Sue's nerves and invisibility included. Whenever she did venture out of her front door, people always forgot to serve her – or bumped into her – or trod on her feet. It was as though they couldn't see her. She'd spent so many years hoping nobody would notice her, it was as though her wish had come true. She'd become invisible. *But not today*, she thought with a smile. Today she'd been noticed. And the person who'd seen her had touched her too. Not a bump or a nudge or a brush as they hurried to somewhere important – this was a deliberate touch. Beneath her coat, her elbow felt hot from the builder's hand. It was as though her whole arm was blushing at the contact. And the more she thought about his strong, steady grip, his economical but polite 'Sorry, love, didn't see you there', the more Sue felt her face follow in tandem. But then she remembered where she was – or rather, where she wasn't. She pulled her newspaper to her chest, quickened her pace and visualised the safety of her front door.

ROXY

Halfway through the next meeting, Roxy got it.

She'd been zoning out of a Cressida monologue about the Jacobean levels of back-stabbing in modern politics, sitting in the room that interior design forgot – aka Terence's living room. She'd been wondering quite how Tornado Terry had managed to time-travel his house back from 1972. The place was a bilious swirl of oranges and browns, with a carpet that doubled as a migraine. The sofas were decked out with lace doilies, the walls infected with an outbreak of cuckoo clocks, and Roxy had bet herself fifty quid that if she nipped to the loo she'd find a doll in a knitted dress squatting down on the spare bog roll.

And then, just as she peered at their host – lounging, cardigan-clad, on a mustard, wing-back armchair – inspiration hit!

Roxy almost yelped with joy.

Her Terry strategy was clear. A comeback slot as the home-owner on *DIY SOS*, followed by a garden makeover on *Ground Force*, an MOT from Gok Wan and chat-show repentance with

Titchmarsh. It was easy – career rehabilitation in four simple
steps.

'Bingo.' She grinned over at Woody.

'Nutcase,' he replied with a smile.

ROXY

It took her longer than usual to walk to Woody's. It was still early and the sun was too wimpy to melt the frost on the pavements. Top Shop stilettos were good for many things, but grip on unsalted surfaces wasn't one of them. But she was here, in one piece, at last. Roxy gripped her Tupperware box and took a long, deep breath. This was it: business time – time to separate the wheat from the chaff, the yolk from the egg white, the pink and yellow Battenberg squares. Mentally, she switched off her flirt switch. And then she power-walked up Woody's short drive.

She knocked on the door. It opened. And Roxy tried not to gasp.

Woody was topless.

Wet-haired and bare-chested, his T-shirt was in his left hand. *Talk about being tested at the first hurdle!* She tried not to ogle his muscles. It took a Herculean effort, but she wrenched her eyeline up.

'We need to talk,' she managed to squeak. Somewhere in his house, the radio was blaring. 'You know – diaries and strategies and all that. I brought us a business breakfast.' She held up her box of fruit salad.

Woody shrugged his T-shirt on.

'Sorry. What? I haven't got time for breakfast. I've got to go to work.' He patted his pockets for his wallet.

'But this *is* work! We need to brainstorm and cook up some plans.'

'Plans for what?'

'Duh! World domination!'

Woody looked at her blankly.

'For the group,' she explained with a laugh.

He frowned. His chest was now double-wrapped in a sweat-shirt. 'Rox, what on earth are you on about?'

'You know – last night! All that stuff about me staying with the group? The code about us working together.'

'But we *are* working together. We're *all* working together.'

He bent down to put on his work boots. Roxy had to stop herself from craning her neck to check out his arse.

'Yeah, 'course,' she agreed, enjoying the unexpected power rush of having Woody at her feet, 'but I think we can work better, don't you? Now, if I could just come in, I've got a few ideas to run past you. I thought we could draw up a schedule.'

Woody finished his laces and stood up.

'But we've got a schedule. We meet every Thursday.'

'Not that kind of schedule – an *action* schedule. For Project Spotlight.'

He laughed, and shook his head, bemused. And then he picked up his coffee mug from the ledge by the door. 'Sorry,

Rox – I've got to go.' He drained his coffee and looked at his watch. 'Actually, I'm already late. I should've been up my ladder ten minutes ago.'

'Tonight, then – after your round?' she pushed. 'I'll bring a bottle.'

'I can't. I'm meeting someone.'

'Who?' the motormouth asked. 'Jennifer?' But luckily Woody didn't hear. His mobile was ringing. He darted away to find it.

'Yep. Sorry, Mrs Henry,' she heard him apologise. 'I'm . . . Yes, I know I'm a bit late. I'll be with you in a couple of minutes.'

Standing on the doorstep, Roxy heard him switch off the radio and pick up his keys. She tried not to imagine him and Jennifer tonight. What would a date with Woody involve? Candles? Dinner? A long, hot soak in the tub? *Sex?* She shook her head to clear the mental pictures. Damn, this Woody-cold-turkey thing was going to be tougher than she'd thought. She needed to beat a tactical retreat – and fast!

'Look, Rox, I think it's happened again,' Woody said, making his way back to the door. 'I think we've got our wires cro—'

'Yep, whatever!' she blurted, reversing down the drive in top gear. 'Things to see, people to do. Some other time, yeah?'

Woody nodded and watched her leave. And then his phone started ringing again.

To: Roxy Squires
From: *Celebrity Juice* INTERN

Hiya Roxy,

Thanks for contacting *Celebrity Juice* to ask if you could be a
contestant. I'm on work experience this week, but I asked the
producer and he said no. But could you send a signed photo for my
dad, please? He used to fancy you, years back, and Mum reckons
he's having a crisis.

TERENCE

Terence opened his front door to an enormous parcel. And Roxy Squires.

'What the . . . ?'

Even to his own ears he sounded alarmed. He'd been expecting the postman. He hadn't been expecting . . . *well* . . . he wasn't sure how to describe Roxy's appearance. He hadn't been so close to this much exposed flesh since his wife left. Roxy's legs were bare right the way up to . . . Suddenly self-conscious in his slippers, he brushed the bump of his stomach to dislodge the toast crumbs.

'Morning, Tezza.' Roxy propped up her sunglasses and grinned over the top of the cardboard box. 'I've been having a clear-out and thought I'd bring you some stuff.' She put down the box and straightened up.

'Stuff?' Terence echoed tightly. He didn't know where to look. Not at Roxy's legs, obviously. But now the box was on the floor, a vast expanse of cleavage had revealed itself too. Roxy's top was so low-cut, he could practically see her break-fast. Didn't she know about today's stiff north-easterlies and fifteen-per-cent chance of sleet? Maybe she was still drunk from last night – he'd heard she was free and easy with the bottle. He averted his eyes altogether and focused instead on the frost on his cloud-shaped bush.

'Yeah, just some clothes an old boyfriend left lying around,' Roxy continued. 'Complete bloody disaster, he was. Anyway, I was just about to sling them when I thought, *hang about* – you're roughly the same build – maybe some of them would be good for you.'

Terence forgot about the topiary.

'But I don't need clothes – I've got plenty.'

'Yeah, but I thought you might want newer ones.'

'Newer ones?' he was confused. Why on earth would he want *newer* clothes? None of his outfits had holes in and most of his trousers still had their creases. Besides, if he wanted new clothes he could buy them himself. 'Now, look here, young lady . . .' he waggled his finger. 'I don't like what you're implying. I don't need your charity.'

'It's not charity,' Roxy snorted. 'No, it's a . . . a *mutually beneficial arrangement*. I get a corner of my wardrobe back, and you get to – you know – rebrand.'

Terence opened his mouth to speak, but couldn't think of a single thing to say. He closed it again with a snap.

'Look, Terry – I'll be blunt. The slacks-and-knitwear look really isn't working for you. I know you're off duty nowadays, but that's no reason to just give up.'

'It's just an old cardigan I wear around the house . . . And what do you mean, "just give up"?'

'But Tezza, it's not *just* the cardigan . . . It's the whole Fusty Uncle look you're rocking.'

'Fusty *what*?'

'You look like you've got a rod up your arse.'

'Now just a minute—'

'Look, Tezza – if you want to get back on the telly, you need to sharpen up. Even weathermen are fashion-forward these days. You can't just rock up at meetings with TV execs looking like that; you're not doing yourself justice. You're a very attractive man!'

Terence's mouth fell open again. Had Roxy Squires just called him *attractive*? Did this mouthy, seasonally-inappropriate young woman actually find him appealing? Stranger things had happened, he supposed. She must have been a fan of his forecasts. It was amazing what television did to a woman's libido. And he *had* caught her staring at him at the last meeting. He straightened up and sucked in his tummy.

'Come of it, Terry. You're as old as my dad.'

'I didn't think—' His belly popped back out.

'Yeah, course you didn't.' She laughed. And then she lowered her voice and leant in. 'Anyway, we both know I'm not the one you've got your eye on.'

'You're not?' Terry spluttered, before realising how wrong that had sounded.

'I've seen the way you look at her.' Roxy winked.

'You have?'

''Course.'

Terry's mouth went slack yet again. Had he been that

obvious? He was mortified! But then it struck him: the way he'd looked at *whom*? He wasn't aware he'd been looking *that* way at anyone. Was Roxy seeing something he wasn't?

'Look, Terry. Do us *both* a favour, eh?' Roxy continued. 'Take a look through the box and try some bits on. If you don't like any of it, fine – give it to the charity shop. But there's some really great clobber in here, and I think a little ramble away from the brown pallet might help *both* your causes. A new image will take ten years off you.'

'Are you trying to say I look old?'

'No! Well – yes. But it's nothing a few new shirts won't fix.' Roxy turned to go, but then suddenly turned back.

'Ooo, I nearly forgot. Can you sing?'

'Sing?'

'Yeah – songs and stuff.'

And this time Terry's mouth fell open and stayed open.

WOODY

The ornate iron gates slid open with a muted electric hum.

'All right, fellas?'

'Hiya, Woody.'

'Shift up a bit, would you? Need to get my ladders through.'

The photographers shuffled aside to give Woody passage through the gates. As he passed, someone fired off a shot. He grimaced. The offending photographer shrugged.

'Just getting something in the bank in case the local rag runs a knobbly knees competition. Knees like that, you're bound to win.'

'And to think I let you sleep in my penthouse when your hotel room fell through in Rome,' Woody replied sternly. 'I should've left you out in the rain.'

'Yeah, well, if you'd been a real host, you'd have shared that tasty Italian model you were partying with in the next room.' The photographer turned to the rest of his mob. 'No manners, these floppy-haired pop tarts.'

'Oi!' Woody set down his ladder and coolly eyeballed the

snapper. 'Less of the floppy!' And then the two men burst into laughter. 'All right, Ken? Good to see you, mate.'

Woody and the photographer man-hugged.

'You too, you old bastard.' Ken rubbed the top of Woody's head. 'Hey, you doing Austin Jones' windows?'

'Yep.'

Ken frowned. 'Isn't that a bit weird?'

'Nope.' Woody tried to move on.

'Well, if you're heading down there, any chance of a—?'

'You had more chance with the Italian model.'

Ken grunted and played up to the other photographers again. 'She couldn't keep her eyes off me, that one. Fancied my bloody arse off. She only went with Woody as a warm-up.'

Woody chuckled and strode past the photographers with a backwards wave.

'Come on,' someone tried their luck. 'Just let one of us sneak up with you . . .'

'Or at least let us stick a digital in your bucket.'

'See you later, lads!' Woody called over his shoulder.

The gates slid closed behind him. Woody adjusted his hold on the ladder and crunched up the long, winding drive to Austin Jones' multi-million-pound pad.

The thought came as he passed a huge bank of hydrangeas. He didn't want to do this. Not the windows (although Austin's place was so vast it took two days to get them all clean). No, it was the windows' owner that was the problem. And until now the windows' owner had always been absent.

Woody wasn't surprised the group wanted to recruit Austin.

Actually, it was surprising nobody had suggested him before, even though he'd previously spent more time in the Hollywood Hills than Lavender Heath. And technically there'd always been the small point of him still *having* a career, of course. But even allowing for his recent retirement, Austin Jones was definitely one of the group's crappier ideas. They had no idea what they were letting themselves in for. They all thought Austin Jones was the same Austin Jones they saw on the big screen. They hadn't a clue about the non-fictionalised, non-airbrushed, non-PR'd Austin.

Woody negotiated his ladder around the final bend in the drive, past the tennis court and the moat-like infinity pool, and into view of the house. As he took in its manicured lawns, immaculate orangery and hushed, moneyed air, Woody was struck by a sudden feeling. He hadn't had it for so long he'd almost forgotten what it felt like. But here it was again – the queasy lurch of unease.

When Woody walked away from the music business, he'd vowed to never ignore his instincts again. He'd wasted *years* agreeing to things he shouldn't have agreed to, muting the voice that nagged in the back of his head. Each thing by itself was tiny but, month by month, year by year, the minuscule concessions to his time and sanity ate rivets into his soul. Naturally polite and easy going, he felt too up himself to look the pop-mag journo in the eye and refuse to pose for her daft photo shoot, or to tell his manager he'd rather *not* record that cover he hated or give up the week's only free hour to chat to a DJ about his favourite trainers/colour/vest. So what if he had to croon his way through that cover version for every TV show on the planet? It wasn't like he was working down a coal mine. Who was he to say no to requests? So he kept saying yes, and rewarded himself with a never-ending whirl of VIP enclosures and backstage parties. And women – *lots and lots of women*. After all, his conscience couldn't keep him awake at night if the latest model/actress/cocktail waitress was keeping him awake instead.

But that inner voice wouldn't stop nagging. Did he really need to get up at 4.30am for hair and make-up? A quick splash of water and a comb would do for Joe Bloggs. And what did it matter if the lighting on his latest video was that fraction too blue? Was it really worth the money to reshoot? When was he going to get a real job? Was it *right* that his brain was filled up with ridiculous stuff, like knowing that eight and a half minutes on a sunbed gave him the most natural tan for TV, that housewives preferred minor keys and that the best way to make teenagers swoon was a six-second gaze into camera three before dropping his eyes in Mills-and-Boon regret?

Instincts, Woody discovered, were awkward buggers; they always won in the end. And when his finally cut through the recording sessions, promotional tours, meet-and-greets, road-shows, video shoots, personal appearances, record signings and parties, *parties*, PARTIES, Woody suddenly stopped dead. He was on the set of a TV show, his band poised behind him – everyone waiting for the cue that they were about to go live. Beneath the MAC foundation, Woody's face went ashen and his eyes went dead. That was it – enough – career over. Without thinking of anything, he walked out of the studio, and home.

Of course, the papers called it a breakdown, but Woody knew better. Something in his brain had fused – a connection made; a spark created – a switch had flicked itself on. It may have *looked* like he was slobbing on his sofa – his stubble growing longer, sleeping in his clothes . . . but beneath the disappearing highlights, fading tan and greying white vest, things were happening. Like Dr Who, Woody was regenerating.

Progress was initially slow. But he eventually re-emerged, blinking at the sun. The world had been busy without him. Homework completed, chores tackled, love affairs started, babies born, the rat race run . . . The sleeping pop star had long been forgotten.

Rejoining the world was the first half of his recovery; rejoining the world of work was the next. What Woody needed, his instincts told him, was good, honest toil. And this time Woody didn't ignore them. Scrubbing windows at the top of a ladder – the breeze blowing around his ankles, the sun beating on his head, his modest, genuinely-earned wages nestling in his pocket – gave him something all his quickly-won pop-star riches had never been able to buy: self-respect. He may have hit adulthood years beforehand, but it was only now Woody felt he was a man.

Woody knew instincts were ignored at your peril. So why, he wondered as he surveyed Austin's beautiful Georgian mansion, was he here, ignoring his? He should have said no the moment Austin was mentioned. He wanted to help the group, not implode them. Any sane person wouldn't go within a mile of this Jones.

But what Woody's instincts hadn't factored in was the un-factorable presence of Roxy Squires. She'd looked at him in that way of hers, like she was setting him a challenge and he'd better measure up. It was the kind of look she used to be famous for, the unpredictable, fun-loving ladette, as likely to lure you into a never-ending duel of tequila shots as a tussle between the sheets. Woody knew she was winding him up. She, at least, must have encountered enough stars to guess what Austin was *really* like. And he couldn't believe she didn't know their history.

'Well, well, well!' a voice suddenly said behind him. 'They told me you were my window cleaner but I thought they were taking the piss.'

Woody turned, and his ladder turned with him, almost knocking Britain's most successful Hollywood export in the face. A distinctly off-duty Austin Jones was leaning against the wall of his quadruple-length garage, wrapped in the world's biggest parka, his eyes shielded from the January gloom by an expensive pair of Ray Bans. But even off-duty and unshaven, Austin was still undeniably an extraordinarily good-looking bloke.

Austin lifted a lazy finger and pushed the tip of Woody's ladder from his nose. An eyebrow appeared above the Ray Bans.

'Working your way down the career ladder?'

A muscle moved in Woody's jaw. 'Just got back from the job centre?' he replied. 'Or is "no more movies" just a stunt so your agent can screw an even bigger pay packet for the comeback?'

'No stunt,' Austin said evenly as he contemplated his infinity pool. He stood stock-still, barely moving. 'I'm done with Hollywood and its poison. If I had to listen to one more leading lady strop because I've got a bigger Winnebago, or throw a tantrum because I had four more lines . . .' he trailed off darkly.

'All those years in LA . . . You never got a shrink then?'

'I'd rather shrink my own balls. No, I just packed my bags and got the hell back to Blighty. Besides, I kept hearing on the grapevine how much you were enjoying retirement. Thought I'd give it a whirl; spend some quality time with the Bentleys. No point bloody having them if I never bloody drive them. Beer?'

'Booze and heights – not a good mix.'

'You always were a pussy, Woods. Speaking of which . . . Cleaning bedroom windows the only way you get to see naked women these days?'

Woody grimaced. 'You're just as I remember you, Austin.'

Austin took off his Ray Bans and grinned.

A few uneasy hours and too-easy beers later, Woody cut across Austin's immaculately trimmed lawn, through his copse of Canadian redwoods and towards the seven-foot boundary wall. He didn't fancy heading back past the paps – too many unanswerable questions to answer. Austin had told him the best place to scale the perimeter wall and slip out, and he'd left his ladders at the manor house. There was no point taking them home – he'd had too many beers for more cleaning. He'd needed the beers not to be angry – not that Austin had noticed. Thick-skinned as ever, Austin had been too busy hitting the vodka. In the old days, Woody would have kept up. He could remember the hazy outlines of a few lost nights they'd had together: the golden boys of British film and music drinking their way around Soho, a trail of beautiful women in their wake. But these days he couldn't compete.

He found the section of wall Austin had mentioned, with the jutting brick that gave a good leg-up. He looked behind him and, sure enough, there was the little red light of the security camera.

'My escape route,' Austin had told him. 'Clive and the security boys keep it monitored in case the scumbags cotton on and get in. Anyone so much as breathes on that section of wall and Clive'll break their legs.'

Woody nodded at Clive, who was undoubtedly watching, put his boot on the brick and hoisted himself up. He dropped over to the other side of the wall, landing far beyond the view of the photographers, on to a quiet, country road on the outskirts of the village.

A couple of minutes later and he was almost back home. He'd just turned in to Blackberry Lane when saw it: the black Aston Martin – engine running, wheel sticking out. Only this time it was outside his house. Woody looked at it warily. This *couldn't* be a coincidence. Was he being followed? Unlikely. Nobody cared who he used to be any more. But then, this was the fifth time he'd seen the Aston Martin in two days. If it was just somebody new who wanted to get on his round, all they had to do was ask – even the local A-listers weren't this melodramatic. And why the hell stake out his house? Enough was enough. He headed straight to the car for an explanation. But then the driver's door opened, and out slid a pair of Jimmy Choo shoes and two long, orange legs.

To: Roxy Squires

From: *Have I Got News For You* production office

Dear Miss Squires,

Thank you for your recent application to be a guest on *Have I Got News For You.*

HIGNFY is an award-winning current affairs comedy quiz show, and as such our guests need to be either topical or amusing. And whilst your application made us laugh, unfortunately it was for all the wrong reasons.

CRESSIDA

It wasn't until she was heading to bed that she found it. Cressida wasn't sure how long it had been sitting there, waiting on her doormat. But she guessed it hadn't been long. The envelope was bright pink and heavy; not the kind of post that was easily overlooked.

She put down her hot milk and bent to retrieve it. Handwritten, with no stamp, the envelope simply said 'Cressida'. There was a little circle above the *i*. Cressida frowned. Who on earth sent post like this? Weren't pink envelopes the domain of the under-twelves? And she didn't know a soul who'd circle-dot their *i*'s. Intrigued, she ripped it open. The letter inside was lilac.

Hey Cressida!

When you get a mo, could you fill out this personality test? Don't stress – it's nothing to worry about . . . Just a few easy questions so I can get a handle on what you're like – the real you, not the cabinet whatsit. You know the kind of thing . . . hobbies, habits, who was your first crush, where you lost your virginity, etc . . .

Cheers 'ears! And gimme a shout when you're thru.

Roxy

X

Cressida frowned again, harder this time. And then she laughed.

'Barking!' she declared to the hallway. And she carried her hot milk up to bed.

11.30am @foxyroxy

#ROXYSAYS: The key to being a celeb = knowing when to keep
your big trap shut. Nothing = more B-list than boasting about
your A-list mates.

11.31am @foxyroxy

eg If BradnAnge invite u 4 dinner, don't blab that Brad sprinkles n
tinkles! No one hits Celeb Siberia faster than a B-list Ms Indi
Screet!

11.40am @foxyroxy

PS – Not that BradnAnge did . . . or Brad would . . . but you get
my point.

SIMON

It was the rarest of moments: a twinless Saturday morning. Simon and Linda cuddled up beneath their king-sized duvet after an unscheduled 11am 'nap'.

'So,' Linda casually cross-examined him as she nestled down into his chest, 'does this unscheduled burst of libido have anything to do with the group's new blonde?'

'Roxy?' Simon did his best to sound innocent. 'How did you know about her?' He hoped his wife hadn't sensed him tense up.

'I bumped into Cressida at the library. She told me about your new recruit. She couldn't remember her name, or what she did, but she gave me a rough description and I know Roxy Squires owns a house in the village. You don't need to be a brunette to put two and two together,' Linda added dryly. When Simon didn't answer, she lifted her head to inspect his expression. 'So?'

'God, no!' Simon exclaimed vehemently, making a point to meet his wife's eye. 'How could you even think that?'

Linda arched an eyebrow. 'That four-bottles-of-cava night?'

'Oh, *that!*' Simon coloured at the memory – from back at

the start of their marriage – of an extremely drunken evening of negotiating the three free sex passes they'd grant each other, and the megastars on whom they could spend them. 'God, that feels like a lifetime ago.'

'It was. Pre-kids. So why didn't you tell me she'd joined?'

'I forgot?'

'Yeah, right.'

Simon tried a little diversion. 'Who were my other free passes?'

'Naomi Campbell and Jennifer Aniston. Like *that* was ever going to happen.'

'It might have done! Me and Jennifer could have been cast in the same movie; Naomi could have presented me with my Best Male Actor BAFTA gong. Besides, weren't yours Bill Clinton, Robert Redford and David Dimbleby?'

'I was in my older-man phase.'

'Older? At least my three had pulses.'

'All of which is a great smokescreen for my original question . . .'

'What question?'

'About Roxy!' Linda watched him closely. 'About whether you having the hots for me today is some kind of frustrated transference of you having the hots for her. It's all right – I'm not complaining. We're married, we've got teenagers: it's a miracle we have sex at all – but, you've got to admit, you *did* used to get frisky on Fridays after her show . . . *and* it's not every day you get to meet one of the three fantasy babes your wife's given you permission to shag.'

Simon sat up in bed.

'Linda, I love you,' he said solemnly. 'I've not looked at another woman since we met.'

'I know,' his wife admitted. 'I'm not saying you'd actually *do* anything. But she *was* kind of gorgeous, in a down-the-pub way.'

Simon frowned. 'Yeah, *was*. She *was*. She's not now.'

'Oh, come off it – she must only be thirty-five. That's about a decade younger than Jennifer Aniston, and look how gnarly she is!'

'No, it's not that. She's still . . . well, you know . . . good looking. But she's just a bit . . .'

'What?'

'Young.'

'*Young?*' Linda roared with laughter. 'Since when was *that* ever a problem for a man?'

'She still goes to nightclubs, Lind! And has hangovers – and wears short skirts and swears and chews gum.'

'She sounds terrible. She sounds exactly the same as when you fancied her.'

'She is.' Simon was unable to argue. He lay back down and thought for a moment. 'She hasn't changed at all. But I've changed – my tastes have changed.'

Linda snuggled back into his chest.

'Well, you no longer play your Steps CD,' she teased. But Simon was too pensive to notice.

'Roxy's good on paper,' he reasoned, 'but I don't want a woman who can drink the bar dry. Or dances on the table, or can name every premier-league player. I don't want a woman who can out-bloke me; life's emasculating enough.'

'Hey, you're all man from where I'm lying.' Linda gave him a nudge.

Simon kissed her and hugged her tightly. 'You know, if Robert Redford knocked on our door right now, I bet you wouldn't fancy him.'

'You offering odds on that?'

'No, really, Lind; you wouldn't – I mean, Redford's all very good in principle – ranch; film festival; still got all his own teeth . . . But the bottom line is, he's *Robert* bloody *Redford*! You don't actually know him. He's bound to have all sorts of issues.'

'Oh, I don't know . . .'

'And it's the same with Roxy,' he declared. 'OK, so I used to fancy her on TV – and yes, she's still hot and fun and bubbly. But I don't want fun and bubbly any more.'

Linda shot Simon *the look*.

'No, ravishingly beautiful defence lawyers are more my thing now,' Simon added hurriedly. Fifteen years of marriage had taught him that speed and extreme flattery were the only appropriate responses to *the look*. 'I don't want to drink in trendy bars with trendy people. I want cosy nights in with the mother of my children – pyjamas and a bottle of red. In fact, you can take back those free passes and burn them – I won't be needing them any more.'

Linda smiled, contented. 'Maybe you're right about Redford,' she conceded. 'They're probably not really his teeth.' She sighed in exaggerated resignation. 'I guess we've just got old, Drennan.'

'*Older*, Lind.' Simon kissed her head and hugged her. 'Just older.'

ROXY

'So?' Roxy demanded, interrupting Cressida mid-flow.

'Sorted,' Woody replied lightly. He shrugged off his coat and dropped it on to the back of Simon's chair.

'You got him?'

'Mmm hmm.'

There was a moment of silence and then . . .

'Fuck!' Roxy screamed. And before she could think the words *professional distance*, she launched herself across Simon's living room. Suddenly her arms were around Woody's shoulders and her face was next to his cheek. And that wasn't all. She could feel the warmth of his body. Woody was hugging her – sort of. Well, he was letting her hug him, anyway. She quickly inhaled the smell of soap and manliness at the base of his neck before professionalism demanded withdrawal. Damn; this Not Fancying Woody lark sucked.

'Steady on, Roxy!' Terence called from the couch. 'There are laws against that kind of thing. Is that ABH, or actual sexual harassment?'

'Sorry,' she mumbled, backing away. 'But, are you serious? Did Austin Jones really say yes?'

'Yep.'

'Bingo!' someone said quietly.

Then there was a gasp from Sue. 'Goodness, Woody, that's *fantastic*!'

And suddenly the whole room was on its feet.

'Yes, good work.' Terence slapped Woody's back in congratulation. 'Got to take my hat off to you – didn't think you'd be able to pull this one off.'

'Austin Jones is a career-changer,' cried Roxy. 'Pack your bags, everybody – we're about to take a fame road trip.'

Woody frowned at the euphoria. 'He's coming to next week's meeting,' he said quietly.

Sue froze. 'But next week's meeting's at my house!'

'Shame he couldn't have made it here today, eh, Si?' Terence smirked. 'Check out how life might have looked if Hollywood hadn't come calling. He's probably forgotten what IKEA looks like.'

'*Heal's*,' Simon corrected reflexively. He was the only one to have remained in his armchair.

'Oh, this is such brilliant news!' Holly clapped her hands in glee. 'Poor Austin, just imagine how terrible it must be having your Hollywood career just *end*. Think how we'll be able to help him.'

'His career didn't just end,' Simon corrected her flatly. 'He ended it.'

'Yes, well, I know that's what they *say* – but what if there's more to it than that? We know you can't believe what you read in the papers. Austin Jones coming to Lavender Heath is a cry for help and, thanks to Woody, we're ready to pick up the pieces.' Holly's face shone evangelically above her buttermilk cardie.

'I can't bloody believe it!' Roxy danced on the spot in celebration.

'Let's just start behaving like rational adults, shall we?' Cressida called the room to order. 'Mr Jones is just an actor. It's not the second coming of Christ.'

'It's *way* better than that!' Roxy laughed and caught Holly's eye. Holly was laughing too. It felt nice. It was the first time Roxy had felt a connection with Holly – and they both knew what a rocking big deal this was. She made a mental note to text Hol about a girls'-night piss-up.

'*Dad!*' a voice suddenly shouted.

Everyone turned to look at the angry-faced teen who'd mysteriously appeared by the door. The happy vibe instantly vanished.

'Couldn't you hear the door? It only rang a gazillion times!'

'Sorry, Euan.' Simon looked limp next to the ire of his son.

Euan eyed the empty wine bottles disdainfully.

'I had to answer it myself!'

'I'm sorry, son.'

'Yeah, well . . .' Euan begrudgingly accepted the apology. 'It's for the window cleaner.'

'Right, great, thanks. I'll take it from here.'

Euan scowled and t[...]

keep the noise down – I ca[...]

He tutted, and slunk off.

And in his space, a pair of six-in[...]

appeared. And the stilettos were attache[...]

orange legs that walked into the centre of th[...]

'Oh!' Roxy's excitement fizzled like a raspberry[...]

'Oh!' said the legs in identical deflation.

'Hey!' Woody hurried over to their owner. 'Glad you cou[...]

make it.' He warmly shook the woman's hand. 'Everybody, this

is Chelle. Chelle, this is everybody.'

Beneath wave after wave of more tonged hair than Roxy

had ever seen on a single human being, Chelle chewed her

gum and blinked. 'Oh!' she repeated, not hiding her disap-

pointment. 'Is this *it*?'

'What do you mean?' Woody asked.

The whole room stared dumbly at the woman's tiny sequined

dress, endless creosote limbs and enormous, pumped-to-burst

breasts.

Slowly Chelle pursed her glossy lips.

'You know . . . Is anyone *else* coming?'

Woody rubbed his head. 'No, this is it. All of us. Well, for

now.'

'Oh! I just thought . . .'

Everyone paused, waiting.

'Yes, yes – you thought what?' Cressida prompted her tersely.

Chelle blinked.

'. . . Like, you'd all be famous.'

...eath. It
...d. Roxy

...v *dare* she?
...ater before

...d pouted at

rned, before firing a last missive. 'And
n't hear the TV over you drunks.'
ruby-jewelled stilettos
to a pair of long,
room.
g balloon.

...hat-d'ya-call'ems

Roxy scowled. ... nd then touched Woody's arm.

'Maybe I should go,' she said, sounding injured. Her eyes had gone big and vulnerable.

'No!' Woody insisted. 'Come on; you tried so hard to meet us – why don't you just stop and say hi. I think you'll be pleasantly surprised.' He took her by the elbow and steered her around the room. 'So, Chelle, this is Cressida Cunningham, the former MP and cabinet minister.'

Chelle blinked, and looked away.

'Charmed,' Cressida muttered acidly. Roxy felt a surge of fondness for the thorny old bird. Woody propelled Chelle along.

'And Holly Childs, the writer . . .'

'A journo?' Chelle suddenly perked up.

'God, no! I'm a novelist!'

'Sorry.' Chelle's blank expression resumed. 'I don't do books.'

'OK, so . . .' Woody ushered her along. 'This is Sue Bunce, the . . .' Sue paled. '*Model and actress*,' he finished gently. 'And this is Simon Drennan, the television star.'

Everyone waited for Chelle to recognise Simon; she seemed a cert for the soaps. But she just chewed blankly.

'Sick Nick?' Simon offered lamely.

Chelle shrugged and gave him a tiny consolation smile. Woody steered her away.

'Right, well, this is leading meteorologist, Teren—'

'Oh. My. God.' Chelle stopped dead. '*I know you!*' She jabbed a hot pink fingernail towards Terence, as he puffed up in pride. 'Yeah, you're Terry Tornado – that weatherman who got everything wrong.' Terence visibly deflated. 'Dwayne, my ex, totally loves you, you crack 'im up! He couldn't believe all those muppets lost their 'ouses!' Chelle rummaged in her It-bag. 'I've gotta text 'im. He'll be well jell!'

Woody quickly moved Chelle along. 'And this,' he grinned, 'is TV presenter and all-round force of nature, Roxy Squires.'

Chelle glanced over her iPhone at Roxy.

'Yeah, well, I've seen *you* before.'

Roxy felt a small twinge of relief. As irritating as Chelle was, she *was* part of her late-night TV demographic. Hell, she was probably even a fan. Maybe they'd got off on the wrong foot, Roxy decided. After all, Chelle must have spent years watching her on the box. She'd probably copied her outfits and wanted her hair. She did her best to crack her a grin.

'Yeah, you're always hanging out at Golddiggaz,' Chelle pouted.

Roxy's grin froze. She turned to Woody in panic. 'It's a night-club! The name's ironic!'

'No it ain't! The blokes have to show their credit cards to get in. No platinum, no entry.'

'But it's work!' Roxy protested, suddenly wishing Simon's floorboards would swallow her whole. 'The paparazzi . . .'

But it was too late. The damage had been done. Roxy looked at Chelle in dismay. Why the hell was she here? She wasn't famous. Roxy's brain was an encyclopaedia of celebrity faces, and Chelle's wasn't in it. So why had Woody invited her? She suddenly noticed how close he and Chelle were standing; how Chelle's long, orange legs were even longer and orangier than her own; how her dress was shorter, her lips glossier, her lashes lusher . . . and suddenly Roxy felt under-done. She knew she should have made more of an effort tonight. Standing before Chelle, Roxy knew with absolute certainty her heels were too short, her tan too pale and her boobs too low. Something inside her sank. It had been bad enough having just Jennifer to contend with . . .

'Um,' Sue piped up shyly. 'Are you Chelle Blowers – wife of the footballer, Dwayne Blowers?'

The room looked at Sue in surprise. Holly gasped.

Chelle straightened proudly and flicked her hair. 'Yeah, that's right.'

'Oh!' Sue's face lit up. 'I read about you in my magazine! You had such a beautiful wedding.'

'*Sue!*' Cressida tutted.

'What? I'm only saying.'

'You shouldn't be wasting your time on *those* kinds of magazines.' Cressida had clearly had enough. She turned to Chelle. 'Excuse me, but taking aside the fact that you clearly lack the maturity to marry, why was a magazine covering your wedding?'

Chelle looked uncomfortable. 'Well, you know . . .'

'No, I don't. Are you accomplished?'

'Am I what?'

'Are you a person of talent? What do you do for a living? What do you do for charity? Have you discovered something, invented something, given to society in some great way?'

'Well . . .'

Roxy grinned. That was it. Her and Cressida – love!

But Chelle wasn't about to roll over.

'No, I ain't got a job.' She blinked defiantly. 'But I'm worth stuff – despite what Dwayne thinks. And I'm gonna get him to give me what he said he would. "For life," he said. Didn't know he only meant a few months. All my mates told me not to sign that pre-nup.' She started blinking again, as though she might cry.

Suddenly, Holly sprang forward. She gently touched Chelle's arm. 'Welcome, Chelle,' she said kindly. 'It's good to meet you; sit down. I'm very sorry you and Dwayne have broken up. I hadn't heard.'

'Yeah, well, this week's edition ain't come out yet.' Chelle sniffed as she allowed herself to be lowered on to a sofa and accepted a large glass of wine. 'I'm announcing the split on the cover.'

'Awwww,' Holly crumpled her nose sympathetically and rubbed Chelle's Fake Bake'd arm. 'You poor thing – how terrible for you. It's bad enough suffering the heartache of a break-up, without having to go through it in public as well.'

Roxy searched Holly's face for irony, but couldn't see any. In fact, Holly seemed to be enjoying her Claire Rayner role.

'I really loved him, my Dwayne!' Chelle blinked fiercely. 'He's my childhood sweetheart. Never thought he'd do the dirty on me – and wiv so many slags.'

'Yes, well, that's very sad,' Cressida said crisply. 'But we're not Relate.'

Holly frowned.

'What?' Cressida innocently protested. 'I'm simply trying to suggest somewhere more appropriate.'

'Woody understands!' Chelle wailed. 'Wivout Dwayne, I'm nuffin'! And 'til he pays me what he said he would, I ain't got nuffin', either. I just need you guys to give me a, you know . . .'

'Loan?'

'. . . leg-up.'

'A leg-up where, exactly?'

'I just wanna have fun – see and be seen. I wanna meet someone new – someone famous.'

'Hang on a minute,' Simon interrupted. 'Are you saying you wanted to meet us to see if you could find a famous boyfriend? No wonder you're so disappointed.'

'I just wanna be kept in the manner I'm customed. You know – new clothes, new clobber, new car . . .'

'What's wrong with the clothes you've already got?' Cressida cross-examined her. But Chelle just pulled a face.

Holly paused from rubbing Chelle's back. 'I don't get it,' she puzzled. 'You said you were announcing your marriage break-up in next week's magazines. Don't those magazines pay for their interviews?'

'Yeah, but not enough. Don't get me wrong; I've got enough dirt on Dwayne to get me covers for a year. But the mags pay peanuts.'

'I heard they pay tens of thousands,' Sue said helpfully.

'And? Tens of thousands'll only last me five minutes, even though Dwayne left me the house and the car. It's expensive being me. I've gotta wear the right stuff, have the right hair, go to the right places.'

Despite herself, Roxy nodded. She had a point.

'No,' Chelle declared decisively. 'Being single won't work. I've gotta be part of a couple, and my other arf's gotta be famous. That's just how it is.' And she set about draining her wine.

Everyone huddled around Woody, except Holly, who was still busy sympathy-rubbing Chelle.

'Woody! What were you thinking?' hissed Cressida. 'She's not like us. She can't possibly stay.'

'But she's had her heart broken,' Sue whispered timidly. 'She needs help.'

'Sue's right,' Terence agreed with uncharacteristic charity.

'And besides, she *is* like us, in a way,' Sue continued. '*We're* trying to work out what to do with our lives after fame, and *she's* trying to work out what to do with her life after marriage.'

'Oh, I think she's already figured out that.' Cressida frowned. 'She's going to piggyback on somebody else's success. Really, Woody; we shouldn't condone this kind of behaviour.'

'What do you think, Rox?' Woody studied her carefully.

Roxy pursed her lips and blew out a long column of air. What *did* she think? Her instinct was to get rid. Chelle was younger and thinner – and obviously desperate to get her hands on Woody. And all that stuff about bagging a rich boyfriend was gross! *But* . . . Chelle *was* getting magazine covers; maybe she could be useful to the group – share her press contacts around. And didn't they say to keep your enemies close? *Arrrrrgh!* What did Woody *want* her to say? She quickly searched his face for clues.

Luckily, Simon interrupted.

'For Christ's sake, everyone – she's embarrassing! She's a gold-digging car wreck in heels! She's going to have to go before Austin joins. He'll think we're a bunch of idiots!'

'Austin?' On the other side of the room, Chelle perked up. 'Austin who?'

The group froze, eyeing each other in panic.

'No one . . .' Simon called out with over-baked innocence. 'Austin no one.'

'Oh. My. God.' Chelle flicked off Holly's arm-rubbing hand in excitement. 'You mean Austin Jones, don'tcha?'

Simon opened his mouth and then closed it, unable to improvise a quick enough lie.

'Austin Jones, the *movie star*!' Chelle giggled. Her blankness was suddenly superanimated. 'Woody – why didn'tcha tell me? Austin's single, right? Wow, *Austin Jones* . . . He'd do perfect! Dwayne'll freak! Is he coming tonight? Get us another wine, Hol, would ya?'

Roxy looked at the group. Everyone's face was registering dread. But that was it – matter settled. Whether they liked it or not, Chelle was joining the group.

To: Roxy Squires

From: *Never Mind The Buzzcocks* production office

Hello Roxy Squires,

Thanks for getting in touch to suggest yourself as a guest panellist for *Never Mind The Buzzcocks*.

Although we don't think you're right as a celebrity panellist, we're always looking for people for the 'where are they now' line-up. We're currently padding out the extras for Whigfield. If you fancy being a red herring, give us a call . . .

ROXY

'Shouldn't you be filming today?'

Roxy frowned and concentrated on applying base coat to Sue's nails.

'Day off,' she muttered darkly. She'd been doing her best to forget the morning's catastrophic round of phone calls. Was it her imagination, or were the people working in telly getting ruder? A few years ago, if she phoned to suggest herself as the presenter for a programme or pitch an idea for a banging new show, people at least listened before they said no. Now they practically hung up before they'd answered.

'All submissions in writing,' one woman (who barely sounded out of her teens) had barked before Roxy's motormouth had even cranked into gear. 'And only via an agent.'

'I don't have an agent.'

'Can't get one?'

'I choose to captain my own ship,' Roxy had retorted with as much dignity as she could muster. 'Girl power,' she added limply.

'Whatever,' the teenager sighed. 'Look, if you want my advice . . .'

Roxy wasn't sure that she did.

'. . . I'd give it a rest. You call us every single week and the answer's always, totally, no. Forget about telly; you're done. Aren't they desperate for nurses?'

Over her years of working in TV, Roxy had learnt to develop a thick skin. And a small part of her – the plain-speaking part – admired the child's bluntness. But the rest of her (the I've-interviewed-more-bands-than-you-could-shake-your-rattle-at bit) wanted to give the jumped-up message-taker a tongue lashing so brutal that it knocked her into the early part of next week. She drew herself up, took a deep breath and was about to get started when she heard a click. The teen had hung up. Furious, Roxy had abandoned the pitches she'd planned for the morning and was now sitting in Sue's kitchen, chain-drinking tea and deflecting a non-stop bombardment of Hobnobs.

'Are you *sure* we should be going for lilac?' Sue eyed the bottle of purple nail varnish with trepidation.

'Mega sure,' Roxy dismissed. 'French is for WAGs; nude is for bores. Red's great, but you need to wear it with attitude. Lilac's leftfield and funky – it's perfect for you.'

Sue nodded uncertainly.

'Well, it's really nice of you to spend your day off doing this,' she ventured gamely as Roxy blew across her base coat to check it was dry. 'I can't remember the last time I had a manicure.'

'Well, you should,' Roxy upbraided her. 'Neglect your nails and the world will neglect you. Manicures are a vital part of your wardrobe!'

Sue looked blank. Roxy sighed and tried another tack.

'Think of your nails like a cardie . . . *or knickers*. You wouldn't leave the house without undercrackers, would you? Nor should you leave without polish.'

'Wearing nail varnish is as important as wearing pants?' Sue's eyes goggled.

Roxy thought for a moment.

'No, you're right,' she conceded. 'Some outfits are rubbish with pants.'

Sue gasped. 'You sometimes go out *without pants*?'

'Course! The paps get a shot of an arse-muncher, and you'll be in all the wrong kinds of spreads.'

Sue blanched. 'I don't go out much, anyway,' she said, relieved.

'No? Why not?'

'Oh, I . . .' she tailed off. She did her best to look offhand, but there was an obvious sadness.

'Why don't you come out with me?' Roxy offered impulsively.

Sue pulled her hand away. It fluttered nervously, nails half painted, at her chest. 'Oh, I couldn't possibly go clubbing.'

'Not clubbing, just a drink.'

Sue looked doubtful. 'I don't know . . .'

'Yes, why not?' Roxy warmed to her theme. Why shouldn't she go drinking with Sue? Just because they had zero in common didn't mean they couldn't have a laugh. Besides, she was developing a soft spot for Sue. OK, she was practically as old as her mum, but Roxy wanted to make her less sad. As she watched Sue struggle to invent an excuse, she was struck by a terrible thought. How long had it been since Sue had got hammered. Months? Years? *Decades?*

'When d'you last have a night out, Sue?' she asked bluntly.

'Last week. With you.'

'Not a meeting. I mean a proper night out – somewhere that doesn't have a kettle.'

'Oh, gosh. Um . . .' Sue's cheeks reddened.

'Right, that settles it – I insist!' Roxy declared. 'Nothing major; just you, me and a bottle of the hard stuff down the Dog and Duck.' She pretended not to notice the fear flooding Sue's face.

'But I haven't got anything to wear,' Sue protested feebly.

'Oh, I doubt that!' Roxy screwed the lid on the bottle of varnish and blew across Sue's new purple nails. 'Come on; lead the way!'

'To the pub?' Sue asked in alarm.

'To your bedroom! I'm gonna check out your clobber – blow the cobwebs off your party outfits. I bet you've got dozens back there!'

But she was wrong.

'Nice!' admired Roxy as she flung open the doors to Sue's wardrobe and surveyed the clothes inside. 'Colour-coded wardrobes – I'm liking your style.' She peered around the bedroom. 'So, where are the other wardrobes?'

'What other wardrobes?' Sue's eyes wandered her own bedroom, confused.

'Very funny.' Roxy was beginning to see a new side to Sue – she'd never had her down as a joker. 'The wardrobes with the colours in them.'

Sue pinkened again. 'There are no other wardrobes.'

Roxy's mouth fell open. 'But all your clothes are black!'

She stared into Sue's wardrobe, agog. It was a cavernous black hole – a dark, deep mass of fabric midnight. It looked like the kind of wardrobe you could walk into and keep walking, and eventually pop out in Narnia.

'Are you telling me you don't own a *single item of colour*?'

Roxy couldn't make sense of such a thing. Her own wardrobe was a riot: a demented mash-up of Eurovision and Barbie. Tentatively, she reached a hand into Sue's clothes and recoiled. Everything was made from jersey – floppy, wide-skirted and elasticated at the waist. There was barely a zip, seam or button to be seen.

'Christ, Sue! What's going on?'

Sue fumbled awkwardly. 'It's just that black's so forgiving. I grow out of things so fast.'

'Bloody hell! I'm all for a nice, black silhouette, but have we just walked into the wrong house? These aren't dresses – they're cassocks! And there's nothing slimming about leisure-goth.'

But then Roxy caught a glimpse of Sue's face. She could have kicked herself. Sue was staring at the carpet, a tart's fart away from tears. The Squires motormouth had struck again.

Chastened, Roxy flopped down on the bed next to her friend. The two women sat in silence, the inky wardrobe yawning before them.

'Black's cool,' Roxy offered after a moment. 'Some of my best underwear's black.'

Sue tried to raise a watery smile. A thoughtful silence resumed.

'You know what I'd love to see you in,' Roxy burst out optimistically. Sue looked at her with big, sad eyes – like Bambi, if he'd just been run over – and Roxy was struck with the momentousness of the task in hand. *This was the Gok moment*, she realised with a tremble. This was way bigger than wardrobes. This wasn't about weaning Sue off her jersey crack – this was about revamping the fabric of Sue, the woman! Sue needed making over from the inside out.

'Duck egg,' Roxy declared authoritatively. 'You'd look mint in a bit of duck egg.'

'Really?' Sue looked dubious and nervous at the same time.

'Deffo! It'll soften you up, let that baby-smooth skin of yours glow.'

Instinctively, Sue's hand crept up to her face to feel its softness.

'You see, black's *good*,' Roxy continued carefully. 'But it would be doubly good to say hi to a few other colours too. Y'know, to *complement* the black.'

'Oh, I'm not sure . . .' Sue looked terrified at the prospect of Pantones.

'Nothing too bright. Just a few soft shades . . . Some greys

and creams. And mushroom; mushroom's very flattering for
. . .' Roxy stopped before the motormouth could blurt *the more
mature lady*. '. . . Your skin tone,' she finished with relief. And
she beamed at Sue encouragingly.

There was a moment of silence whilst duck egg hung in
the balance.

'Oooo, hang about!' Roxy dashed out of the bedroom, before
rocketing back with her bag. She plonked it on the bed and
rummaged its contents. 'In fact . . .' she muttered, as various
oddities spilled out the sides, 'I've got just the thing . . . Ta-
dah!' And she triumphantly waved a pewter cloth.

'What is it?'

'It's a scarf, Sue – a scarf!'

Sue regarded it nervously. Pewter was obviously dangerous
new territory.

'Look, I'm not suggesting you swan about in a dreamcoat,'
Roxy told her. 'All I'm saying is, how about a few *mildly* colourful
accessories? I mean, this isn't a proper colour at all; it's a
demi-colour.'

Sue eyed the scarf as though it were teethed and hungry.
'OK,' she finally agreed.

It was all the encouragement Roxy needed. In a blink she
hoisted Sue to her feet and arranged the scarf around her
neck. The effect was immediate. Sue's complexion brightened
and her eyes sparkled. Roxy span her around so she could see
her reflection in the mirror.

'See?' Roxy prompted, barely able to hide her jubilation. 'A
little bit of *almost* colour goes a very long way.'

Sue's breath quickened. She looked at herself. And then Roxy saw it – a hint of marvel in Sue's eyes.

'Is it my imagination . . .' Sue ventured hesitantly, '. . . or does it make me look a bit . . .'

'Younger? Trendier?' she offered.

'. . . *thinner*?'

Roxy smiled. 'Thinner – yes! Definitely thinner.'

And Sue turned and gave a radiant smile that suddenly wiped twenty years from her face and gave Roxy a glimpse of what she must have looked like when she was Suzi.

'Keep it,' Roxy told her, despite the fact that the scarf was Marc Jacobs and her favourite.

'I couldn't . . .'

'Really – it never suited me, anyway. Have it!'

'Well . . . if you're sure.' Sue grinned, and put her hand up to touch the scarf's folds. Roxy noticed her hand fluttered less than before. And then she clocked Sue admiring her lilac nails against the pewter.

Bingo, Roxy thought proudly. But then her smile faded. 'Sue?' she asked quickly, before better judgement could get in the way. 'What's Jennifer like?'

'Like?' Sue was still entranced by her new reflection. 'Well, I expect she's lovely.'

'You've not met her?'

'No.'

'But you said she was beautiful,' Roxy protested. '*And* dedicated to her job.'

'Well, she *is* beautiful,' Sue automatically insisted. 'Have you still not seen the photos?'

Roxy grunted. She'd not actually managed to set foot in Woody's house since the night of their date-that-never-was. Not that it mattered now, anyway. She was officially No Longer Interested In Woody. So why did hearing that Jennifer was beautiful hurt?

'And I don't think she wears a drop of make-up,' Sue added.

The elastic snapped in Roxy's jaw. *What kind of woman didn't wear make-up?* She couldn't imagine a life without MAC. She made herself up just to make toast. So, unless Woody was going out with a battleaxe (unlikely), Jennifer had to be beyond mortally stunning.

'And *of course* she's dedicated to her job.' Sue patted her scarf, unaware of the meltdown taking place on her bed. 'Otherwise she'd come to our meetings.'

Roxy choked. 'Are you saying she used to be famous?' She suddenly remembered all the beautiful women Woody used to be linked to: Imogen Tattinger . . . Jessica Jones . . . *Petra Klitova.*

'Oh, no! I'm sure Woody would have said.'

'But she lives in Lavender Heath?' Roxy wondered if she'd ever seen her. She couldn't remember seeing any bare-faced supermodel types about. It was the kind of thing she wasn't likely to miss.

'She lives with Woody, silly.'

Roxy stared at the carpet a moment, suddenly wishing she

could lie on it and never get up. It was just as well she wasn't going after Woody. She'd never have stood a chance.

'Anyway!' Roxy clapped her hands and tried to sound unaffected. 'I'd better make tracks . . . Hot date tonight; need to shave my bits.' And she hurried to the bedroom door.

'Oh, Roxy, you dropped something!'

Roxy turned as Sue picked up a thick wadge of paper. It was her latest Visa bill. It must have fallen out of her bag when she was digging for the scarf. But as Sue handed it over, the bill slipped and page after page cascaded on to the floor, covering the carpet in incriminating sheets of black and white.

'Goodness, Roxy; have you been on a spree?' Sue exclaimed. She looked at a page and frowned. 'Are these *all* clothes shops?'

Roxy launched herself at the scattered bill.

'Just a few outfits,' she mumbled as she tried to pull the page out of Sue's hand. 'For work.'

'But aren't these men's clothes shops?'

'Presents – for my brother.' And Roxy ripped the sheet away, stuffing it in her bag with the rest of the bill. 'Anyway, like I said . . . Gotta run.' She scarpered again, but then paused in the doorway. 'And remember, Sue . . . *duck egg!*'

'Duck egg,' Sue obediently nodded.

Roxy grinned emptily, and bolted.

To: Roxy Squires

From: The Regency Television Presenters' Representation Agency

Thank you for your request that we become your official agent for television presenting employment.

However, whilst we are aware of your past body of work, we don't think there's anything we could do with you now.

We wish you the best of luck for the future.

To: Roxy Squires

From: Cast Of Thousands Representation

Thank you for considering us for your professional representation.

Our books are currently full.

However, we do have a gap in our roster for Eastern European women (under 30). Full training given. If you know any, give them our number.

To: Roxy Squires

From: Casting Couch

Hiya. I'm out of the office this week. If you're emailing about *Honey Cassidy's Fresh Melons* supermarket tour, give me a shout on the mobile. For info on *Topless Chess*, give the girls in the office a buzz.

SIMON

'Urgh!' Euan screwed up his nose in disgust.

'What do you mean, "urgh"?' Simon replied, affronted. He'd spent ages slow-cooking the venison-and-chorizo casserole, and it was melt-in-your-mouth perfection. It hadn't been easy; he'd had to drive to Biddington for the pimento-stuffed olives and, in the Lavender Heath farmers'-market shop, he'd practically had to wrestle for the last imported sausage. If that woman hadn't been so worried about her nails, he might never have got it at all.

'Why can't we eat normal stuff, like normal people?' Euan grumbled as he prodded his lunch with disdain.

Simon spiked an olive and did his best not to look hurt. He'd learnt to keep his expressions neutral when close to the twins. Reactions were only used against him as evidence of his own moronity.

'We *are* normal people, Euan,' he countered jovially. 'Everybody eats casserole.'

'Not pretentious casserole, they don't.' Euan turned to his mother. 'Why can't we have Turkey Twizzlers?'

'Ah!' Simon interrupted knowingly. '*Nobody* eats Turkey Twizzlers – not since Jamie Oliver.'

'*Everyone* eats Turkey Twizzlers, numbskull. William Jarrett-Smith's mum gets them imported. Duh – nobody's *seen* eating Turkey Twizzlers – they get them online. Haven't you ever heard of the Twizzler black market?'

Simon studied his son in confusion. Was he joking? Was Euan actually engaging in humour? But one glimpse of his son's curled lip evaporated all hope. Suddenly Simon felt mortified. How come he didn't know about the Twizzler black market? Was there a whole sub-section of black market food he didn't know about? An alliance of Lavender Heath mums secretly feeding their little darlings Angel Delight and Brain's faggots?

'So,' chirped Linda, in an attempt to lift the mood. 'It's your dad's last night in panto.'

'Thank Christ,' muttered Scarlet.

'Why do you say that?' Simon quizzed, before considering the wisdom of asking. In one sense, he agreed with his daughter – he *did* thank Christ it was the last night he had to glue on his eyebrows and slip into his spit-laden beard. This year's panto had run unseasonably, depressingly long (it was 2nd February, for heaven's sake!). But on the other hand, the twins were an empathy-free zone, and any support from them should be treated as suspicious.

Scarlet shrugged.

'Well, it's embarrassing, isn't it?'

Again, Simon had to agree. Treading the boards of a second-rate theatre *was* embarrassing. He should be strutting the stages of the West End! He looked at his daughter in wonder. He'd never realised he had an ally.

'Yeah, everyone else's dad's a CEO,' she continued lethally. 'But *ours* wears tights for a living. And that's when he's actually working – the rest of the year he's a dole-ite.'

'Scarlet!' Linda scolded angrily as Simon recoiled from his daughter's betrayal. 'Your father is a highly respected actor! And, anyway, what's so wrong with pantomime? You used to love it when you were a little girl.' She lifted a hand to silence Scarlet's counter-argument. '*Plus* you know full well that it's perfectly normal for an actor to have downtime between jobs. You should be pleased your father's so choosy. If he took everything he was offered, he wouldn't be able to drive you to all your lovely activities.'

But Scarlet was unimpressed. 'Anyway, I'm glad the panto's over.' She eyeballed her father witheringly. 'Give those zits time to recover.'

Simon's fork fell on his plate with a clatter.

'Zits! What zits?' His fingers searched his cheeks for their Braille.

'Duh! The zits covering your whole, entire face! You're like the *before* bit in a Clearasil ad. It's putting me off my lunch.' And underlining her point, Scarlet put down her knife and fork and pushed her casserole away.

'It's the make-up! Stage make-up's so horribly thick—'

'We *all* wear make-up, Dad. Doesn't mean we go around with a plague face.'

'*Scarlet!*' Linda scolded her again.

'What? I'm only saying!'

A few minutes later and, mercifully, Linda granted the twins liberty from the dinner table. Within seconds, they'd scarpered back to their iPads and Xboxes, their bedroom doors articulately slamming behind them. A blissful silence swept into the kitchen, and then Simon crumpled with the release of the superhuman effort it took to remain upbeat in front of his kids.

'She doesn't mean to be vile,' Linda consoled him. 'It's just her crap DNA.'

'But, she's right, isn't she?' Simon wallowed. 'Panto *is* embarrassing. *I'm* embarrassing. Kids want to respect their dads. Nobody wants one who's just meals and wheels.'

'Oi! We *both* agreed you should take your time and hang out for the quality projects. And whilst that's happening, it's great that you can pick the kids up from school and give them a home-cooked meal. One day they'll thank you for it!'

'One day they'll hang me for it,' he mumbled darkly.

'Hey!' Linda came over to his side of the table and gave him a friendly poke. 'You're officially hanging up your eyebrows for another year. I thought you'd be pleased.'

'I *am* pleased.'

'So why the long face?' She pulled Scarlet's chair up beside him and gave him a gentle, teasing kiss.

Simon sighed and relented. He never liked to keep things from Linda. Actually, he found it impossible. She had a way of cuddling things out of him.

'It's the group,' he admitted heavily.

'What, your famous-friends group?'

'My *formerly*-famous-friends group,' he corrected bleakly. 'Yeah, well, it looks like one of us isn't going to be so formerly famous.'

Linda peered at him quizzically. 'What do you mean?'

'Austin's joining,' he declared, depressed.

'Austin who?'

He tutted. 'Austin Jones!'

Linda laughed. 'Austin Jones is joining your support group? What? *The* Austin Jones?'

'It's not a support group,' insisted Simon. 'We're a collection of friends who meet to share our experiences. And yes, *the* bloody Austin Jones!'

'Friends? You can't stand half of them!'

'That's not true.'

His wife raised an eyebrow. 'The only one you like is Roxy,' she teased, nudging him fondly before cuddling back up. 'Well, well, well. *The* Austin Jones, eh?'

'I don't know why you find it so funny.'

'I don't, honey. It's just, the most successful rom-com actor in the world is joining your group, and you think it's *bad* news.'

'It *is* bad news.'

'Yeah? On what planet?'

Simon struggled to think of a reply. He knew he was being childish, but he couldn't help it.

'You daft sod!' Linda fondly ruffled his hair. 'This is a brilliant opportunity, silly. Think about it . . . *You* love rom-coms

– *he* knows rom-coms inside out. *You* want to get into them – *he* wants to get out. What better opportunity for my handsome, talented, criminally under-cast husband to pick Austin Jones' brain for some tips? He can give you all the inside info. He might even help you on your way. Simon, this is great news! This could be the opportunity you've been looking for!'

Simon knew it made sense, but his bad mood had dug in too deep.

'He's thirty-seven!' he protested bleakly.

'So . . . ?'

'"So"?' Did he really need to spell it out? His brilliant wife could defend watertight accusations on the most oblique and complicated loophole. How could she not see *this* glaring injustice? 'So, he's thirty-seven and has done fourteen movies that have grossed hundreds of millions of dollars around the world. I'm thirty-nine, have done precisely *no* movies and spend six months a year living off the joint account.'

Linda scooched a little closer. 'It's just the luck of the draw, sweetheart. Austin isn't more talented – he's luckier. He just happened to be in the right place at the right time.'

'Yeah, and now he's in his multi-million-pound mansion and I'm in panto!'

'Bloody Barrington.' Linda suddenly sat straight. 'You *have* fired him, haven't you?'

'Everyone loves him, Lind,' Simon whined extra loudly, to divert his wife from his lack of answer. 'The whole world loves Austin Jones! Everyone thinks I'm a murderous, kiddy-fiddling pervert . . . if they even think of me at all.'

'Now, you listen to me, Simon Drennan.' Linda fixed him with a no-nonsense stare. 'You are a great actor – too great! That's why everyone still thinks you're Sick Nick – because you were so brilliant at pretending to be him. Now that's what *I* call talent.'

Simon grunted, determined to resist her logic. He stared at the twins' discarded casserole to keep himself feeling down-beat.

'Come on, cheer up.' Linda slapped his back and stood up. 'I'm sure you and Austin'll be best mates within the week. Who knows? Maybe he'll introduce you to some of his contacts. Hey, get him to give you his agent's details. That'll wipe the smirk off Barrington's smug little face.' And she started clearing the plates. Forlornly, Simon watched as she loaded the dishwasher.

'*The* Austin Jones, eh?' She grinned as she stacked dirty dinner plates. Trapped in his gloom, Simon didn't see the teasing look she threw in his direction.

To: Roxy Squires

From: Holly Childs

Hi Roxy,

Thanks very much for your message(s). I don't often go out in the evenings, but yes, OK . . . I suppose a drink might be nice!

Shall we meet in the Dog and Duck at 7.30?

x

ROXY

'Oh!' Roxy's face fell. 'You bought Chelle.'

'You don't mind, do you?' Holly asked sweetly, as she joined Roxy at the corner table and sat down. She was wearing a peach blouse and cardie. 'She's having a bad day.'

Roxy looked over to the bar. Chelle didn't look like she was having a bad day. She was wearing six-inch heels, a silver mini and more make-up than a synchronised swimmer.

'You know me,' she mumbled. 'Two's a chat; three's a party.' She took a swig of her beer and tried not to feel resentful as a ruddy-faced Dave asked Chelle for her order. Dave didn't blush when *she* ordered drinks – not unless you counted that time she asked for a Slippery Nipple. But Chelle was unaware of Dave's hormones, tapping away on her iPhone and ceaselessly rearranging her hair.

'Does she realise she's in the Dog and Duck and there's no pole?' Roxy muttered.

'Bottle of champers, girlies?' Chelle hollered over.

'Ooo, lovely!' Holly cooed excitedly.

'What's wrong with her then?' Roxy asked as Chelle went

into slo-mo looking for her purse. 'Not got her acrylics into any millionaires this week?'

'Roxy!'

'What? It's what she wants – she said so herself!'

'If you must know,' Holly corrected, 'she's a bit blue. She just needs a girly chat to get things off her chest.'

'Epic,' replied Roxy dryly, as she eyed Chelle's plastic boobs. She'd wanted a natter with Holly; she had important comeback ideas to discuss. But now Chelle would be turning the night into a spotlit weep-fest.

'Bloody 'ell, that took yonks!' Chelle arrived at the table with bubbly, Dave and a tray of glasses in her wake. 'I can't believe this place don't take AmEx. What're we doin' 'ere, anyway? I thought we was goin' up town?'

Dave scuttled back to the safety of the bar.

'To London?' Holly froze.

'Yeah; up West, down East, round Mayfair . . . It's all farmers and coffin dodgers round 'ere. We should be struttin' our stuff somewhere glamorous!'

'I don't really think . . .' Holly adjusted her cardie.

'Oh, come on, Hol! Live a bit, would'ya?'

'But you've just bought champagne.'

'We can drink it in the taxi!'

Holly groped for a different excuse. 'But aren't they all members' bars in London?'

'So?'

'So – Roxy and I aren't members!'

Roxy was about to protest. She didn't want to be trumped

in the membership-of-cool-bars stakes. Besides, membership was for wimps. There wasn't a velvet rope in the world she couldn't get past if she put her mind to it and her slap on. But Chelle didn't give her time to butt in.

'Don't be stupid!' she snorted. 'You're with me, I'm a member everywhere!'

'Really? Gosh, that sounds expensive.'

'I don't pay! Nah, I get sent membership cards for free. Or, at least, Dwayne does.' Suddenly Chelle stopped and looked sad.

'Yes, well, I don't really fancy London,' Holly said quickly. 'Too much hassle, isn't it, Roxy?'

Roxy decided to play along. If she was going to be forced into a night with Chelle, it had to be quick. There was no way she was prolonging it by clubbing.

'Haven't you heard?' she declared archly. 'London's over! Locals are where it's at now.'

'Really?' Chelle instantly brightened. 'Wicked!'

For all her talk of clubbing, Chelle – it turned out – was a lightweight. After just thirty minutes of drinking, she'd gone distinctly last-season green.

'Shall I take you out for some air?' Holly rubbed her arm in concern.

Chelle shook her head and gripped her seat. She concentrated very hard on just breathing.

Roxy seized her chance. 'So, Hol, we need to talk about something.'

'We do?'

'You!'

But Holly was distracted by Chelle.

'Why d'you give it up, Hol?'

'Give what up?'

'The books, the writing, the fame!'

Now she had her attention.

'Oh, I was never really famous.' Holly's forehead rumpled into a frown.

'Don't be daft, you were mega successful!'

'Well, a bit. But success and fame are two different things. I wasn't a star – I was at school.'

'But Holly, your book was made into a film! And not just any film – a bloody big, bank-busting blockbuster!'

Holly looked at her obtusely. 'I don't get your point.'

'My point is, you could have been J. K. Rowling! Or . . .' Roxy tried to think of some other authors. 'Enid Blyton.'

'It was just a bit of fun,' said Holly. 'And then I gave it up.'

'But I don't get it.' Roxy slapped the table in exasperation. 'If it was fun, why stop?'

Holly shrugged. 'My parents thought education was important.'

'My parents thought Cliff was important.'

'They wanted me to study science.'

'So? Nobody does what their parents tell them.'

'I did,' Holly said simply. 'They said being high profile was vulgar.'

'Being high profile is ace!'

Holly pulled a face. 'I don't think I would have liked it. I'm not really one for big parties. My mum said I wasn't the type.'

'You were fifteen. You could have *become* the type!'

For a moment Holly looked lost. 'I don't know. I already had lots of money. And making up stories just seemed a bit silly. Besides, I had lots of ideas when I was younger. But I don't any more.'

'That's because you don't *do* anything!' Roxy cried. 'If you stepped a few feet out of Lavender Heath, you'd find tons of juicy stuff to write about.'

'I'm not su—'

'Hol, you've *got* to start writing again!'

'Oh, I don't—'

'If *you* don't have stories, *use mine*. I've been there, done that – with knobs on. I'm a walking one-woman bonkbuster!'

'I miss Dwayne!' Chelle suddenly wailed.

Holly's attention instantly vanished. She pulled Chelle into a hug.

'Awww, you poor thing! Oh, let's see if I've got a tissue for your nose.'

Irritated, Roxy topped up her glass. If she couldn't get what she wanted from Holly, she'd settle for Plan B and get pissed.

'All I ever wanted was Dwayne's babies!' howled Chelle, her eyes muddying with mascara, a rivet of snot glistening next to the gloss on her lips. 'Imagine how beautiful they'd be!'

Holly dabbed at Chelle with a tissue. 'He doesn't deserve your tears,' she consoled her. 'And you can still have babies. With someone more deserving than Dwayne.'

'But Dwayne *is* deserving!' wept Chelle. 'I love him, Hol; I really do.'

'I know,' she clucked sympathetically. 'But you'll find someone else. Won't she, Roxy?'

'Yep.' Roxy drained her glass and tried to remember how many calories were in crisps.

Chelle swayed giddily. 'I just don't get why we can't be together!'

'Well . . .' Holly started in surprise. 'Well, because you *can't*. Because of the other women, remember? He cheated on you; you can't take him back. Tell her, Roxy.'

'Girl power!' Roxy roused, whilst signalling to Dave for another bottle of fizz. As irritating as Chelle was, even *she* deserved a bit of dignity. When the shit hit the fan and men did the dirty, girls had to stick together. 'He's hardly the dream package,' she said bluntly. 'He's a two-timing, wick-dipping love rat!'

'He's *my* dream package,' Chelle sniffed. 'And he's not what you think.'

'I think he's an arse!' Roxy scoffed. 'Come on, Chelle – channel your inner Beyoncé!'

'You've been so brave,' Holly added. 'You walked away; you've already done the hard bit.'

'Nah, you don' geddit,' Chelle slurred. 'I didn't walk away – *he* did.'

Holly frowned. 'He left you for another woman?'

'*Women*,' Roxy quietly corrected.

'*What* other women?' Chelle bawled.

And then she spilled her drink (right over her latest It-bag).
And then she spilled Dwayne's secret.

The night didn't last long. Holly took Chelle home in a taxi
and Roxy drained the last bottle of champagne on her own.
She zigzagged back to her house. She'd tried to feel sorry for
Chelle, she reasoned, as she wobbled into the side of a bush.
In life, she made it a policy to like people. Liking people was
good karma and stuff. But she just *couldn't* like WAGs. It wasn't
their designer lifestyles and endless supply of free handbags
. . . it was that WAGs got famous without trying. And Roxy
was forged from pure Irene Cara. Fame cost, and you had to
pay for it in blood, sweat and legwarmers. Or, at the very least,
in lads' mags, calendars and late-night cable TV.

But still, Roxy had to hand it to her – even snotty, wailing
and pissed, Chelle had still managed to look glamorous. Roxy
inspected herself in the moonlight. She'd been letting things
slip a bit lately. She was still wearing heels, but her tops had
got baggier and longer and, beneath her Seven jeans, she knew
she was at least three shades lighter than Chelle. What the
hell was happening? Maintenance was Roxy's middle name!
Had she become so preoccupied with other people's careers
that she'd started neglecting her own? With a sinking heart,
Roxy realised she'd missed her last appointment at the Tan
Hut. And she'd forgotten the beautician! She *never* forgot the
beautician! She went religiously, like other people went to
church. But lately her legs had begun to sprout stubble, and
she didn't want to *think* about the state of her ladygarden.

Nope, there were no two ways about it: Roxy needed to beauty-up – else the Chelles of the world would take over. It might be ten thirty at night, but there wasn't a minute to loose.

To: Roxy Squires

From: *Celebsville* Magazine

Dear Roxy Squirls

Thanks for your email asking if you can come to the celebrity launch party of *Celebsville* Magazine, the number one destination for all the hottest gossip from planet celeb.

Unfortunately our guest list is full.

However, don't forget to buy the first edition for just £1 when it hits news-stands next Tuesday!

Luv

The *Celebsville* Editorial Team

x

8.30am @foxyroxy

Fuuuuccccckkkkkkkkk!

8.31am @foxyroxy

#ROXYSAYS: never drink and self-tan! Am dead ringer for a
fence.

ROXY

She was going to die – she knew it.

If she took one more step, she was one hundred per cent certain she'd explode. The only evidence Roxy Squires had ever existed would be an orange splat and a pair of silver Nikes. But, even as she fought for breath and searched her soul for anything that approximated willpower, Roxy couldn't help but feel proud. She was such a pro! Even at the point of death, she was *still* calculating the small screen potential. Just think, she consoled herself gleefully, she'd be a real-life case of spontaneous human combustion. She was bound to be in a Channel Five documentary with that. And a TV appearance was still a TV appearance – even if it was posthumous . . . it'd still count as a credit on IMDb!

And then the fleeting pride was gone, and only the sweat and pain remained.

That was it, she told herself – enough! Sod legs like Alexa Chung – this was bloody agony! She didn't have the strength to propel herself a single centimetre more. So she stopped. Or rather, collapsed.

Roxy nosedived sweatily on to somebody's garden wall and then – because merely sitting wasn't quite enough – she lay on it, pressing her cheek into the coolness of the shrubbery. She closed her eyes, blotted out the world and desperately tried to suck air into her body.

Christ – why did people jog?

Were they masochists, or just mental?

As air began to filter back into her lungs, Roxy heard a moaning noise. She could barely hear it at first, over the roar of the blood in her veins, but it was definitely there: a low, agonised note, broken only by her wheezing for breath. It was a note that sounded as broken as she felt. She liked it! She enjoyed it for a moment before realising that what was making the noise was her. And then there was another noise too.

'Roxy? Roxy? Can you hear me?'

Woody's face was hovering above her.

Roxy choked. *Christ!* What was he doing here? Especially with her looking like this! She let her mouth drop open. *Quick! What would Liz do if she was caught in daylight with hair stuck to her forehead and a complexion like forty-per-cent burns?* She tried to blend into the wall.

'Are you OK?' Woody asked. His eyebrows were knitted in worry. 'Come on, Rox – focus! What day is it? Who am I? What's your middle name?'

'Wha—?'

'How many fingers am I holding up? Look, don't panic! Just stay where you are; I'm going to call for an ambulance.' And then his face moved out of her vision.

'An ambu . . . ?' Roxy wheezed. 'No! No! I'm OK!' She tried to sit up.

Woody hesitated. He was already several steps away. Now that she was upright she could see his ladder, abandoned in the middle of the pavement. His bucket had rolled into the gutter.

'But you're making a whining noise, and you've gone a really weird colour!'

'I'm fine. I was just . . .'

He hurried back, took her face in his hands and scrutinised her carefully. His face was very close. Roxy stifled a whimper. But then Woody pulled back, picked up her wrist and felt her pulse.

'Whoa!' he jumped at its vigour.

'. . . jogging,' she finished lamely.

'Jogging?' Woody paused for a moment. 'Well, that explains the sweating and shortness of breath. But I still think we need to get you to hospital. Your whole body's jaundiced.'

'I'm just hot.'

'No, Rox, you look . . .'

She hoped the next words out of his mouth would be 'attractively tousled'.

'. . . like you're having organ failure. Roxy, you're *mustard*! And not Colman's . . . I mean on-the-turn, call-health-and-safety stuff! I don't care what you say – I'm definitely phoning an ambulance.'

'Wait!' Roxy quickly weighed up which was the larger indignity: an ambulance, or telling the truth? 'I'm not jaundiced. I had a run-in with a bottle of Fake Bake.'

Woody paused. 'Tan?' He looked at her lurid legs. 'You're telling me *this* is fake tan?'

Roxy nodded miserably.

Woody stared at her for a moment. And then he threw back his head and guffawed.

'I know,' she conceded. 'I look like a traffic cone! Normally I'm really good at it, but yesterday I was a bit . . .' she tailed off. For some reason she couldn't bring herself to say 'drunk'.

'Roxy Squires, you're totally bonkers!' Woody sat on the wall beside her, still laughing. 'God, you had me worried for a minute. I thought you were seriously ill!'

'Just seriously orange,' she admitted sheepishly. And then they grinned at each other. Gradually her breathing became normal.

'Will it wash off?'

'Nope. I'm destined to be Tango Woman for at least five days. I thought a jog might sweat out the worst of it.'

'It was *worse*?' Woody laughed.

Roxy examined her limbs. Had it got any better? It was hard to tell.

'I know I'm in no position to judge, being a former vain pop tart and all.' Woody smiled. 'But why do you bother with all the fake tan stuff, Rox? You're already gorgeous!'

'Yeah, right,' she spluttered. She put her inner armour on. She wasn't going to fall into *that* trap. Woody didn't mean it – he was just being kind. 'Gorgeous' was Jennifer and her natural beauty, not Roxy and her colour-block face.

There was a pause.

'So, I didn't know you're a jogger.' Woody grinned.

'You don't know *everything* about me.'

'I know you're a bit out of practice.'

'Bloody cheek!'

'Want to come running with me sometime?'

'No!'

'Why not, Rox? Frightened you can't hack it?'

'No!' But it was true. She wasn't *frightened* she couldn't hack it – she *knew* she couldn't! Jogging four streets had practically killed her. But she was buggered if she was going to admit it (Jennifer probably ran marathons for fun). 'If you must know, I'm busy. Some of us still work for a living. *Proper* work!'

'How about six thirty?'

'I told you; I'm working!'

Woody gave her a look. 'What? Seven days a week?'

'Not all seven, no . . .'

'So, let's do it; three times a week, then – just you and me.'

'I . . .' Roxy started, and then stopped. Had he really said just her and him? Now that *was* tempting – for professional reasons, of course. A private, one-to-one jog would be an excellent opportunity to discuss strategies. The breakfast meeting hadn't worked and Woody seemed to live up his ladder. But this would be uninterrupted time for them to talk tactics, to come up with a solid set of career plans for each member of the group.

'I can hear your brain clunking,' Woody teased. 'You're thinking about it!'

'I . . .' she stalled. But on the other hand – OK, so she officially No Longer Fancied Woody, but did that mean she had to abandon *all* vanity? Did she really want him seeing her sweat? Some people looked hot when they exercised . . . Jessica Ennis, Davina, Cher . . . But Roxy just looked *hot* – like a sausage on the run from a grill.

'Come on, Rox – I'll make it easy. Just a few gentle laps of the village.'

She looked at him. *Oh, bollocks*, she thought. *Where's the harm?* He'd already seen her flailing like an upside-down tortoise, the colour of a seventies condiment. And she *did* want to lose a few pounds . . .

'OK,' she heard herself mumble.

'Great!' he grinned. And then he scooped his bucket out of the gutter, shouldered his ladder and started striding away. 'See you in the morning, then!' he called.

'The morning?'

'For a jog!'

'You said six thirty!' she called out in alarm.

But he was already too far away.

SUE

There were ninety minutes to go, but Sue already felt sick. Every little bit of her was anxious. She paced from room to room, searching for a magazine to straighten as she tried to relax her nostrils enough to let in air. Of all the weeks Austin Jones could join the group, why did it have to be the week the meeting was at *her* house? She'd been dusting and polishing for days, but she was still sure something, somewhere would let her down.

Sue looked at her hands for comfort. She'd surprised herself by liking her lilac nails. She'd not worn nail polish for years – not since she was married to Jeff. It wasn't that she had anything against polish, it was just polish reminded her of *her*. *She'd* always painted her nails in pretty pinks and reds. But Sue wasn't the kind.

But still, she *did* like the lilac. And she liked it enough to try to make it last. It had been days since Roxy had given her the manicure, and those days had been hard on her hands. She'd scrubbed the baths, scoured the toilets and even bleached the grouting with a toothbrush. The rest of the rooms had been sruced up as well – even the bedrooms, none of which anyone was likely to visit, let alone inspect for dust. But she hadn't minded the work. Her frenzy of cleaning had been the only thing to tether her nerves. She'd worn her marigolds religiously, for fear of chipping the lilac. Some days she'd even hoovered in gloves.

Of course, a clean house was just the half of it. There were dozens of other worries to fret about too. What drinks should she offer? Should she lay out a few plates of biscuits, or organise professional catering? Normally Simon brought a tub of home-made cakes, but could she expect him to bake again? It felt rude to phone him and ask. And which room should they sit in? The living room? The study? Reception? The dining room was largest, but she didn't normally go in it. And the conservatory was lovely by day but full of reflections at night. She was on edge enough as it was – she didn't want to keep catching herself mirrored in the glass.

In the end she'd plumped for the kitchen. It wasn't the biggest room, but it was where she felt most comfortable. Her table sat six, and there were stools and squashy chairs too. And it meant Roxy wouldn't keep leaving to top up her wine. She wanted Roxy with her – she felt safer with her around.

But her biggest fear of all was the fear of Austin arriving early. What if he was the first to turn up? She'd have to talk to him all on her own! Sue's nights had been interrupted by nightmares. She'd woken up sweating, heart racing, from the stress of having to summon up small talk interesting enough for a star. In her dreams her tongue got fatter and fatter until it filled her mouth and she couldn't speak at all – and the house would fall silent and Austin would look at his knees and curse Woody for persuading him to come. And Sue would cry – real tears, in her sleep – desperately longing for Woody to arrive and take over the responsibility of conversation.

Sue stopped pacing.

She'd paced all the way into her bedroom and up to her mirror. She looked at herself. She barely recognised the woman before her; her face was pinched with nerves. She didn't want to be this lady, so pale and frightened in her big, black clothes. Quickly, she found Roxy's pewter scarf and put it on. And then she remembered something else Roxy had said, and scooped up her hair at the back.

And then, just as she was grappling with some bobby pins, the doorbell rang. Sue stopped breathing. He was here; Austin was here. *And he was early*. Her tongue began to thicken. Where were the others? Where were Woody, Simon and Terence? Where was Roxy with her never-ending chatter? Where was Cressida, even? She couldn't do this on her own. Should she pretend she was out? Should she pretend she was ill? *Should she find a place to hide?*

BING, BONG.

The doorbell rang again.

And suddenly, Sue's legs were heading for the stairs – and her hand was on the front door. She pulled back its oak protection. Her heart stopped as she looked at her doorstep and prepared to see Austin Jones.

'Hiya!'

'Chelle?'

'Duh!' Chelle swanned past Sue and into the house. Immediately she gawped at the hallway. 'Nice place. Big!'

Sue reminded herself to breathe. She hadn't drawn breath since upstairs with the bobby pins.

'My ex-husband's,' she blurted, suddenly dizzy with relief. 'He was big in plastics.'

Chelle's stiletto scraped to a halt.

'Surgery?'

Sue blinked. 'Plastics. Just plastics.'

Chelle looked disappointed. But she resumed her nosy inspection. As her heartbeat returned to normal, Sue took in Chelle's appearance. If possible, Chelle was even more dressed up than before. She looked beautiful – like a doll. Her hair was thick and luxuriant, and longer than Sue remembered, and her outfit was tiny and shiny. From her chandelier earrings to her jewel-studded toes, Chelle was done up to the nines. Sue had never seen anyone so glamorous . . . not even Roxy.

'You're early,' Sue stated, and immediately blushed at her own rudeness. 'Not that it's a problem. In fact, what was I thinking? I haven't even offered you a cup of tea! Would you like one? I've got all kinds – Darjeeling, Earl Grey, Yorkshire . . .'

'Caffeine gives you cellulite,' Chelle sniffed.

'Oh.'

Sue didn't know what to say – even Roxy drank tea. Without the diversion of brewing a pot, she didn't know what to do, so she gestured Chelle into the kitchen and over to the table.

Both women sat, and Sue wedged her hands beneath her to stop them from flapping. She tried not to stare at Chelle's eyelashes. She'd never seen lashes so thick. They looked like a ribbon of ebony velvet.

'Yeah, I know I'm early,' Chelle abruptly piped up. 'But the early bird catches worms.'

Sue nodded uncertainly.

'Duh, *Austin*!' Chelle said with a scowl.

Sue looked at her blankly. And then the penny dropped. So *that* was why Chelle was dressed to kill! How silly she'd been not to realise! Chelle had been clear enough at the last meeting . . .

'Yeah, when he gets here, I want me to be the first person he sees.'

Sue perked up, suddenly warming to the possibilities. 'When the doorbell rings, would you like to answer it?' she offered.

Chelle gasped. 'Could I?'

Could she? Sue could almost kiss her!

'Oh, yes!' she declared with relief. 'Be my guest. Answer away – any time.'

'Brill.'

That settled, Chelle looked around the kitchen, pouted and then switched off. Sue sneaked a look at the kitchen clock. There was still fifty minutes to go. She thought about opening a packet of biscuits, but remembered what Chelle had said about cellulite. So she forced herself not to comfort eat, and then the room lapsed into silence.

ROXY

As usual, Roxy was the last to arrive . . . or rather, *almost* the last. The whole room sagged as Chelle half-heartedly led her into the kitchen.

'No need to be so excited to see me!' she said. But they were all wound too tightly to smile. Sitting rigidly around the kitchen table, everyone – even Cressida – was anxiously awaiting the arrival of the world's most famous Mr Jones.

Roxy frowned. Was it her imagination, or had they all scrubbed up that bit harder for tonight's meeting? It went without saying that Chelle's clobber was set to stun, but this time she wasn't alone. Everyone was a maxed-out version of theirselves. Holly was extra squeaky-clean, her pastel knitwear glowing like the starring twinset from a Daz ad. Sue may have been hyperventilating as she fluttered along the kitchen cabinets, but her hair was up and the pewter scarf was on. Simon – hardly eager to meet their soon-to-be guest – was sporting a new, uncharacteristically trendy hairdo, and Terry had finally cracked open one of his new Paul Smith shirts. Even Cressida wasn't immune to the excitement and had assembled her hair into an even more brittle helmet than usual, before going the whole hog and pinning a brooch to the front of her blazer. Only Woody was normal, in battered jeans, scuffed-up boots and faded grey T-shirt.

'Cinnamon doughnut?' Holly offered, her eyes glued to the hallway. 'Straight from the Simon Drennan patisserie!'

Roxy waved the plate away.

'Hey, Rox,' Simon greeted her suddenly, as though he'd only just noticed her arrive. His fingers drummed the kitchen table. 'Working late?'

'Huh?'

'Those TV make-up ladies always overdo it.'

'Oh . . . yeah, right.'

Self-consciously, Roxy pulled her sleeves further down over her glowing hands. She still couldn't get used to sleeves, let alone trousers that finished lower than the thigh. She tried not to think about tonight's depressing ensemble – but she only had herself, two bottles of bubbly and a pint of Fake Bake to blame. And, until the tan faded into something more human, she needed to cover up. She'd spent hours rummaging in the back of her wardrobe for clothes that actually covered her up. Eventually she'd stumbled across a bag of black basics. She hadn't worn a polo neck for years – *and full-length leggings!* She'd hidden her last millimetres of neon neck under a scarf and stuffed her feet into a pair of boots. She looked as wrapped as a parcel and as chaste as a nun. Thank Christ everything was Lycra!

Roxy perched herself on to a kitchen stool and threw Sue

a rallying grin. And then a heavy silence resumed. The only noise was the sound of Simon's fingers. The whole room was consumed with waiting.

'Bloody hell, you lot!' Roxy blurted, making Holly jump in fright. 'What's this? Civvy central? Anyone'd think you guys had never met a megastar before!' She nodded at the seating arrangement.

Everyone looked where Roxy was looking. A single chair – taller than the rest – had been left empty at the head of the table. They'd all angled their seats towards it.

'Christ!' Simon scraped back his chair, his complexion paling to a new tone of ash. 'We're sitting in bloody *worship!*'

Everyone jumped up and hastily started rearranging the seating. After some hurried consultation, the table was pushed aside and the chairs thrust into a circle.

From her perch on the stool, Roxy grinned. 'Now you look like you're all AA!'

'Well, how *should* we sit?' Simon asked wildly, his eyes beginning to bulge in panic.

Roxy shrugged. 'Just be normal!'

'Normal. Right . . .' Simon ran his hand through his hair. 'What's normal?'

'Around the table will be fine,' Woody said calmly. 'Maybe with Sue at the head.'

'Me? Why me?' Sue froze.

'Well, you *are* the host,' Holly reasoned.

'But . . .' Sue's protestations were interrupted by a tussle.

Cressida and Chelle were grappling over the chair in front of Austin's.

'But I wanna sit there!' Chelle demanded.

'Whatever for?' Cressida tried to muscle the chair away. 'You can sit over there.'

'But I *want* to sit *here*.'

'Worried he'll miss you if you're not in his eyeline? He's got about as much chance of missing the Blackpool illuminations!'

'I don't know why you care anyway.'

'I don't,' the former Secretary of State for Work and Pensions insisted primly. 'I merely want to be comfortable.'

'Well, park your arse over there then.' Chelle nodded towards an ancient armchair tucked in the corner. 'It'll be better for you, at your age, Grandma. Not so hard on your hips.'

Cressida puffed up, ready to strike, but was halted by the sound of the doorbell. Everyone froze.

'*He's here!*' someone hissed. '*Austin Jones is here!*'

'Relax,' Woody said calmly. 'I'll get it.'

'NO!' shrieked Chelle. '*I'll* get it!' and she proceeded to pull out her compact. The room watched in incredulous silence as lipgloss was topped up, blusher reapplied and strands of hair minutely adjusted.

Seconds stretched agonisingly by.

'For Christ's sake, Chelle!' Simon exploded. 'Tonight would be good – before he changes his mind and goes home.'

'Quick!' Holly cried out in panic.

The doorbell went again.

'All *right*,' Chelle snapped, as she flipped shut her compact, took a deep breath and slowly sashayed out into the hall.

The whole room sighed with relief. And then, as though moving to a choreographed cue, everyone leant forward to eavesdrop.

There was the sound of Chelle fumbling with the latch and then . . .

'*Ding* fucking *dong*,' came a deep voice – like a super-sexed Leslie Phillips on his way to addiction-clinic. 'So that window-cleaning ponce *can* still pull 'em! I'd heard his knob'd been on the bench so long it'd filed for a transfer!'

'Whose knob?' Chelle asked girlishly, at least an octave higher than normal. 'Oh, I'm not with *Woody*!' She emitted a bubbly giggle that sounded like pink champagne in a frosted glass. And then her voice suddenly became adamant. 'No; I'm single.'

'All right, Single? I'm Austin. Got anything to drink? My tongue's drier than a sailor's gonad.'

There was the sound of material crumpling. Either Chelle had fainted, or Austin had tossed her his coat. Then footsteps . . . and then there he was, rounding the corner and filling up the kitchen with his presence.

Roxy gasped.

The man voted 'Most Handsome Male Alive' by cinema-goers four years in a row – the man whose drop-dead gorgeousness was the stuff of legend, whose name alone had opened a dozen movies and made weak-kneed wives look upon their once-treasured husbands with marriage-altering disappointment – was standing just a few feet away. And he looked . . . he looked . . .

'He's *fat!*' said Roxy incredulously.

'Shh!' somebody hissed.

'*Austin Jones is fat!*' she repeated, oblivious. But surely she'd just seen his photo in the papers and he was thin. But here he was, standing right in front of her, more pork pie than California rolls. Nobody could get fat *that* quickly. She stared in disbelief at his face – so familiar, but unfamiliar too. It was like he *was* Austin Jones, but he wasn't. The same sparkling green eyes were there, the same famous hair, sumptuous lips and even white teeth, but it was as though someone had pumped him up. But how could Austin Jones, *the* Austin Jones – darling of red carpets, *Vanity Fair* photo shoots and women's nocturnal fantasies worldwide – turn into a podgy bloater? Where was his pride? His self-respect? *His staff?* Didn't he have an army of people paid precisely to make sure this never happened? And what, Roxy thought in an epiphany of outrage, *what* was with the manky chin tufts? Was he trying to grow a *beard?* Any anorak'd idiot knew beards were cosmically, epicly wrong – even Brad Pitt couldn't pull one off!

Roxy was about to splutter, but Austin got in first.

'Bloody hell, Woodster. What's this? A fucking knitting group?'

'Evening, Austin,' Woody replied tensely.

'Like-minded people, you said.'

'Similar situations, it was.'

Austin looked momentarily gobsmacked. But then he took a step backwards and laughed.

'Is this a wind-up? Have I walked into some care-in-the-community thing by mistake?'

'*Austin!*' Woody warned sternly. And then his tone became more relaxed. 'Look, come on . . . chill out, say hi. Fancy a beer?'

'I fancy something stronger.'

The group had been stunned into silence. This wasn't the Austin Jones they'd been expecting. Where were the endearing one-liners, sensitive eyes and winning smile? Where was the chat shows' easy-going affability, and the red carpets' classic designer suits? This Austin's shirt looked ready to fire off its buttons, such was the strain over his gut.

'Oh!' Sue blushed as she brought herself to Austin's attention. 'Oh – sorry. Would you like some tea, Mr Jones? Or maybe a, um, whisky?'

'Meths ought to do it,' he drawled. Sue froze, confused. But then Woody nodded gently and she scuttled off for a bottle of Scotch.

Again, the room fell into silence. Austin peered at everyone in turn.

'Go on!' Holly whispered, nudging Simon. 'Offer him a cinnamon doughnut.'

Simon jabbed her sharply and did his best to blend into the wall.

Nobody spoke. Sue hurried back with the Scotch. She nervously leant over Austin – like a snack over the jaws of a pitbull – and set the bottle and a glass down before him. Austin didn't move. So, hands shaking, she leant back across him and poured out an ultra-large measure. Austin drained it in one gulp.

He arched an eyebrow at Woody. 'So this lot have just retired from Tinseltown? What were they? Catering crew?'

'I didn't say they were like you *exactly*. I said, *like you*, they were all successful in their fields. And, *like you*, they've now opted for a change of career.'

'Change of career?' Austin rapped his glass for a refill. 'I'm opting for *no* career. I'm opting for long lazy days yanking my chain.'

Cressida tutted. Austin turned the full force of his green eyes upon her. 'Problem?'

'No problem,' she replied primly. 'I just happen to believe that manners and industry are preferable to sloth and masturbation.'

Roxy gasped. Had Cressida really just said *masturbation*?

Austin regarded her coldly.

'If I want to wank myself into senility, that's my prerogative. As retirement activities go, it's got to be better than golf.'

'Retirement?' Cressida scoffed with disdain. 'You're a young man! You shouldn't be giving up – you should be thinking about what you can give.'

Austin looked at Woody and laughed. 'Is she for real, or have I slipped myself mind-altering drugs?'

'Of course I'm real!' Cressida replied.

Austin held up his hands in surrender. 'All right, I give up; who are they all?'

Woody made the introductions.

'This is Chelle Blowers, the former partner of Dwayne.' After her early bout as door monitor, Chelle had gone suspiciously quiet. She was staring at Austin's spare tyre. But on hearing her name she extended her chest, batted her lashes and flashed him a lipglossy smile.

'A WAG,' Austin summarised lasciviously. 'Not that I'm complaining. The world needs decoration.'

Chelle froze, trying to work out if she'd just been slagged off.

'And this is Terence Leggett, the UK's most famous weatherman,' Woody continued.

'No need for weathermen in LA – the weather's always the same.'

'And this is a fellow actor for you to chat things over with – our very own small-screen superstar, Simon Drennan.'

'Yeah?' Austin mimicked interest. And then he instantly cut it off dead. 'Never watch telly.'

'What, not even *Down Town*?' Terence asked.

'You're in *Downton*?' Austin looked surprised. He eyed Simon, impressed.

Simon hesitated. And then he reluctantly confessed. 'Not *Downton*; *Down Town* – the soap.'

'Never heard of it,' Austin sniffed.

Terence stifled a laugh.

'The problem with the small screen is that it's just too small,' Austin plucked a cigarette from his pocket and lit up. 'Unless it's HBO. Done any HBO?'

Simon looked sick.

'Thought not.'

'And this is our host for tonight,' Woody interrupted. 'Our Queen of the Crossword, Sue Bunce!'

'Bunce?' Austin suddenly snapped to attention. He turned and peered at her closely. Sue backed into the cabinets. 'Fuck! Sue Bunce? *Really*? I had your picture on my wall! Seriously – you're *Sugatits Suzi*?'

Everyone looked at Sue in surprise. Of all of them, Sue seemed the least likely to be recognised by Austin. Or by anyone. But Austin was drinking in every inch of her body.

'Austin . . .' Woody warned. But he didn't seem to hear.

'Fuck me!' he declared with a snort. Like lightning, he leapt over to Sue, circling her in predatory inspection. Within seconds Sue started to wilt. But Austin just threw his head back and laughed. 'You're kidding, right? *You* can't be Sugatits Suzi! Sugatits Suzi was *hot*!'

'Now look here!' Terence sprang to her defence. 'She *is*—' He momentarily looked a bit lost. 'And she's just Sue these days, if you don't mind!' he added crossly.

'Too right she is!' Austin grinned. 'The only thing sugary about *those* tits is that they've dangled in her doughnuts.'

Everyone looked down – and, sure enough, Austin was right. The sugar crusting of Simon's home-made cinnamon dough- nuts was dusted across the bottom of her breasts. Roxy cringed. *Poor Sue.* How the hell had *that* got *there*?

'Now, that really is enough!' the weatherman demanded bravely. 'You owe Sue an apology!'

Austin flopped back into his seat.

ELEANOR PRESCOTT   231

'For what? Telling the truth?'

'You rude bastard!' Roxy jumped off her stool. 'I don't care how many movies you've starred in – you apologise right now, lard arse!'

'Yes, Austin,' Woody agreed tightly. '*Apologise.*'

Austin looked at him strangely, as though Woody was speaking a language only they could understand. 'Fine,' he shrugged, nonchalant. 'Sorry. Christ, can no one around here take a joke?'

'Aren't we all looking at one?' Roxy growled.

Austin turned and looked at Roxy anew. And then a smile played upon his lips.

'So, who are you, Feisty?' The flame of flirtation suddenly ignited in his eye. Roxy gasped as her breath whooshed out her body. The way his lips moved around the word 'Feisty' was so sexual! Just *those lips* and *that word* had given her lady shivers. And now Austin Jones was looking at her – *really* looking at her – she felt . . . *she felt like she'd been fired on a rocket!* Immediately his weird beard and big belly vanished and Roxy was dumbstruck by how achingly, meltingly, *supernaturally* handsome he was. *This* was the Austin Jones they'd been expecting, the Austin Jones the camera loved, the public adored and the supermodels queued up in a line for. It was as if the Austin of the last ten minutes had never existed; all she could see were the tempting pools of his eyes, the impossible perfection of his cheekbones and the sensual promise of his mouth. How could she ever have thought Austin Jones wasn't her type? Austin Jones was every woman's type!

'Hey, I *know* you!' he suddenly grinned. 'Didn't we . . . ? A few years back . . . ?'

Roxy felt the weight of the group's eyes upon her. Holly clasped her hand to her mouth in shock.

'Um . . .' Roxy mumbled limply. Had they? Her brain was sure they hadn't, but her body was telling her they had. Or they should – right now – as fast as humanly possible. Lust was charging her veins, lighting weird sparks in her head. *Wow!* What was it with Lavender Heath? A few weeks ago it had been a sexual dead zone – but suddenly it was awash with man-totty! It was like the ley lines of shag and hotness had crossed and all the UK's pheromones had converged at this spot.

'Yeah, I'm sure we did . . . In a club somewhere . . . In the gents'.'

'No,' Roxy replied a little more strongly. But her nipples had fizzed into action, like a twinset of Pinocchio's nose. *Imagine it!* Her and Austin in a gents' toilet! It'd be the wildest, filthiest shag of her life! She could almost feel the thump of the dance music reverberating through the floorboards, the hard metallic nub of the door-lock as it rubbed against her back.

Somebody coughed.

It was Woody.

And – *bollocks!* – Roxy fell back to earth with a bang. Gorgeous, scrumptious Woody didn't have a beer belly, or a chin-rug. Woody wouldn't insinuate a rude sexual history, or freak out a middle-aged lady in her own kitchen. It was a sex-life sod's law; a shag-fest Catch-22. And OK, *yes*, she knew Woody was taken – and *yes*, he probably didn't give a monkey's either way – but his good opinion of her mattered. She didn't want him thinking she was *like that*. And she *definitely* didn't want him thinking she was like that *with Austin*!

'I didn't!' she announced emphatically, crossing her arms and trying to force her nipples back down to her chest.

'My mistake.' Austin winked. 'So many toilets; so many blondes.'

'I'm not just some *blonde*,' she retorted angrily. 'I'm a television presenter!'

Austin turned towards Simon. 'Chin up, Downton; you're not bottom of the food chain, after all!'

'I interview Hollywood stars,' she told him frostily. '*Real* Hollywood stars.'

'Ouch!' Austin pretended to be scalded. 'Hey, Sugatits – you got a gents' here? Reckon me and Feisty'll be paying it a visit in precisely two and a half minutes.'

'I believe Sue's toilet has a mirror. I'm sure you and your reflection will be fine,' Roxy replied.

But Austin had already turned back to Woody. 'And what about Vidal Sassoon?' He pointed at Cressida. 'Does the barnet come with a name?'

'Watch it, Austin,' Woody growled. 'You're at the end of everyone's patience.'

'My name is Cressida Cunningham,' Cressida answered crisply. 'Former Member of Parliament for Biddington Borders, and Secretary of State for Work and Pensions.'

'Lovely,' replied Austin with a yawn. And then he spotted Holly and her notebook.

'Oi! Anne Frank! What're you writing?' His voice was hard and aggressive. Holly froze. 'Are you a bloody journalist?'

'No,' she squeaked, her voice extra small.

'Why are you taking notes then?' Austin glared. Roxy suddenly felt sorry for Holly. She looked like a bunny in the track of a juggernaut.

'Get off her case!' Roxy told him. 'She's a writer! She's not doing any harm. It's like an artist doing a doodle.'

'Sorry.' Holly shakily stowed her notebook in her bag. 'I didn't mean . . .' She looked so frightened Roxy thought she might cry.

'For goodness sake, Austin – don't you recognise her?' cried Terence. 'She wrote your first ever movie! She's Holly Childs!'

'Yeah?' For a moment there was a flicker of interest. But then Austin was diverted by the doughnuts. 'Calories; Christ, how I've missed you.'

'I've changed a bit since then,' Holly mumbled, embarrassed.

Austin reached forward and looped one off the plate. 'You look so good I don't know whether to eat you or shag you,' he addressed the doughnut.

'But you must have met her on set?' Terence persevered. 'You could hardly have missed her, for heaven's sake, she was *thirteen*!'

'Thirteen?' Austin echoed, his mouth full of half-eaten doughnut. 'What're you insinuating, Rain Man? Are you a complete cloud-headed pervert?'

And then he scraped back his chair and headed to Sue's toilet. He didn't bother shutting the door.

Everyone stared at the table, silently nursing their egos. The sound of Austin urinating filled the room. Roxy concentrated very hard on the globules of doughnut that surrounded where Austin had sat. Anything was better than looking at Woody. God knows what he thought of her right now.

'I didn't,' she whispered, as the sound of urine hitting water subsided. 'Not with him . . . in the gents'.'

And then Austin yelled out from the toilet. 'Oi, Feisty! How about you and me head back to my place? I've got a crate of tequila and a stack of Brazilian porn. They'll do anything, those Brazilians. Whadd'ya say? Let's make a night of it!'

'I'll take him home,' Woody said grimly.

'What a silly little boy he is,' Cressida suddenly piped up. 'Such a fatal mix – money, success and a penis. I've seen this so many times before.'

Roxy looked at her in surprise. Surely Cressida couldn't be *used* to hanging around with super-sexed A-listers? She was a posh, frumpy spinster – not exactly top of anyone's guest list.

'Everyone likes to think we politicians do nothing more than lounge around the Commons, fiddling our expenses,' Cressida continued sagely. 'But we see ten times more of life than your average man on the street. When you go everywhere from homeless shelters to black-tie dinners, you see life in all its inglorious varieties. Mr Jones, here, thinks he's special, but he's no more than predictably average. Still –' she stood up and brushed down her blazer – 'he's come to the right place, hasn't he, chaps?'

Everyone looked up in alarm.

'Weren't you all desperate for a lost soul to nurture? Well, it looks very much to me like you've found one.'

'Austin's not a lost soul,' Simon whispered. 'He's a spoilt, self-indulgent millionaire, too lazy to do a day's work.'

'Exactly,' Cressida replied with a smile. 'You've made my point exactly.' And she headed for the door and for home.

To: Roxy Squires

From: The Marketing Team, Vanish Cleaning Products
(Laundry Division)

Dear Mrs Squires,

Thank you for contacting our advertising agency, Pritchard &
Pritchard, and suggesting a new plot for a VANISH ad – starring you!

We're so glad our adverts have come to your attention. We work
hard on making them appealing to housewives. We're always being
contacted by women facing the battle to remove stubborn stains –
grassy knees on trousers, felt-tip on school-uniform shirts . . . But we
LOVED your idea featuring your attempts to remove 'alternative'
stains – cocktails, baby oil, kebab sauce (plus that other stain, that
would never get past Ofcom!). How wonderful of you to send it to us
as a joke!

We're sending you a bumper bottle of VANISH as thanks!

ROXY

'Bollocks!'

Despite the fact that Roxy was the owner of no less than eleven sets of on-trend gym wear, none of them had been worn for actual exercise (bar the kit from the other morning, which was still in a sweaty ball in the corner of her bedroom), and none of them were right for exercising with Woody. She had all the right brands . . . Sweaty Betty, Lululemon, Stella – even some No Balls (because she'd been web-shopping, drunk). But which should she wear today? Should she opt for maximum cover-up to hide her orange skin? Or should she say 'sod it' and go for a sexy crop top and shorts? If the other morning's exertions were anything to go by, she'd sweat buckets, so maybe covering up wasn't a good option. Besides, what was the point in hiding? Woody had already seen her at her technicolour worst.

Or had he?

Because, wardrobe anxieties aside, Roxy had something bigger to stress about: the fact that she'd agreed to go jogging with Woody at all. What the hell had she been thinking? She couldn't jog – the other morning had proved it. And she certainly couldn't jog next to Woody. He wouldn't know what to laugh at first: the fact that her face would be neon pink by the time she'd reached the first lamp post, or that the first lamp post would be as far as she'd reach. The whole prospect spelt humiliation on a see-it-from-space scale.

But then there was a knock at the door, and it was too late for freaking. Woody was here. She opened the door.

'Ready?' he asked.

'As Brek,' she replied with empty bravado. Yet again she had to force her libido to heel. What was it with Woody, she wondered? Did he never look bad in *anything*? Because even at six thirty in the morning, in shorts and a fraying Stones T-shirt, Woody still looked like sex on her doorstep. It was no bloody wonder no one ever saw Jennifer. If *she* woke up to the sight of Woody every morning, she'd probably stay glued to her bed sheets as well!

'And how long are you planning for this morning's bout of torture, Mr Grey?' she flirted.

'Nothing too terrible. Just a few laps of the village.'

Trying not to whimper at the words 'just a few', Roxy closed her front door. They hadn't started running yet, but already her palms were sweaty. *Must be the nerves*, she decided, as she wiped them on her leggings. She'd plumped for Lululemon in the end. They were the most expensive. Hopefully Woody would be wise to the cost and be rendered so stunned at the extravagance, that he'd fail to notice she was marginally less fit than a darts player.

And then, to her surprise, they were suddenly jogging – two sets of feet pounding the pavement in perfect synchronicity. For a few brief moments Roxy felt elated. She and Woody were together! Well, not *together* together, but the next best thing . . . *working* together – as a team. Was this the joggers' high everyone banged on about? This was bloody brilliant! If she'd known jogging felt this good she'd have started yonks ago.

'So,' she started brightly – there was no point fannying around – 'about the group; I was thinking a good plan of action for Sue would be—'

And then the joggers' high was nuked by something else – something Roxy remembered from the other morning: painful side, leaden lungs, burning cheeks, nauseous tummy – and the absolute certainty that all her internal organs were in crisis. She stopped, raised her face to the heavens and desperately tried to suck in some breath.

'You all right?' Woody doubled back to find her.

She tried to say 'Uh huh', but it came out 'Urghhh'.

'Were we going too fast? We can slow down.'

She made a rasping noise that seemed to come from the pit of her soul.

Woody looked at her closely. 'OK, enough – Rox; bend over.'

She tried to make another Mr Grey quip, but couldn't.

'Put your head between your knees and just breathe.'

So she did.

'Maybe I was a bit too ambitious.' Woody frowned.

From between her knees, Roxy tried to blank out Woody's legs and get her bearings. And to her mortification, she saw they'd only made it as far as the pub. For a moment she wondered if it was open (the morning might not be a complete loss, after all), but then she remembered it was six thirty-five.

'Just rest a minute, and we'll start again.'

'Again?'

'You're not giving up already!'

She was dying to say yes, but she couldn't lose face (even if that face was dripping like a sponge).

'Give up?' she wheezed. 'Never! Eat my dirt, Pop Boy!' And she forced herself out of recovery and up the road.

In the end, Roxy lasted two full laps of the village, before collapsing on Woody's front doorstep.

'Not bad, Squires.' He grinned at her. He barely had a bead of sweat on him. Roxy was sure the Lululemon was squelching. 'Breakfast?'

She wheezed out a 'Yes', and he unlocked his door.

Despite her struggle for breath, Roxy felt a thrill of excitement. They were alone, just the two of them, in Woody's place! But then excitement gave way to fear. Was she about to come face-to-face with Jennifer? Whilst Woody had been taking her jogging, had Jennifer been lounging in bed?

'I should go!' she blurted.

'Why?' Woody replied in surprise.

'I don't want to gatecrash.'

'You're not gatecrashing – I invited you, you nutter.'

'But, Jennifer . . .'

Woody smiled. 'Jennifer's not *here*. Look, come in, Rox – sit down. No jog's complete without breakfast and you're in luck, because I happen to make the world's best ever sausage sandwich!'

But Roxy's anxieties were not over. As she followed Woody into his kitchen–diner, her mind whirred. A sausage sandwich meant bread, and bread meant CARBS. Could she ask for a no-bread sausage sandwich? Liz Hurley would and nobody would bat an eyelid. But if she did it, would Woody think she was nuts? Maybe she should just carb herself up. After all, on the jog she'd been too busy trying to breathe to talk tactics, and ingesting bread seemed a small price to pay for prolonging the chance to talk career strategies with Woody. So she decided to button her lips and stay schtum.

As Woody got busy with the sausages, she wandered over to the shelves for some casual spying.

'So . . . Austin, eh?' She made diversionary conversation as she searched for a picture of Jennifer. Sue had said the place was littered with them. But the first few frames were just of coffin dodgers.

'He's not the man of the movies,' Woody replied darkly as he started slicing some bread.

'D'you reckon Chelle's in with a chance?' Her eyes skipped to the next shelf – and suddenly her heart stopped dead. There was a picture of a woman – laughing into the camera, eyes sparkling, hair glossy brown, face entirely absent of make-up. And she was beautiful – totally, ravishingly beautiful. Roxy's stomach hit the soles of her feet.

'With Austin?' Woody was looking right at her. 'I hope not,

for Chelle's sake. But that's not really the question you want to ask – is it?'

'It isn't?' Guiltily, Roxy inched away from the shelf. Had Woody just seen her snooping? Did he actually just read her mind? How did he know she wanted to ask about Jennifer? He was looking at her with a strange expression – brooding and kind of pissed off. Roxy shifted uncomfortably – the sausages sizzled loudly – and then mercifully her eye fell on a pile of CDs. She quickly pretended to immerse herself in their covers. There was a very long moment – and then Woody turned back to the pan.

'So, d'you reckon Austin *really* had a thing about Sue?' she babbled, trying to lighten the mood. She tried not to think about the woman with the glossy brown hair and concentrate instead on Woody's CDs: *Nirvana, Muse, David Bowie* . . .

'Probably,' Woody said normally. 'Sue was incredibly famous back then. And incredibly beautiful.'

'She still is!' Roxy mumbled in protest. 'All she needs is a makeover.' *Jimi Hendrix, Iggy Pop, Debbie Harry* . . . DEBBIE HARRY! 'God, Woods, your CD collection's really . . .'

'Really . . . ?'

'Cool!'

'Don't sound so surprised.'

'I'm not! It's just . . . I kind of expected . . .'

'Wall-to-wall ballads?' He smiled. 'Just because I *sang* shit doesn't mean I *listen* to it too.'

'Your stuff wasn't shit.'

'Oh, come off it, Rox.'

'But I loved your shit! "Could It Be I'm Falling In Love?" was ace!'

'"Could It Be I'm Falling In Love?" was dire.'

'OK, so maybe it *was* a bit cheesy . . .'

'Cheesy? It whiffed like a blue-veined Stilton!'

'But you sang it really well!'

'I sang it like I had a rod up my arse.'

'Why do you find it so hard to take a compliment?'

'I don't. I just don't like to have smoke blown up my backside.'

'No extra room, with that rod?'

'Exactly!'

They grinned at each other before Woody scooped the sausages out of the pan and on to the bread.

'Sauce?'

'I thought you'd never ask!'

Woody laughed and shook his head. He put a dollop of ketchup on her sausage and handed her a plate. In another room, his phone started ringing. He headed out to answer it.

As soon as he'd gone, Roxy kicked herself. She officially No Longer Fancied Woody. So why the hell was she flirting? And *why* had she been checking Jennifer out? Woody's girlfriend was none of her business! But, even as she scolded herself, she still had to resist the urge to scoot back to the shelf for another peek. With an iron will, she stayed in her seat and instead took advantage of Woody's absence by stuffing her ketchuppy bread in her pocket. She didn't care if the sauce stained the Lululemon – stains were easier to get rid of than carbs.

'Hi, Cressida.' She could hear Woody on the phone. 'No . . . no, really, it's no bother . . . Look, I'm just having breakfast – I'll pop over straight after . . . It's probably just a fuse or something . . . Yeah, OK. See you in thirty.'

He returned to the kitchen and sat down.

'What are you? Cressida's Mr Fix It?' Roxy asked as she took a big bite of sausage and nearly moaned. *Damn*, Woody was right; the sausage bit of his sarnie was mint!

'Cressida's a woman born out of her time,' he replied. 'Anything electrical and she's flummoxed. I quite often go over to help out.'

'But she must have loads of money! Why doesn't she get a handyman?'

'Maybe it's not the fixing bit she's after.'

'Meaning?'

Woody shrugged. 'Maybe it's the company she needs.'

Roxy swallowed with a frown. 'Are you saying Cressida's lonely?'

'Haven't you noticed?'

'But she always seems so . . .' Roxy groped for a word. *Bossy? Controlling?* '. . . Self-sufficient.'

'Everyone needs mates, Rox. And, from what Cressida says, friends are pretty scarce in politics.'

Roxy chewed on her last bit of sausage. Cressida, lonely – who'd have thought it? She stood up and took her plate over to the sink. But, as she turned back towards Woody, she noticed a half-open door leading to a utility room. In the middle of the utility room was a washing rack, and hanging out to dry were a dozen . . . She gasped.

'Bloody hell, Woods – *are they your old vests?*'

She pointed at the washing in shock.

'They make good rags for the windows.'

She gasped again, almost choking on the double intake of breath.

'But . . . but . . . but they're your *vests*, Woody! They're famous – pop history! They should be in a museum of rock, or the Hard Rock Café – not used to wipe grubby windows!'

'Breathe, Rox; your lips have gone blue.'

'But . . .'

Woody walked over to the rack.

'Here – if they mean that much to you, have one.' And he tossed one over. Roxy caught it and turned it over in her hands in despair.

'It's not even white any more!'

'They've moved on – new careers and all that.' Woody grinned. 'Look, I'd love to chat about my cruel mistreatment of vests but, sorry, Rox – I'm going to have to chuck you out. Cressida's waiting and I need a shower.'

'Course,' Roxy mumbled as she was shepherded over to the door. She threw one last glance towards Jennifer's photograph. And then she was out on Woody's doorstep, his vest in her hand, using every Jedi mind-trick in the universe not to imagine him in nothing but a towel.

SIMON

Simon frowned and stepped into the blast of the gym's polar air-conditioning. He hated the gym and everything about it.

For a start, the music was terrible . . . and so terribly loud! It didn't make sense; at the times he visited – one thirty until three, Mondays, Wednesdays and Fridays – the place was a morgue . . . almost literally! All the young, thrusting, vital people were at work, so the gym was empty save for the local 'resting' thesps (total of one) and a few doddery pensioners, freewheeling on the bikes, a star-jump away from death. If asked, they'd probably have preferred a bit of Dean Martin. In fact, Simon had a theory that the gym was empty *because* of the music. The old folk were the only ones who could tolerate it – and only because hearing aids came with an off switch.

But the truth was, in his own perverse way, Simon revelled in the awfulness of the gym. Ever since puberty, he'd had an innate weakness for self-flagellation. Secretly he *welcomed* the fact that his gym trips lumped him with society's infirm. After all, it wasn't as if he couldn't go at another time (in the mornings, perhaps, with the yummy mummies). And he could always invest in an iPod. But Simon believed that, if he was going to be miserable, he might as well go the whole hog and make himself really, *really* miserable.

Like a condemned man, he headed over to the rower.

By three thirty, Simon was pink, pumped and parked outside the school gate. In the distance he could see the stirrings of lilac blazers as the children started heading for home. But Scarlet and Euan always took at least fifteen minutes to make the two-minute walk from classroom to people carrier, so he let his mind drift back to last night's meeting and the dreaded arrival of the world's favourite Mr Jones. And smugly, he smiled.

Simon had expected Austin to be many things – egotistical, arrogant, aloof – but not fat. For the first time, Simon pondered his own waist fondly. Yes, there was no denying it, Roxy was right: the great Austin Jones was a lard arse. It was strange . . . he didn't look overweight on screen. But when your status hit the top of the alphabet, maybe nobody suggested a diet. Maybe the crew just made allowances – filmed from flattering angles, cracked out the slimming lens. *Did Austin* – Simon wondered with a shake of excitement – *film in a corset?* Not that it really mattered . . . spare tyre or not, he obviously had more pheromones than an alley cat. *And* a nose to die for. And what eyes! So vulnerable on screen, but so dangerous in the flesh. Despite the deep well of antagonism he felt towards the man whose career he should have had, Simon began to wonder whether *he* wasn't the only victim of casting injustice. Maybe Austin *had* retired prematurely after all. Not because of all the housewives who'd had their hearts broken, but because now the world would never get to see what Austin could truly achieve. In a flash, Simon had a vision of what Austin might have been – a Coriolanus, a Heathcliff, a Lear . . .

The left rear door of the people carrier slammed shut.

'Hello, Euan. Good day at school?'

His son wedged on his headphones and selected an angry-sounding tune.

The right rear door slammed too.

'Hey, Scarlet; is that Venetia I can see over there? I can barely make her out under all that make-up. Her foundation must be two inches thick!'

'Just drive, Dad,' Scarlet commanded icily.

Simon peered at his daughter in the rear-view mirror. The smile she'd worn moments earlier, as she'd larked on the pavement with her friend, was gone. In its place was the impenetrable teenage expression that glowered at him daily, sucking out his every ounce of positivity, and flavouring his every meal with acid indigestion. For a moment Simon contemplated fishing for a morsel of conversation, a few small words of familial communication about his daughter's day. But then he thought better of it. It was best to do as Scarlet ordered.

He crunched his car into gear and just drove.

ROXY

It was ten o'clock in the morning, and Roxy was already hard at work at the kitchen table, flipping through the pages of *Heat*. Her strategies were nearly complete. All she needed were a few more ideas for the former Secretary of State for Work and Pensions.

She frowned.

Cressida was tricky. She didn't have any of the obvious things going for her: youth, looks, popularity, killer legs, a moderately famous boyfriend, a large Twitter following – and the helmet hair didn't help, either. But there must be *something* she could suggest. After all, everyone had hated Widdy before *Strictly*.

She flicked past 'Torso Of The Week' and on to the TV pages.

What were Cressida's plus points?

Well, she obviously had an egghead brain – how else had she been a top political whatsit? And, judging from the pics on her wall, she had some serious A-list connections too. Roxy paused, excited. Maybe there was something in that. Had Cressida ever poked Obama? Had Mandela ever written on her wall? Did Cressida even *have* a wall?

Roxy put down the magazine and pondered.

SUE

'D'you keep a diary?'

'Roxy!' Sue smiled in surprise. 'I'm so glad you're here. I've got something to show you . . . in duck egg.'

'Yeah, sorry; hiya, Sue.' Roxy lurched across the front doorstep and landed a kiss on Sue's cheek. Sue couldn't help it – she recoiled. And then worried. Had Roxy noticed? Oh gosh, she hoped not. She hadn't meant to be rude; it was just she wasn't used to being kissed. People didn't normally do that – not to her.

But Roxy was too preoccupied to notice. She was wearing skin-tight electric-blue jeans, electric-blue boots, an electric-blue top and an electric-blue scarf, wound right the way up to her chin. It made her hair look even blonder, like she was a Barbarella smurf, or a futuristic lady from a pop video. Sue still couldn't get used to this new look. She'd only known Roxy a few weeks, but already it was strange to see her with so many clothes on.

'But do you, though? Keep a diary, I mean.'

'Um . . .' Sue wasn't sure what to say. What she really wanted to say was how pleased she was to see Roxy. She'd been desperate to show her her new purchase. She'd been meaning to take a trip around to her house for days, but hadn't quite summoned the nerve. A trip out was frightening enough on a normal day, but now there was the extra threat of bumping into Austin . . . And, granted, she knew he rarely set foot out from behind his tall, swirly gates – but what if he did? What if he cornered her on the street and looked her up and down again – just him, and her, and that horrible smirk? No, she was safer staying at home. Thank heaven for internet shopping. What with her paper boy and Ocado, she might be able to stay in right the way until the next meeting. 'Sorry, Roxy.' She shook her head. 'I never do anything exciting enough to put in a diary.'

'But *did* you? When you used to go out and do stuff?'

'Oh, yes!'

'When you were S— *her*?'

Sue thought. 'Yes, I think so. I remember writing about all the modelling jobs I did and nice parties I went to, so I suppose I must have done – yes.'

'So when you were seeing that politician – what's-his-name, *Hunt* – and everything went public and the shit hit the fan . . . you were keeping a diary then?'

Sue's insides began to clench. Even after all these years, her tummy still went funny whenever anybody mentioned Hunt, and *the trouble*. 'Sort of,' she said quietly. 'But when everything came out in the papers, I was all over the place. I couldn't focus on anything.'

'But you did write anything?'

'Just ramblings, really. They probably didn't make any sense. Everything was a whirr.'

'D'you still have them – your ramblings?'

'Um, maybe. In the study, perhaps.'

'Mint!' Roxy's face burst into a grin. 'Sue, I think we've just found you a way back!'

Sue blinked. 'Back where?'

'Sue, have you ever thought about writing a book?'

'A book?'

'You know; a kiss-and-tell.'

Sue instinctively shrank back.

'An *autobiography*,' Roxy hurriedly corrected. 'A lovely hard-backed autobiography, with a classy photo and posh jacket. Your story, in your own words. A chance to tell the world who you really are and what falling in love with the wrong man cost you.'

'Oh, gosh, Roxy; I really don't think that would be a good—'

'The housewives would love it! A real-life tale of sex, power and betrayal!'

'About me?'

'Yeah, why not? Everyone remembers the scandal. And Hunt and his wife are always gurning in *Hello*, introducing their new living-room rug, or whatever flimsy pretext their agent's managed to spin. Why should they come out smelling of roses, and not you?'

But Sue wasn't listening. The only word she'd heard was 'agent'. Why would Hunt have an agent? He was a politician – not a celebrity. Or rather, he *used* to be a politician. Actually, now that she thought about it, she didn't have a clue what he did any more. All she knew was that he'd had to give up his seat when the scandal broke and that, all these years later, he and Deirdre were in *Hello* quite a lot. Even though she normally devoured *Hello*, Sue could never bring herself to read the articles about them. She tried to flip those pages over before any of the pictures could register. But even the moment- ary flashes her eyes refused to miss told her that the Hunts were still together – happy, with their white teeth, golden tans and sunkissed hair.

'Don't you reckon it's time you showed the world your side of the story?' Roxy's voice permeated her thoughts.

'Oh; I don't think—'

'There's sod-all money in books, of course, but that's not the point – the book's just the means to the end. Serialisation's where the big bucks are. I reckon the *Mail* would be the best place for you.'

'The *Mail*?' Sue echoed, her voice full of fear.

'Yeah! We could stagger the revelations; string them out over a few Sundays. Then there'd be the book tour, of course . . . maybe a few after-dinner speeches at the WI . . .'

'Do you mean the *Daily Mail*?'

'It'd be great practice before getting you on to telly. Daytime would be gagging for you, Sue. Phil and Hol'd kill to get you on their sofa.'

Sue quivered. 'I can't go on anyone's *sofa!*'

'And then a few choice magazine interviews. Trendy ones, with glossy photo shoots. Nothing with any puzzles in it.'

Sue's whole being had frozen. The words 'glossy' and 'photo shoot' had stopped her lungs inflating.

And then Roxy pulled out her trump card. 'M&S!' she cried. 'That's what we'll get you! A Marks and bloody Sparks ad! You know, you're still a very beautiful woman. And you've got loads of modelling experience. You'd be right up the street of the forty-plus gang. Hell, why should Twiggy get all the bloody work?'

Sue stared at Roxy aghast. Had she gone mad? Had Roxy actually gone insane? What was she on about with Twiggy, and book jackets, and the WI? Didn't Roxy know she found it hard enough to get to the village shop, let alone whizz around the country doing speeches? Didn't Roxy realise she'd spent the last thirty years hiding from the world and everyone in it? Why on earth would she draw attention to herself now? Sue opened her mouth to explain, but nothing came out.

'Hey, what was it you wanted to show me?' Roxy suddenly sounded sane again.

'Huh?'

'You said you had something to show me. You were excited.'

'It doesn't matter now,' Sue replied flatly. And it didn't. All the excitement of her new purchase had been flattened under serialisations and sofas.

'Of course it matters! *You* matter!'

'No, really; it doesn't.'

Roxy grinned. 'Didn't you say something about duck egg? Sue, have you splashed out on some *colour*?'

Despite herself, Sue couldn't help but begin to smile. 'Well, if you've got a minute . . .' And she scuttled off to her bedroom for her purchase. Shaking, she hurried back and handed Roxy a package wrapped in thick tissue and tied with an expensive ivory ribbon.

'I found it online. I thought it might fit your description.'

She could barely breathe as Roxy unwrapped the tissue.

Roxy's eyes widened in wonder. 'Oh my God, Sue . . . Is this *cashmere*?'

'Mmm hmm,' Sue replied, a slight wobble in voice. Had she imagined it, or had Roxy sounded impressed? Or was it surprised? No, it was more than just surprised; she was staggered!

The knee-length coatigan fell luxuriously open.

'I've never seen cashmere so thick,' Roxy marvelled as she held the material to her face in awe. 'It's so soft!'

Sue bubbled over with excitement. 'Do you like it?'

'Like it? I could shag it! It's gorgeous! Put it on.'

Nervously, Sue accepted it back and shrugged her arms through the sleeves. The heavy cashmere felt wonderful. Instantly, she felt transformed. Suddenly she wasn't just a former bit of tabloid trash whose mother had told her she didn't want to know her . . . She wasn't the woman Jeff had got bored with, or the person nobody noticed in shops . . .

She was a *somebody*; a mature but stylish *somebody*. She held her breath as she waited for Roxy's verdict.

'Bloody hell, Sue! You hot, sexy mama!'

Sue blushed. 'Don't feel you have to be polite . . .'

'*Polite?*' Roxy roared. 'When am I ever *polite*? Sue, you look absolutely bloody rocktastic! Ten pounds lighter and ten years younger.'

'I know it's only a cardigan . . .'

'It's not a cardigan – it's a statement!'

Sue beamed.

'And it must have cost a bloody fortune.'

Sue's cheeks burned again. She didn't like to say it, but she hadn't even looked at the price tag. Her marriage to Jeff may have been short, but it had been lucrative. How else had she been able to stay in Lavender Heath all these years?

'Right – that's it,' Roxy declared decisively. 'Grab your duck egg; it's time for an unveiling!'

Sue looked at her blankly.

'The pub, love – we're going to the pub.'

'The pub? As in public house?'

'Nowhere fancy. Just the Dog and Duck. I'm meeting Terry there in . . .' Roxy checked the time on her phone. 'Fifteen minutes ago.'

'Oh, no, I couldn't . . .'

'Why not? There's bugger all on TV and you've got a new purchase to show off! There's no point looking hot-to-trot if nobody's there to see it. Come on; I'm buying.'

'No, really, I can't . . .' Sue began to panic. How could she explain to Roxy that she hadn't been to a pub since, well . . . since she used to go with Jeff? The thought of going to one now terrified her, even *with* Roxy. What if she had to go up to the bar to buy drinks? It wasn't the money – she didn't mind paying. It was just, how on earth would she get the barman's attention? She'd be left standing there for hours! Didn't Roxy know how invisible she was?

'Can't what?' Roxy teased. 'Can't have a quiet drink with friends?'

'I'm . . . I'm waiting for a phone call,' she fumbled.

'Bring your mobile.'

'I don't have one.'

Roxy snorted. 'You don't have a mobile? Are you for real?'

'It's from Australia. The call. I can't miss it – not with the time difference . . .'

Roxy looked at her strangely for a few moments. Sue did her best to look confident, like a person who really was expecting an important phone call from the other side of the world.

'OK, you win,' Roxy said eventually. Sue tried not to sag with relief. 'But, Sue . . .'

'Hmmm?'

'You can't resist me forever. I *will* get you to come for a drink with me some day.'

'OK,' Sue conceded tightly. *Some* day sounded better than *to*day. At least she'd have time to prepare, build herself up to it, work out a few conversation topics.

'We're going to be mates, you and me.' Roxy winked as she backed up along Sue's garden path. 'Whether you like it or not, we *will* be friends!'

And then she was gone.

To: Roxy Squires

From: Red Carpet Premieres PR

Hey Rox!

V sorry, but our new boss has ordered a shake-up of our celebrity invitation database . . . and I'm afraid she's taken you off it!

Brutal!

She says we can only invite celebs to our movie premieres with newspaper / magazine profile from the last twelve months. It's an austerity thang. So – bottom line is – I can't send you tickets for our West End premieres any more . . .

Soz! ☹

xx

PS. But if you suddenly get into *Heat*, give us a bell!!!!!

ROXY

'Two more of your finest tequilas, please, landlord. And one for yourself whilst you're at it.'

Roxy rifled her purse for another twenty whilst Dave peered at the tequila suspiciously.

'I don't drink continental,' he told her. 'You know where you stand with a Bass.'

'Well, Bass yourself up on me, then, sweet cheeks! And give me two lager chasers whilst you're at. I'm dizzy with all these trips to the bar.'

'So, you'll be needing my wheelbarrow, then?'

'Eh?'

'It's the only way you're going to get Tornado home, the rate you're going.' Dave nodded over to where Terence was sitting, a lone figure amid a sea of empty shot glasses. 'He normally just has a mild.'

'Really?' Roxy stared at Terence. His face was screwed up in confusion (or was it after-burn from all the tequila?). 'Nah, you've got Terry all wrong – you've just got to find his party button, that's all. Besides, there's no way he's going home in a wheelbarrow; that's Comme des Garçons he's wearing.'

'Comedy-guff-on, more like.' Dave eyed Terence's blouson and drew himself a Bass.

Roxy strode back to the table.

'You seriously want me to make a *record*?' Terence asked, the moment her bottom hit the chair.

'It'll be epic!' She pushed a tequila into his hand. 'You see, Tezza, it's page one in your chapter of my masterplan – the one I've been designing to get you all back to the top. You had me stumped for a while; you're an awkward bugger, and your age doesn't help. At first I was thinking a three-sixty makeover . . . You know – *Fat Club*; Gok; Nick Knowles . . . *Bottoms up!*' She knocked back her shot in one. 'But then it hit me . . .' she continued gruffly as the tequila inflicted its burn. 'You need to show the public that you're *more* than just that weather guy. You can't let a bunch of *other* TV personalities reinvent you – you need to grab the world by the goolies and reinvent yourself!'

'Grab the world by the *what*?'

'Obviously, *Strictly*'s top of the list . . .'

Terence choked.

'. . . but every celeb on the block's gunning for that one. And we shouldn't put all your eggs in one handbag. We need a multi-thonged attack.'

'A *what* attack?'

'Which gets me back to the record.' Roxy grinned. 'Comic Relief's next month. What d'you reckon about doing the official single?'

'You seriously want me to *sing*?'

'It'll be fun!'

'Fun?'

Roxy prised the empty tequila glass from his fingers and inserted the lager instead.

'You *do* know I was the only boy to get barred from school choir? I was seven.'

'Even more reason to do it. C'mon, Tezza – even *you* must see it's a laugh. More than a laugh – a way back.'

'But a way back to what, exactly?'

'To fame! To being fab, and famous, and on telly!'

Terence stared for a moment, his whole body rigid.

'Dave!' Roxy called over her shoulder. 'Bring us a couple of brandies, would you? Tezza's gone into shock!'

'Don't take this the wrong way,' Terence said finally, after Roxy had wafted a Rémy Martin under his nostrils, 'but I don't think you're from this planet. This whole evening is an out-of-body experience! You do know who I am, don't you? I'm Terence Leggett, professional meteorologist. I used to present premium-quality weather forecasts on prime-time television. On what planet would parading about like a tone-deaf village idiot, or cancanning in a sparkly cat suit, get me back my job? It would be complete career suicide.'

'Your career's already dead,' Roxy scoffed. 'It's stuffed and mounted – the full rigor mortis.'

'Oh, don't hold back – heaven forbid you spare my feelings.'

'I'm just being honest. No point blowing smoke up your arse.'

Terence self-anaesthetised with a very large brandy. 'And what would you have me sing?' he asked warily.

'"It's Raining Men"?'

He made a popping noise, like one of his organs had imploded.

'At least I didn't say "White Christmas".'

'The bloody tabloids made me a joke – and now you want to wheel me out for round two!'

'All right, Tezza. Keep your hair on . . .'

'"Let's go for a drink," you said. "Have a tequila," you said. But you're just like the bloody papers. You want everyone to take the piss out of me *again*!'

'I don't want everyone to take the piss out of you,' Roxy snapped. 'I want everyone to love you, you muppet. The others might be happy to trowel on the sympathy, but that's not the kind of woman I am. I'm telling it like it is – stay as you are and you're over.'

'You . . . *you* . . . YOU—'

'Oh, quit the dramatics and listen. You'll get nowhere flogging a dead horse. If you want to get back in the saddle, face facts – your old career's over. Like it or lump it, you're not Terence Leggett any more – you're Tornado Terry. Embrace the change and move on.'

'By singing homosexual disco anthems?'

'Christ; you don't even know the basics, do you?' Roxy sighed. What was she working with here? Even Z-listers knew all this stuff. 'The first rule of fame: know your market. You need to be a showbiz Lazarus. The great British public may love chopping down a tall poppy . . . but what they love *more* is a poppy that gets back on its feet with a smile. Which leads me to lesson number two: self-deprecating humour. You can get away with bloody murder if you laugh. Careers are reborn on taking the piss out of yourself – did you never see George Michael's video for "Outside"? Trust me . . .' She leant forward, cupped his face and slapped him lightly around the chops. 'You'll get nowhere being a grump. Love your inner Tornado and the public will love you back.'

'They will?'

'With knobs on,' she promised.

For a moment Terence looked thoughtful. '"It's Raining Men", you say?'

'Hallelujah!' she replied with a smile.

2.07am @FoxyRoxy
#ROXYSAYS: Tequilla *RRRRROCKSS!*

To: Roxy Squires
From: Red Carpet Premieres PR

Why didn't you say the tickets were for Tornado Terry??? I love him!!!!! He's sooo lol!!!!!

Course I'll send you a couple of tickets. I'm biking them over right now!

☺

x

SUE

Sue stared.

And stared.

She'd spent the last forty minutes at her vanity table, scrutinising her reflection for a sign. She'd turned on the overhead light. She'd tried with and without her glasses. She'd gazed for so long, and from so many angles, that the daylight had faded and her tea had gone cold. But it made no difference – she still couldn't see Suzi.

Was she still in her, Sue wondered. Was the pretty, laughing, *sexy* girl who'd enchanted Hunt – the one who'd magnetised men without trying – was *she* still in there . . . even a trace? Could it be that, despite the years, Suzi was lying dormant under the neglect and the biscuits, waiting to be set free?

Sue blinked.

She'd read that Marilyn Monroe had been able to switch herself on or off at will . . . that the ultimate screen idol could, at any time, switch to plain old Norma Jean and walk down the street unspotted. But then – in a grocery queue, perhaps, or a diner – she'd flick back to being her. A pinning back of the shoulders, a roll of the hips, a minuscule adjustment to her expression – her eyes – and *bang*! Suddenly she was Marilyn again, and shoppers would blink in dumbfounded amazement, staggered to be standing next to a star.

Was it the same with her, Sue wondered as she gazed at her own reflection. Was it just that when she'd hidden in Lavender Heath, she'd unknowingly turned off her Suzi button and forgotten where to find the switch?

She smiled.

Nothing.

She smiled again, wider.

But then she remembered something else – something snide she'd heard on the radio about a famous businessman's hair. His hair, it was argued, was like a time capsule buried in a garden. Vain, powerful people were supposed to subconsciously freeze their look at the peak of their success, hence one celeb's devotion to her bubble perm, or the rock star's refusal to cut his grey locks.

And Sue wondered . . . had this happened to her too? Was she mummified in time? Although it wasn't her hairstyle that had frozen, but her heart – her mind – her nerves. Had *her* peak moment been the scandal? After all, it wasn't *normal* to be fifty and frightened; it wasn't *healthy* to hide behind doors; it wasn't *right* to pine for a man who'd made his decision thirty years ago and scuttled back home to his wife. And then Sue wondered . . . did she really still love Hunt? Or was he just an excuse? Was the truth *actually* that she was stuck as that nervous nineteen-year-old, forever frozen in the headlights of scandal, preserved in perpetuity like a pickled onion in a jar?

She looked at her reflection. Out of the corner of her eye she saw the cashmere duck egg hanging on the front of her wardrobe. And Sue decided . . .

She didn't want to be an onion.

She'd had enough of being pickled.

CRESSIDA

Cressida was doing her best to look unruffled. Politics had given her a lifetime of training: when it came to greeting bad news, she could put on a brave face in her sleep. But this was jolly difficult. She ignored the icy wind at her ankles, wrapped her dressing gown more tightly around her and nodded at the young fireman who'd momentarily returned to the engine.

'Is there a neighbour you could wait with?' he asked kindly. 'It's pretty parky out here.'

'I'm perfectly fine, thank you.' She waved him away with a hand that had gone blue.

'I'd let you wait in the cab . . .' He motioned towards the huge shiny fire engine dwarfing Cressida's drive. 'But, health and safety . . .'

'Really,' Cressida assured him, 'I'll survive.'

The young fireman headed back into the house.

Alone on her lawn, Cressida surveyed the small column of smoke that still plumed into the section of sky above her kitchen. She couldn't possibly disturb her neighbours – she didn't *know* her neighbours. And this was hardly the time to introduce herself – at dawn, in a terry-towel robe. She thought about calling Woody, but her phone was indoors and the fireman had told her that under no circumstances was she to re-enter the house – not until they'd made a full structural inspection and issued the all-clear. Heavens, it had only been a few flames: hardly the inferno in the Great Hall at Windsor. Still, rules were rules . . .

But she *was* freezing. And, despite the brave face, it *was* embarrassing being in her nightie on the lawn. A bit like standing on election night hustings with a ladder in your tights. Thank goodness the village was quiet!

Suddenly Cressida's fragile equanimity was shattered by a deep, growly roar. A low-slung sports car came towards her, its driver slowing for a gawp. Cressida didn't know a thing about cars (other than that they should display a valid tax disk, stick to thirty in towns and emit no more than 130 grams of CO_2 per kilogram), but even *she* knew this car was ludicrously expensive. It looked like something from a Bond movie car chase.

And then there was a whistle – loud and sharp, and dropping a tone at the end – the kind of whistle that workmen were reputed to be fond of.

'Niiice slippers!'

Cressida grimaced. This was just what she needed – a wise-cracking loudmouth. She dipped down and, sure enough, Austin Jones smirked back from the driver's seat.

She tightened her dressing gown. What was *he* doing up at this time? She knew the chances of being spotted by someone *in flagrante* were quite high, but she never imagined it would be by him. Surely he should be languishing in a coffin somewhere, waiting for the emergence of dusk?

'You all right?' He grinned from behind movie-star sunglasses.

'Perfectly,' she replied tartly, wondering what glare he was expecting from a February dawn.

'Been trashing your house?'

'A minor fire in the kitchen.'

'Need to go to hospital?'

'No, thank you.'

'I could give you a lift?'

'Not necessary.'

'Come on, Cressida; it's bloody arctic out there. There's a poodle frozen solid down the road. At least come and sit in my car.'

'I'm perfectly fine where I am.'

'It's got heated seats.' He raised an eyebrow.

Cressida folded her arms.

'So, what happened?' He nodded towards the fire engine. 'Overheat your rollers?'

'My bacon, actually,' she said primly. 'It exploded. In my microwave.'

'You *microwave* bacon?'

'It's quicker than frying.'

'So? That's what staff are for.'

'You *have staff* to cook your bacon?'

'You *don't*?'

Cressida thought for a moment. 'Maybe I should,' she conceded. 'I never *can* work my blasted grill. Cookers are so complicated: more knobs and dials than NASA.'

'Exactly! Leave cooking to the professionals. They love all that danger.'

Cressida scanned Austin's face for sarcasm but, strangely, none seemed to be there. And then, before she knew it, she told him . . .

'I only went into the hall for my post, but I got distracted by the cover of *Pensions Weekly*. And the next thing I knew, the smoke alarm was ringing. So I dashed back into the kitchen, found the microwave ablaze, and—'

'Your bacon was bacon,' he finished solemnly.

'Well, quite.' And then she sagged. 'Apparently it was the tin foil that did it. The fireman told me I should never have put it in the microwave.'

'How were you supposed to know that?'

'Everyone knows it, apparently.'

'Everyone knows who won *X Factor* – doesn't mean we should, too,' Austin reasoned.

Cressida smiled at the good sense of his point. 'I'm a bit of a novice at home economics,' she admitted.

'Me, too. A total cookery virgin, with no plans for being seduced.'

'When I was an MP, I had a cook. I worked twenty-hour days – I didn't have time to boil a kettle.'

'And why the hell should you? There are plenty of kettle-boilers on the dole. Give them a job, that's what I say!'

Surprised, Cressida regarded him again through the open car window. He was being three-hundred-per-cent more charming today. And as she looked, he took off his sunglasses, dropped his chin and fixed her with puppy-dog eyes. A naughty puppy dog, that was – one that had probably just widdled on the carpet, or tried to make love to someone's leg.

'Come on, Cressie,' he drawled. 'Drop your frozen backside on to my nice, warm seat and let me whisk you back to mine for unthawing. I'll get Cook to make you some breakfast. Hell, she could even do you a bacon sandwich. Although, I always had you down as more of a sausage girl.'

Cressida folded her arms and tried to think of all the good reasons why she should say no . . . Austin's vile behaviour at the meeting, his rudeness, his arrogance, his juvenile car . . . the guarantee of his complete indiscretion . . . the fact that he would doubtless tease her forever about her state of undress. Of all the people she could hope to be rescued by, Austin Jones was bottom of the list. But then again . . . he *was* being surprising civil and she *had* gone numb from the nose down.

'I don't bite,' he promised teasingly. 'Unless you ask.'

And just as she was feeling herself being lured by his heated seat, Cressida remembered her senses. 'Why are you up so early?'

'Is it early? I thought it was late.'

'Have you been to bed at all?'

'Is that an offer?'

'Just answer the question, Mr Jones.'

'Are you always this nosy, Ms Cunningham?'

'Only when my personal safety depends on it.'

'I'm offering breakfast, not a tour of my severed head collection.'

'Are you drunk? Because I cannot condone drinking and driving.'

'That's OK – you won't be doing the driving.'

'Oh, for goodness sake – where have you *been*, Austin?'

He grinned. 'A couple of casinos, cocktails with Peter Stringfellow, several sublime hours of sexual depravity and infantile submission with a few of my large-chested chums . . .'

'I thought as much.'

'Really? But I'm not the one hanging out in lingerie, kerbside.' He lasciviously eyed the terry-towelling. 'The way I see it, Cressida, I'm the best offer you've got. Oh, come on – hop in. What's the worst that can happen?'

Cressida thought for a moment. The village was quiet, traffic was light and Austin's house couldn't be more than a minute away. Surely the statistical likelihood of him crashing was microscopic. And she was rather hungry, and more than a little bit cold.

'I'm not dressed,' she reasoned half-heartedly.

Austin shrugged. 'You're wearing more than most of my visitors.'

Cressida looked back at her house. There was no sign of the fire crew re-emerging.

'No speeding,' she instructed, as she scooted to the passenger door and hopped in. 'I've got my reputation to think of.'

'Me too.' Austin grinned, and he noisily revved up the engine.

ROXY

It wasn't the ideal start to the jog. Roxy hadn't had a hangover so bad since . . . well, since January 2nd. Concentrating on everyone else's career had turned her into such a nun, she'd barely had time to get bladdered. She almost missed the feeling of death rot. But last night Terry had been a surprise. Who'd have thought the Tornado could sink so much tequila? With shaking hands, she buried her forty-per-cent-proof sheen under an extra layer of slap and bent down to tie up her laces.

The knock on the door came at six thirty.

'Ready for round two?' Woody grinned.

Roxy grunted and then they set off. And this time, to her amazement, she made it to the pub with ease. Her mood lifted. She'd always had a theory she functioned best on a hangover. Some of her best telly had been done still pissed. Her Liam Gallagher interview had got five stars in *The Sun TV Mag*, and she'd thrown up twice between takes (once over his Adidas shell toes). Maybe it was the same with jogging, she wondered. This didn't hurt half as much as the other day. Next time she wouldn't bother with a bottle of water; she'd run with a vodka and tonic instead.

'Good night?' Woody interrupted her thoughts.

'Huh?'

'With Terry?'

'How do you know about that?'

'He booty-called me. Actually, it was more of an SOS. He was so drunk, he got his key jammed in his front door. He rang for help getting in.'

'Is there no end to your talents?' Roxy teased. She was beginning to feel feisty. She'd forgotten how liberating hangovers were. It was as though all the alcohol sloshing in her system had washed her motormouth free of restraint. 'So you clean windows, fix fuses and come to the aid of weathermen in distress . . . Seems like the only thing you *can't* do is see the wood for the trees.'

Woody looked at her askance.

'Meaning what, exactly?'

'Meaning, what the hell are you doing with your life, Woody? You've made your point; you don't *need* to be famous – I get it! But when are you going to get back to what you're *really* good at?'

'I'm *good* at cleaning windows.'

'You're good at being a pop star!'

Woody sighed. 'Roxy, I've already told you, I don't want my old life.'

'But what's so bad about being successful?'

'Nothing.'

'So why don't you give it another try?'

'No.'

They turned into Cherry Blossom Drive. Roxy thought for a moment and then tried another tack. 'If you thought your version of "Could It Be I'm Falling In Love?" was cheesy, why did you release it?'

'Because my manager said that I should. Because I was young and polite and didn't like saying no.'

'Is that why you shagged so many women?' she asked cheekily. 'You were just a boy who couldn't say no?'

'The stories of my sexual prowess were greatly exaggerated.'

'So you *didn't* shag half of London?'

'Just a third,' he replied, straight-faced. For a moment Roxy wondered if he really was joking.

'Are you poor?' she blurted.

'Am I what?'

'You *have* got the smallest house in the village!'

'Bloody hell – size isn't everything, Rox.'

'Only men ever say that.'

'I've got enough money; I get by,' he said tersely.

'Woody, you *clean windows* for a living.'

'I clean windows for a life. Not everything's about money and status.'

Roxy frowned. 'But seriously, Woods, how many number ones did you have?'

Woody sighed again before answering. 'Seven.'

'And weren't you constantly on tour?'

'Mmm hmmm.'

'So you should be totally wadded! Where's all your money gone?'

'Not that it's any of your business,' he stressed, irritated, 'but I bought my parents a house and paid for my sister to go to uni. Plus, I wasted crazy money buying huge houses I never even lived in, throwing parties that lasted for weeks—'

'That's more like it!'

'. . . And, when I quit, I had to pay compensation – *and* give the label back my advance.'

'Sounds like your bank manager would tell you to be famous again,' she baited.

'Roxy, do you ever give up?'

'Are you frightened of being famous again?'

'No!' Woody snorted in exasperation. But still Roxy didn't see the signs.

'Has this got anything to do with Petra Klitova?' she demanded.

'Petra?' Woody's stride faltered as he looked at her in shock. 'No!'

'When did you guys split up?'

'A long time ago,' he replied tightly.

'How long?'

He frowned and stepped up the pace.

'Did she dump you because you weren't famous any more? You two *were* a golden couple.'

'Whatever that means,' he muttered.

'Was *she* the reason you quit? Did Petra break your heart?'

'For Christ's sake, Rox, shut up!'

He stopped running. Roxy ground to a halt too and, to her surprise, she realised they'd already done three laps of the village. But then she noticed Woody's expression. He was looking seriously pissed off.

'No, Petra didn't break my heart,' he stated angrily. 'No, I'm not hard up and, no, I don't want to be famous again. Does that answer your questions? Now can we finish our jog in peace?'

'OK,' Roxy said meekly. Woody's profile was angry and hard. Maybe he really didn't want to be famous, she realised. After all, she'd given him enough chances to change his mind. He must actually be happy as a civvy. But what she still didn't get was why. And before she could reach for her inner handbrake, the motormouth leapt into gear.

'Is it Jennifer?' she heard herself blurt. 'Is she frightened of losing you to showbiz?'

'No,' Woody replied in a flash. 'Jennifer's pretty . . .'

There was a long pause; too long. Suddenly all Roxy could see was the laughing woman with the glossy dark hair; 'pretty' didn't even begin to cover it.

'. . . low maintenance,' he finished flatly.

And beneath her peroxide hair, double-layer MAC foundation and implausibly tanned skin, something inside Roxy began to shrivel. And a second later, her hangover hurt like hell.

TERENCE

Terence frowned at his empty doorstep. If it was local kids playing knock-down-ginger, he'd be livid. Not that Lavender Heath kids did that kind of thing – they were usually too busy with their ponies and junior trust funds – but, if they did, and he caught them, he'd give them short shrift. Because Terence's head felt like someone was hitting him repeatedly with a sledgehammer, and the effort it had taken to haul himself to the door had been colossal. He hadn't had a hangover like this since the morning Barbara had left him. And he hadn't had a tequila hangover since . . . *well*, since . . . Terence gave up thinking. Mexican spirits seemed to have wiped whole tranches of his brain.

And then, just as he was turning back into the house and the welcoming embrace of his wing-back armchair, he saw it . . . an envelope on the doormat. He slowly bent to retrieve it, trying not to wince at the extra pressure in his head. He frowned again and turned it over. The envelope was blank and unsealed at the back, a card poking out from its folds. He slid it out and nearly gasped in surprise. It was a blank Valentine's card, two tickets for the cinema inside.

Perplexed, Terence looked up and beyond the garden. And through the haze of hangover and hedge, he caught a glimpse of turquoise sequins, moving fast towards Gates Green Road.

To: Roxy Squires
From: Holly Childs

Hi Roxy,

Thanks for your messages inviting me for another night out. Your offers of trips to dance at Mahiki, dine at NOPI and drink at the Roxy (where else?!) were very kind, but I'm afraid I'm going to say no. You see, I don't really go out much and, if I'm being honest, I like it that way. And whilst I'm very flattered that you want to spend time with me, I think I'd only be a disappointment. I don't like loud music, prefer orange juice to cocktails and like my clothes practical and warm.

I'm sorry! I know you like to call a spade a spade, so I thought you'd appreciate an honest answer.

See you at the next meeting, though . . .

Luv
Holly
;-)
xx

ROXY

Roxy emptied a carrier bag of magazines on to Cressida's coffee table. The brightly-coloured pages of *Heat*, *Reveal* and *Star* spilled across the mahogany.

'Why are you here?' Cressida peered at her closely.

'I thought you'd be pleased! I brought *The Economist*.' She waved the latest issue and grinned.

'Of course I'm pleased; I haven't spoken to a soul since Sunday.'

'But that was two days ago!' Roxy cried. She could have kicked herself for not coming sooner.

'It's the price one pays for age and unpopularity.'

'You're not unpopular – I like you.'

'Well, thank you. But fifty-two per cent of the Biddington Borders voters would beg to differ.'

There was a pause.

'Oh, and I meant to say you're not old,' Roxy added. 'Come on – you're only sixty.'

'Fifty,' Cressida corrected.

Roxy suddenly became aware of a grandfather clock ticking. It was the only sound in the room.

'Anyway –' she clapped – 'I'm here now. I thought we could, you know . . . *natter*.'

Cressida looked cockled for a moment. 'Yes, all right then; why not?' she decided. 'Let's natter!'

'And check out some mags whilst we're at it.' Roxy grinned, surreptitiously slipping *Hair* magazine into the pile. She was going to gently coerce Cressida into a new look.

Cressida eyed the multiple Jennifer Aniston covers disparagingly.

'I haven't read my *Telegraph* yet. How about I just read that?'

'Oh, OK – if you like.'

The two women sat down and opened their respective reading.

'Great smell, by the way,' Roxy said.

'Smell?'

'The paint! There's nothing like the smell of emulsion! Other than Tipp-Ex and poppers.'

'Woody repainted my kitchen. I had a spot of bother with my microwave.'

Roxy nodded. Woody hadn't mentioned he'd done Cressida's decorating. She awkwardly looked down at her magazine.

'*This is nice!*' she declared conversationally about nothing in particular. She flipped through eleven pages of Kim Kardashian and the February shoe diary of Lauren Pope. The next page was a photo-spread of Valentine's gifts for him. Lucky him – if he liked chocolate golf balls. 'So, any plans for Valentine's?' she small-talked.

'Only to sit in my armchair and wrestle with my Sky TV remote in an attempt to find a channel that hasn't completely given itself over to schmaltz.'

'Yeah, it's a bugger, all the stupid hearts and guff,' Roxy agreed. 'It's bloody hard being single on Valentine's.'

'I dare say I'll survive,' Cressida replied archly.

'Me, too. I mean, it's just another night, right?'

'Well, quite.'

Roxy flipped on a few pages, suddenly sad. This was no good – she was supposed to be bringing Cressida up, not down. Although, she had to admit, Cressida didn't look too down, peering at her *Telegraph* through her half-moon glasses. But Roxy couldn't help it. Valentine's always gave her a downer. She hated it, with its bouquets and chocolate-measured love. Although she'd had dozens of flings, they'd always flung off before Valentine's – and the guitarists who booty-called weren't the Interflora type. So, over the years, in the interests of ego-preservation, she'd developed her very own brand of 'VD tactics' ('VD' being an appropriate abbreviation for Valentine's Day, seeing as the two buggers were equally unwelcome). She'd leave home mega early, looking dishevelled. Or – even better – head straight to work from a nightclub. That way she could legitimately swan around declaring she hadn't had the chance to pick up her cards yet (whilst secretly quashing the hope of a card-tower on her return).

'Oh, for heaven's sake, Roxy – cheer up!' Cressida called over. 'Why don't you have a nice cup of coffee?'

Roxy perked up at her kindness.

'Thanks, Cressida; that'd be mint.'

'The kettle's in the kitchen, second on the right. I have mine milky; two sugars.' And she returned to the pages of her *Telegraph*.

Obediently, Roxy stood and made her way to the kitchen. There was something about Cressida that required compliance. She didn't know how fifty-two per cent of Biddington Borders had dared defy her. As she flicked on the kettle, she admired Woody's new paintwork; 'Farrow and Ball, Stone White', the tin said. And then she looked out of the window and marvelled. She'd never really thought about windows before, but she suddenly noticed that Cressida's were superclean! Yep, she had to hand it to Woody . . . a skill was a skill, no matter how unglamorous . . . *and Woody cleaned a damn good window!*

SUE

For once, the crossword could wait.

Sue settled down at the kitchen table with her tea (Assam) and biscuits (ginger creams) and opened her laptop. She double-clicked excitedly on her inbox. It wasn't a Friday, so there was no email from Holly with the minutes, but that didn't matter. Sue's inbox was bustling with three new emails – *three!* – all tracking orders for yesterday's purchases.

She was getting the hang of this online shopping thing. The duck egg had been just the start. Sue was amazed; shopping had become so easy! All you had to do was point and click, and a nice young man brought your purchases right to your door. And it wasn't just the novelty of hearing her door-bell ring that made it so exciting . . . it was the whole new world of colour and fabrics that Roxy had opened her up to. Clothes didn't need to be black, stretchy and elasticated at the waist. They could be sculpted and tailored – in every shape, colour or pattern you could imagine.

Yes, the duck-egg coatigan had unleashed a beast that Sue hadn't realised still lurked inside her. Like any woman, she'd been born with a propensity for shopping – it came as a given with the longer eyelashes and extra rib. She used to love it, back when she was Suzi and everything she wore looked good. But Sue hadn't been shopping for years. High streets were too full of eyes to visit voluntarily, and besides – clothes weren't fun once your middle had gone spongy. But now that she could shop from the safety of her kitchen, and not have to worry about changing-room mirrors, disparaging assistants and the looks of recognition she got on public transport – well, shopping was actually *fun*! Filling up her online basket over breakfast was exhilarating – and tracking her orders was like monitoring the arrival of Father Christmas. Admittedly, she hadn't actually *worn* any of her purchases yet, but that wasn't the point. The point was . . . *the point was* . . . Actually, she didn't know what the point was, but she was pretty sure it was good. At the very least, Roxy would call it progress. Even if the clothes just hung in her wardrobe, at least they broke up the black.

Sue clicked out of her inbox and into hobbs.co.uk. Happily, she started to browse. Roxy had told her to look out for soft purples. She dragged a silk heather blouse into her shopping cart and smiled.

And then something out the window caught her eye. Her chest went tight and her mouth suddenly dried. There was a man at the edge of her garden.

Was that *Terence*?

She frowned as she tried to focus on the figure loitering at the end of her drive.

This Terence was smarter than usual. He was wearing a navy jacket and a flowery blue shirt. Even his hair was different: neatly combed with a parting. He looked strange . . . thinner, younger – less angry than he did in a cardigan. And then, before she'd had the chance to stop frowning, Terence raised his hand, gave a strange little smile, and hurried away up Chestnut Avenue.

Sue's cheeks burned and her breath came out short. Why had Terence been there? And why had he been so dressed up? Had he been looking at her for long? Had he seen her eating biscuits, or caught a side view of her double chin? But then she told herself off for being silly. Of course Terence hadn't been looking at her! Why on earth would he? No, he must have dropped something and been looking for it – that was all. Something must have fallen out of his pocket and hidden itself in her gravel. He was on his way somewhere important – hence the shirt, and the jacket, and the hair – and only waved to be polite because he knew how easily she frightened. *Yes, that was it.* It was obvious, really.

Deflated, Sue picked up her Assam, turned back to her computer and shopped.

ROXY

Roxy woke from her dream with a start.

'Bollocks!' she cried to her bedroom. Everything had been about to go stellar.

Her fanny was fizzing and her nipples rock hard. *Could women actually come in their sleep?* she wondered. She knew boys did it as easily as farting – *but women*? She could have cursed her 6am alarm. Who the hell went jogging at night?

Frustrated, she dropped her head back on to her pillow and tried to remember the dream. Damn, she knew Austin was flabby and bearded in real life, but *Christ*, he gave a bloody good rude dream! He'd arrived for their date in his chopper, before whisking her off to wine her and dine her at the top of the Eiffel Tower. And then he'd led her into the lift for a bloody good shafting. He'd been utterly consumed with her pleasure and had spent so long perusing her ladygarden that the chopper had run out of gas. He'd sent his pilot to fill up at the chopper garage, with strict instructions to come back with Curly Wurlies.

Roxy sighed. Still, dreams were just dreams – and reality

was totally different. The real Austin couldn't come close. She'd bet her house on him being a selfish sod under the duvet. All take, no give – *and* he'd expect breakfast in the morning.

She threw back her duvet and got up.

ROXY

'So you really think "It's Raining Men" will get Terence his job back?' Woody asked as they came to the end of lap three, their feet – as before – pounding the pavement in perfect time.

'Yes!' Roxy insisted, her cheeks as red from the mission as the running.

'And that Simon should present cookery programmes and Cressida be a talent-show judge?'

'Yes, yes! You see, I'm making plans – writing strategies. *Fame Again*, I'm calling it. I'm even working on a strategy for Holly.'

Woody frowned as they turned at the postbox.

'And have you asked Holly if she wants a strategy? Or, for that matter, *Fame Again*?'

'Well, no, not yet. But she'll definitely want it. I just need her to stop being so modest.'

'So you don't think there's a reason why she's *not* famous again already?'

Roxy rolled her eyes. 'Just because her parents didn't want her going to parties—'

'Something other than that?'

'Well, I know she thinks her inspiration's run out – but I've got a few ideas for that too.'

'But maybe Holly doesn't *want* to be famous. Maybe she's got different priorities.'

'Priorities? Come off it.' Roxy laughed. 'Holly's diary's as empty as space.'

'What about looking after her mum?'

'Her mum?'

'She's old and ill, and Holly's the only family she's got.'

Roxy ran a few steps before Woody's words sank in. '*But . . .* But what about Holly's dad?'

'Died – years ago. Didn't you wonder why we never have meetings at Holly's house?'

'I . . .' she didn't want to admit she hadn't noticed.

'Holly lives with her mother. She's her carer.'

'Oh!'

For once Roxy was silenced.

'Look, Rox, it's great that you're so passionate about helping everyone. But have you checked that what *you* want for them is actually what they want too?'

Roxy frowned as she ran. Poor Holly; imagine having to give up your life to look after your mum. What patience she must have – what kindness. Roxy couldn't begin to imagine the sacrifices she must have made – they certainly went beyond jacking in Kit Kats. She suddenly felt guilty for every bad thing she'd ever thought about Holly's twinsets. It was no wonder she always wore them – she probably hadn't had the time to go shopping in years.

'One more lap, then back to mine for a sausage sandwich?' Woody asked, upping the pace.

Roxy nodded, her head too full of Holly for a meat-based double entendre.

WOODY

It had chucked it down ever since he'd got back from the jog. Rain might be manna for gardeners, but for window cleaners it was torture by water. Wet ladders were slippy and dangerous, and for men who liked to be outdoors, there was nothing worse than twiddling your thumbs. But the rain had eventually cleared and Woody had spent the afternoon on fast-forward, trying to catch up with his round. By three thirty he'd managed six customers, but already the daylight was dying.

He'd just finished Mrs Dewsbury-Fox's windows and was about to head down his ladder when he caught sight of two boys skulking in lilac school blazers. They'd hidden themselves in the hydrangea bushes that ran along Lime Tree Walk and, puffing out of the bushes, was a thin cloud of smoke. And, *if Woody's nostrils weren't mistaken* . . . As one of the boys inhaled, he lifted his face. It was one of the twins – Simon's son. In a flash, Woody hurtled down his ladder, bolted up Mrs Dewsbury-Fox's drive and rounded the corner.

'Euan!' he boomed as he burst through the bushes. Frightened, the mate quickly legged it, but Euan's reactions weren't as fast. Realising he was busted, he flicked his home-made cigarette further into the bush and did his best not to look scared.

'What are you doing?' Woody asked sternly.

'Nuffin'.' Euan gave a half-hearted suck of his teeth. His fear had already been replaced by surly teenage indifference. Woody dug deep and did his best to look strict. He wasn't a dad – he didn't know how to do this kind of stuff. The last time he'd got angry was in 1997.

He settled on raising an eyebrow. 'It doesn't smell like nothing.'

Euan shrugged and studied the fence. 'I'm just doin' my own t'ing.'

Woody tried not to smirk at Euan's gangsta. He saw a clear plastic bag peeking from the pocket of his school blazer. Quick as a flash he whipped it out. It was a large bag of weed.

'What's this, mate?'

'Cooking herbs?'

Woody laughed. 'Do you think I'm as daft as I look? What I mean is, what are you doing wasting your time on this?'

Euan sucked his teeth again.

Woody paused. It was difficult to come down hard on the kid; he was only doing what all teenagers got up to and, Christ knew, *he* was in no position to judge. He'd wasted years on his sofa with 'cooking herbs'. But still, Simon was a mate – he had obligations.

'Look, I know this seems like a cool thing to do when you're fourteen . . .'

'Fifteen!'

'. . . but, trust me, it's not.'

Euan continued to stare at the fence. Woody tried another tack.

'Do your parents know you smoke weed?'

Euan shrugged again.

'Thought not.' Woody held up the bag. 'I'm just wondering who I should tell first – your parents, your school, or the police?'

Now he had Euan's attention. 'You don't *need* to tell no one!' he barked nervously, looking him in the eye at last. 'And besides, it's nuttin' to do wit' you!'

'I'm a friend of your dad!'

For a moment they held eye contact. But then Euan's gaze moved back to the fence.

Woody sighed.

'Euan, mate, this really isn't the way to go. You need to be concentrating on other stuff – like school, and music, and sport.'

'Yeah, right,' Euan scoffed. 'And what makes you the oracle? You're a poxy window cleaner.'

'There's nothing poxy about being a window cleaner. It's a good, honest job.'

'For retards.'

'Christ, Euan! Since when did you get so obnoxious? Do you know what? I reckon I'll hold on to this for a while . . .' He gave the bag of weed a little shake. 'See if we can't sort this out, man to man. I think a bit of good, honest work is in order.'

Euan stiffened. 'I ain't goin' up no ladder.'

'Yeah, ladders – scary, aren't they,' Woody replied. Two could play at being sarcastic.

'I ain't scared, I just ain't going up one. Ladders are for ponces.'

'Ponces?' Woody laughed. 'How about buckets – are they heterosexual enough for you?'

Euan stubbed at the earth with his foot. Woody watched him for a moment.

'I don't know what your fancy school's teaching you, Euan,' he said eventually. 'It's obviously nothing that makes any sense. But never mind; I've got just the teacher for you.'

'Teacher?' Euan sounded alarmed.

'Think of it as an information exchange. You'll teach, and you'll also be taught.'

'No way! I ain't doing any teaching wit' you.'

'Not with me. With a lady.'

'A lady?' Euan couldn't hide the gleam in his eye. Woody tried not to grin. He suddenly remembered what it felt like to be fifteen.

'Yes – she'll be right up your street. She's fifty and eats gobshites for breakfast.'

The gleam disappeared.

'No way!' Euan dug his heels into the mud. 'I ain't doing it.'

'Fine. I'll just give your dad a quick ring . . .' Woody waved the bag of weed with one hand and reached for his phone with the other. He switched the phone to speaker and dialled.

Euan did his best to not look bothered. He sucked his teeth with a squeak.

'. . . *And* your mum,' Woody finished with emphasis.

Suddenly Euan looked worried. As the phone began to ring, he shuffled. And as someone picked up, he lunged.

'What's this lady going to teach me?' he blurted.

'Manners,' Woody replied dryly. 'She's going to teach you manners.' His eyes locked on Euan's, he slowly hung up the phone. 'And if you do the right thing and are really, really lucky, she might just kick your sorry arse on to a career path.'

Euan looked dubious but no longer rebellious. 'You said "information exchange". What am I supposed to be teaching her?' He tried to keep his voice hard, as though he was in a position to bargain. But the middle-class accent was back.

'Nothing you can't handle,' Woody replied airily. 'What this lady needs most is a gimp.'

'A gimp?' Euan squeaked. 'No way! I won't do anything kinky!'

Woody dangled the weed yet again.

'Like I said . . .' he warned. 'For breakfast!'

And he stepped out from the bushes and back to his ladder, doing his best to stifle his laugh.

To: Roxy; Cressida; Sue; Holly; Simon; Terence; Chelle
From: Woody

Guys – It's almost Thursday, and our next meeting. Given his performance last week, do you still want Austin to come? I'm happy to tell him to sling his hook . . . ?

Come over tonight if you want to discuss. (I've got a fridge full of wine and beer.)

W

ROXY

As usual, Roxy was the last to arrive. She could have kicked herself. Her strategies were finally finished and she was dying to show them to Woody. But Simon's got stuck in the printer and she'd spent so long yanking the jam she was late. By the time Cressida answered Woody's front door, the whole gang was already in there, hotly debating Austin. Woody was sitting between Simon and Chelle, so there was no chance to pass him the Barbie-pink A4 envelope. Instead, Roxy sat down and placed the envelope on her knees, ready to grab him as soon as a private moment came up. She tried not to peek over at the picture of the laughing woman with the dark glossy hair. She forced herself to pay attention to Terence instead.

'He was bloody rude!' he was insisting, jabbing the air in disgust.

'Like you were head boy at charm school,' Simon muttered.

'He had zero respect for Sue. He called her . . . *that name.* He implied that she . . . that she'd . . . *Christ;* he practically harassed her in her own kitchen.'

'He was showing off.' Cressida shrugged.

'*He didn't even flush the bloody toilet.*'

'He wasn't *so* rude.' Sue gently defended Austin in his absence. 'He's right that I've put on some weight. He didn't say anything that was technically untrue.'

'He said he'd shagged Roxy in a toilet!'

'Which he *didn't*,' Roxy added quickly. She tried to catch Woody's eye but he was looking elsewhere. She rocked the envelope with her knees in a bid to get his attention.

Chelle turned to Roxy and frowned. 'But why didn'tcha? I mean, he's Austin Jones – right?'

'He can't possibly come to the next meeting,' Terence interrupted.

'Why not?' Simon piped up.

'Because . . . Because . . . Because of all of the reasons outlined above.'

'Can he come if he promises to flush?' Roxy smirked.

Holly laughed.

'What do you think, Hol?' Woody asked. 'Austin: in or out?'

Holly froze, suddenly awkward. 'I know he was a bit anti-social,' she ventured timidly. 'But maybe it was a cry for help.'

Terence snorted.

'So is that an "in" or an "out"?' Woody pressed.

'Ummm . . .' she trailed off.

'Chelle?'

'What?' Chelle blinked.

'Should we let Austin stay?' Woody asked.

''Course! He's Austin cockin' Jones!'

'Si?'

Simon looked uncomfortable. 'He's not one of us . . .' he said hesitantly.

'So that's an "out",' Terence jumped in.

'I didn't say that *exactly*.'

Terence rolled his eyes. 'You never say anything exactly.'

'What do you mean?' Simon demanded, affronted.

'I mean, why don't you shuffle along that fence 'til you hit a post? It might just give you a backbone. You hate Austin – admit it.'

'I don't *hate him* hate him.'

'Just dislike him intensely.'

'I . . .'

Terence rolled his eyes again. 'For Christ's sake, Woody; *he's not welcome!*'

'Says who?' Roxy piped up.

'Says me!' Terence exploded. 'Says anyone with a molecule of sense. He treated Sue abominably. He said rude things about her breasts.'

Sue blanched.

'Isn't it up to Sue to be angry about that?' Simon needled. 'Sue doesn't need your protection.'

'I'm not protecting her,' Terence blustered unsteadily.

'Have you ever considered that she might get sick of you defending her? That she might like to speak for herself?'

'But—'

'Because you actually aren't joined at the hip.'

'I . . . We're . . . *Christ!* You wouldn't understand.'

'Wouldn't we?' Roxy stirred, eyebrow cocked.

'Look at his ears,' sniggered Chelle. 'They're bright pink.'

Terence looked like an angry raspberry. 'Sue and I aren't like the rest of you,' he said angrily.

'How do you mean?' Woody frowned.

'We didn't just fall out of fashion. Sue and I – *we're different.* We didn't bring this all on ourselves. We didn't pick the wrong projects, or get bored. We're not famous. We're *infamous. Notorious.*'

There was a pause and Cressida snorted.

'Our very own Bonnie and Clyde.'

'It's all right for you to snigger,' he snapped. 'You lost an election – you weren't personally screwed by the papers. They didn't make it impossible for *you* to find new employment. And you –' he turned to Woody – 'you just decided to stop! And you –' he pointed at Roxy – 'well, you've had your fifteen minutes. And you –' he rounded on Simon – '*you* did it to yourself! You gave up a once-in-a-lifetime TV role. You weren't savaged by the press like Sue and me.'

'For God's sake, Terry – you weren't savaged,' Simon tutted. 'Don't you think it's time you got off your high horse?'

'*No*, I bloody *don't!*' Terence exploded. 'I got blamed for families getting kicked out of their homes – for children having to take their Christmas presents back to the shops. The newspapers made me a pariah – and they did exactly the same to Sue. So if anyone wants to be snide and make something out of this that it's not, *they can bloody well just fuck off!'*

There was a long, awkward pause. Sue stared at her knees in mortification.

'Maybe we should just stick to the point of the evening,' Woody suggested gently. 'We're here to talk about Austin. Is *anyone* in favour of having him back?'

'Yes!' both Roxy and Chelle declared.

'Anyone not making a judgement with their groin?'

There was another long pause. Terence started looking triumphant.

'Yes,' Cressida declared suddenly. '*I* think Austin should come back.'

Woody looked at her in surprise.

'But he called you Vidal Sassoon!' Terence cried.

Cressida shrugged. 'He's rich and spoilt. He's not Genghis Khan. He just needs to get Hollywood out of his system – get his feet back on British terra firma.'

'She's got a point,' nodded Holly.

'Sue?' Woody asked gently.

Sue hesitated. 'Everyone deserves a second chance.'

'And he might get us into cool parties!' added Chelle.

'Oh, well, that's all right then!' Terence thundered, as Woody's mobile started to ring. 'Welcome back, Austin – all is forgiven! Just carry on spouting your poison and take us to a party when you're done.'

But Roxy was no longer listening. She was focusing on Woody. She sat up straight to catch a glimpse of his phone as he brought it to his ear. But then her heart sank at the name on the screen . . . The letters that flashed were 'JJ'.

'All right, baby?' Woody's face lit up as he headed to the door. 'When are you coming home?'

Roxy clutched the pink envelope tightly.

Home – Woody had said *home*.

So Jennifer *did* live with Woody, after all. Even with Woody in the hall she kept straining to hear. And, over all the noise and kerfuffle of the group, she was sure she heard three little words: 'I miss you.'

Roxy's insides turned to lead.

That was it; game over.

She officially stood no chance whatsoever, under any circumstance, with Woody. She knew she'd told herself that before – that fancying him was wrong and bad karma and not very girl power. But, deep down, a tiny part of her had still harboured hope. But now everything was different. This was cohabitation – a whole new level of love. Cohabitation was serious and permanant and proper. Woody definitely loved Jennifer. And she'd had no right to ever hope otherwise.

She stood up. She'd lost her appetite for the evening.

'I'm knackered,' she said quietly, interrupting the Austin debate mid-flow. The lure of her Wonder Woman pyjamas was suddenly very strong. Actually, the lure of climbing into her Wonder Woman pyjamas and not climbing out for a week was pretty strong, too. She didn't want a private moment with

Woody. What she had with Woody was *business* – she'd email the strategies instead. And, without interrupting his phone call to say goodbye, she slipped out the front door and back home.

SUE

Sue dropped her head between her knees and let her arms flop by her ankles, her cheeks pulsating hotly.

'Really stick your bum out!' Roxy instructed. 'Go on! Feel your back-door funbags getting tighter as you really nail it with the stretch!'

Upside down, and from between her legs, Sue screwed up her face and tried to feel her backside getting tighter. Could five sessions a week really give her the pert bottom Roxy promised? It seemed unlikely. Her bottom hadn't looked like a bottom in years – more like a landslide of flesh. Definitely for sitting on, not display.

'Good work, ladies!' Roxy cried from the TV. 'Follow this workout and you'll be bikinilicious by the end of the month. Straight up – the most booty-beautiful babe in the nightclub!'

Sue frowned. There was a big lump of fluff under the sofa.

'And lift yourselves back up! Pull your right arm across your body and *sstttrrreeeettccchh*!'

What was 'bikinilicious', exactly? Sue wondered as she hoisted herself painfully up to standing. And 'booty-beautiful', come to that? Were they things she wanted to be? Still, she thought as she tugged her right arm across her breasts and tried to clamp it down with her left, it *would* be nice if Roxy could make her bottom a bit less unlovely. And after dusting her DVD for the last six weeks, it seemed only polite to give it a try. After all, nobody could see her doing it, and it wasn't like she had anything else planned. The crossword barely took twenty minutes and she couldn't internet-shop for the *whole* of the rest of each day.

'Now *that's* what I call a stretch!' Roxy grinned. 'No more bingo wings for you lot!'

Sue looked at Roxy's image on screen. How old was this Roxy? she wondered thoughtfully. Twenty-three? Twenty-five? She certainly looked younger than the real Roxy: happier, sunnier – more relaxed. Sue stared as TV-Roxy started a set of dizzying head rolls. So what was the difference? What made young Roxy so natural and carefree? Sue tried to concentrate.

Well, normal Roxy's hair was long and white-blonde, and tumbled down her chest like an old scarf. And it had lots of curls at the end and looked like it hadn't been brushed. But TV-Roxy's hair was short and flippy – cute like Meg Ryan in *You've Got Mail*. It was blonde – but more golden than white – and it was held in place with a bright, sparkly clip. And then there was the make-up. Yes, TV-Roxy *was* wearing make-up, but not in the same quantity as normal Roxy. And Sue felt bad for even thinking it, because time was kind to no woman . . . but TV-Roxy's skin was perfect! Bright and radiant and luminous, and not in the least bit orange at all. And TV-Roxy's smile! How much prettier Roxy looked when her teeth were, well . . . *tooth*-coloured.

'And lift the shoulders!' TV-Roxy grinned. 'And keep 'em there for ten.'

Surely Roxy could look like that again, Sue thought as she hoisted her shoulders to her ears. It wasn't as though Roxy was old. Her skin was probably still just as radiant under all her make-up. If she'd only wear her hair up a bit more so everyone could see her pretty face . . . And maybe teeth-bleach wore off after a bit.

TV-Roxy was cheering.

'You've done it, girls!' she whooped. 'Session over! Now hit the shower, be gorgeous and meet me back here tomorrow! I'm Foxy Roxy, and remember – it's just twenty-nine more days to a foxier, funkier you! And, if you're going to G and T, make it slimline!'

She winked and the credits rolled.

Sue stared at the screen for a moment. TV-Roxy was gone. The DVD was finished. And suddenly it hit her . . . *Roxy's DVD was finished!* Which meant she, Sue Bunce, had done a whole fitness workout! She couldn't believe it. It had been her first bit of exercise since Lord-knows-when and it hadn't been *too* terrible. Admittedly, her face felt hotter than a three-bar fire . . . but she'd survived.

Buoyantly, she headed to the kitchen for a glass of water, trying to gauge whether her bottom was already tighter. She opened the cupboard, reached for a glass and was about to turn on the tap when . . .

There he was again . . . standing at the end of her drive! His face broke stiffly into a smile and he was just lifting his arm up to wave . . .

Sue dropped to the floor in panic.

It was Terence!

Had he seen her? He was the *last* person she wanted seeing her like this – hot and sweaty in an old, saggy tracksuit.

What on earth would he think? Had he seen her tummy bulging over her waistband? Had he seen her hair stuck to her neck?

But what was he doing out there? He *couldn't* be waiting to see her. Had he dropped something again? Maybe there was a ridge in the pavement outside her house that kept making him trip? Or maybe he'd stopped to take a phone call and had just hung up the instant before she'd seen him.

And where on earth, she puzzled hardest of all, did he get that gorgeous new coat?

ROXY

Although Roxy had lived in Lavender Heath for seven whole years, she'd never made it as far across the village as Hawthorne Close. Hawthorne Close was the very last road in the village and not what estate agents called 'optimum location'. But this morning was different. Des res or not, she pulled out her phone, downloaded a map app, and set off.

As Roxy whizzed down Gates Green Road, along Chestnut Avenue and into the High Street, her head buzzed with plans. She was a glass-half-full kind of girl and, as she'd whipped off her Wonder Woman pyjamas that morning, she'd determined to put Woody behind her. Industry was the answer. Industry was *always* the anwer. And besides, this helping-out-the-group stuff was fun. She'd only thought of charity work as a career-boosting opportunity before (TV-friendly stuff involving poppies, Pudsey or cute, plucky grannies recanting stories of dancing with GI's = good; mental illness, infectious diseases or dribbly, incontinent grannies holding your hand very tightly and not letting go = not good – and, actually, a little bit scary . . .). Not that Roxy was anti old people – she had a monthly direct debit to Age Concern – it was just, despite the rest of the world thinking she was a top-volume loudmouth, old people could never hear her. She knew she should talk slower, louder and repeat everything *ad infinitum*. But talking slowly didn't come naturally and life was too short for repeats. So, when it came to old folk, Roxy was uncharacteristically quiet, self-banished to the sidelines like a miniskirted lemon.

But this kind of charity was different.

This kind of charity was cool.

It was as if coming to the rescue of beleaguered micro-celebs was her vocation. She liked it! It made her feel good. After all those years of attacking her career like the *Total Wipeout* assault course, it was a relief to think about others for a change. And, bit by bit, she was sure she was making progress. Sue was looking for her diaries and Terry was practising scales. Slowly but surely they were dragging themselves out of their ruts. And today it was Holly's turn to get the Roxy treatment. She couldn't wait to see her face when she explained!

Distractedly, Roxy stepped off the pavement to pass the gaggle of paps huddled by Austin's gates. She strained her eyes as she peered through Sue's hedge. Was Woody doing Sue's windows today? She was dying to know what he thought of her strategies. Why hadn't he called? She'd sent the email thirteen hours ago – surely he must have read it by now! She'd half expected to find him on her doorstep this morning, rendered speechless by her career-resurrection genius, awestruck by her out-of-the-box plans. She fought off her disappointment and pushed on.

A few minutes later she arrived at Hawthorne Close and scuttled up its pavement to find Holly's house. She stopped at number fourteen. It wasn't a typical Lavender Heath home – it was semi-detached, for a start. And whilst the place wasn't overrun exactly (the grass was cut and the windows were sparkling), there was a definite air of neglect. The paint on the door was peeling and the window box was crammed with rotting flowers.

Roxy felt a sudden surge of sadness. Poor Holly, looking after her ill mother. How epic she was to dedicate herself to her care. If the stiletto was on Roxy's foot, she knew she wouldn't be up to the job. So, if Holly didn't fancy Mahiki, fair enough. She didn't have to go out to have a good time – she could stay in! And Roxy had just the solution . . . She'd spent ages researching home spas, and everything was already paid for. She'd found a masseur who did home visits – plus a hot-stones specialist, reflexologist, mobile hairdresser, home-stylist, make-up artist and a manicurist-on-wheels who promised the best mani-pedis outside of zone one. All Holly had to do was name the day.

Beaming excitedly, Roxy knocked on the door.

And waited.

And knocked again.

And waited some more.

Eventually a small, wizened lady answered.

'Yes?' She peered at Roxy suspiciously, her extraordinarily lined face rumpling, confused.

'Hello, Mrs Childs.' Roxy beamed and tried to speak extra

loudly, suppressing the urge to recommend a good night cream. 'I'm Roxy – Holly's friend. Is she in?'

'Who?' the old lady replied shrilly, her forehead furrowing further.

'Roxy; I'm Roxy. She must have mentioned me?' Her smile became a little unsteady. She'd only met the old lady a few seconds ago, but already she was beginning to feel like that lemon.

'*Loxy?*'

'*Roxy!*'

'Yes; no need to shout, dear; I heard you!'

'Oh.' Roxy awkwardly shifted her weight. 'Well, is Holly there?'

'Holly?' The woman looked confused again.

Roxy raised her voice even higher. 'Your daughter!'

'My daughter? Here?'

'I just want a quick word. It won't take long.'

'Don't be silly.' The old lady looked at Roxy as though she'd said something crazy. 'Holly's in the Shetlands.'

'The Shetlands?'

'Up north,' Mrs Childs replied bluntly. 'But you should know that. You're her friend.'

'Of course!' Roxy laughed quickly. She slapped her hand on her forehead ostentatiously. If old folk needed loud talking, they probably needed big gestures too. 'I forgot! Brain like a goldfish!'

'Fish? In your drain? You need to get a man around about that.'

'No, my *brain*! Like a goldfish! Never mind.'

'Only comes back at Christmas,' the old lady grumbled. 'And not every Christmas, at that. Lavender Heath's too busy, she says. *Too busy!* She always was selfish, that girl.'

Roxy's grin wavered. Holly had to be the least selfish person alive. And why was the old girl banging on about Scotland? She was as nutty as a bag of dry roasted. She'd have to come back when she was napping. Either that, or nab Holly when she was out in the village.

'Is there anything I can get you, Mrs Childs?' Roxy shouted kindly. 'Some milk or a newspaper, perhaps?'

'Milk? Don't be silly!' the old woman scoffed. 'Holly brings me that.'

'Holly . . . Right; of course,' muttered Roxy. 'Look, don't worry! I'll send her an email,' she added loudly.

'Right you are, dear,' the old woman replied. 'And spuds and curly kale.'

The front door promptly closed.

Roxy let out a deep breath.

Damn! Plan A thwarted – for now. She headed back down Holly's mum's path, to the pavement. But then she delved into her bag, fished out her phone and typed in a new postcode. Directions to Cressida's house popped up. And Roxy set off back into the village, ready to action Plan B.

ROXY

'Hell's bells, Simon; this is *delicious*!' Cressida waggled her fork ecstatically at the slice of carrot cake. 'Really, Chelle; you should try some!'

Chelle recoiled as though burned. 'A moment on the lips . . .'

'Is what?' Cressida scoffed. 'Oh, for heaven's sake; live a little!' She inched her plate towards Chelle.

Sat on her sofa, Roxy groped for serenity. But it was hard. It was now twenty hours since she'd emailed Woody the strategies – *twenty whole hours* – and not a dickie bird! Even *if* Jennifer had just come home, it was no excuse. He'd arrived late and had sat next to Holly, so Roxy hadn't even been able to ask if he'd read them. *And* it was just three hours to go 'til bloody Valentine's. And, *bollocks* – that carrot cake looked good! So, with an iron will, Roxy dragged her eyes over to a happier sight – the results of Plan B: Cressida's hair. There were no two ways about it – Cressida's new barnet was a hairdressing triumph. She'd been shocked at how little resistance the former Secretary of State for Work and Pensions had shown to a chestnut rinse and pair of curling tongs. Maybe Austin's Vidal Sassoon comment had hurt. But still, no pain no gain, and the autumn waves took years off her.

Serenity restored, Roxy relaxed. But then the armchair grunted.

The autumn waves swivelled.

'Did he just snore?' Cressida asked incredulously.

The group eyed the shambolic sight of Austin Jones slumped in Roxy's armchair, Chelle on sexy stand-by to the side. He looked – if it was possible – even worse than last week. His beard matted, his hair was greasy and there was a crusty stain on his shirt.

'He definitely *looks* asleep,' whispered Sue.

'He's an actor. He could be acting asleep,' Terence hissed.

'Well at least he's being no trouble.' Woody shrugged.

For a few moments everyone watched Austin's gut rise and fall as he slept.

'Anyone thinking what I'm thinking?' Terence asked evilly.

'What?' Chelle blinked. 'Thinking what?'

'That maybe Austin didn't quit Hollywood, after all?'

Holly gasped.

'What?' Chelle's head swung from one to the other. 'What? I don't get it!'

Terence gave a thin-lipped smile. And then he wrinkled his nose. 'Is it just me, or can everyone smell him?'

The room collectively inhaled. There was a definite whiff of BO.

'Well, that's a turn up for the books,' smirked Simon.

Chelle screwed up her face. 'That's minging.'

'For goodness sake, Roxy,' Cressida cried, wafting her airspace with a napkin. 'Haven't you got any air freshener?'

Roxy shrugged. 'I normally squirt the radiator with perfume. Makes the house smell mint. Want me to get some?'

'*Yes!*' everyone cried.

Roxy rummaged down the back of her sofa, pulled out a bottle and doused the room in Obsession.

Terence pointed at Austin. 'You'd better do him as well.'

'Really?'

'*Yes!*' everyone cried again.

Roxy crept up towards Britain's highest-grossing box-office star, aimed at his armpit and squirted. Austin Jones grunted, sneezed and then fell back to sleep. The group squeaked with silent laughter. Even Chelle afforded a smile.

'He'll smell like a tart's parlour,' Terence gleefully predicted. 'No offence, Rox – *you* smell great.'

Roxy settled back on to the sofa, zoned out the cake and smiled. It was a rare moment of group unity – and it felt ace! Maybe Woody hadn't read the strategies, but it didn't mean she shouldn't get cracking. And with everyone so happy and relaxed, wasn't now the perfect time to lob them a few pearls of her wisdom?

'OK, gang . . . It's time we stopped fannying about and said hello to the bloody big elephant in the room.'

'What elephant?' Chelle looked over her shoulder.

'*Reality TV!*' Roxy cried out with passion. 'And what it can do for you.'

The room collectively groaned.

'No, really, guys. Pick the right show and it's complete career rejuvenation! Just look at Myleene, and Widdy, and Andre.'

'Andre who?' Cressida asked with a frown.

'*Peter* An— Oh, it doesn't matter. The point is, reality TV can make you. You just have to get the right show.'

Suddenly Simon sighed, right from the bottom of his diaphragm. 'I can't believe I said no to *Big Brother*.'

'You were offered *Celebrity Big Brother*?' Roxy goggled him, amazed. *CBB* was seriously big league.

'Another classic Drennan career choice,' he said glumly. 'I'd give my right arm to do it now – even on Channel Five.'

'Some dweeb phoned to offer me *Wife Swap*.' Terence frowned. 'I thought he was taking the piss!'

'*Celebrity Love Island* offered me six figures.' Holly looked up from her minutes.

'And I said no to *Who Do You Think You Are?* And *Celebrity Masterchef*, and *Dancing On Ice!*' Simon continued morosely.

'I was asked to do *Strictly*,' piped up Sue. 'Do you think I should have done it?'

'*Bloody hell*, Sue; *yes!*' Roxy choked.

'But I don't know how to dance.'

'That's the whole point!'

'I got offered *The Salon*,' Chelle joined in through a mouthful of gum. 'And *Most Haunted Live*, *Celebrity Coach Trip* and my very own version of *The Bachelor*.'

'*The Bachelor Hunter*?' Cressida asked tartly.

'*The Bachelorette*,' Chelle replied with a frown.

Roxy was speechless. Even Chelle had had offers!

'What about you?' Holly asked Woody. 'The TV bookers must have been fighting to get hold of you.'

Woody rubbed his head. 'I think I've been approached by them all. I said no to everything, of course. Apart from the *Pop Dinosaurs* comeback tour. I quite fancied that. There'd have been a whole bunch of us has-beens in a crappy old tour bus, playing pubs and eating at Little Chefs. It could have been a laugh.'

'Don't talk to me about bookers.' Cressida put down her plate with a scowl. 'That jungle-show woman was a pest. She called every day for six months. I'd a mind to report her for harassment.'

Roxy's mouth fell open. '*You* were offered *I'm A Celeb*?'

'That's the one!'

'But why didn't you do it?'

'Because I am not a "celeb".'

'Fuck!' the armchair declared. 'I *knew* I'd seen your arse!'

Everyone turned with a jump. Austin had woken. And he was staring right at Roxy.

'I knew I knew you!' He grinned. 'You're the bird that got a colonic! I saw it, live on TV!'

Everyone gasped.

'Bloody hell, Roxy!' exclaimed Simon.

'A colonic?' Chelle momentarily broke off from pouting at Austin. 'What, where someone sticks one of them pipes up your—'

'*Yes!*' everyone cried out again.

Roxy swallowed hard. This wasn't quite the pearl of wisdom she'd intended. As a rule, she didn't believe in regrets – but the colonic was the exception. Her mum had cried for a week, her fan mail had halved and her agent had actually fired her. Roxy looked around the room, apprehensive. Everyone was staring, appalled. She didn't dare look as far as Woody – God knew what he thought of her now.

'It was terrestrial TV; Friday night,' she offered limply.

There was a long pause . . . incredibly long. And then Cressida frowned. 'Was it a medical experiment?'

'A desperate bid for fame, more like,' someone muttered.

'Oh, Roxy.' Sue looked at her sadly.

But Simon scratched his head. 'Did it work?'

Roxy laughed, awkward. 'In a deep-cleaning sense?'

He looked sheepish. 'In a fame sense.'

'Um . . .' Not even *she* could blag this.

Austin sniffed. 'Bloody good telly though,' he said loudly. 'I laughed my cock off!'

'Not quite the reaction I'd hoped for.' Roxy managed a weak smile.

'Still . . .' Austin yawned and stretched. 'I've got to hand it to you – you've got balls, Feisty! You've got to be brave, desperate or retarded to have a shit on TV.'

He stood up and wandered into the kitchen. A few moments later there was the sound of Roxy's fridge opening.

Roxy had never understood the expression 'praying for the ground to swallow you up'. Not until now, that was. And, sitting on her sofa – with Woody quieter than a sound-proofed coffin in a graveyard vacuum, all her new friends mute with disgust – Roxy offered up a plea to the gods. And then she offered up another to the goddesses of the golden triangle. But even Liz, Debs and Mossy had gone AWOL.

And then she heard it: a farty-sounding snort. And she looked up and saw Woody's shoulders beginning to shake.

'Are you . . . ?' She stopped herself dead. *Surely not. Surely Woody wouldn't be . . . ?* But the shakes were getting bigger, the farty snort sounds louder, and Woody looked as though he was biting his lip.

'Oh my God; are you *laughing* at me?' she demanded.

And then it came – loud, unmistakeable and infectious . . . a huge, gurgling Woody guffaw.

'Yes!' he managed between snorts, tears starting to roll from from his eyes. 'I'm sorry, Rox, but a TV colonic?' And then his whole body convulsed in a bellow.

'OK, so it wasn't one of my better moves . . .' she said crossly. How dare Woody laugh at her? At least she'd been being pro-active. At least she hadn't been sat waiting for the phone to ring. At least she'd been *doing something* about her career! But Woody was really going for it – holding his sides, his gorgeous face creased into an expression that was halfway between pleasure and pain.

'I've never heard anything so . . .' he managed to squeak out between convulsions.

Roxy folded her arms. 'Go on – say it,' she said tartly. '*Desperate!*'

'. . . *insane!*'

And now the others were sniggering too. And the sniggers were turning into laughter, and the laughter into hoots.

'Oh, come on, Roxy, admit it: it *is* funny!' Holly giggled.

'You're as driven as a bus!' Simon roared.

'You're mental!' Chelle grinned through her gum. 'I'd never show anyone my bum. Not without photo approval.'

Roxy looked around her. Everyone was in fits of laughter. But they weren't laughing unkindly. For years, the colonic had haunted her. She'd got such stick about it from the papers, such disgust from her family and friends that it had never occurred to her it was actually funny.

And then she just couldn't stop herself – a smile began to play on her own lips.

'Yes, yes. As career choices go, I agree it was shit,' she admitted, and everyone howled all over again.

'But that's why we need to talk about reality TV . . .' she insisted as the room started quietening down. 'So you don't make the same gaffes as me.'

'I'm so glad I didn't do *Strictly Come Dancing*,' Sue said thankfully, wiping a tear from her eye.

'*Strictly* would have been an *excellent* move,' Roxy assured her. 'As reality TV goes, it's the best!'

'It is?'

'Lordy, Sue!' Cressida recovered her composure. 'All you have to do is waltz around in a frock. It's not like being parachuted into the jungle and buried in a box of rats.'

'Rats?' Sue clutched her cup of tea to her chest. 'Oh, I don't like rats.'

'I wonder if I've still got the number for *Wife Swap*.' Terence mused. 'Maybe I should call them back.'

'You'll need to find a new wife first,' Roxy reminded him.

'Rats, snakes, scorpions, fifteen million viewers . . .' Simon raised his eyebrows at his own stupidity. 'And *I* chose a season in panto. Barrington should have forced me into that jungle at gunpoint.'

Terence leant towards Sue. 'I don't suppose you can remember the name of that contact at *Strictly*?'

'I love *I'm A Celeb*!' bubbled Chelle. 'I can't wait for them to ask me – I've already bought the bikinis.'

'Fuck!'

The smell of Obsession was back. In their mirth they'd forgotten about Austin. But he was leaning against Roxy's wall, quietly taking it all in. 'Tell me something . . .' he said slowly. 'How did you lot end up in Lavender Heath?'

Everyone fell silent. The only sound was the scratching of Holly's pen as she diligently took down the minutes.

'Austin . . .' Woody's voice was loaded with warning.

'No, seriously, I'm curious . . .' Austin pushed on. 'The tabloids might make out I'm out of touch with reality, just because I don't drink with bricklayers, or know how much a pint of sodding milk is, but I've not disappeared so far up my own arse that I've missed the fact that Lavender Heath's an exclusive kind of village.'

Roxy was about to pipe up about her 2000 calendar paying off her mortgage, but Terence opened his mouth first.

'What's your point, Austin?' He brushed a carrot-cake crumb off his stomach.

'My point, *Rain Man*, is *exclusive* means *rich*. Exclusive means having enough money to keep the right kind of people in and the wrong kind of people out. I may not have a degree in economics, but I'd bet my house on the fact that none of you lot have earned money in years . . . Apart from Woody, of course, who, for some crazy-arsed reason, has decided to pick up pocket change peering through married women's bedroom windows . . . Oh, and Kenny Branagh here –' his eye fell on Simon – 'who wears tights for the kids at Christmas.'

'And this from the man who's a stranger to a bathtubs?' Terence muttered.

'You guys aren't has-beens,' Austin said simply. 'You're never-weres.'

'*Austin!*' Woody growled.

'What? A man can ask questions, can't he? And my question is this: how the fuck can you McNobodies afford to live in a posh corner of real estate like Lavender Heath?'

'Oh, that's just charming,' Terence muttered.

Woody put down his drink. 'I think it's time I took you home. I'm not sure group activities are your thing.'

'Oh, group activities are *definitely* my thing.' Austin grinned wolfishly at Roxy, his Hollywood magnetism suddenly switching on. He moved to the sofa and sat next to her, his hand resting on her thigh.

Roxy gasped, oblivious to Chelle's angry tut. Again, all logical thought about Austin disintegrated – the beard, the rudeness, the overpowering smell of ladies' perfume – all forgotten against the power of his superstar pheromones. *Austin Jones was touching her thigh.* And not just the bottom of her thigh, either – the bit that was right up the top! She knew she should move away – people were watching; *Woody* was watching – but she couldn't. She was paralysed by the electricity emanating from Austin's fingers, surging through her whole body, firing up her libido and heating up all her rude bits.

'I keep getting flashbacks of your arse.' He grinned. 'I like a girl who's up for anything. Fancy seeing in Valentine's with a poke from *my* pipe?'

Roxy gasped yet again. She knew she should slap him, but for some reason her arms seemed glued to her sides. All she could feel were his fingers on her thighs and their tantalising burn on her flesh.

'Hey, Suga!' Austin heckled Sue. 'What was that trick you used to get up to with Hunt? I've never been able to look at a tube of smarties the same since. And I've fulfilled all my boyhood fantasies, *except one*.' His fingers started climbing Roxy's thigh. 'So, what d'you say, Feisty? Why don't we give this lot something to *really* talk about.'

Woody jumped up – expression unreadable.

'Right; that's it, Jones – we're going. And no –' he heaved Austin off the sofa as he turned to protest – 'it's *not* open for negotiation. Next week, everyone, let's meet in the Dog and Duck.' He slapped Austin's back. '*You're* not invited.'

'A public house?' Cressida straightened up. 'That could be fun.'

The room erupted into chatter and everyone got to their feet. The meeting was over. And just as everyone started pulling on their coats, there was a quiet voice in Roxy's ear.

'Be careful with Austin.'

She turned. Woody was standing close behind her.

'I think I can handle Austin,' she said tersely. She'd forgiven the others for laughing at the colonic, but she couldn't quite bring herself to forgive him.

'Can you?' His eyes searched her face for an answer.

'What's your beef with Austin, anyway?' she grumped.

'There's no beef. I just don't want you getting sucked in. He doesn't think about the consequences of his actions. He breaks things.'

Roxy laughed. She was about to tell Woody she wasn't daft, that she wasn't gullible enough to be flattered into submission, that she'd met enough megastars to know the person they loved most was themselves – and that there was no way on earth Austin could ever break her heart. But then she stopped. *Surely Woody can't be jealous?* He certainly looked uptight. His face was closed and unsmiling. And suddenly Roxy realised she *wanted* him to worry.

'My private life is none of your business,' she declared tartly, and then deliberately turned back to the group.

Everyone was discussing the pub. Cressida was already phoning ahead to book them the upstairs room for their meeting.

'It's a great chance to show off the duck egg,' Roxy quickly told Sue.

'Sugatits in duck egg?' Austin raised a salacious eyebrow. 'In which case, count me in!'

Cressida rolled her eyes. 'For goodness sake, Woody, take that oversexed imbecile home.'

'Come on, Jones.' Woody gave him a prod. 'You've outstayed your welcome.'

'Me? Impossible! I'm number one on the Netmums fantasy shag list.' But a moment later Austin had been bundled out of the door.

For a split second Roxy's house fell silent. And then, just as she was trying to work out how she could possibly explain to the group why she hadn't walloped Austin's wandering hand into next week, there was an unexpected explosion, stage left.

'He's such an ungrateful, undeserving *bastard*!' Simon was suddenly puce. 'He doesn't *care* that Richard Curtis begs him to be in his films, or that Cameron and Angelina fight over being his co-star. He doesn't have a clue what it's like to have *nobody* fight over being your co-star, to have *nobody* beg you to be in their film – *or* their series, *or their bastard CBeebies mime show* . . . And, as for anyone offering him an ad . . .' He started to cackle manically.

And then, as quickly as his outburst had started, it stopped. His body mass suddenly halved.

'It's all right, Si,' Roxy said, and he limply sagged into her shoulder.

'It's not fair, Rox.'

'I know,' she said. And she did.

It was time to put the strategies into action.

To: Roxy Squires

From: Biddington Hospital Radio

Hi Roxy,

WOW!!! I never expected to get an email from FOXY ROXY! It really made my day (What am I saying? It made my year!!!!). I've always been a fan, from way back, when you got fined for saying the F-word on kids' TV (classic!!!). And I've bought every single one of your calendars since 1997! (BTW, have you done any calendars recently? I've looked everywhere, but haven't been able to find anything post 2002 . . .)

But back to the point . . . RADIO! Well, I never knew you fancied the move into radio. It's a cracking idea – you'll be BRILLIANT! But I had a word with my boss (small man – very narrow minded) and the idiot only said no! He reckoned 'hospital radio isn't a place for any Tom, Dick or Harry to try their hand at broadcasting'. Obviously I told him you're not just any Tom, Dick or Harry – that you're one of the best TV presenters Great Britain has ever seen, and that your series of interviews with A-listers in toilets is legendary, but he wasn't having any of it. But I think you would have been brilliant cheering up the patients . . . a real shot in the arm (boom, boom!).

But WOW! Stay in touch, yeah? It would be great to have a real celebrity friend. Maybe you could pop in and sign your old calendars? (Although, sorry – the May and October pages for 1997 are a little bit, um, water damaged.)

Sue woke with a start. A noise had penetrated her dreams, a noise that sounded like . . . feet, *on her driveway*. She checked the clock at her bedside . . . 6.05. Her stomach filled with fear. It was too early for the postman, but someone was definitely there. Who'd come into her garden so early? And why? Terrified, she forced herself up. She crept over to the window, took a deep breath and peeped out. Nothing. Her garden looked quiet and peaceful. Heart beating wildly, she inched out of the bedroom to the landing.

As soon as she reached the top of the stairs she saw it . . . An envelope on her mat. She let out her breath. So it *had* been the postman, after all. With relief she headed down and picked it up. But then she frowned. There was no stamp or postmark. It must have been hand-delivered – but by whom? And why now, so early in the morning? Worriedly, she opened it and then gasped. Inside was a card – red and shaped like a heart.

Simon grunted and sleepily rolled over. Eyes closed, he groped for the alarm clock and its deafening, set-to-stun sound.

'Shurrup!' he mumbled as his fingers sought the right button. 'Shurrup!'

His hand landed on the tiny knob in the corner and the clock reset to snooze. Simon rolled back, almost asleep again already. But then something stuck to his cheek. Blearily he reached to unstick it. His eyes creaked open. Linda had already left for work, but she hadn't forgotten. She'd left her mark on her pillow. Smiling, Simon opened the card.

* * *

Under the eyemask, Chelle was completely unconscious. Her mouth was open and there was the faintest purr of a snore. She was totally unaware of the single red rose being placed on her doorstep.

ROXY

As starts to Valentine's Day went, this one particularly sucked.

As per her new routine, her phone had started chiming at six. She had thirty minutes to caffeinate, throw on some make-up and squeeze herself into her gym kit. Roxy tried not to think about the significance of the day – today was just Friday, like any other Friday, and she was merely about to go jogging with her pop-star window cleaner . . . *What could be more normal than that?*

She threw herself into some stretches.

The knock came at the door and she pulled it open to greet Woody. She swallowed the (fleeting) disappointment that he was brandishing a bottle of water, not flowers, and reminded herself that Woody was merely her business partner – and that any flowers he might brandish wouldn't be at her. He could stick his sodding flowers, anyway. She could still hear his laughter from last night.

'We should go faster today,' she declared stiffly as their feet started their now-familiar rhythm on the pavement.

Woody looked at her in surprise, but she kept her eyes locked firmly ahead. She stepped up the pace to *cracking*.

Yes, work is the key, Roxy told herself as she tried to regulate her breathing. All the hearts and flowers of the day were just a crappy distraction. Blokes came and went, but careers were with you forever. Roxy's one true love had always been work. Yes, she, Roxy Squires, was Mistress Of Her Own Destiny, Girl Power General, a Lieutenant in the Army of Ladette. Only muppets moped over a card. Real women threw on their heels, set their brains to Beyoncé, and powered off to their mega-bucks jobs.

And this morning's jog was part-and-parcel of that. She'd gym-dodged too long, she decided. TV was a fat-free zone and presenters got skinnier by the day. Goji berries couldn't do it alone (she knew; she'd tried). She *had* to exercise and it *had* to hurt. That coffin-dodging rake Jane Fonda had been right all along . . . if there was no pain, there was no gain. If she wanted to get hired, she had to feel the burn. She gritted her teeth and ran faster.

'All right?' Woody asked as he matched her suicidal pace.

'Fine,' she barked, ignoring the pain in her calves. 'So,' she asked tersely, 'did you get my email?'

'Ah!' Woody smiled. 'The strategies.'

'Yes, the strategies,' she snapped. 'The ones I've been working on – have you read them?'

'Yes, I read them.'

'And?'

'And I think they're great . . . in theory.'

Roxy narrowed her eyes. 'And in practice?'

Woody ran a few steps before answering.

'Rox, are you sure fame's what they all need? I mean, *really need*?'

'Why are you sure that it isn't?'

'I—'

'I mean, what makes you so bloody sure about everything?' Suddenly she was properly angry. And not just that he'd ignored the strategies for thirty-one hours and twelve minutes – or that he'd laughed at the colonic, or seen Austin turn her on, *or that it was yet another bloody sodding cardless cocking Valentine's.* She was angry about 'gorgeously natural' and 'pretty low maintenance' and 'Hi, baby; when are you back?'

'I'm *not* sure about everything,' he replied calmly. 'I just think what suits *you* might not suit everyone else.'

'So you reckon they're all better off now? Feeling bitter, and sad, and like failures?'

'No . . .'

'That Cressida should fade away into incontinence and Sue should hole up at home with the biscuits?' She was suddenly furious. Who'd given Woody the monopoly on being right?

'But that's why I'm trying to help,' he protested. 'To make them see they have friends, and opportunities, and *other* ways to be happy.'

'And why is your brand of happy OK, but not mine?'

'I'm not saying that.' Woody rubbed his head. She could feel him looking at her but she doggedly kept looking ahead. 'I'm just saying *your* way might not be their way. Sue and

Holly are fragile. Falling out of nightclubs won't make them happy.'

'So you don't reckon Simon'd jump at the chance to get back on telly? Or Terry wouldn't pimp out his own granny for good press?'

Woody hesitated.

'You think I'm shallow, don't you?' she bludgeoned. 'You think that, just because I want to be famous, I'm stupid and shallow and an airhead.'

'I don't think you're like that at all!' he cried in exasperation. 'I think you're ballsy, and brave, and bloody barking.'

'God, you're so sodding *sanctimonious*!' she exploded before she could allow his two compliments to seep in. She didn't want compliments – she wanted his head on a stick. 'Just because *you* don't want to be famous, doesn't mean *we* can't want it. Just because *you* couldn't hack it, doesn't mean *we're* not built that bit stronger.'

'Roxy—'

'The only person too fragile for fame is *you*! You wussed out, Woody, and you know it. You had it all and you bottled it. And now you're hiding in Lavender Heath, just like the others – but you're worse than them because you're a liar. You pretend to be happy, but you're bricking it. You're just another washed-up failure, too frightened to give it another go!'

'Christ, Roxy! You're so bloody wrong!' he exploded. 'Listen to yourself! You're not thinking about them – you're thinking about you. You're bullying everyone back into the spotlight because that's where *you* want to be!'

'And you're holding everyone back!' she yelled. 'Don't make *me* out to be selfish. You're a bloody hypocrite, Woody. You want everyone to live *little* lives – just like you!'

Fuming, Roxy sprinted on. What she really wanted was to leave Woody far behind her, but they were hurtling in the direction of home, so there was no point in turning away. Plus, their pace was already scorching; physically, she couldn't run any faster. So the silence deepened and lengthened, with just their ragged breath and fast, angry feet to break it.

Finally Woody spoke. 'I'm just a bloke,' he said, his voice tight.

'You don't say!' Roxy snorted, still angry.

'I fart, and I hog the remote, and I forget people's birthdays . . .'

'And your point is?'

'Just see things as they are, Rox – not how you want them to be.'

Roxy growled at the sky in fury. 'You're a man. You're rubbish. I get it.'

They ran the last hundred metres in silence. As they arrived at her house, she stopped. There wasn't a cat in hell's chance of Woody suggesting breakfast. Not that she'd go, anyway.

Woody stopped too. They both panted hard on the pavement.

'Look, Rox, about the strategies . . .' He touched her arm but she brusquely shrugged him away.

'Your hands are rough,' she mumbled accusingly.

'Occupational hazard.'

He held up his hands and for the first time Roxy saw they were cracked and dry.

'They look knackered,' she said harshly, before turning on the heel of her trainer and marching into her house. She slammed her door behind her, shutting the world – and Woody – out.

She stomped up her hallway, raging. How dare Woody say she was selfish? After all she was doing for the group! *And how bloody dare* he make out she was out of touch with reality? *She* wasn't the one with her head in the clouds . . . it was *him*, perched at the top of his ladder. She was the most in-touch-with-reality person in the village . . . *wasn't she?*

And then suddenly it came – fast and deadly – and the barricade that had confined all of the nagging voices broke down . . . *Was* she out of touch and deluded? Was that why the TV companies wouldn't take her calls? Why didn't Woody want her? Why did all her emails start with 'no'? Why was she single, *again*, on Valentine's Day? Where was her life going? Where was her career going? Did she even *have* a career any more?

Roxy gritted her teeth.

Why wasn't life better?

She closed her eyes and slumped on to the stairs.

Everything had started so well. She and Tish had been the hottest girls in London. Everyone wanted them: newspapers, party organisers . . . hot boys in bands, with skinny trousers . . . the secret gang of showbiz fairy godmothers whose sole purpose was to search out stars and give them free stuff. Life was a whirl of fun. But then the axis of cool had shifted. The change was so tiny, Roxy hadn't even felt it. But one day she'd turned around and the free-stuff fairy godmothers had vanished and the boys in bands had moved on and, somehow, somewhere, a cool party was happening that she didn't know about. Tish got married and Roxy was on her own, the wrong side of the velvet rope – the magical pool of TV work slowly, imperceptibly seeping away. It wasn't fair! *She* hadn't changed – not much. OK, the clothes, hair and make-up had evolved a bit, but that was fashion. At her core, she was the same as she'd always been. If anything, she'd only got better! She was blonder, thinner and had even whiter teeth; her tan was deeper, her lashes thicker. She'd kept up with new music, still knew every premier-league score from the weekend and she could still pull a bloke in skinny jeans if she had to. Hell, she was two dress sizes thinner! *She'd been hungry for nine years.* NINE WHOLE YEARS! All that willpower, gritted teeth and starvation . . . All those mealtimes with just a bowl of cherries to sustain her in the hope that, one day, another Friday-night Channel-Four job would come knocking.

Roxy opened her eyes.

She was starving.

Not just slightly starving . . . absolutely, totally, utterly, insanely, eat-her-way-through-a-Tesco's-delivery-truck *famished*. Images of Simon's cakes swam before her . . . all that calorific temptation she'd so desperately wanted to gorge on . . . the cheesecake, the French fancies, the cinnamon doughnuts! She closed her eyes again as she tried to blot out the vision of carrot cake. Her mouth watered. What had she been so frightened of? It was carrot cake – how bad could it be? *It was made from bloody carrots!*

Roxy stood up.

She scrambled down the hall, into the kitchen and to her larder. That was it . . . nine years of restraint was enough. *She was bloody well going to eat, and she didn't give a shit what the golden triangle said about it!* Manically, she rifled through her groceries, scattering boxes of cup-a-soup in search of something with calories. But her larder was a fat-free zone. Undeterred, she ransacked the fridge, tossing aside the mangetout and endless bags of spinach, desperate for *anything* with more than 0.1 per cent fat . . . a chocolate bar, an egg custard – hell, even a full-fat yoghurt! But there was nothing.

'Carrot cake!' Roxy yelled to the empty kitchen. 'I must have carrot cake!'

The kitchen was silent.

'Sod it!' she swore with a surge of girl power. She would not be thwarted. It was as if the last few years of set-backs and rejections had stacked into a mountain – and she was *damned* if it was going to grow a single millimetre higher. She was going to have her cake and there wasn't a single thing life could do to stop her from sinking her face right into it. 'I'll bloody make one!' she vowed with a snarl.

She'd done home economics at school. She'd baked cakes. OK, so it was twenty years ago, but how hard could it be? All she had to do was chuck together some carrots and butter and stuff, and bung it in the oven. She ran upstairs, pulled off her gym kit and – without bothering to shower – threw on an outfit and heels. And then she surged back downstairs, grabbed some money and checked the time on her phone: 7.48am. Mint! The village shop opened at eight. She'd google the ingredients on the way.

She steamed along the road towards the High Street. As she marched, she could see a bunch of paps loitering by Austin's ahead. For a moment, she considered stopping, ringing the buzzer and seeing if Austin had been serious about that poke from his pipework. Hell, why should Valentine sex be just for the loved-up? She could do with a pick-me-up bonk, and Austin was the dictionary definition of filthy shag. But she didn't slow down. Cake trumped sex and, besides – it was five to eight! Austin would be sleeping, like any other borderline-sex-pest Hollywood heart-throb. And, as much as an X-rated romp with Austin Jones might make her feel better, scaling his gates to get it might not. She knew his type . . . all innuendo and no trousers.

She powered on.

The village shop loomed into view with its promise of full-fat butter, demerara sugar and artery-thickening cream cheese. Roxy's mouth watered again. All she could think about was cake . . . sinking gum-deep into criminally calorific cake.

But suddenly she stopped.

Forty feet ahead, right outside the village shop, two women were ensconced in a tête-à-tête. And not just any old tête-à-tête: a girly tête-à-tête. They were standing very near to each other, their voices low, their faces so close they were almost touching. One of the women was nodding and rubbing the other one's back. The other woman was upset. Clutching a rose, her cheeks glowed with a colour that could be high emotion or NARS Super Orgasm blush. The woman with the cheeks was Chelle. And massaging her back was Holly.

Roxy stood for a moment, paralysed. She should move, keep walking, say hello. But something kept her rooted to her spot. What was it? Nosiness? Suspicion? *Jealousy?* Roxy was winded by a pang. Something stirred, deep inside her. Buried beneath a scattered pile of messy nights out was a set of memories of moments like this . . . when everything would stop as she and Tish spilled out whatever tiny thing was bothering them and together they put the world bang-to-rights. As Roxy stared, she tried to swallow the unexpected envy she felt. She shouldn't feel jealous of Chelle! Chelle was thick and vacuous and totally the wrong shade of orange. Chelle was a celebrity-husband hunter, on a mission for her next designer-clad millionaire with a magazine cover thrown in.

And yet, Chelle had Holly and her sympathy.

And suddenly the tête-à-tête was over. Before Roxy could blink, the two women had swept into a double-parked Aston Martin, fired the engine and roared off. Roxy pulled herself back to life and stumbled the last few steps to the shop. There was serious business at hand . . . Carrot cake was on the menu for breakfast.

SUE

Nine down (seven letters): To overcome, suceed.

Something, something, *E*, last letter *L*.

No matter how hard she tried, she just couldn't concentrate. She'd been doing the crossword for an hour, but couldn't get further than nine down. Her attention kept wandering from the black and white squares on the paper to the red heart on the worktop. She had a Valentine's card! She hadn't had one since Jeff and, even then, he'd forgotten at least two of the three years they were married. Sue resisted going over and picking it up and, for the thousandth time since breakfast, she racked her brains as to who could have sent it. She'd have sworn it had been put through the wrong letterbox, but the name 'Sue Bunce' had been scrawled on the envelope.

She was still puzzling nine down when the doorbell rang. The delivery-man was standing on her doorstep, yet another Hobbs parcel in his hands.

'We must stop meeting like this,' he said, and then winked.

Sue almost did a double take. Had the delivery-man just flirted with her? She was sure that he had. Could *he* be the one who'd sent her the card? But before she had the chance to talk herself out of the possibility, he thrust his electronic pad forward.

Clutching her parcel with one hand, she numbly scribbled her name.

'Keep shopping!' He tipped his cap, grinned and turned away. And that's when Sue saw him: Terence – at the end of her drive – *again*.

Even from a distance she could see him colour slightly, before lifting his hand up to wave. She froze, suddenly nervous, her package tight to her chest. Three times he'd been there now. Even *she* knew the statistical likelihood of Terence having dropped something three times in the same spot was nigh on impossible. But why was he there?

The delivery-man receded down the drive, whistling loudly.

'Lovely morning for it,' he called to Terence as he crunched past.

'Um, yes; lovely,' Terry coughed. 'Apart from the north-easterlies, of course.'

And then the delivery-man was gone, and it was just Terence and Sue, standing awkwardly at opposite ends of the gravel.

There was a pause.

'Would you like a cup of tea?' Sue hesitantly called over.

Terence cupped his hand to his ear.

'I said, WOULD YOU LIKE A CUP OF TEA?'

'TEA? YES – FANTASTIC!' he hollered back. 'I MEAN, THANK YOU. THAT WOULD BE VERY NICE.'

Another moment passed and then, as if remembering his legs, Terence lurched into action and walked towards her.

Sue was shocked. She'd never seen him self-conscious before. He was always so assured at the meetings. She turned into the house to spare him the embarrassment of being watched. Nervously, she fluttered in her hallway. Should she wait for Terence here, or in the kitchen with the kettle on? She'd never been on her own with Terence before, and she panicked. Should she just say hello? Shake his hand? *Kiss his cheek?* And then she remembered the heart-shaped card on the worktop and she whizzed into the kitchen and stuffed it into a drawer.

'That's the thing about north-easterlies,' Terence announced loudly as he entered the kitchen, stiff-limbed. 'You can never be sure they won't bring rain.'

Sue nodded uncertainly, unable to think of a single appropriate reply. Terence was wearing that nice coat again. It was even nicer close up . . . soft-looking; like it was cashmere.

'Sugar?'

'Oh, no, I'm watching my . . .' He patted his stomach. He stood ramrod straight as Sue boiled the kettle.

'I'm not stalking you!' He suddenly laughed tightly.

'Sorry?'

'By standing at the end of your drive. I know it probably looks like I am, but I'm not – stalking you, I mean. Obviously I *am* standing – or I was.'

'Of course!' agreed Sue, confused.

The kettle turned itself off with a click. Gratefully, Sue turned away and poured hot water into the teapot.

'Please, Terence; you're making me nervous,' she said over her shoulder. 'Would you please sit down?'

'God – sorry!' Terence jumped into a seat. 'I didn't mean . . .'

Happier now that he was seated, Sue carried the tea (PG) and biscuits (custard creams) to the table. She'd always thought Terence was a custard creams man.

'The thing is . . .' he said suddenly. 'The thing is, there's something I've been meaning to ask you.'

'There is?'

'And each time I got here, I kind of . . .' He looked at Sue hopefully, willing for the penny to drop. '. . . *chickened out.*'

'Oh!' Sue nervously picked up a biscuit.

'Sue, would you come to the pictures with me?'

'The pictures?' Sue's cheeks fired with shock. She put the biscuit back on the plate.

'A week next Tuesday.'

'Umm.'

'As friends, of course. I didn't mean—'

'Of course! I wouldn't presume . . .' she reassured him, suddenly feeling a bit flat. 'It's just that . . . I'm . . . Well, I'm . . .' How could she explain that going to the cinema wasn't something she did?

'Busy, of course,' he surmised. 'It was silly of me, really, to expect . . .' He stood up. 'Right, well, I'd better be leaving. I'm sorry to have wasted your time.'

He was about to head for the door.

'But your tea. It's only just brewed!'

Terence looked for a moment and then abruptly came back and sat down.

There was another awkward pause: a very long one.

And then Sue heard herself break it.

'What were you planning to see?'

'Hmm?'

'At the pictures, next Tuesday?'

'Do you know – I don't even know.' He ran his fingers through his hair, embarrassed. 'It's just, I think Roxy left me these tickets, and it's in London – a premiere, and I've got no one else to ask.'

'Oh!'

'I mean, obviously you're my *first* choice.'

Sue didn't know what to say. The whole conversation was rather perplexing.

'Anyway, you're busy. And that's perfectly fine. It's just that . . .' He tailed off again, lost.

'A premiere?' Sue asked. 'With crowds, and photographers, and a red carpet?'

'Yes. I thought it would be exciting, but the more I think about it, the more it sounds—'

'Frightening.'

He nodded.

They both stared at their tea.

'She says it would be good for my profile,' Terence said after a moment. 'She says I need to get out of the "weatherman zone"; let people see me in unexpected locations.'

Suddenly Sue felt sorry for him. Beneath the new coat, he looked like the wall of his chest had just crumpled.

'I'll give the tickets back,' he determined.

'Is that what you want?'

He went quiet for a moment. 'I know the thought of going to a premiere is, well . . .' He shrugged. '*But what if she's right?* I can't stagnate in Lavender Heath for the rest of my life; I'm still a young man!' His middle-age spread wobbled earnestly. 'I don't want my life to be over already. And it's not as if the meteorological broadcasting fraternity is beating down my door to beg me to come back. I know Woody says fame isn't everything, that we need to work out what we want to do with the next stage of our lives; but what if what I want *is* to be famous? What if I *want* to be back on TV – to be recognised, and respected – to actually have things to *do* in a day? Does that make me a terrible person?'

He stared at her, waiting. Sue realised her answer was important. 'No! No, it doesn't!' she said. And it didn't. Just because *not* being famous was right for her and fine and dandy for Woody, it didn't mean it was right for *everyone*. And Terence obviously needed his old life back. He certainly wasn't happy without it.

'I know she's loud and orange and wears seasonally-inappropriate clothing,' he continued, 'but Roxy's the only person who's actually helped me. Not that I'm saying . . . Well, you all – Woody and everyone – obviously *you guys* have helped me. Actually, you've all been kinder to me than anyone I can remember. But Roxy's the only one who's helped me *get back*.'

Sue nodded, thinking of all the little ways Roxy had helped her too: the duck egg, the hair tips, the girly chats over shared pots of tea . . . It wasn't as if *she* wanted to be famous again, but she realised that she did feel a bit better about herself lately. It was as though Roxy had given her a piece of her old self back.

'I'll do it!' she suddenly declared, making Terence's teacup rattle in its saucer. 'I'll come with you, to London!'

'To the premiere?'

'Yes!' she cried before she could talk herself out of it. Already she felt a bit sick. What was she saying? She hadn't been to London for years. She'd have to get the train. And there'd be people – crowds and crowds of people. And cameras. *And people.*

'You'd really do that?' Terence asked. '*For me?*'

Sue looked at him. How different he seemed, with his new clothes and honesty. She watched his face as excitement pushed aside the bitterness and blurred out the frown lines. He looked rejuvenated, exhilarated . . . *happy!*

'Yes. Yes, I will,' she confirmed. She tried to ignore the fact that her whole body was screaming for her not to. She felt tense from her toenails to her eyeballs. But something made her say yes. After all – she tried to be rational – she *did* have a dozen new outfits to wear, and it was pointless having them if they never came off the hanger. And Terence had looked so wretched when he'd thought she was busy. Besides, she'd only be there as moral support. Everyone would be looking at him. Surely she'd hidden long enough to be forgotten by now?

'Thank you, Sue; thank you so much!' Terence cracked with relief. 'You're amazing!' And, beaming broadly, he stood up to leave.

Sue picked up her tea and tried to relax enough to sip. She felt a hundred different things, but amazing definitely wasn't one of them.

'It's "prevail", by the way,' Terence smiled.

'Hmm?'

'Nine down,' he pointed at the crossword, half finished, next to the teapot. 'Seven letters; something, something, *E*, last letter *L*. "Prevail".'

SIMON

'Help!' cried a voice on the doorstep.

Simon opened the front door and there was Roxy Squires.

'Please, Si,' she begged as she shivered in the February air. Clutched to her chest was a Union Jack tin. 'You're the only one who can!'

Thrilled to be needed (it wasn't every day his assistance was beseeched), Simon let her in. There was something even wilder than usual about Roxy today – and it wasn't just the Lilliputian proportions of her clothing. Of course, she was dressed more for the Balearics than for Britain and had managed to leave home without a coat . . . but that wasn't it either. Roxy always looked like she'd just fallen out of bed, but normally it was in a wanton kind of way. But today she looked like she really *had* just fallen out of bed. Her eyes were wide, her expression frantic and her eyeliner was smudged so low it could have doubled as goth blusher.

He ushered her into the warmth of his kitchen.

'What's the problem, Rox?'

'This!' She thrust the tin into his chest.

Gingerly, he peered inside.

'You see, I had this urge . . . this *uncontrollable urge*. And it was because of you – well, your cakes – and suddenly I was hungry; I mean, *really* hungry – like I could rip the head off a passing chicken, or stick up a garage for its Kit Kats. And then everything went funny and my mouth went dribbly and all my food morals went out the window . . .'

'So you baked a cake?'

Roxy made a weird noise – somewhere between a sob and a snort.

There was a moment of silence.

'May I?' asked Simon. Carefully, he opened the tin, broke off a tiny chunk and popped it into his mouth. Roxy winced.

'Not bad,' he said kindly. 'Carrot?'

'You can tell?'

'Of course – it's a good cake! All the basics are there. The balance of flavours is great. The only thing wrong is that it looks like—'

'Shit! It's all right; you can say it. It's a steaming great pile of cake turd!'

'It looks like you put a bit too much oil in,' Simon finished gently. 'Carrot cakes are tricky – much harder than sponge or fruit. It's hard to get the sunflower oil right. I'm guessing you didn't measure the oil out right and then couldn't get the mixture to smooth.'

'You see!' Roxy cried, her face suddenly alight. '*This* is the stuff I need to know! You're right; it was an oil-fest – total

Ann Summers stuff. God, Si, *please* will you help me? Will you teach me how to make cake?'

'My pleasure,' he answered lightly, and Roxy squealed with joy. He tried to hide how chuffed he felt. The twins were more interested in mastering their Xboxes than learning their dad's skill of baking. He couldn't believe he'd have a pupil – a *willing* one – at last! 'Although, really, this is a very good effort,' he told her. 'Other than a few presentation and decoration tricks, there won't be much I can teach you.'

'Can we start now?' Roxy did the running man in his kitchen. 'Now?'

'I don't see the point in long engagements – you might see me without my make-up and call it off. So, anyway, I took the liberty of bringing the ingredients. I want to beat this baking bollocks and then I want to eat carrot cake for dinner – all of it – nothing else; not even a dressing-free side salad.'

Simon hesitated. The kids had after-school clubs and it wasn't as if he had any scripts to learn. There was no point pretending he was busy – he wouldn't be busy for months. And Roxy seemed *so* keen . . .

'Right,' he magnanimously acquiesced. 'We'd better get to work.'

Roxy whooped and tipped her ingredients on to the counter. Simon switched on the oven and reached for his pinny, before quickly stopping himself. Normally he'd never dream of sieving icing sugar without an apron, let alone beating in sunflower oil – but then, normally he didn't bake with an apprentice . . . and certainly never with a TV-presenting, former free-shag-pass apprentice. Not that he fancied Roxy any more; he'd told Linda the truth. But he'd be lying if he said it didn't give him a larger than medium thrill to know that he, Simon Drennan, was about to give a personal, baking master-class to a former number twenty-three on the *FHM* chart of babes. Expectantly awaiting his bidding was a ladette – a woman whose name was forever prefixed in print by the word 'foxy' – someone the world best knew slathered in baby oil and dressed as a PVC air-hostess. Simon cleared his throat and wondered if he could get Roxy to call him 'Chef'.

Fifteen minutes later the carrot cake was nearly ready to go in the oven. The carrots had been grated, the fruit zested and the nuts folded into the bowl. Roxy was a surprisingly diligent pupil, carefully listening to his instructions – even tapping the key points into her iPhone. She hadn't even raised an eyebrow when Simon had been unable to resist any longer and had finally tied on his apron. He was enjoying himself more than he had in years. And, as Roxy obediently double-lined the base of the tin, he realised he hadn't felt this good about himself for ages. The daily struggle to master his career felt like walking a flimsy plank, but here – in the kitchen – he could stride on solid ground. Like Gordon Gekko on Wall Street, or Bond in a Monte Carlo casino, behind a mixing bowl, in a pinny, was where Simon Drennan was king.

'Just do it!' Roxy instructed as they weighed the butter for the cream-cheese frosting. The delicious aroma of baking already filled the room.

'But it's funeral insurance!' Simon protested, surprised. He'd never expected Roxy to tell him to do Barrington's ad. He thought she'd tell him to shove it up his—

'Just take the money and run. I would.'

Simon looked at her incredulously. Surely she, more than anyone, would lambast him for stooping so low? 'But what if anyone saw it? I'd have no credibility left at all.'

'Credibility's overrated,' she said dismissively. 'And, besides, everyone does ads. What about Clooney's Nespresso?'

'Yes, but George Clooney's George Clooney. He could open an Aldi and look cool.'

Roxy frowned. 'And doesn't Ewan McGregor do ads in Japan? For kilts, or beards, or something?'

'Again – it's McGregor,' Simon countered glumly. 'We're not exactly comparing like for like.'

'Oh, rock off!' Roxy cried, disgusted. 'Honestly, Simon, you need to bitch up and be confident. You're every bit as good as McGregor, you berk. You could have done *Star Wars* – easy. You just weren't in the right place at the right time. And, let's face it, you were *epic* as Sick Nick.'

'I was?'

'Monumental! You scared everyone's keks off *and* you can do panto. I bet McGregor'd chop off his exhaust pipe to be as versatile as you.'

'But it's for funeral insurance, Rox – it's so *unsexy*.'

'So? Everyone's got to pay the mortgage. I've done more crap ads than you've made hot dinners.'

'You have?' Simon was taken aback. He didn't know Roxy had done any adverts – let alone crap ones. Surely the only

kind she'd do would be for fast cars or intoxicating per-
fumes?

'Didn't you know you're looking at the voice of Britain's
top-selling high-absorbency solution for bladder weakness?'
she batted her lashes flirtatiously.

'I am?'

'Not to mention that cream for lady itches . . .'

'Crikey!'

'Easiest money I've ever made. Ninety minutes in a voice-
over studio and, six years on, they're still paying repeats.'

Simon was stunned. 'You're still getting paid for work you
did *six years ago*?'

'Mint, isn't it?' she laughed. 'I'm telling you, Si, ads are
cool! And besides, didn't Ridley Scott do ads?'

Simon nodded numbly.

'Bread, wasn't it? *Unsexy* sliced? See! Your funeral-ad director
might be tomorrow's Ridley Scott! Think what a tit you'd be
if you turned him down.'

Simon thought for a moment. She had a point.

'What's all this about tits?' A voice cut across the kitchen.
Simon jumped. Linda was standing by the door. Simon couldn't
help it – he blushed. Luckily Roxy didn't notice – her mobile
was bleeping. But his wife certainly did.

'Linda, hi! You're home early. We're just cooking. Cake. Carrot
cake. See?' And he pointed at the peelings on the counter.
Suddenly he was aware of how hot the oven was, how discreet
Roxy's top wasn't and how a big smear of icing sugar had
somehow smudged itself across her left breast.

Linda raised an eyebrow and looked over at Roxy, who was still totally engrossed in her phone.

'Fucking hell!' she declared. '*Jesus Christ!*'

Linda and Simon exchanged glances.

'I don't believe it. I don't rockin' believe it! I've got a job!'

'Congratulations,' Linda said politely. 'Hello, I'm Linda. You must be Roxy Squires.'

Roxy looked up, her eyes shiny and filled with excitement. 'Hi, Mrs Drennan. *I've got a job!* Filming tomorrow! *A job!*' And she whooped in frenzied delight.

'Tomorrow? That's a bit short notice,' frowned Simon. But Roxy was too ecstatic to hear. She enveloped him in a barrage of kisses so forceful he nearly fell over.

'Steady on, I'm a married maaa—'

But Roxy *had* already moved on and was now crushing his wife to her chest.

'I've got a job!' she sang out ecstatically. She span round and round the kitchen, with Linda forced to spin in her arms.

'Well, that's great, Rox.' Simon scratched his head as he watched his wife rotate. 'But you've always got jobs. You're fully booked 'til Christmas, remember?'

'Yeah.' Roxy stopped dead . . . Dizzily, Linda sank into a chair. 'But this is a *job*! Christ, *there's so much to do!*' And she flung her belongings into her handbag and hurtled out into the hall. 'Oh – Si; cheers for this afty!' She popped her head back and winked at his pinny. 'It's been epic! Nice to meet you, Mrs Drennan!' and she hurtled out again.

'But what about the cake?' Simon called after her.

'That piece of crap? Give it to your dog!' Her voice echoed along the hall.

'Not that one; the cake we're still making! The one you're having for dinner!'

'Give that to your dog too – it's not like *he* gives a monkey's about wide-angle lenses!'

The door slammed and there was the crunch of stilettos on gravel as Roxy rocketed away up the drive.

Simon looked at his wife and messy kitchen.

'But we don't have a dog,' he mumbled aloud.

To: Roxy Squires
From: Mungo Elliott, Cool Britannia TV

Roxy, you old tart! I hear you're still touting your wares . . . Wanna job? Got something right up your alley. New channel . . . 'Cool Britannia'. Retro stuff – does what it says on the tin. Look-back documentaries – Tony Blair with fluffy hair, Robbie off his face, social historian wankers bleating on about the importance of the Spice Girls . . . blah, blah.

I'm exec producing a show, *When D:Ream Ruled The Waves* – 're-examining the giddy days of Britpop . . .'. Interviews with all the usual bastards . . . Noel, Damon, Jarvis, that bird whose naked arse was blown up on the houses of parliament . . . yawn. Need a presenter to string it all together. Fancy it?

Just a day's filming – tomorrow. Some old studio cupboard in Camden. No need for stylist / make-up – just wear whatever it is you're passing off as clothes these days. Fluffy tops, skirt belts . . . Just keep it decent, for Christ's sake – no *Basic Instinct* stuff.

Will get some infant assistant to email the script. They're younger than ever these days. Am working with a bunch of effin' embryos. Half of them still not in long trousers. Let's get shitfaced sometime, like grown-ups . . . Make our livers bleed and pretend it's the old days. Presenters now so bloody boring. Most too busy opening their chakras to open a bottle.

M

Rarely, in the history of high heels, have a pair of Louboutins moved so quickly.

At exactly 2.39pm on a damp, grey Valentine's Friday, the fastest thing Lavender Heath had ever seen on two legs exited a driveway on Cherry Blossom Drive, hurtled towards the post office, and turned left at the Dog and Duck pub. Every few seconds, heel scraped metallically on pavement – but it was barely heard by the shoes' owner above her own heavy breathing and issuings of the words 'ROCKIN' EPIC!' At precisely 2.41pm the Louboutins made a sharp right into Chestnut Avenue, scuffed loudly against the wobbly sixth paving stone (still unrepaired by the council, despite Mrs Barrington-Stanley's written complaints), turned left into Gates Green Road and zipped up to number eleven. The door slammed loudly, causing birds in the trees to start. And then peace was reinstated. Order returned to the village.

* * *

Now that she was home, Roxy didn't know what to do. She paced around her kitchen, flushed and breathless, ready to erupt with glee.

She had a job!

She was going to be back on TV!

ROCK AND ROLL!!!

She laughed out loud. She *knew* TV would come begging, if she could just keep the faith. And her career second wind had just gusted. Cool Britannia would be just the beginning . . . Once everyone saw her back where she belonged – on the box, interviewing rock stars and stuff – they'd *all* see the light. Producers the length of London would stare – flabbers gasted – wondering how they'd managed *not* to book Roxy Squires for their last eighteen jobs. And then there'd be a whoosh – so enormous that actual wind would blow across Soho – as hands simultaneously reached for phones to dial Roxy's number . . . And then a groan, as deep as thunder, as all the two-bit agents who'd told her she was 'just too millennium' dropped their heads on their desks and wept.

'I'm back!' Roxy roared to her empty kitchen. '*I'm bloody back!*'

And then nothing . . .

Her smile froze.

What now?

How should she celebrate her news? It seemed weird

opening bubbly alone – and besides, if she was filming, she should probably detox. So, what else . . . ? Instinctively her hand grasped her phone. She knew who she wanted to tell. The person she most wanted to share her news with was *him*. She wanted to see his eyes sparkle – his face burst into that big, dazzling grin that made her tummy flip and her chest go as fizzy as cola. She wanted to see him light up with happiness as he took her in his arms and whirled her around and around in celebration over the career break she so obviously deserved.

'Arghhhh!' Roxy growled. Was there anything in the world more frustrating than having just had a barney with the man you most wanted to speak to? Oh yes, she remembered – there was. *It was that man already having a Jennifer.*

She gritted her teeth. This wasn't a day to feel down. This was *exactly* the Valentine's she'd wanted – a CV-changer! And if she couldn't celebrate with Woody, then she'd celebrate in the next best way she knew how . . . with a frantic bout of shopping and a good hard tweet. Roxy zoomed into the hall. Yes, virtual friends and shopping – that was the solution. After all, Mungo had said to wear her own clothes and, despite having four wardrobes bursting with outfits, she was sure she didn't have quite the right thing. A quick trip to London was called for; just her, her credit card and Westfield . . . plus a pit stop on the way home at the Tanning Shop. After all, her drunken self-tan had nearly faded back to mere orange and she couldn't rock up at Camden a ghost. Not now she was going to be on TV! *Not now she was back!*

2.48pm @FoxyRoxy

To all the lily-livered talent bookers who lost my number – grow a pair! Mungo's got bigger whatsits than the lot of you!

2.50pm @FoxyRoxy

When D:Ream Ruled The Waves? *Roxy Rules The Waves*, more like! Stand back everyone; it's time for another surfs-up!

2.54pm @FoxyRoxy

No, I am not drunk!!! Just high on success, people . . . *high on success!*

To: Roxy Squires

From: Quercus Publishing

Dear Ms Squires,

Thank you for your email detailing two outlines for non-fiction manuscripts you'd like us to publish.

First, it is with regret that we inform you that, whilst your idea for the self-penned volume *1001 Ways To Party (And Still Be At Work By 9)* is interesting, it isn't suitable for our list at present.

However, your idea for a 'warts and all' memoir of Suzi 'Sugatits' Bunce is something we are very keen to pursue! Can you organise for us to meet Ms Bunce and discuss this further? However, prior to meeting, there were a couple of points in your email that puzzled us . . . Firstly, is Ms Bunce your legally signed literary client? And secondly, is the author actually in agreement that she *wants* her story told?

ROXY

Despite her vow to have an under-eye-boosting early night, Roxy was still up and flicking through the TV channels. She couldn't remember being nervous about a shoot before. In the old days, she'd always been too busy. She'd just learn the script and head off to party. If anything went wrong, she just blagged it. But this time everything was different. This time she had to be perfect.

She eyed her Cool Britannia script and tried to stay calm. She was pretty sure she'd learnt it word-perfect. It hadn't been hard – it was short. They must be keeping it lean for her interviews. She looked at her new shoot outfit, hanging up on the door. It was perfect – fantastic – she knew it! But still she felt freakily frightened.

She grabbed her phone. It rang twenty-three times before being answered.

'Um, timing?' Tish's voice sounded sarcastic. There were restaurant noises behind her. With a cringe, Roxy remembered the date.

'Romantic nosh-up with the Guy-ster?'

'Top table at Nobu.'

Despite sounding peeved, Roxy knew Tish was pleased. There was no point having the top table at Nobu if nobody knew you were there.

'Sorry, Tish – it's just I've got a major shoot tomorrow and I was thinking . . . Why don't we hook up afterwards – paint the town red, like the old days? We could knock back the sambucas, throw a few shapes and pass out with kebab on our faces.' Roxy paused for the squeal of delight. But she could only hear chopsticks on china. 'Or we could glam up, wear black and sip the night away in a posh cocktail bar; let Guy think they're non-alcoholic . . . ?'

'Rox, babe, you know I'd love to. But it's Seraphina's school play.'

'That's OK. What time does it finish? Seven?'

'Eight.'

'Eight's perfect! The shoot probably won't wrap 'til then. That'll give us both enough time to glam up, hop in a cab and meet in the middle.' Again, Roxy waited for the squeal. Again, it didn't come – just mutterings from Guy about boundaries. 'Come on!' She tried to entice her. 'You're always moaning you never go out; here's your chance. I'll drag Mungo out too, if you like?'

'Mungo Elliott?' Now she had Tish's attention. 'That old cokehead? Isn't he extinct with the rest of the dinosaurs?'

'He was the one who got me the job. Didn't you pick up my tweets? He's executive producing the show. It sounds as if he's practically running Cool Britannia single-handed.'

'Running it into the ground, more like. Didn't he get fired from every TV company he worked for?'

'Did he?' Roxy tried to think back. 'I just remember him being a good laugh. And he's got amazing shows on his CV.'

'From the last millennium,' Tish snorted. 'He's been travelling ever since 2000.'

'Travelling? Cool! Where's he been?'

'Nowhere, silly. Nobody travels when they say they've been travelling. They only go as far as the Priory. *Excuse me; are you sure that water's been* triple *purified*?'

Roxy was shocked.

'Mungo's been in rehab?'

'Does Russell Brand like sex?' Tish scoffed. 'Mungo's recession-proofed the industry.'

'Oh!' Roxy felt stupid. 'I didn't know.'

'How could you have *not* known? I'm not even on the circuit and *I* know.'

'Well, let's not invite Mungo then,' Roxy said hurriedly, trying not to feel out of date. She could hear Guy telling Tish to hang up. 'Let's just keep it old school – you and me! And – who knows? – I'll be interviewing loads of the bands we used to hang with; maybe I could get a few of them to come out with us too.'

For a moment Tish sounded tempted, but then her voice slumped.

'I dunno, Rox. Guy's got a really early tee-off.'

'I'm not going to force you to have a good time!' Roxy laughed.

'Cheers, hun; I knew you'd understand. Ooo, that noodle salad looks *delicious*!' And suddenly Tish was gone.

Roxy put down the phone and tried not to feel hurt. She forced herself to look on the bright side. Yes, it was a bummer Tish was busy, but the crew would be up for a night out. No self-respecting TV shoot would dream of ending without an almighty piss-up – and given this was one of Mungo's TV shoots, the partying was bound to be epic. In fact, maybe it was best Tish couldn't make it. Everyone knew partying with the production team was the best way to get your next job – and Tish always did have a way of stealing the show.

Roxy hugged her knees to her chest.

It was no good . . . she still felt nervous. So she asked herself, *What would Mossy do, the night before a career-altering shoot?* A hot bath? A few calming fags? An all-night bender with a pickled Rolling Stone? Roxy sat back, breathed hard and tried to channel some Mossy.

7.21am @FoxyRoxy

Sooo excited! Big shoot today! Hardly slept a wink – too happy!
Am gonna kick serious TV butt + remind world

7.22am @FoxyRoxy

. . . (or rather media world, so butt-kicking refined to W1, WC2 &
small patch of Salford) . . .

7.23am @FoxyRoxy

. . . that ROXY is still FOXY! #ROXYSAYS: watch this space!

7.25am @FoxyRoxy

eek! Got 4 layers of Bobbi Brown to administer, funny chin
whisker to pluck + final coat of St Trop to slap on . . .

7.26am @FoxyRoxy

. . . AND I'VE NOT EVEN BREWED UP YET!!!

WOODY

'At last! I thought you'd forgotten!' said Cressida as she peered at the teen on her doorstep. 'Is this my gimp?'

'Wha—?' Euan freewheeled back in alarm.

'One gimp, as promised,' Woody replied cheerily. 'He's got an attitude to rival Piers Morgan, but his dad says he's great with his thumbs.'

Euan stared wildly and whimpered.

Cressida looked Euan up and down with a frown. Her gaze lingered on his high-top trainers.

'How old are you, boy?' she demanded.

'Fifteen.'

'Have you ever read a broadsheet? What's the IMF? What's the name of the Chancellor of the Exchequer?'

His eyes fell to his feet.

'Too busy playing computer games and frittering time on the internet?'

He gave a small nod.

'Perfect!' She stuck out her hand. 'Cressida Cunningham. Ms Cunningham, to you. And you are . . . ?'

'Euan,' he squeaked, his eyes beginning to water from her grip.

'Euan what?'

'Drennan.'

'Simon's son?'

'The very same,' Woody replied. 'And, despite his liking for herbal cigarettes, I think he might be just the young man that you're after.'

'Herbal cigarettes?' Cressida eyed Euan sternly. 'So your father's sent you here to be punished?'

For the second time that minute Euan whimpered.

'Not quite,' said Woody. 'Think of his gimping as community service. If he fails to put in the hours, he'll be putting in an appearance at the court of Mum and Dad. But I doubt it'll come to that. I'm sure you can whip him into shape.'

Euan made a noise like a choke.

'Hmmm.' Cressida looked less than convinced. But then she clapped her hands together with a crack. 'Well, don't just stand there like a wet blanket! Come in and make yourself useful.'

She turned and disappeared into the bowels of the house.

From the safety of the doorstep, Euan faltered.

'Go on,' Woody nudged him over the threshold.

'But I don't want . . .' Euan replied, more with fear than actual resistance.

'I know,' Woody agreed. 'But you're going to do it anyway. Like I said, think of it as an exchange. You could learn a hell of a lot from Ms Cunningham. Pay attention and she could be the making of you.'

'You can start with the coffee machine,' Cressida instructed brusquely from somewhere inside the house.

'You've got a coffee machine?' Woody was surprised.

'Oh, yes . . .' Her voice bounced down the hall. 'Now I've got a gimp, there'll be no end to my purchasing of gadgets. Euan, I have milk and one sugar, and you can have squash and a biscuit. And when you've made the coffee, you can set up my new i-telephone. And after that, you can teach me how to DDM.'

Euan inched reluctantly into the hallway, as though imminently meeting his doom.

'Go on,' said Woody. 'You heard her. It's time you made yourself useful.'

And as Euan inched in a fraction further, Woody closed the door and left him to his fate.

ROXY

It was no good. No matter how deep she dug, Roxy couldn't summon the golden triangle – not even the tiniest yellowy corner. After yesterday's shoot, even Mossy, it seemed, had disowned her – and everyone knew she had a soft spot for pariahs. Sighing, Roxy pulled her duvet even tighter around her and miserably contemplated her bedroom ceiling.

Was this what working in TV had come to? Maybe Tish had been right, after all . . . Maybe she too should have got out before the new generation had got in. Yesterday had made her feel sixty years old and six centimetres tall.

And then her ceiling began to get fuzzy. Roxy panicked and blinked like the clappers. This wasn't the way to go. Ladettes didn't do tears (unless they were at *Glee* and ironic). Ladettes didn't do wimpy, or self-pity, or Radiohead. Ladettes had a laugh, had a drink and got on with stuff. There was no point crying over spilt milk – or crap shoots. Yesterday was nobody's fault but her own. Roxy was a firm believer that, in life, you captained your own ship. That way, nobody could nick the credit when things were good. And if the good shit was all down to your brilliance, then the bad shit was down to you too. The trick was to avoid the bad shit in the first place. But after all this time, shouldn't she have developed a bad-shit radar? After all, Hurley had had her fair share of career ups and downs. But when the chips were down, would Liz have agreed to *When D:Ream Ruled The Waves*? Would she have signed up for a show where you had to buy your own wardrobe, make your own sandwich and do your own hair with a set of mouldy rollers in the corridor by the loo? No, she bloody wouldn't! Liz would *never* have contemplated a TV show based around a one-hit wonder, never have got out of bed without the guarantee of a hand-delivered Carluccio's (no bread) sandwich and would *never* have deigned to anything less than luxury rollers administered by a hairdressing god. Hell, Liz would never have even *read* Mungo's email – and Roxy never should have, either.

But . . .

Roxy couldn't help thinking . . .

But . . .

Was it *really* her fault? Was she *really* to blame for not knowing what everyone from the spotty runner to the bespectacled director took for granted . . . that Mungo was a washed-up, over-amphetamined used-to-be and that any casting suggestion to come from his direction, on the one day a month he was sober enough to make it to the office, was to be treated like a poo-filled grenade? Was she really responsible for this bad-shit decision? After all, she'd been between jobs for so long, she didn't have a clue that yesterday's shoot would be so epicly, buttock-clenchingly bad.

Roxy got out of bed and pulled on her leopard-print dressing gown. Caffeine – that was what she needed. Caffeine and the immediate onslaught of amnesia. She stumbled down the stairs to the kitchen.

Roxy listened to the sounds of the kettle cranking into life as she absent-mindedly wiped off yesterday's make-up with a washing-up sponge. It was no good, she decided. There was no point pretending *D:Ream* hadn't happened. She didn't need to wait for it to be broadcast for the world to know she was a pillock . . . Thanks to Twitter, she'd probably been a laughing stock from the moment the shoot wrapped. No, she was going to have to face this one out like a man. Or rather, a ladette.

She got out her phone and typed.

> **10.30am @FoxyRoxy**
>
> Bollocks. Think I might be the world's biggest tit. Was I the only plonker on the planet who thought *WHEN D:REAM RULED* was a winner? Ouch!

And then she frowned for a moment before typing . . .

> **10.32am @FoxyRoxy**
>
> PS: To all the TV bookers I slandered as lily-livered + small of testicle – erm, sorry about that . . .

> **10.33am @FoxyRoxy**
>
> . . . is clear the only pecker in the pack is me. #ROXYSAYS: SOZ!

And then, her fingers already whirring, she couldn't stop herself . . . She typed again. And then she put down her phone, drifted over to the larder and pulled out the ingredients to bake.

An hour later, the doorbell rang. Woody was standing on her doorstep.

'Rox!' He looked at her strangely. His grin was unusually absent. He was probably still cross about their fight. 'I got your text.'

'Great,' she said flatly. 'Come in.'

'You're not dressed.'

Roxy looked down in surprise. She brushed flour off the front of her dressing gown.

'I've been baking.'

'Right – OK. Well, I guess I'd better . . .' He held up his bucket between them.

Roxy stepped aside and then followed him into the kitchen. And, despite the *D:Ream* depression and the cut-with-a-knife tension from their tiff, she couldn't help but notice that, even from behind, Woody looked good: so fit, and firm, and strong. She suddenly realised she needed a cuddle so badly it had actually begun to hurt. Woody would give amazing cuddles. Not just warm and meltworthy and delicious, but strong and resolute too. He'd give the kind of cuddles that told you the world wasn't such a bad place and that everything would work out in the end because *he* thought *you* were worth cuddling.

'You missed our jog this morning,' he said.

'I had a late night,' she mumbled. 'I was working.'

He didn't reply. He just inspected her kitchen window with a frown.

'You know, I only cleaned your windows last week, and I'm pretty sure I didn't miss one. Are you sure one's dirty already?'

'Rancid,' she replied, too fast.

Woody fixed her with his infinite blue eyes. Roxy's breath went funny and she completely forgot the script she'd concocted in her head. And, just when she was on the point of confessing, Woody mercifully turned back to the window. 'Well, this one looks OK.'

'It's upstairs,' she said in a hurry. 'In my bedroom.'

He eyed the hallway warily.

'Courgette biscuit?' She held up a plate of warm baking. Despite the tension, Woody couldn't resist.

'Courgette?'

'I'm experimenting,' she brusquely replied, embarrassed at her display of domesticity. Showing him her biscuits felt as revealing as showing him her bottom (or worse: her birth certificate). 'The courgettes bulk up the biscuits, with none of the fat of butter.' She winced. It was the first rule of ladettedom; never discuss calories with a man (the second rule being to profess an unending love of beer).

But Woody didn't notice her gaffe. He picked up a biscuit and took a bite.

'Wow, Rox; these are *good*!'

'They are?'

'Are you kidding me? Are they seriously made from courgettes?'

'I'd never kid about vegetables.'

The tension dissolved around them.

'You know, this is pretty unique, Rox. I've never heard of courgette biscuits before and, trust me, in this job you get offered *a lot* of biscuits. But these are delicious!'

'As one door closes . . .' she mumbled.

'What d'you mean?' He looked at her intently. 'Come on, Roxy! What's wrong?'

She looked into his kind eyes and was paralysed. She'd wanted him here all along. She needed a friendly face . . . not just any friendly face – *his* friendly face. She'd thought about phoning her mum, but that would only have provoked a lecture on how she should have married someone nice before she'd blown all her chances by sitting in baked beans in a bikini and burping pop songs on national TV. And then she'd thought about calling Tish, but Tish would only have laughed, before telling her off for doing crappy jobs on crappy channels without stopping to think that maybe the non-crappy jobs on the non-crappy channels were totally out of her reach. Desperate, Roxy had even considered calling her brother, but had chickened out in case *she* answered the phone. Her sister-in-law still hadn't forgiven her for borrowing her daughters on the promise of visiting a museum, but whizzing them past the paparazzi at a *Harry Potter* premiere instead. Roxy's insistence that it had been educational had fallen on deaf ears and she'd been banished to sister-in-law Siberia. It hadn't been worth it. She hadn't even made it into the *Express*.

But as she stood in her kitchen, transfixed by the amazing aura of Woody's Woodyness, even just being in his presence felt good; more than good – *it felt right*. If she could only open her mouth and tell him, everything would instantly be better. All she need do was move her lips and the words would come out and he'd know how sorry she was for their fight; how she'd cocked up and made a mistake; how awful the *D:Ream* shoot had been; how she'd only been hired to present the show to be the butt of its jokes; how it had been her first TV job in years and how, once everyone saw it, it would almost certainly be her last.

But she stopped.

How could she possibly admit failure to this gorgeous, sexy, wonderful man – the man she most wanted to impress in the world; the man who made a happy, smiling success of everything from conquering the music business to life up a ladder with a squeegee?

'Nothing's wrong,' she stubbornly insisted.

There was a long moment of silence. And, for once, Roxy didn't fill it.

'Well –' Woody slowly rubbed his head, making Roxy's knees feel as though they might buckle – 'I'd better take a look at that window.'

She nodded and then stood for a moment after he'd gone, listening to him clanking his ladder. And then she walked up to the bedroom to dress.

Woody had been gone a long time. So long that Roxy could have made his tea several times over. As it was, she'd already

ransacked her wardrobe for an outfit, bundled herself into a
cupboard and dressed. She'd even had time to throw her hair
into a ponytail and whizz on a slash of lipgloss (nude, today,
not red). And now she was standing in her kitchen, grasping
the tea she'd made him in her favourite Chesney Hawkes mug.

'Hey, Rox; come out here for a sec,' she heard him yell from
outside. She found him next to his ladder, which was propped
up to her bedroom window.

'Wanna help?' he asked.

'Help? Why would I want to do that?'

'OK, I'll rephrase . . . *You're helping.*'

Roxy froze. Had Woody gone off his rocker?

'Come on.' He beckoned her over.

'What? Up the ladder?'

'I reckon you'll have your work cut out, cleaning it from
down here.'

Roxy stared, perplexed.

'Isn't the great Roxy Squires up for anything?'

'Yes, but—'

'Come on then.' He rattled the ladder encouragingly.

'I . . . I'm . . .'

'Chicken?'

Roxy hesitated, trying to think of a lie. But her motormouth
beat her to it. 'I don't like heights!'

'A ballsy girl like you?' Woody laughed.

'Everyone has their Achilles heel,' she said tightly. 'Besides,
you're the window cleaner. Why can't you do it?'

'I'll do it, if you do it.' Woody shrugged.

'But *why* do I need to do it *at all*?'

Woody raised an eyebrow. 'Why do *you* need to clean ground coffee off your *own* window?' he asked archly. 'Ground coffee that I reckon's only been there than an hour – and could only have got there at all if someone angled her hand out the bedroom window and splattered it over the pane.'

'Ah . . .'

'Rox, if you want to talk to me, you only have to ask.'

Roxy turned away in embarrassment. But there were only two directions to face: Woody or the ladder. The ladder won. She slipped her Ugg on to the first rung.

'Bloody hell, Woody!' she shrieked as the ladder buckled flimsily beneath her. She breathed deeply. 'If this is a ruse just to see up my skirt . . .' She tried to joke as she started moving upwards. 'Because, I'll have you know, these are leggings, not stockings, and they come with a crotch.'

'You're doing brilliantly, Rox.' Woody laughed. 'You're halfway there already.'

Halfway? Roxy closed her eyes and clung on. But then she heard the ladder creak below. Woody was climbing up behind her. And then somehow she'd miraculously made it, and she was nose to pane with her messy bedroom.

'Oh my God, you can see right in!'

'And that's surprising because . . . ?'

'But, you can see *everything*!' Roxy cried in horror as she peered through the coffee splatters. Her room was always a mess, but somehow, up a ladder, on the other side of the glass, it looked as though her whole house had been turned upside down and shaken.

But then she was suddenly overwhelmed by Woody's presence behind her. It seemed impossible! They were standing about a thousand feet above ground, perched on a creaky bit of aluminium in a force ten gale, and yet his body was right alongside hers, balancing in perfect equilibrium, the ladder suddenly as solid as a rock staircase. And he was touching her, but not touching her . . . His body pushed against hers, but was actually pushing her nowhere: separate but utterly with her at the same time. She could feel his heat up and down her back, feel his shelter as he cocooned her from the wind. She could sense his face close behind hers, his mouth, his lips . . . He was just centimetres away. It felt safe, protected, *exciting*. It was the most erotic experience she could remember (even hotter than that Meg Ryan/Marc Ruffalo DVD, where she was the lady rediscovering her libido and he was the moustachioed cop) and yet she and Woody weren't actually touching and everyone's clothes were still on. It was spooning, but up a ladder, in jumpers.

Shakily, Roxy exhaled.

And then suddenly, her hand was in his, and it was warm and wet and in a bucket. And, before she could even realise what was happening, she felt his fingers gently close her fingers around a sponge and guide them on to the pane. She felt tiny rivers of water course down her arm as, Woody's hand over hers, they rubbed circles across her glass. Roxy's breath left

her body and her bedroom disappeared behind a wall of soapy
bubbles.

'And rinse,' Woody said softly, returning his hand to the
ladder.

Numbly, Roxy plunged the sponge back into the bucket and
then obediently wiped the suds away. The window was clean.
But she could no longer see the messy bedroom; she could
only see Woody's reflection. And his reflection was making
her shake. What she really wanted was to stand there forever,
to tell him how she'd fancied him from the moment they'd
met, how his very presence made her warm up from inside
like Ready Brek, how every time she saw him she was rendered
almost limp with longing, just for the touch of his skin. But
she couldn't say all that . . . she didn't dare. So instead she
stared at the windowsill, took a deep breath and confessed to
the other thing she'd been hiding.

'It's crap. My career: it's crap.'

Behind her, Woody stood still. He didn't say anything, so
Roxy talked on.

'I did a job yesterday. Not one of my normal, made-up ones,'
she admitted, ashamed. 'A real job. And it was terrible. *I* was
terrible. The whole thing was completely humiliating.'

Gently, Woody let go of the ladder and placed his hand
back over hers.

'I thought I was . . .' Roxy faltered. 'I mean – I didn't realise
I'm . . . that people think I'm . . .' She swallowed hard. What
should she say? An idiot? A has-been? A laughing stock?

'It's OK,' Woody said gently.

'They didn't know who I was! The director thought I was a courier; he told me I'd got the wrong address.'

'Ah.'

'It was the *dregs*, Woody!' she cried. 'The job was the dregs, but I'd been so happy to get it.'

The first tear came. Roxy tried to blink it back but three more sprang up in its place.

'I don't think telly's what I cracked it up to be,' she said quietly. And then she dropped her head, closed her tears behind the walls of her eyes and said it: 'I think my career's over.'

Woody squeezed her hand and let his chest touch Roxy's shoulders like an embrace. 'It's all right, Rox,' he whispered. 'It doesn't matter.'

And standing there, hovering in the air outside her messy bedroom, clinging to a pair of rickety aluminium stairs whilst the career she'd fought her whole life for died around her, Roxy suddenly realised he was right.

Ladder-spooning with Woody, nothing else mattered at all.

To: Roxy Squires

From: The offices of Merchant & Gervais

Dear Roxy,

Thank you for your letter suggesting Ricky and Stephen consider Terry 'Tornado' Leggett for any future '*Extras*-style ventures they're writing'.

Whilst Ricky and Stephen currently have no plans to write any further episodes of *Extras* – or indeed anything that specifically suits Terry – they have said that they're aware of his infamous broadcasts, and they'd be happy to meet him for a drink.

Please don't take this as any guarantee of future collaboration. Think of it more as a 'chemistry coffee' to see if the boys all get on . . .

TERENCE

'Do you want to be famous again?'

'Are you on drugs?'

Standing on Terence's doorstep, grinning like she was plugged into the mains, was Roxy Squires.

'It's a simple question, Tezza – fame: yes or no?'

'Yes . . .'

'Rocking!' She beamed and waltzed right into his house.

Terence frowned and checked his watch. 'Why are you here? I wasn't expecting you. *And why are you so freakishly happy?*'

Ignoring his questions, Roxy pirouetted up and down his hallway, humming as she headed for the living room.

'I haven't got any tequila, if that's what you're looking for. I don't keep hard spirits in the house.'

'Who needs the hard stuff?' she chimed back. 'Life's wonderful enough.'

'High as a kite . . .' Terence declared to the walls. And then he followed her into the living room to find her studiously examining his chairs.

'Mega!' she declared as she selected an old, brown swivel

chair and wheeled it to the window. She beckoned Terence over. 'Come on, Tezza, park your peachies down here!' She tapped its seat invitingly.

On the far side of the living-room carpet, Terence stalled. 'Now look here, Roxy . . .'

'Nah, ah, ah!' She waggled a finger. 'You promised!'

'I know what I promised you, but . . .'

'But what? You know you want to.'

His buttocks clenched. 'I'm having second thoughts.'

'Forget 'em. Thinking's overrated.'

'And third, fourth and fifth—'

'You'll look a million times better.'

'I doubt that very much . . .'

'Terry . . .' She patted the seat again. And then she delved into her handbag and pulled out a shiny instrument of lady-torture.

Terence couldn't help himself. 'But it might hurt!'

'Don't be a tart. It's painless!'

Terence could tell she was lying. And yet somehow, against every atom of his sensible judgement, he crossed the room. A split second later, Roxy's hands were on his shoulders and she was gently forcing him down. As his bottom hit cloth, she sighed.

'You've literally no idea how long I've been dying to get my hands on these babies!'

'I don't want to look like that idiot Shane Warne,' Terence grumbled. 'I saw what he looked like after that Hurley woman got her hands on him.'

Roxy gave an injurious gasp. 'Fear not, my little storm cloud,' she said after a moment. 'You are going to put the "Met" into *met*rosexual. Once I've had my way with you, you'll be a new man: the kind of man women stop in the street to ogle; the kind of man whose career is going places.'

'But I'm *me*, Roxy,' Terence cried in exasperation. 'A walking, talking blunder on legs! As welcome as a cold front at a picnic; as predictable as rain at a Wimbledon final. I'm boring old Terence Leggett. Emphasis on the boring. *And* on the old.'

'No, that's where you're wrong,' she insisted. 'You *used* to be gaffe-ridden Terence, more obsessed with isobars than cock-tail bars. But now you're Terry. And Terry is a hot, tasty ladykiller.'

Terence sighed. 'Look, Roxy, it's not that I don't appreciate your efforts but, as the saying goes, you can't polish a turd.'

Something in Roxy's eye gleamed.

'Ah, but you *can* roll it in glitter, Terry,' she declared as she leant over him, lady-torture instrument in hand. '*You can roll it in glitter.*'

ROXY

'Tish! Thank God! I really need to talk.'

On the other end of the phone Tish sighed dramatically.

'You've seen it then?'

'Seen what?'

'Oh, come off it, Rox. You read the tabloids before you even open your eyes! You've *sooo* already seen it.'

Roxy frowned. *Sooo already seen what?* Her mind quickly scooted through the stories she'd been working on for the group.

'No, really, Tish; that's not why I'm calling. It's just, a really weird thing happened to me yesterday, up a ladder, and I really need your advice. See, my window was dirty and the wind was blowing and we held the sponge and I started crying and I know it sounds mad, but I think I might actually be in with a chance with Woo—'

'No bloody respect for my privacy! Honestly, I'm so embarrassed,' Tish declared, sounding anything but. 'All the school mums were just giving me daggers. How was I supposed to have known there was a photographer? I'd never have worn that vest if I had. It's not even Stella McCartney.'

'A photographer? On the school run?' Roxy was confused.

'No, stupid – at the yoga class. Well, on the way out of it. They can't think for a minute I set it up – I'd never do it in full daylight like that. And *never* with my hair pulled back! I could hear them all gossiping behind me – *and* it's PTA tonight. And Guy's gonna totally freak. Oh my God, you really haven't seen it, have you?'

'No, Tish, I haven't.'

'But you've read the tabloids, right?'

Roxy padded into the hall to retrieve the neglected newspapers.

'I'm on the Nicola Blunt page! Main photo – *in leggings*!'

Nestling her phone against her shoulder, Roxy picked up the *Daily Post* and flicked to the Nicola Blunt page. Sure enough, straddling the paper like a super-toned colossus was a very large (and very gorgeous) picture of Tish. 'DE-TISH-IOUS.', praised the headline. And beneath it was Tish, looking luscious, her yoga mat rolled under one arm. Her hair was tied back post-yoga, immaculately Cheryl Cole glossy. Her make-up was natural and understated. She looked a bit shiny, but not in a sweat-drenched-Madonna-leaving-the-gym-in-a-flat-cap kind of way, more '90s-Cindy-Crawford-working-out-on-a-Malibu-beach.

'But Tish, you look great!' Roxy declared honestly. She battled the twinge of jealousy trying to take root in her gut. *She'd* never made it on to the Nicola Blunt page; but Tish had without even trying.

'I look minging!' Tish replied with some force. 'A right wobbly-thighed munter.'

Roxy looked at Tish's thighs; they were as taut and perfect as Kylie's.

'Why me?' Tish moaned unconvincingly. 'I'm just a mum – I haven't worked in yonks. Not that being a mum isn't work, of course; I mean, I know I've got the nanny and the cleaner and the tutors, but there's always so much to be done. And I've been out of the game for ages – I can't believe the tabloids still care,' she cried, sounding as chuffed as nuts that they did.

'But you must have known the photographer was there,' Roxy reasoned. She'd scanned the page to see if her *When D:Ream Ruled The Waves* shame was in there – it wasn't. 'You're smiling right into the camera.'

'Well, *of course* I knew he was there when I stepped on him,' Tish snapped. 'But what I want to know is, how did he know *I* was there? It's not fair . . . *we* can't hide behind a silhouette. I mean, if nobody knows what Nicola Blunt looks like, how're we supposed to avoid her? That bitch could be anyone.' Tish thought for a second before adding, venomously, 'There's a woman at yoga whose dolphin planks are crap – *and* she's always hungover. I bet it's her. I don't reckon she's really even vegan.'

'Honestly, Tish, relax. This is nothing to worry about,' Roxy reasoned. 'You look amazing, Guy won't be cross and all the mums will come round.'

'That's what you think. But it's warfare out there in the playground.'

It was time for Roxy to seize her chance.

'Look, Tish, I'm sorry if my timing sucks again, but I badly need your advice about Woo—'

'Not now, Rox,' tutted her friend. 'If they've papped me once, they could pap me again. Consuela, the cleaner, is going to drive me to the salon to get my hair done. Obviously *I* can't drive – who knows how many lenses are lurking. So I'm going to lie in the back under a blanket. Don't even ask if her licence is valid because, frankly, I don't want to know. And Christ knows if we're gonna make it there anyway; I just hope my satnav does Venezuelan!'

And two seconds later she was gone.

WOODY

It had been a long day. Woody stowed his ladder in the garage, looking forward to a bath and a beer. He rubbed his head with a yawn, dug his keys out of his shorts pocket and headed over to the front door.

And that's when he saw it . . . A pot of something sat on the doorstep, wrapped in a red satin bow, a handwritten note attached.

He bent to retrieve it.

Peace offering.
Sorry for being a nobber. You didn't wimp out – you rock!
But your hands are as rough as a badger's proverbial!
Try this.
Rox.
x

Woody laughed.

Beneath the note and the ribbon was a pot of hand cream.

ROXY

So, was she going bonkers, or not?

Roxy tortured herself for possibly the eleven thousandth time since her jaunt up Woody's ladder, as she made the short walk to the Dog and Duck. Did Woody *really* have feelings for her? The question was driving her nuts.

She frowned. Blokes weren't normally confusing: Beer, footie, fast cars, shoot-'em-ups, uninhibited nut-scratching and unambiguously available women = good . . . Talking, thinking, Smart Cars, rom-coms, hugs-that-didn't-end-in-sex and women who required any effort = bad.

But Woody . . .

She *wasn't* going mad . . . They'd definitely had 'a moment' up his ladder. He'd reverse-cuddled her, for God's sake! And you didn't reverse-cuddle someone without feeling *something*.

But then again . . . she'd only been up his ladder in the first place to clean the window *she'd* deliberately dirtied. It wasn't Woody's fault she'd decided to 'fess up to her crap career and got sad enough to necessitate the hugging thing.

And, at the end of the day, there was still the matter of Jennifer. There was *always* the matter of Jennifer.

Roxy arrived at the pub none the wiser.

'All right, Rox?' Simon's voice came from the left.

'Mega,' she shot back, trying to force her eyes over in his direction. But her eyes had a will of their own and they were already locked on Woody, standing in checked shirt and jeans at the bar. He looked so good – *he was so good* – it was all she could do not to sigh. But then she noticed the rest of the group beside her. And the group was collectively frowning.

'He was already here when we arrived,' Simon said quietly. 'According to Dave, he's been here quite some time.'

And that was when Roxy noticed the figure next to Woody. Sitting at the bar, looking like he'd rolled through three fields to get there, was Austin. He was wearing a grubby anorak and his skin looked waxy and damp.

'Apparently there's a big awards ceremony in London,' Holly whispered over her orange juice, 'so all the photographers at his gates have left. Otherwise he'd never have got out.'

'He wants to come to our meeting,' added Simon.

'But Woody said he wasn't invited!' said Roxy.

'Maybe he realised he needs help,' offered Holly.

'Maybe he realised he's got no friends,' Terence muttered.

Roxy frowned at Woody and Austin. You could practically *see* the tension between them. But why? Woody liked everyone – why was he so weird about Austin? And why did he think she'd get hurt? And, talking of whys, why *did* Austin want to come to the meeting? It didn't make sense – he'd made it clear that he didn't really like anyone, and she was sure he wasn't here because of her. As flattered as she'd been by his exploration of her inner thigh, she knew he wasn't really serious. He was like her – born to flirt. It was rude-dream stuff – not stuff that would ever be real. Surely Woody realised *she* knew better than that!

But then her attention was distracted by a fast-moving boob tube. Like a supersonic, man-seeking missile, Chelle hurtled in, in a strip of silver elastic. She expertly placed herself between Austin and Woody, her cleavage sandwiched perfectly equidistant between them.

'I'm gagging for a Bacardi and Coke!' she pouted. Woody and Austin stopped talking. There was a long, awkward pause. And then Woody nodded at Dave.

Chelle simpered and they waited in silence for her drink. It finally arrived. Chelle took a tiny sip from its straw.

'Wow, what's with all the sexual tension?' she giggled. 'Honestly, you guys – get a room!'

Austin eyed her with glassy disinterest from his bar stool. 'Parole Officer Woody was just deciding if I can come to tonight's meeting.'

'Wicked!' Chelle dropped her hand on to his thigh. 'It wouldn't be the same without you.'

'Not everyone's as enthusiastic about the prospect,' he said darkly. He glanced over at Woody and his crossed arms.

Chelle turned the full force of her cleavage towards Woody.

'Oh, come on, Woody – let Austin come!'

Roxy saw how her eyes doubled in size as she implored him. Instinctively her palms tightened.

'I mean, the others are all right,' Chelle continued, 'but none of 'em is as famous as Austin. And this is supposed to be a famous persons' club, right?'

'Yeah, come on, Woodster; I'm cool,' Austin drawled.

Woody looked over to the group. His eyes rested on Roxy. She gave a small, almost imperceptible nod. For the briefest of moments, Woody looked disappointed. And then he turned back to Austin, face stern.

'There'll be no rude behaviour,' he told him. 'No cruel digs, nasty names or sexual advances.'

'Oh, I don't know about that!' Chelle swivelled her cleavage back to Austin.

'And you'll have to open up.' Woody frowned. 'It's the whole point of the group. You need to talk about yourself and your situation.'

'But I'm my own favourite subject.' Austin grinned.

'And, contrary to popular opinion, this *isn't* a famous persons' club.'

'You're telling me.' Austin eyed Chelle.

Woody scrutinised Austin for a moment. There was a very long pause. 'I'm warning you, Austin – last chance.'

'Magic.' Austin saluted and grinned. And then he slapped his empty glass on the counter. 'Fill me up, Dave; I'm in.'

Dave stepped forward and relucantly filled the glass.

'Let's dispense with the foreplay, shall we, Davey-boy?' Austin grabbed the whisky bottle from his hands and unsteadily rose to his feet. 'Put it on my tab. In fact, put drinks for everyone on my tab! Let Lavender Heath get pissed on me. Come on, gang . . . let's get *analysing*!' And, holding the whisky bottle aloft, he headed towards the stairs.

Grumbling quietly, the group shuffled along behind him. 'Thanks, Woody,' Chelle smirked. 'You're amazing!'

'Amazingly stupid,' he replied grimly, and followed the group up the stairs.

Roxy ordered a drink, feeling weird. Had she been wrong to nod about Austin? Woody hadn't seemed pleased – although he *never* seemed pleased around Austin. She suddenly had a sense of foreboding.

By the time she arrived in the upstairs room, everyone was already chatting. Numbly she laid out the cake she'd baked for the meeting. Simon came over to help.

He gave a low whistle. 'Apple and cider: that's pretty adventurous for a beginner!' He cut a slice and took a quick bite. 'Mmmm, and made with . . .' He paused for a moment, trying to work it out. 'Actually, what *is* it made with?'

'Parsnip,' she answered hollowly.

'Of course: the low-cal alternative to butter!' He smiled.

They both joined the group and sat down. Roxy sank into the far edge of an old springless sofa. She tried not to feel miserable as she looked up to where Chelle was perching between Austin and Woody, nipples freakishly pert in her boob tube.

'You look well,' she heard Sue compliment Terence. 'Younger; more relaxed.'

Despite everything, Roxy smiled. Terence self-consciously stroked his new eyebrows and avoided meeting her eye.

'Yes, Terence, you look *divine*,' Austin declared loudly. 'A real honey.'

The room suddenly felt tense. Eight pairs of eyes searched for an empty space on which to focus.

'So, you're writing again?' Cressida declared. Everyone turned to see who she was addressing.

'I . . .' A flush started to grow across Holly's cheeks.

'Don't look so startled. A friend in publishing told me.'

'Well, yes. Yes, I am.' Her entire face was now fuchsia.

'But that's wonderful!' Cressida told her. 'What's the new book about?'

Holly looked awkward. 'I'd rather not say, if you don't mind.'

'Oh, gosh, how rude of me! Of course.'

'Early days and all that,' Holly offered meekly. 'Sorry.'

'Well done, Holly. That's brilliant.' Woody smiled.

'Yeah, good on you, Hol,' agreed Simon. 'What made you start writing again?'

'Oh, you know . . .' Holly tailed off with painful embarrassment.

Roxy decided to dive in. 'Leave the poor woman alone. She'll tell us when she's good and ready.'

Holly smiled at her gratefully.

Woody turned to Austin, who was working his way steadily through his bottle of Jack.

'So, Austin, seeing as you were so keen to join us tonight, why don't you talk about yourself?'

'Yeah, go on, Austin – tell us stuff!' Chelle angled her breasts towards him.

Austin looked at Woody and shrugged. Roxy suddenly wondered how many bottles of Jack he'd already gone through. He didn't sound drunk, but his eyes gave him away. His eyes told her he was definitely – dangerously – bladdered.

'Not much to say . . .' He poured himself yet another drink. 'I'm as rich as Donald Trump, as happy as Forrest Gump and busier in the sack than Hugh Hefner. No problems here.'

'Yes, you're the model of well-adjusted,' Cressida observed.

But Simon couldn't hide his curiosity. 'But what about your recent change in lifestyle?'

'My what?'

'Well, your . . . you know . . . retirement.'

'What about it?'

Simon blushed. 'Well . . . how do you like it?'

Austin surveyed him for a moment, like a shark. There was a long pause. 'It's peachy,' he finally declared.

'But you must miss your old life?' pressed Roxy. 'Aren't you itching to get back to all the Hollywood parties and premieres and private yachts?'

'And miss our meetings?' he replied, deadpan.

'But what do you *do* all day?' puzzled Cressida.

Austin took a long sip of whisky. 'Get up, watch TV—'

'Crack a Special Brew,' muttered Terence.

'And that's it?' Cressida frowned.

'I might spend a few hours on my Xbox.'

'So you don't do anything productive, or useful, or helpful?'

'Christ, not this again.'

'You really do nothing at all?' Holly frowned.

'Some days I get dressed—'

'And you're happy to waste your life like this?' Cressida asked.

'Fuck, what is this – *Judge Judy*?'

'Nobody's judging you,' Woody told him. 'Cressida's trying to help – we all are. We're trying to offer you friendship.'

Austin turned to Holly and grinned. 'Wanna be friends? I've not made friends with a virgin for ages.' He dropped a grubby hand on her knee.

Chelle tutted and visibly deflated.

'Oi!' Roxy piped up. The last thing Holly needed was a mauling.

'Jealous?' he asked with a wink. 'Don't worry, Feisty, I've got enough friendship to go around.'

'*Austin* . . .' Woody growled.

'All right!' he held up the offending hand in surrender.

'But why did you do it?' Simon blurted. 'I don't get it. Why walk away from success?'

'I was bored.'

'Spielberg and Myers were queueing up to work with you!'

Austin pulled a face and swigged.

'But you've got so much talent . . .' said Simon. 'You're not just good; you could be a great. Not just a British great – an all-time, Brando-style legend. The rom-coms were just the beginning. Any fool could see you're capable of more.'

Austin looked at Simon strangely. 'I went to LA for one thing, and one thing only. And believe me, Downton, when you've pulled one pair of Hollywood beef curtains, you've pulled them all. It's not just their faces that all look the same.'

'Beef curtains?' Cressida frowned.

'You don't want to know.' Roxy and Woody told her together. And for the briefest of moments their eyes met. But before Roxy had a chance to go tingly, Austin was looking at Chelle's mouth.

'You'd better shut that, sweetheart – you don't know what I might put in it. You sure you haven't done her, Woods? Going floppy in your old age?'

'He was so nice on *Parkinson*,' Cressida lamented.

'Why did you come tonight, Austin?' Woody asked harshly. 'No bullshit – tell us the truth.'

Everyone looked expectantly at Austin. Slowly, he shrugged and then laughed.

'Bloody fantastic,' declared Terence sarcastically. 'We're officially nothing more than a "laugh".'

'My career's not a laugh,' Simon said quietly, his voice low as he looked at his lap. 'I've cried blood, sweat and tears for the Bard; I've begged every casting director, swallowed every indignity, eaten every possible variety of humble pie. And *you* . . .' He looked up and pointed, shakily, at Austin. '*And you* . . .'

But he couldn't finish.

'I think what he's trying to say, Austin,' Sue offered gently, 'is that we're all a bit confused about why you've turned your back on your career.'

'Why did *you* turn your back on *your* career, Suga?' Austin snapped. 'Or was gorging yourself into obesity the plan?'

'You arse!' Roxy exploded. 'I'd forgotten what wankers stars are.'

'Yes, don't listen to his poison,' Terence told Sue. 'You're a beautiful woman.'

'No, she *was* a beautiful woman,' corrected Austin. 'Now she's just fat.'

'Enough!' Woody jumped up, pulled Austin to his feet and marshalled him over to the door. 'You've had more than enough second chances. You shouldn't have had any at all. Get out!'

'*Oh, fuck off!*' Austin spluttered, indignant. 'You can't throw me out – it's a pub! I could buy it a million times over.'

'I said, out!'

But Austin didn't move. He just stood and looked at Woody coldly.

'What the fuck's happened to you, Woodster? Where's the real Woody gone? The one who drank the bar dry and humped anything in a skirt? Did you wake up in some supermodel's bed one morning and decide, "*No*, I *won't* give that top-quality snatch another hammering – I'll find a bunch of nobodies to nurse through their mid-life crises. I'll search out a load of saggy-titted, no-bollocked non-entities, without a single achievement between them . . . A feeble, washed-up gaggle of wannabes – not even the smallest dribble of talent or shagg-ability to kee—"'

There was a sudden crack of knuckle on bone, and Austin slumped to the floor.

'Shit!' Roxy stared open-mouthed. Woody had punched Austin out cold.

Woody rubbed his knuckles. 'At last,' he said quietly to himself.

'Oh. My. God!' declared Chelle as she peered over Austin's crumpled form. 'You've just knocked out *Austin* cockin' *Jones!*'

And then, just as everyone was looking at the unconscious figure of a megastar and wondering what on earth they were supposed to do next, an agonised howl pierced the air. But it wasn't Austin – it was Sue.

'I don't want to be Sue any more!' she wailed, her face coated in tears, spittle and snot. '*I JUST WANT TO BE SUGATITS!*'

Everyone stared, astonished. The word 'Sugatits' seemed to echo around the room. And then, as quickly as it had come, the volume of Sue's upset receded and she dissolved into silent tears, her mouth fixed into an anguished 'O'. Terence patted her arm stiffly. And then Austin groaned and threw up over his chest.

'I need a drink,' he declared, eyes whirling. 'Fill me up, Dave!' And he passed out again.

Cressida frowned. 'Do you think we should take him to hospital?'

Roxy shook her head. 'The newspapers would have a field day.'

'But we can't just leave him here. I know he's unpleasant, but he's still a human being.'

'Debatable,' Terence muttered, as he comforted Sue.

Woody looked Austin over. 'He'll be fine. He needs to sleep it off, that's all. I'll take him home.'

'Do you really think that's a good idea?' Roxy frowned. 'You *did* just knock him out.'

'She's got a point,' agreed Holly. 'What if he goes for round two?'

'He's my mistake, my responsibility,' Woody said grimly.

'No,' Simon suddenly declared. 'No, he's *our* responsibility – all of us. Let *us* help *you*, for once, Woody. You're the last person he'll want to see when he wakes up. I've got the people carrier outside. You get off – *we'll* get him home.'

'But—'

'No, really – we've got this. You go.'

Woody rubbed his head. 'Are you sure?'

Everyone nodded.

'Really?'

'He's the last person *you* should have to help.' Simon looked at him significantly. Woody nodded.

'Sorry about . . .' He gestured to where Austin was crumpled.

'Don't be.' Cressida smiled. 'Seeing you punch Austin was more fun than I've had in ages. Makes me yearn to be back in the Commons!'

'Go home, Woody,' Roxy said softly. 'Ice your hand.' She looked up at him in his lumberjack shirt: the kind-hearted man who'd just decked someone for everyone's honour. Suddenly, more than anything she could ever remember wanting, she wanted to look after him . . . to take him home, tend his hand, nurse his wound. He couldn't afford to damage his hand – his hands were his living. The thought of his cut, swollen knuckles, frozen up a ladder in February, almost brought a tear to her eye.

'Oh my God, he's pissing himself!' shrieked Chelle, pointing a pink nail at Austin's groin.

Woody paused reluctantly in the doorway.

'I'll ring you in the morning,' Simon told him, ignoring the pool of liquid spreading out from Austin Jones. 'Tell you how it went.'

'There's piss everywhere!' yelled Chelle as the puddle surrounded her. 'It's all over my cockin' shoes!'

Woody hesitated, nodded and then left.

'Aw, that's disgusting. They're peep-toes!' Chelle wailed.

'Right!' Simon clapped his hands together. 'Let's get this joker downstairs.'

Two vomits later, Austin was safely bundled into the people carrier. Simon was driving, Cressida alongside; Roxy, Holly, Terence and Sue were in the back, with Austin slumped at their feet.

'Where's Chelle?' Roxy asked, looking around.

'Tactical retreat,' said Holly. 'She couldn't stand the smell.'

'It *is* pretty strong,' remarked Sue, back to her old self at last.

'There's nothing like the whiff of vomit to dampen the ardour.' Terence smiled. 'Or someone's piss in your shoes!'

'I saw your soap . . .' Austin suddenly croaked from the footwell.

'*Down Town*?' Simon asked in surprise. '*You* saw *Down Town*?'

'I called the producshion company; gothem to send a deeveedee.'

'You did?'

'You were quite . . .' Austin drunkenly tailed off. Simon clenched the wheel as he awaited the verdict. '. . . Good.'

Simon drove in stunned silence. 'Thank you,' he finally replied. 'I'm so flattered . . .' But Austin was vomiting on his mats.

'Bloody hell!' Terence drew up his feet. 'Anyone would think he actually cares.'

'He watched my shows!' Simon grinned, oblivious. 'I can't believe he watched my shows!'

'I can't believe he made a phone call,' muttered Cressida. 'It must have been his busiest day in months.'

'And he actually said I was *good*.'

'*Quite* good,' Terence reminded him.

But it didn't matter. Chuckling with delight, Simon took a left and swept into Austin's drive. Everyone fell silent as they sped along its length, the vast, up-lit manor house sliding into view.

Roxy let out a whistle. 'Now *that* is what I call epic!'

'It's enormous,' said Holly with a gasp. 'How much do you think it's worth?'

'Six point two million,' Cressida replied crisply. 'Don't any of you read the local paper?'

'Six point two million?' Terence spluttered. 'For swanning around in a few films?'

They drew up at the front door. A dusky-skinned woman came out to meet them. Even in the dark, Roxy could see she was stunning.

'We're just bringing Austin home,' Simon explained as he got out of the car. 'I'm afraid he's a bit worse for wear.'

The woman opened the rear door, recoiling slightly as she was hit by the aroma of Jack Daniel's, vomit and piss. She surveyed the mess inside.

'Os-tin Jones! You get up rye now!' she ordered fiercely. Her hair shone glossily under the lamplight as she spoke.

'He might have a bit of a sore head in the morning,' Simon offered sheepishly. 'He gave it a small bump getting in the car.'

'I'm sure eet ees ze least ee deserves,' the woman said. 'Zank you for bringing eem 'ome. I know ee is not eeasy when ee ees like zis. Ee's lucky ee 'as such good friends.'

Everyone examined the ground shiftily, too embarrassed to meet each other's eyes. And then, as if on an unspoken order, Terence and Roxy started hoisting Austin out from the car.

'I'm Simon.' Simon offered the woman his hand. 'And this is Cressida, Sue, Holly, Terence and Roxy.'

'Carmen Bonitta,' the beautiful woman replied. 'Os-tin's girlfriend.'

'Thassa lie,' Austin slurred from the depths of his anorak. 'I'm single!'

'Of courz you arr, Os-tin,' Carmen agreed wearily as she wiped a chunk of bile from his beard. 'And ze sky ees also purple.'

'You're his *girlfriend*?' Roxy was stunned. *Austin Jones* had a *girlfriend*? How could anyone have a beard and a gut and a girlfriend like Carmen Bonitta? 'Wow!' she blurted in awe.

'Yes, wow,' Carmen replied sardonically. 'Luckee me.' And then, staggering under his weight, she expertly half-led, half-carried him back into the house. 'Come on, Os-tin.' She tried to rouse him. 'Coffeee time!'

They all stood in the glow of the manor house up-lighting.

'How can he have a girlfriend?' Terence hissed. 'He practically begged Roxy for sex.'

'She thinks we're his friends,' Roxy whispered. She suddenly felt very ashamed.

Holly ran after Carmen. 'Can I come in? It's just, I need to wash sick off my skirt.'

'Bee my guess,' Carmen called over her shoulder. 'Zair ees guess bathroom, third door on left.'

'We'll wait,' Simon told Holly.

'Don't,' Holly called back. 'I'll cab it – I can't stand the smell. Besides, Carmen might need some help.'

Everyone piled wordlessly back into the car. They all sat in mute contemplation. Simon stared out through the windscreen at Austin's house.

'You know, maybe I'm not cut out for success,' he mused quietly. 'Maybe panto isn't so bad, after all.'

And then he started the engine and drew away from the manor house, the people carrier reeking of A-list Hollywood chunder.

To: Roxy Squires

From: *The Daily Telegraph*

Dear Ms Squires,

Thank you for contacting us with your idea for a new, no-nonsense agony aunt column, to be penned by the former Secretary of State for Work and Pensions, Cressida Cunningham.

We love it!

Cressida Cunningham has long had a reputation for plain talking with a sensible, old-fashioned approach. We have often marvelled at her disregard for tact, diplomacy and fashion, whilst simultaneously admiring her ability to 'hit the nail right on the head'. She'll be a perfect agony aunt.

Many thanks for this wonderful suggestion. We've asked our legal team to draw up a contract of employment . . .

ROXY

Roxy breathed deeply and concentrated on keeping her pace. She'd decided not to run with Woody this morning. She'd told him she needed a lie-in – but the truth was she needed to think. There'd been lots of surprises about jogging – the fact that she liked it being the first. But one of the other surprises had been space. Pounding the pavements gave her the perfect time and space for some thought – although thinking still needed a soundtrack and, without Woody, she needed her iPod. She hadn't changed so much that silence was golden.

Familiar sticky-sweet notes started chiming.

Of course, if she'd wanted real clarity of thought, she probably shouldn't have picked Woody's back catalogue as her playlist. It was hard to be rational when his voice caressed her ears like warm honey. But then, it was hard to be rational about Woody full stop. Ever since the ladder-spooning, she'd felt different – as though everything was completely upended. Her career was over – she knew that now. But, strangely, she didn't feel depressed. And, whilst a few days ago she may not have liked where she stood with Woody, it was as though, when she'd climbed up that ladder, she'd stepped off one piece of ground and stepped back down on to another. But what she couldn't work out was this: was where she stood *before* the ladder better or worse?

Woody had reached his famous chorus.

It's funny, she thought, but when she was fifteen, his cover had meant nothing more to her than its video. The words and tune were hardly the point – she'd loved it because Woody wore his vest. Fast-forward to a few weeks ago and she'd thought that the song was cheesy. But today, as she jogged with it on her iPod, it was cool. For the first time, she listened past Woody's lyrics and heard what was happening under-neath . . . the delicate bongos, the soaring strings, the rich but understated brass . . . and suddenly she heard the whole song. And she liked it.

And as the music reached its crescendo, Roxy was struck with a thought that made her heart beat faster and stop at the same time. Was *this* what she was doing with Woody?

Could it be that *she* was falling in love?

SIMON

Something magical had happened to Simon.

Last night he'd gone to bed as normal Simon, but this morning he'd woken armour-plated. Or maybe Teflon-coated. But, whichever miraculous substance had covered him, it meant that nothing the twins could hurl at him managed to get through. He'd woken up to discover he was invincible!

'Rank,' Scarlet sniffed, the nanosecond she got into the people carrier. Simon had been waiting, engine running, for Scarlet to finish burying her natural features in make-up and deign to throw herself into the car. 'It smells like someone's just hurled!'

Simon whacked the people carrier into gear and expertly reversed down the drive. If he put his foot down, he might still get them to school on time. Not that the twins cared whether they were on time or not – they didn't give two stuffs! Normally Simon would have given a stuff that they didn't give two stuffs. He'd have got stressed and uptight – blaming himself for his teenaged children's inability to get themselves dressed, showered and breakfasted in under two hours and cursing himself for his inability to provide authoritative alpha-male leadership via a string of prominent Hollywood roles.

But today was different.

Today, nothing could chink his good mood. Because today he wasn't just Simon Drennan, moderately successful provider of his kids' five-a-day, and major embarrassment of a dad . . . Today he was Simon Drennan, winner of the Austin Jones seal of approval and proud owner of the professional appraisal 'quite good'.

He eyed the scowling fruits of his loin. Suddenly he had a suicidal urge to impress them.

'Very observant, Ms Drennan,' he cheerfully praised his daughter. 'Your nasal skills are top notch. Someone *did* indeed hurl in our car . . .' He paused – a touch longer than an *X Factor* reveal, but just shy of a Chris Tarrant *Millionaire*. 'Austin Jones!'

'Austin Jones?' deadpanned his daughter. 'What, Austin Jones, the Hollywood megastar?'

'That's the one!'

She curled her lip with a snort. 'Yeah, right.'

'What do you mean, "Yeah, right"?' Simon buoyantly quizzed her, her disbelief in his A-list connections bouncing off his armour like a squash ball on a court. 'Is it *so hard* for you to believe that I was out drinking with my friend, Austin Jones, and that after a few too many he "hurled" in the back of my car?'

'You're embarrassing yourself, Dad,' Euan informed him, his eyes glued to his phone.

'Big time,' Scarlet agreed. 'As if Austin Jones would be mates with *you*. He's, like, mega famous.'

'He's an actor,' Simon replied mildly. 'Just like me.'

'Yeah, just like you,' his son snorted.

'Austin Jones is *juice*, Dad,' Scarlet informed him. 'You're just an ungoogleable.'

'I'm on Google!' Simon protested.

'Duh! As if *that's* what it means.'

He shrugged. 'I'm telling you, *that vomit* came from Austin Jones' stomach. And you, my lovely children, are breathing in molecules of A-list thespian chunder.'

Scarlet pulled a face in disgust. 'You're gross, Dad.'

'Retarded,' Euan concurred.

But Simon just smiled, impervious. He drove on in maddening silence.

And then Scarlet couldn't help herself. Despite a lifetime of disinterest in every word ever uttered by her father, she asked, 'You're seriously trying to tell us that, of all the cars in the world Austin Jones could throw up in, he chose to throw up in ours?'

'Uh huh.' Simon grinned happily.

'You're sick, Dad, you know that?' she told him. 'And not in the good sick way.'

'Sick Nick,' Euan traitorously sniggered, psychologically kicking his dad where it hurt most. 'Sick Nick and his fantasy friend.'

For a brief, micro-fraction of a second, Simon felt metaphorical pain. But then the Teflon took effect and his children's insults slipped harmlessly away. He couldn't blame their scepticism, he reasoned. No teenager's impressed by their parent. And six weeks ago *even he* wouldn't have believed Austin Jones would throw up in his car. But, one day, Euan and Scarlet would admit to their error. One day, they'd regret their casual dismissal of their father's acting prowess and big-league celebrity connections. One day they'd understand that he was indeed 'quite good'.

And to the annoyance of his offspring, Simon started to whistle.

ROXY

Roxy stepped out of the shower, wrapped herself in a towel and sat numbly on the edge of her bed. Was she in love with Woody? The very thought was making her shake.

She'd been in lust before – loads of times. It was usually a two-week shagathon with a band member, fuelled by booze and post-gig-high sex. When the tour bus moved into the Chunnel, she'd scoot back home to everyday life, memories of her latest all-time-favourite-shag-ever receding faster than Calum Best's hair.

But this was different.

This time, she'd not even kissed him.

This time she'd fallen in love.

But what the hell should she do about it? It felt like a milestone moment – a sing-it-from-the-rooftops piece of info; a hug-strangers-on-the-street piece of news. Surely you weren't supposed to just *sit* on this knowledge? If you loved someone, you told them . . . *right*?

But what if the person you'd fallen in love with was awaiting the homecoming of his girlfriend? What if he was definitely, totally attached? Did you risk humiliation and upset? Did you tell him your big news, even if only to get it off your chest?

Suddenly Roxy stood up. She knew what she'd do . . . She'd do what every girl did in a crisis – she'd nip to the shop for some beetroot. There was a new recipe she wanted to try: a beetroot-based Christmas chocolate log. OK, so it was about ten years 'til Christmas . . . but she hadn't had chocolate since 2007 and suddenly, more than anything, she was desperate for the taste.

She flung off her towel and got dressed.

WOODY

At the top of his ladder, Woody flexed his knuckles. Austin's jaw had been surprisingly hard. He hadn't had a fight since . . . well – ages. Not since that scuffle with a photographer in Stuttgart. He just hadn't had many reasons to be *that* angry since quitting showbiz. But finally punching Austin had felt good. He could see why people went on about closure. He no longer cared about what Austin had done.

He dropped his hand back into the bucket of water, grasped his sponge and started sudsing Mrs Kippington's bedroom window. Luckily, it was sunny and mild. Normally the February wind would bite into cuts on his hands, but today's weather was unusually kind. The sun warmed his back as he worked.

Woody thought back to last night. He definitely owed Roxy an apology. When he'd got home he'd replayed the evening over and he'd suddenly realised that Roxy was right. He *was* a hypocrite. He *had* made judgements without asking. His motives may have been decent, but he *had* been holding the group back. Yes, they were damaged and fragile – but it didn't mean that fame would damage them *more*. And if Roxy was right about him, maybe she was right about them all? Maybe recapturing their success *would* be healing for the group? After all, they'd been pretty tough last night. When he'd decked Austin they'd all pulled together. They'd never have done that a few months ago. They'd never have done that before Roxy.

Woody looked over towards Austin's. He couldn't see as far as the house – just the gates. A solitary photographer stood outside. Woody smiled. He doubted he'd get shots today – Austin would be growling into his duvet, hungover. He watched the photographer drop his cigarette butt and immediately light up another.

Woody's smile deepened into a grin. Yes, he had to hand it to Roxy, she was a one-woman force for good. She cared about the group just as much as he did. She wanted them to be happy too. And – if her method got results, then great! It wasn't a competition. The group was definitely happier. And didn't having her around make *him* happier too?

Feeling lighter than he had in years, Woody twisted and looked around him. He could see Simon driving back from the school run. Outside the post office, Terence checked his hair in the glass. And on Lime Tree Walk, a determined-looking Sue was limbering up for a jog. And then, between sprigs of early spring blossom, he saw Roxy hurtle towards the village shop. His eyes followed her for a moment. From his spot on the ladder, he could see dark roots starting to poke through the blonde. But it didn't matter. If anything, Roxy looked softer, more human. She was wearing jeans. In fact, the miniskirts had been absent a few days now. He missed her legs, he realised with a pang.

Suddenly there was a rap on the window. Mrs Kippington was indignant and naked.

'I'm not doing this for the ventilation,' she scolded. 'Are you coming in, or not?'

Woody's face broke into a fresh grin.

'Sorry, Mrs Kippington – I'm taken!'

And then he thoughtfully finished shammying the window.

SUE

Sue stood on her doorstep and soaked in the unseasonal sunshine.

She was going to do it.

Just two hours since her jog she was pushing herself out of the house (and her comfort zone) again. And this time she was wearing the duck egg.

She tried to forget the terror churning like acid in her tummy. She tried to ignore the nervous thrill of the duck egg's first outing. She even tried to block out the cheerful chirrups of the birds in the laurels.

She had to focus.

It was only a few minutes' walk to Blackberry Lane; just down the road, along the High Street, sharp right and then left. She didn't even know if the workmen were still fixing the hole. But she was going anyway. Suzi would have done it, and so would she.

She took a last, dizzy breath, let go of the door handle and walked.

She was doing it! For the second time that day, she'd left

the house on un-vital business. The soaring high she'd felt after her jog had outweighed the terrible pain during it. It hadn't mattered that she'd sweated buckets, nearly punctured a lung, or run at a pace that wouldn't challenge a snail . . . the point was she'd tried, and trying had felt great. And now, as – step by step – her feet took her closer to the hole in Blackberry Lane, that high began to return.

Sue ruffled her new fringe as she walked and caught sight of herself in the post office window. Roxy had been right: a fringe *did* suit her. And wearing her hair up *did* make her face look slimmer too. As the sun shone, she thought she caught a glimpse of cheekbone in her reflection. She tried not to laugh in delight.

And then, before she knew it, she was there . . . Blackberry Lane. And there, too, was the hole and the workmen.

For a moment, Sue doubted her sanity. What was she doing? Builders were the people she most wanted to hide from. Back when *it* had happened, most men had taken a while before calling over – they'd have a few drinks, gather some mates, build up the requisite bravado. But not builders. With their loud whistles and ever-ready patter, she could barely step out her front door without a builder yelling, 'Show us your sugatits!' They seemed to have a sixth sense. Any attempt at hiding beneath a headscarf was pointless; their cheerful obscenities were a leper's bell, alerting the world to her presence. She dreaded them. No matter where she went, or how she disguised herself, builders always *just knew*. And their crudeness cut her to her quick.

But now here they were: three workmen in yellow hats, down a hole in Blackberry Lane. And it was Sue's very own feet that had delivered her to them. And now those very same feet had stopped.

He was here . . . The builder who'd knocked into her in the newsagent's . . . The one who'd actually noticed her presence. And he was doing something buildery with a hammer and a pipe.

Sue hesitated as they continued their work, oblivious. She waited a moment – the longest moment she could ever remember. And then her heart skittled in panic. She'd got it wrong; she shouldn't have come. She was still the same . . . still invisible. Still Sue.

She started to turn back towards home, but was stopped by a noise: a funny, off-beat chink of a hammer not quite hitting its mark.

She turned back.

He was looking at her. The builder from the newsagent's had stopped working and was looking at her.

Their eyes locked. Sue held her breath. He was an ordinary-enough looking man: neither young nor old, neither hand-some nor plain. But that wasn't the point.

And then slowly – ever so slowly – he smiled. And then he nodded, tipped his hard hat and winked.

'Afternoon.'

Sue inwardly gasped. She seemed to take an hour to reply. 'Afternoon!'

And then she span on her heel and away. Not breathing –

not needing to breathe – she walked off home with a singing heart.

He'd noticed! *She* had been noticed! She wasn't just Sue any more. She didn't look back. It didn't matter if he was still looking or not. The point was, he *had* looked and things need never be the same ever again.

4.48pm @foxyroxy
My chocolate log ROCKS! CHOCOLATE ROCKS!

WOODY

Woody was holding his breath. He wasn't sure why, but he suddenly realised his lungs were stuck on pause. He forced himself to breathe out, check his watch and knock again.

Still no answer.

She was out.

He shouldn't have been surprised. He should have come round sooner. Roxy wasn't the type to stay in in the evenings. She was probably whipping up a storm on a dancefloor some-where, knocking back tequila in a dress so short it came with an arrest warrant. Woody tried not to feel disappointed. He was *glad* Roxy was out. After the last few days she'd had, she deserved to have a good time. Woody nodded, as if confirming something. And then he turned and headed back down Roxy's front path. He'd come back in the morning to apologise instead.

As he walked down a dark Gates Green Road, he thought back to the other night, in the pub – to Roxy, and Terry's eyebrows, and the punch. And, halfway along Chestnut Avenue, his lungs went on pause once again. God, he hoped she wasn't at Austin's! After all, Austin *had* been as subtle as a donkey on heat about Roxy, and he wasn't a man who was often told no. Woody knew *that* better than anyone. When Austin decided to be seductive, women seemed unable to resist. And, Austin's objectionableness aside, why *should* Roxy resist? She was young, free and single. And hadn't he just told himself that she needed a good time?

Woody frowned into the darkness. He picked up the pace as he strode home. And, as he rounded the corner to Blackberry Lane, he saw her: the black Aston Martin, double-parked – and Chelle in a bundle on his doorstep.

ROXY

It was 8.30am in Roxy's kitchen.

Confessing felt surprisingly good, Roxy thought as she waited for her flapjacks to brown.

She'd always prided herself on being a computer-says-yes kind of girl. There was nothing she wasn't prepared to go on the record about, from waxing her tash to her old school reports. But over the years, and much to her surprise, Roxy had developed taboos.

The first had been her date of birth (the precise digits of which she'd told so many lies about, that the filling in of an official form – like a passport application – now necessitated a phone call to her mum).

But Roxy's major taboo was her career – or rather, her career's demise. Gradually she'd become uncharacteristically cagey about the state of her work diary. Since being relieved of the services of her final agent ('There's nothing more I can do for you,' she'd smiled sadly. 'Go home, dust off your GCSE certificates and remember your fifteen minutes with a smile'), nobody had been privy to the secret of quite how empty Roxy's schedule had been. Even Roxy had barely known. Looking at her diary, with its endless pages of snowy blankness, had freaked her out so badly she'd decided not to look. Why torture herself? The truth only ever got her down, and everyone knew that to be hired you had to be up, up, up!

Looking back, all the denial had been exhausting. It took more effort to lie about being busy, she now realised, than it did to actually *be* busy. She was dizzy from all her own spin.

But coming clean, telling Woody, 'fessing up to her unemployment . . . Roxy felt like a great and terrible weight had been lifted from her. It was far more effective than the colonic. She felt lighter – literally *stones* lighter. She felt giddy with freedom, like gravity had been switched off and her feet couldn't stay on the ground. Even getting puked on by Austin hadn't fazed her. She wasn't Roxy Squires, Failing TV Presenter Perpetually Hunting Down The Next Job . . . She was just . . . well, she was Just Roxy Squires, and being Just Roxy Squires felt great. If she'd known 'fessing up was so amazing, she'd have done it yonks ago. Maybe the Catholics were on to something.

The oven timer pinged.

Roxy frowned.

Of course, there was still one big taboo left, eating away at her like the knowledge of a Mars bar in the cupboard . . .

Woody.

It was now twenty-four hours since her moment of self-discovery. And lying in bed that morning, her mind uncluttered by the list of potential jobs she should be chasing and

TV execs she needed to poke, Roxy had made a decision. She was going to be true to herself. She was a heart-on-her-sleeve girl. She wasn't a procrastinator, long-game player or dweller of fences – she was a plain-spoken, no-fannying-about motor-mouth.

She'd heard people say that the way to a man's heart is through his stomach, and so Roxy's plan of action was flap-jacks. After all, her armoury of micro-skirts and tit-tops was now balled in a corner of her bedroom and, since she'd dis-covered the comfort of jumpers, she wasn't sure she could welcome them back. No amount of breast-wobbling or smutty innuendo would work with Woody, anyway. And, short of challenging him to naked arm-wrestling, strip poker or truth-or-dare drinking games, that was it . . . all of her pulling tech-niques exhausted.

Flapjacks were the only course of action.

Because it was time to tell Woody the truth.

The truth.

She wouldn't be sly about it. She wouldn't try to talk him into anything. If Woody wanted Jennifer – fine. She wasn't a man-stealer. She'd wish him good luck and then scarper. But . . . *but* . . . if he was having any doubt about Jennifer . . . *any teeny, tiny molecule of uncertainty at all* . . . then surely he needed to know how she felt? And what Roxy felt, felt massively like love.

It was a high-risk strategy. But, hey – dignity was overrated. And so she picked up her flapjacks and set off.

The whole way over, she rehearsed the script in her head:

Woody. I know you're with Jennifer, but just in case you're ever <u>not</u> with Jennifer, I just wanted to let you know that I, Roxy Squires, am available . . .

Woody. I think you're wonderful and kind and handsome and lovely, and I'd be honoured if you'd consider me for the position of your girlfriend . . .

Woody. I fancy the arse of you; always have, always will . . .

Woody. I think that I might . . . that I might lov—

Oh, she was just going to have to wing it . . . to cross her fingers and hope the right noises came out of her mouth. Because it was too late now – she was here. Her feet scraped to a halt at the end of Woody's drive.

This was it: no turning back.

She took a deep breath and walked up to the door. But before she could knock, it opened.

'Roxy Squires? What the cockin'ell do you want?'

Roxy froze.

Standing on Woody's doorstep – as bold as brass and dressed in something only marginally more sturdy than a negligee – was Chelle.

Roxy's body turned to lead. Her heart clattered around her ankles. Was Chelle . . . ? Was Woody . . . ? *Were Chelle and Woody . . . ?*

'I was . . .' she floundered as she saw Chelle's bonked-all-night bed hair. 'I was just . . .'

Chelle raised an eyebrow.

'Spit it out! We're busy.'

Roxy's mouth flopped as she tried to find the power of

speech . . . but inexplicably the motormouth was silent. Every word in the English language escaped her. All she could hear were Chelle's words.

We're busy.

We.

Chelle and Woody were a *we*. And *we* were busy.

Busy doing what? Nausea flooded her. But then her brain contracted tightly as protection against the visions.

How could she have missed this development? Surely there must have been signs . . . lingering looks, jointly-timed exits, body language impossible to ignore . . . ? Yes, Woody had a reputation that preceded him – but he seemed so different to the tabloid stories of his past. And Roxy had never thought he'd be the kind of man to do *this*. She thought he was better, kinder, more honourable.

'But Jennifer . . .' she managed to utter.

'Who's Jennifer?' Chelle screwed up her face.

'Woody's girlfriend!'

But Chelle's only reaction was a shrug. 'They for Woody?' She eyed up the flapjacks then leant forward and whisked the Tupperware out of her hands. 'See ya, then.'

And then the door closed and Roxy was left staring nose first at Woody's woodwork, wondering where all the thousands of words she should have said had just flown to, and how on earth she could have got Woody so wrong.

To: Feisty; Rain Man; Downton; Vidal; Sugatits; Head Girl; Woodster; the WAG

From: Austin Jones

Hello. Is Austin's girlfriend, Carmen Bonitta, here. Austin is very sorry for the other nite and would like to invite you to hes house tonite to say sorrey. Please come. He is not horrible all the time, I promise! He knows he has been (is this right word?) plonker.

Love,
Carmen

ROXY

'Now *this* is something I have to see,' grinned Terry evilly as they crunched up the long, winding drive to Austin's manor house. 'Austin Jones, forced to eat humble pie by his girlfriend: priceless!'

'It must be a difficult transition,' reasoned Holly. 'He *was* a movie star a few months ago.'

'Yes, well, everyone has dreams that get broken,' said Cressida. 'It doesn't give him licence to be rude.'

'Can't we just hear him out?' asked Simon. 'The man wants to apologise!'

'Oh, hark at you now,' sniped Terence. 'Just because he watched *Down Town*.'

'I just think everyone deserves a second chance.'

'And a third, and a fourth, and a twenty-fifth . . .'

The uplit mansion swung into view. Everyone fell silent as they took in its grandeur once more. Terence was the first to recover. 'Holly, did you bring your notepad? Because, if Austin's going to say sorry, I definitely want it in the minutes. I want to be able to reread it, word for word, over breakfast.'

'Terence!' Sue scolded him gently. 'I hope you're going to be gracious.'

'Anyway, I don't know what *you're* so grumpy about,' Holly grumbled. 'He wasn't even that horrible to you. He called me a virgin!'

Chelle stopped dead in her tracks. 'Ain't you?'

'I couldn't care less what he says about *me*,' insisted Terence. 'But he was damned rude about Sue, and it's not right!'

'I didn't mind,' Sue said mildly. 'Maybe I needed to hear what he said.'

'Nobody *needed* to hear what he said!'

'Oh, let's just get this over and done with, shall we?' interrupted Cressida. 'And then we can retire to the pub.'

'The pub?' Woody laughed in surprise. 'Congratulations, Cressida; you've just re-entered normal life.'

Everyone laughed except Roxy. She wasn't in the mood for laughing. She hadn't been in the mood for *anything* since the flapjacks and Woody's doorstep. She walked at the back of the group, looking for signs from Woody and Chelle. So far, they'd been totally discreet. If they'd been at it like rabbits an hour earlier, there was no way of telling; they'd exchanged no secretive glances and were walking several metres apart.

As the group reached the door of the mansion, Carmen stepped out to greet them. Despite herself, Roxy couldn't help but marvel. Carmen was even more stunning than before.

'Hi, everybodee!' She warmly embraced them. 'Zank you so much for coming. Eet is probably more than ee deserves.'

'She said it . . .' Terence mumbled.

Roxy saw Chelle check out Carmen for the first time – eyeing her up and down with a mix of jealousy and awe. With her orange skin, unnatural highlights and plastic chest, Chelle was a freak show next to Carmen's organic beauty. Roxy suddenly felt relieved she'd worn her jeans.

'Thanks for inviting us,' Woody smiled.

'Come een; come een.' She gestured them indoors excitedly. 'Os-tin is waiting. We 'ave sangria, but I 'ear that you, Sue, like tee; so we 'ave sangria and tee – all kinds.'

'Oh, lovely.' Sue smiled at her kindness. 'I'd love a cup of Assam, please.'

Roxy glumly trailed them in. They followed Carmen through a vast, cavernous hallway and into an immaculate, supersized kitchen.

'Jesus Christ!' Terence stopped dead. 'What the hell is *that*?' Everyone looked at where he was pointing. Roxy blinked in disbelief. There was a strip of deep water starting at the breakfast bar and running through the middle of the kitchen.

'Sweemming pool,' Carmen replied nonchalantly, as if it was the most ordinary thing in the world to have a swimming lane snaking through your kitchen. 'Eet goes threw every room in the 'ouse. Os-tin wanted it. Zee workmen took forever.'

Chelle made a noise like somebody choking.

'O.M.G. – that's just *awesome*!' she cried.

'But where does it go?' Simon puzzled.

Carmen shrugged. 'Evereewhere.'

'Of course,' Terence deadpanned. 'Why walk to the kitchen when you could swim?'

'Oh, Os-tin never swims.' Carmen flicked her hair with a laugh. 'Ee said ee would, but ee never. Ee uses it for toy boats and submareens. And for sometimes sailing ees dinner into ze living room.'

Cressida wasn't impressed. 'It sounds a bit Willy Wonka to me.'

'Who's he?' asked Chelle. 'An interior designer?'

Carmen followed the swimming lane and led them into an enormous living room. White leather sofas sat alongside the swimming pool and bubble chairs were suspended in each corner. There were illuminated red neon side tables, original film posters on the wall and an enormous, roaring fire with a red perspex mantelpiece.

'Oh my God, is that . . . ?' Simon trailed off in awe.

'His BAFTAs!' squealed Holly.

'How many's he got?' Simon marvelled, swivelling his head as he tried to count them all.

'Eight,' Carmen replied.

'Eight!' exclaimed Cressida. 'Goodness, that *is* impressive. And isn't that . . .' She pointed over to another perspex shelf with its very own spotlight.

Simon gasped. 'His *Oscar*!'

'Austin won an Oscar?' Even Terence was impressed.

'Only Best Actor in a Supporting Role,' Austin offered modestly. Everyone turned in surprise. The room was so large they hadn't realised he was in it. 'Not the big one.'

Everyone regarded him open-mouthed. Cressida was the first to break the silence. 'You've had a bath!'

It was true; Austin looked neater and cleaner than they'd ever seen him. His shirt was ironed, his hair was brushed; even his beard had been trimmed into submission.

'Tsk! Os-tin!' Carmen scolded. 'Ee es very bad,' she told the group. 'I stay in LA to fineesh my studies and eet all goes to pot! Ee knows ee should not drink so much. Ee forgets to make bath when ee ees drunk.'

Terence sniggered.

'Anyway, sangria ees ere on ze table,' Carmen continued lightly. 'I go make ze tee.' And she left them all in silence.

'Would anyone like to sit down?' Austin asked stiffly.

'Thought you'd never ask,' Cressida grumbled.

Everyone made for a sofa. Roxy frowned as Chelle dropped her bottom next to Woody. She grumpily tried to lever herself into one of the swinging bubble chairs, but every time she reversed her bottom in, the chair swung maddeningly away. She didn't want Woody seeing her being beaten by a chair, so she decided to lean against it instead. But the chair still kept swinging and although Roxy tried to look comfortable, she wondered which of her muscles would pull first.

There was another tense pause. Woody was the only member of the group without his arms crossed. In fact, he seemed more relaxed than he'd been in ages. 'So, Carmen's back?' He broke the ice.

'Thank God,' Austin replied.

'She staying?'

'I think so. If she's passed her exam, she can practise anywhere.'

'What's she been studying?' Holly asked.

Austin looked at her for a moment before replying. 'Physiotherapy.'

'Useful,' she offered politely.

'Sorry,' blurted Chelle, 'but have I missed something? Is that foreign lady actually your *girlfriend*?'

'My better half.' He grinned sheepishly.

'But I thought she was your maid!' Chelle seemed angry. 'You said you was single!'

'I said a lot of stuff that was rubbish. Carmen told me what state I was in the other night. And Woody came round this morning to tell me I'm a knob.'

'You came to see him?' Terence asked Woody in shock.

Woody shrugged. 'I thought he should know he was an idiot. Besides, we had stuff we needed to get straight.'

'About Petra?' Holly suddenly piped up.

Roxy wobbled against the bubble chair in surprise. *Petra Klitova? Why would Woody and Austin be talking about her?*

The two men shared a glance, and then Austin turned to Simon. 'Sorry about your car. I hear I gave it a spray job.'

'It's OK.'

'No, it's not.' Austin took something from his pocket and passed it to him. 'I got this, to say sorry. No hard feelings?'

Simon looked at his hand. A key card rested in his palm.

'Is this . . . ?' He stopped in surprise.

'I upgraded you. Imported from Germany this morning.'

'You bought me a *new car*?'

'Yeah, well, vom smells last for ages.'

'But you didn't need . . . I mean, this is crazy!' he protested. But he looked so pleased he could burst.

Carmen slipped back into the room with a tea tray.

Terence tightened his arms across his chest. 'You can't just buy us off, you know!' he warned Austin. 'It takes more than a flash car to say sorry.'

'I know,' Austin agreed. 'And I *really am* sorry . . . about all of it. I just wondered if I could . . . you know . . . start again? I'm not normally such an ignorant bastard. I'd been on a bender since my last film wrapped. You know what it's like – that end-of-term thing. The only thing was, the film wrapped five months ago but I just kept on drinking. Daft really; real vodka-on-the-cornflakes stuff.'

'But you weren't drunk *all* the time!' Holly frowned. 'Sometimes you were sober and horrible.'

'I can drink a lot before I seem pissed. And, as for being horrible . . . Hollywood doesn't exactly exercise your "nice" muscle. I was a complete arsehole on set and everyone pretended it was fine.'

'Ee says that ee 'ates 'ollywood, but I don't think eet ees true,' piped up Carmen. 'I think ee likes being an arsehole.'

Austin shook his head. 'I've had enough of acting. I'm through.'

'I am not so sure.' Carmen smiled.

Austin turned to Sue. 'Sue, can you forgive me? You probably won't believe me, but I really *did* fancy you when I was little. I don't know why I was such a cock. Hormonal flash-back, I reckon.'

Sue's cheeks went pink. 'Really, Austin, it's fine.'

'Is there anything I can do to make it up to you?'

'There's no need. You were telling the truth.'

'I was talking bollocks. I was totally out of line.'

'Yes,' Terence interrupted with anger. 'Yes, you were!'

Austin turned to him. 'Terence . . .' He was careful to use his right name. 'Cressida, Woodster, Roxy, Holly – *all of you* . . . I'm sorry. But Carmen's back now; she'll keep me in line.'

'You need to learn to keep yourself een line, Meester Jones!' Carmen scolded him. 'I am not your mother. I do not want boyfriend like baby. You want mee to stay, you must deserve mee to stay.'

'Girl power!' Roxy half-heartedly punched the air, and nearly slid off the front of the bubble chair. As she righted herself, her eye fell on Chelle. Chelle was sitting arms-crossed and stony-faced – pouting like a teenager who'd just been grounded. And then Roxy saw it: the tell-tale sign she'd been looking for. Woody turned to Chelle, smiled sadly, and mouthed the words, 'You OK?'

'So, what d'you reckon?' Austin was asking contritely. 'Can I come to the next meeting? Start again?'

But Roxy heard nothing. Her heart had smashed on the floor.

'Hey, Rox; wait up!'

Roxy could hear Woody's voice in the darkness behind her.

She hadn't hung around. Austin had said his bit, the group had forgiven him and everyone was chatting idly. Chelle had scarpered first, stiff-backed with a face like thunder, a concerned-looking Holly in her wake. If it was a deliberate ploy to put the group off the scent, it was working. Woody had done a brilliant job of pretending not to notice Chelle leave, and the others hadn't even seen the change that had happened between them. But Roxy had, and she'd had enough. She was sick of the evening, sick of the group and sick with herself. And being so close to Woody was confusing. She didn't know whether to ache with longing or slap his two-timing face.

She speeded up, but he strode after her regardless.

'I came to see you the other night,' he told her.

'Yeah?' she muttered with venom. 'Looking for another idiot to shag?'

'What? No! Rox, look – what's up?'

'You know full well what's up.' She fixed her eyes on Austin's iron gates and kept marching. She wasn't turning round to look at him – no way.

'Are you upset about Austin and Carmen?'

'Upset about Austin . . . ? Are you nuts?'

'I thought you and him had a thing.'

'Oh, rock off!' Roxy thundered, disgusted. 'Austin flirts like breathing. I'm not a complete bloody amateur, you know!'

Furiously, she tried to walk faster. Why wouldn't Woody just leave her alone? She didn't want to talk to him and she definitely didn't want him being kind. She knew her anger was fragile. One little smile from him and it could all tumble apart. That's why she needed to get home, and fast.

'So, what is it? Are you pissed that everyone forgave him?'

'No!'

'So, what then? I'm confused.'

'Confused?' Roxy spat the word out. 'Well, isn't that just typical of a man?'

'Eh?'

'"I'm not bad; I'm confused."'

'Roxy, I don't have a clue what you're on about.'

'*You!*' Roxy shouted incredulously. 'I'm on about *you*! I can't believe I actually fell for all that shit about you being reformed . . . all the shagabout, Woodeniser crap being behind you!'

'It is! I am!'

'You make me sick!' Roxy was almost running now – the wave of her anger was so strong. 'All that pious group-hug, caring rubbish – when, beneath it all, you're just a randy vagina miner!'

'A randy *what*?' Woody laughed in surprise.

'You heard me! You should be ashamed of yourself, cheating on Jennifer.'

'On Jennifer?'

Even through her rage, Roxy could tell he was surprised.

'With *who, exactly*?' he asked.

'Don't be cute with me.' She wasn't going to fall for his innocent act again.

'I'm not! Cheating on Jennifer with who?'

'You *know* who!'

'No, I don't. And actually, Rox, there's something I've been meaning to tell you about Jennifer—'

'What? Don't tell me! She *doesn't understand you* . . . ? You're *only staying with her to be kind* . . . ? You *haven't had sex in years* . . . ? Well, button it, Woody; I don't care! And to think I thought you were special!'

Suddenly Woody stopped walking. 'You think I'm special?'

'Grrrrraaarggghhh!' she threw up her arms in fury. '*How* could you have been *so stupid*, Rox?' she shouted up at the stars. And she powered through Austin's gates and away.

ROXY

6am, Lavender Heath High Street.

Roxy's feet powered over the pavement, her trainers punching the ground with intent. She was running suicidally fast, her music loud and hard in her ears. Her iPod was set to her rage list: The Prodigy; Sex Pistols; Nine Inch Nails. No Woody. Very, very definitely no Woody.

SUE

Sue's bedroom hadn't seen such activity in decades. The floor was littered with discarded clothes and the windows had steamed up from the excitement. A glass of Dutch courage lay drained on the bed. Sue couldn't believe she was doing it . . . that she was *actually* going to do it. She sucked in her tummy, screwed her eyes tight and tried to breathe just from the very top of her lungs.

'Try now!' she cried, and braced hard.

There was a tug at her bottom, strenuous straining and a cheer.

'You're in!' Roxy flopped breathlessly back.

Sue opened her eyes.

It had taken three attempts, two Roxy pep-talks and one Spanx bodystocking, but they'd done it! Slowly, she let herself breathe. It felt tight, but nothing broke, ripped or popped. She was actually wearing the dress!

She looked in the mirror, agog. The dress was simple, but absolutely stunning. Floor-length, cream, with a fitted body and wide, drapey sleeves that tapered to a point under each wrist . . . It was classy, expensive . . . *and tight*!

She frowned nervously. 'Do you really think I can get away with it?'

'With knobs on!'

'But my bottom . . . ?'

'What bottom? The Spanx has nuked it.'

'And my tummy . . .'

'Sue – you look a billion dollars!'

'A billion?' she laughed at the very idea.

'Any old WAG can be a million. But you, Sue Bunce, are a classy billion.'

Sue looked in the mirror again. She couldn't quite believe what she saw. The woman looking back wasn't the old Sue; her hair was up, her cheekbones shone and her make-up was glamorously classic. But this woman wasn't Suzi, either. This Sue was someone new: a perfect blend of them both. Prettier, happier, more confident than Sue, but subtler, less naïve than Suzi. She was her old self grown wiser, grown dignified, grown up.

'Come on, Cinders.' Roxy gently nudged her. 'Your people carrier awaits.'

Sue nodded. It was too late for second thoughts now.

Terence and Simon were waiting in the hallway.

'Good God!' Terence exclaimed as Sue descended the stairs. Beneath his bow tie and dinner jacket, he was speechless. He stared in mute admiration.

'Wow!' Simon grinned. 'You look beautiful, Sue – really beautiful. Kind of Princess-Leia-meets-Donna-Karan.'

'Every boy's fantasy, come of age,' Terence murmured in a trance.

Sue felt her cheeks burn with embarrassment. She hadn't had compliments in years, other than from Roxy – and she always thought Roxy was just cheering her up. She couldn't quite remember how she was supposed to react to flattery, so she looked at the carpet and blushed.

'Right –' Simon jangled his keys – 'we'd better get going!'

Terence was still staring in awe.

'Now, you listen up, Mr Leggett.' Roxy waggled a finger. 'You look after Sue – you hear me? Treat her like a lady. That means no being your normal self and moaning about stuff. No nightclubs, casinos or strip bars. And *definitely* no kebabs!' She winked at Sue. 'They make your breath ming in the morning.'

'Thank you,' Sue whispered. 'For everything.'

Roxy gently readjusted Sue's hair. 'No problem.' She smiled. 'Now, go on, you lot – rock off! There's a premiere you're supposed to be at!'

Nervously, Sue let Terence help her into the back of the new people carrier. She carefully arranged her dress as she sat.

'Gosh!' she marvelled when her eyes finally took in the sumptuous white leather interior. The car seats were plumper than her sofa. And there were TVs on the back of each headrest.

'When Austin Jones says top of the range, he means Top Of

The Range.' Simon grinned. He sped smoothly away from Lavender Heath and towards London, the sound of the engine just the tiniest hum.

'It's good of you to drive us,' Terence thanked him stiffly. Sue hid a smile. Being pleasant to Simon didn't come naturally to Terence. His fingers tugged at his shirt collar, as if the niceness needed help getting out.

'No problem,' said Simon easily, his eyes on the dark country road. 'Any excuse to try out the new wheels.'

'But you really don't need to wait around and bring us back. I mean, it must be inconvenient. We'll be perfectly fine on the train.'

Sue held her breath. She'd been so grateful when Simon had offered to drive. It was terrifying enough facing the eyes of Leicester Square, let alone the prospect of public transport.

'It's OK,' Simon replied. 'I'll just wander around the West End – take in the lights, sniff the greasepaint . . . torture myself with all the hit plays I'm not starring in. I'll be fine.'

Sue exhaled in relief.

'Well, it's jolly decent of you,' Terence gruffly thanked him again.

'No problem. That's what friends are for.'

Sue sat back, savouring his words as she watched the countryside morph into the suburbs of London.

Friends: that's what Simon had said. And then she suddenly realised that that's what Roxy and the gang were . . . that she, Sue Bunce, the sleazy, undeserving harlot, the crossword-

obsessed, biscuit-loving, overweight recluse, had somehow
found herself *friends*.

And suddenly nothing seemed frightening any more.

Terence and Sue stood at the start of the red carpet. Ahead of
them was an organised riot: a VIP corridor of people, noise and
light. It wasn't a premiere, it was a bunfight – a scrum. Autograph
hunters hung over the barriers, screeching at Hollywood stars
to smile into their camera phones and record messages for their
mums. Harassed PRs in air-traffic-controller headsets officiously
patrolled the carpet, thrusting anyone famous into the arms
of the nearest film crew. There were TV cameras, radio microphones and the blinding whirl of spotlights. Celebrities glittered
celestially as they chatted to news crews and dazzled the
ordinary crowds. Thick-set security guards glared ominously in
their wake. It was deafening, demented, Dantesque. And, at the
far end of it all, a seething swarm of photographers lay in wait.

Terence looked at her nervously. 'OK?'

Sue swallowed hard.

'I mean, we don't have to . . . I could ring Simon; we could
just go home.'

'No,' she heard herself insist. 'We're here now. And this is
important to you.'

She sensed Terence soften. 'Thank you. I don't think I could
face this on my own. Too terrified everyone will laugh.'

Sue looked at him, surprised. This wasn't the Terence she
knew: the bitter, angry weatherman who thought the whole
world had mugged him of his old life.

'They won't laugh,' she replied simply. 'You're Terence Leggett, esteemed meteorologist.'

'No,' he smiled. 'I'm Tornado Terry, and I've just got to get over it.'

They looked at each other for a moment. Slowly, Terence offered his arm.

And then they were doing it: they were walking down the red carpet and into the riot, past the autograph hunters and the spotlights and the security guards, past the news crews and the radio mics and the PRs. And then a voice cut through . . .

'Hey! Tornado! Over here!'

They froze.

'Ha! I thought it was you!' the voice continued. It was coming from deep within the mass of photographers. 'A couple of quick shots before you go inside?'

Terence hesitated.

'Go.' Sue smiled encouragingly. 'It's what we came for. Go and get back your old life.'

Terence nodded, looking frightened. But then he stiffened his shoulders, lifted his chin and stepped forward. Sue stayed where she was, barely breathing. This was it – make or break – Terence's future hanging in the balance. She watched his silhouette, dark against the flashing of the cameras. Squeezed into just a few feet of Leicester Square's pavement, a hundred photographers towered before him, crushed against barriers, balancing on ladders . . . a living, braying, petrifying wall of lenses.

'Tornado Terry! This way!'

'On your left, Mr Tornado.'

'Just a few shots over here, please!'

'Lovely, Mr Tornado! And again – this way, please!'

Sue exhaled in relief. The photographers weren't being rude. They weren't mocking. They were just doing their job. And Terence was doing all right. His shoulders were relaxed; he was smiling – *he looked happy*. It was going well; it was going *really* well!

'What're you working on now, Terry?' someone asked.

Sue tensed, waiting for his bitterness to show.

'Nothing! Haven't you heard? I'm unemployable!'

The photographers laughed. But it was *with* him – definitely not at him.

'Who's your lady-friend, Terry?' somebody asked.

Sue blinked as a few shots were fired in her direction. And then she felt the eyes of the pack upon her. Terence turned, his face a silent question. And to her amazement, Sue felt herself nod.

Gallantly, Terence took her arm and led her forward. Bulbs started flashing with more urgency.

'This, gentlemen,' he declared proudly, 'is the very lovely, extremely beautiful, Sue Bunce.'

'*Bunce?*' In the middle of the pack, a camera dropped down. A lone human face was revealed. 'What, *the* Sue Bunce? From ages ago? *Sugatits Suzi?*'

And all the air was sucked out of Leicester Square, and all the noise seemed to switch itself off. Even the rowdy autograph hunters fell silent and the traffic stopped as the whole of WC2 seemed to hang on Sue's reply.

Sue paused. At her side, she could see Terence ready to jump in and rescue her.

She took a deep breath.

There was nowhere to hide, no front door to hurtle back to, or cup of tea to run off to make. It was time to meet the world once again.

'Yes,' she said, as loud as she could, her voice tiny in the vast London night. 'Although, I'm really just "Sue" these days.'

There was a moment of silence . . . and then a roar.

'Sue! Sue, this way!'

'Miss Bunce! Miss Bunce! The picture desk's gonna go nuts!'

'Sue, please, over here! Look at me, please, Sue! *Look at me!*'

And the air heated up and the warm wall hit her, and the whole world suddenly shone with the light of a thousand dazzling flashes.

To: Roxy Squires
From: *The Book Show* production office

Dear Ms Squires,

Thank you for your intriguing email about the author, Holly Childs.

Obviously we'd be more than interested in having the phenomenal
Ms Childs as a guest on *The Book Show* . . . In fact, we'll clear the
whole show in her honour! We'd given up hope of ever booking her.
We'd heard that she refuses to grant any interviews. (Actually, we'd
heard that she'd dropped out of society entirely and was living in a
tree house on an island . . . *how do these rumours get started?!*)

Is Holly available to record the interview next week? Please let us
know her green-room requirements . . . Champagne, oysters,
anything . . . !

To: Roxy Squires

From: *Loose Women* production office

Dear Roxy,

Are you kidding??? God, we'd *kill* to have Cressida Cunningham as a guest!

We on *Loose Women* pride ourselves on telling it like it is. Nobody calls a spade a spade like Cressida Cunningham – she's our heroine! Do you *really* think she might be interested in coming on our show?

We've got everything crossed in anticipation!!!

WOODY

Euan opened the front door.

'All right?' he nodded. 'Cressida's online.'

'Online?' Woody stepped inside and tried not to smile. He glanced at the teenager beside him. He certainly looked like he'd lost some rough edges. The sullenness had receded and, although he wasn't smiling exactly, he'd at least stopped glaring like you were shit on his shoe.

'Is that Woody?' Cressida trilled from the study. 'Tell him I'm just finishing my blog!'

Woody raised an eyebrow. 'She blogs now?'

Euan shrugged. 'And tweets, trends and BBMs . . .'

'Coffee, Woody?' Cressida called out.

'I'll stick the kettle on!' he replied with a laugh. He knew the drill.

'She's bought a Nespresso,' Euan mumbled.

'But can she work it?' Woody asked dryly.

'Course! But it's OK – I like to make it.'

Woody choked down another laugh and headed into the

study. Sitting at her desk, Cressida was just hitting *publish* with a flourish.

'There; that'll do for now,' she declared. 'I'm going to Skype my followers this afternoon. I want to hear what they think about the new baccalaureates.'

'It's working, then, this home-gimp business?' Woody grinned.

'What? Euan? He's a poppet. I don't know what all the worry was about.'

'I don't think Si would call him a poppet.'

'You've just got to show teenagers who's boss. They're like dogs: give them too much freedom and they'll worry the sheep, but show a firm hand and they soon walk to heel.'

Woody bit his lip to stop himself laughing. But Cressida didn't notice. She was too busy beaming at Euan, who'd just appeared with a tray.

'Thank you, Euan.' She cleared a space on her desk next to the newspapers. 'Oh, and biscuits too – jolly good! Tell me, how did you get on with that economics homework I set you?'

'Finished,' he replied, a hint of pride briefly flitting across his features.

'You're setting him homework?' Woody asked. He wasn't sure what to be more shocked by – the homework, or the pride.

'He's a bright boy; he can handle it!' Cressida told him. 'Besides, if you want to learn, you need to go off-piste. Otherwise all you get is the grade.'

'Any parrot can get a grade,' added Euan, witheringly.

'Quite!' agreed Cressida. 'Well, you'd better head off now, Euan, else your mother will start wondering where you are. I'll text you later if I get stuck with the Skype.'

'OK. Bye, Cressida.' And with the smallest hint of a smile, Euan was off.

Woody stared into the space he'd just vacated.

'He likes you!' he said in amazement. 'Teenagers hate everyone, but he actually likes you!'

'I'm not here to be liked. I didn't build a career on being liked.'

'So what happened to "Ms Cunningham", then?' Woody teased.

Cressida tutted. 'I'm not a complete dinosaur. We got beyond all that pomp in the first week. Besides, you can't be too formal in chat rooms; it's a whole new language in there. If I sounded like myself, I'd sound ludicrous. Correct parlance is "totes inappropes".'

Woody laughed. 'You're phenomenal, Cressida, d'you know that? The world's only government-minister-turned-teen-whisperer.'

Cressida pulled a face. 'Amazeballs.' She shrugged and sipped her Nespresso.

7.51pm @FoxyRoxy

Fame, work, It bags, Nanoblur, men . . . all overrated! When
chips down & fan shitty, nothing in world beats a girly night in.

7.52pm @FoxyRoxy

The girls are on their way over!
#ROXYSAYS: BOTTOMS UP TO THAT!

CRESSIDA

Cressida peeled the cucumber slices off her eyes and leant forward to examine the newspaper.

'*LOOK WHAT THE TORNADO BLEW IN!*' read the headline.

Restricted by the cement of her face pack, she made a loud, clucky tut. 'And on a scale of one to ten, how well has Terence taken his upstaging?'

'Terence has been a real sweetheart,' Sue declared earnestly, her eyes shining with the three bottles of fizz the women had so far downed between them. It was shaping up to be a vintage girls' night in: pink booze, a mountain of cakes and Shirley Bassey's greatest hits on shuffle. 'He was just worried about me, the lamb.'

'Hmmm,' Cressida murmured at full volume. 'Somehow I think only *you* could have got away with it.'

'What do you mean?' Sue asked, confused.

'What I mean is –' Cressida tried to speak without cracking her face – 'I don't think he'd have been such a "lamb" about having his big moment overshadowed if it had been one of us lot doing the overshadowing!'

Sue looked blank for a moment.

'Oh!' she exclaimed, as the penny dropped. 'Oh, no; it's not like that – we're just friends.'

'Yeah, right,' Roxy smirked as she popped the cork on bottle number four (Asti, not champagne – now that she was a civilian she had to economise). 'That's not what the papers say.' She topped up Sue's glass and read from the paper. 'Sue Bunce made her return to the spotlight last night at the UK premiere of *Fluffy Love Stuff*. Ms Bunce – who gained nationwide notoriety when her affair with the former cabinet MP, Rupert Hunt, was revealed – almost three decades ago – had been living in obscurity since the scandal. Her unexpected appearance in London's Leicester Square came on the arm of her . . .' Roxy raised an eyebrow at Sue '. . . close friend, former TV weatherman, Terence "Tornado Terry" Leggett . . .'

'See?' Sue protested. 'They said "friend".'

'They said "*close* friend".'

'I can't help it if they added a "close". Besides, Terence knows it's not like that.'

'Of course he does,' Cressida agreed ambiguously.

Sue frowned. 'Are you laughing at me? Because I can't tell with that face pack . . .'

Cressida replaced the cucumber slices over her eyes and slid back to a recline.

'All of which is missing the point,' Roxy interrupted, as she stared at Sue's picture in the paper. Sue looked radiant as she posed on the red carpet, Terence beaming proudly behind her. There was no mistaking what a beauty she'd been. The poise of her modelling days had not deserted her. Her hip was forward, her leg extended and she was looking into the lens like she owned it. 'You know what, Sue?' Roxy marvelled. 'You've still got it!'

Sue wriggled happily across the sofa to scour the picture once again. 'I didn't think I had it in me,' she beamed.

'It was just a short walk across Leicester Square.'

'Not just that – all of it! The dress, the hair, the confidence . . .'

'Confidence is a trick. You just need to practise.'

Sue nodded, tipsy and happy. 'The dress *is* spectacular,' she conceded.

'*You* are spectacular!' Roxy cried.

'I have to agree,' Cressida declared suddenly, discarding the cucumbers and sitting up. 'You put a point on the board for the older woman last night. You blew all those underdressed, undernourished teen-women out of the water.'

Sue looked at her, dumbfounded. Suddenly her eyes dampened. 'Thanks Cressida,' she croaked drunkenly. 'That means a lot.'

'Yes, well . . .' Cressida shrugged. 'Can you please release me from this blasted cast, now, Roxy? I feel like I'm being mummified.'

'*Beautified*,' Roxy corrected.

'Hmmm.' Cressida eyed her toes – rammed into separators and painted scarlet – with suspicion.

Roxy sighed happily and drained her glass. 'It's a shame Holly and Chelle couldn't make it,' she mused as she started melting Cressida's face mask with warm water, 'because I reckon this is the life!'

'This?' Sue echoed, surprised. 'What, here . . . ? With *us*?'

'Yeah, this is *way* better than going through my checklist in some nightclub – spending the whole night blagging my way into VIP, only to discover there's nothing "I" about the "P"s that are in there – before freezing my tits off for the paps.'

'Oh, Roxy, what a lovely thing to say!' Sue gushed, touched in a fourth-bottle-of-Asti kind of way.

'And, you know what?' Roxy added thoughtfully. 'I don't want to be famous any more.'

'*Roxy!*'

'It's too much effort . . . I can't be arsed.'

'At last!' smirked Cressida, under the remains of her face mask.

But Sue was confused. 'But being famous . . . Roxy, it's who you *are*. Are you seriously giving it up?'

Roxy nodded.

Sue frowned. 'But if you're not going to be famous, where does that leave the rest of us?'

'Page seven of today's newspaper,' Roxy laughed. 'Oh, Sue, I'll let you in on a secret. I haven't been famous in ages.'

'But . . .' Sue protested, perplexed. 'But what about all those jobs, and the showbiz parties, and your celebrity clothes, and your famous-person teeth—?'

'All bollocks.' Roxy dismissed them with a wave. 'The jobs were invented, the parties crap and the clothes were too small. And, as for the teeth – I'm going fallow.'

'Yellow?'

'Fallow. Like a field!'

Sue furrowed her brow as she thought. 'Does that mean they'll go back to being tooth coloured?'

'Hallelujah,' Cressida said dryly.

'I'll look like Stig of the Dump, but who cares? It's not like I've got anyone to impress.' Roxy looked glum. 'No, I'll leave all the impressing to Chelle.'

'Hah!' Cressida cried. 'Chelle couldn't impress her way out of a paper bag.'

'I don't think Woody agrees.' Suddenly Roxy had had enough booze not to be angry. Suddenly she was fourth-bottle-of-Asti depressed. She took a deep breath. 'Woody and Chelle; they're together.'

'Don't be ridiculous,' Cressida snorted.

'They're keeping it hidden, but they're shagging.'

'Woody's not interested in Chelle,' cried Sue. 'He's totally in love with Jennifer!'

'He's *cheating* on Jennifer,' Roxy told her.

'He wouldn't. Not after what happened with Petra.'

'What happened with Petra?' Roxy asked.

'She cheated on him with Austin, of course!'

Roxy's mouth fell open. How had she never known that? She was a walking who's-doing-who on celebs. But now everything was beginning to make sense. *That* was why Woody and Petra split up . . . why Woody was grumpy with Austin . . . and why he'd warned her not to fall for his charms! Roxy felt a massive whoosh of sympathy. *Poor Woody* – having to put up with the man who'd stolen his girlfriend. And then sympathy turned into guilt as she remembered that it was *she* who'd made Woody ask Austin to join the group.

'No wonder he punched Austin's lights out,' Cressida chortled.

But Roxy frowned. Something still didn't add up.

'But there's definitely *something* going on between Chelle and Woody,' she insisted. All she could see was the memory of Chelle in her undies, marking her territory on Woody's front doorstep.

'Chelle's not interested in Woody,' scoffed Cressida. 'She's got her eye higher up the food chain.'

'But who could be higher than Woody?' Sue frowned.

'Austin,' Roxy replied in a daze. *Of course – Austin!* How could she have missed something so obvious? Chelle had always been clear about her game plan – and Austin was definitely richer and more famous than Woody. *And* she'd been flirting for Britain in the pub the other night. *And* she'd legged it just after finding out about Carmen.

'And as for Jennifer . . .' Cressida continued smugly, eyes twinkling as she regarded her Asti. There was a very long pause – torturously long. 'Well . . . isn't it obvious?' she smirked.

To: Roxy Squires

From: *Have I Got News For You* production office

Dear Ms Squires,

We hear from some of our industry colleagues that you represent Cressida Cunningham, Sue Bunce, Terence 'The Tornado' Leggett and Holly Childs. If possible, we'd like to book all of them for our forthcoming series. Whatever your conditions, we agree! We'd even like to offer you a host slot, as thanks.

Yours in anticipation . . .

ROXY

Roxy lay in bed, miserably staring at her ceiling. Last night had been confusing through the blur of a fourth bottle of pink, but morning had not made things any clearer. *What* was obvious about Jennifer?

Of course, she hadn't wanted to come out and admit that what was obvious to Cressida was as clear as a mudbath to her. She'd had enough confession that week. So, instead, she'd dug out her Wham! CD and kicked off the dancing. But as she'd cancanned around her living room, she hadn't for a moment stopped puzzling. *What* was obvious about Jennifer? And, come to think of it, *who* was bloody Jennifer? And was she *ever* going to bother coming back?

She sighed and groped for her phone on the bedside table. Her fingers closed around it and switched it on. Immediately, it started beeping. She had messages. She touched the answerphone icon and Tish's voice filled her ear.

'Rox the fox, you bad, bad girl!' Tish's voice bubbled with unstoppable excitement. 'I just hope that bitch mega-paid you. No, seriously, hon – it's hilaire! Haven't laughed so much in years. I *knew* there had to be a reason why you'd hidden away in suburbia, or the countryside, or wherever it is you live these days. When I saw it this morning, I shrieked so hard my pelvic floor nearly gave way . . . *Thank God for pilates and Davina.* Even Guy raised a smile, and you know what he's like with the tabloids. And O.M.G! *Austin Jones – what a munter!* All that money and he looks like a homeless! Does he smell? *Just imagine the knob cheese.* And all the other little hobbits in the gang – what a funny bunch of freaks they all are. Anyway, babes – call me – immediately! I want all the goss; every last, gory drop!'

And then there were fourteen messages from her mother.

Roxy had barely finished her mother's fretful messages when Simon's text had come through. There had been no time for make-up; she hadn't even brushed her hair. She'd thrown on some leggings and was hurtling up Simon's drive as the people carrier pulled up. Panting from the rush, she watched as Simon got out, did a secret-service-style three-sixty inspection, and then opened the rear passenger door. Wearing shades and a hoody, Austin slid out. Simon ushered him urgently into the house.

'It was the only way he could get here,' he told Roxy, the excitement of his mission making his eyes shine. 'It's a bunfight outside his gates: so many paparazzi, they've blocked the whole road! I had to wait around the corner with the engine running. He climbed over the wall and escaped!'

'Rocking hell!' exclaimed Roxy. Overnight, the world had gone mad.

Inside, the house was like emergency headquarters. The group was sat in a daze, with Linda cooking bacon butties and issuing tea. Despite the extra sugar in hers, Sue was visibly shaking.

'I was so frightened.' She wrapped the duck egg tightly around her. 'They were all at the end of my drive! I couldn't go out. I couldn't even go downstairs to make a cup of tea because I'd left the curtains open and their lenses were all pointing in. Luckily, Woody saw the commotion. He brought his ladder round the back. We came out over the fence.'

There was a noise at Simon's front door. Everyone froze.

'The paparazzi,' hissed Chelle, her voice laced with as much excitement as dread. 'They must've followed us here!'

Linda marched into the hall, guns blazing. But a moment later she returned with Woody.

'It's not good,' Woody admitted as he dropped a stack of *Sunday Post*s on to the table. 'I bought all the copies in the shop – not that it'll make a difference. The story's already out there.'

'It's probably in Honolulu by now,' Roxy told them. 'Things go global faster than you can fart.'

Somebody whimpered. Everyone picked up a paper and read.

'It's mainly about you,' Woody warned Austin.

Austin looked grim but unsurprised. He examined the front page. 'One for the cuttings book, I see!' he said wryly. 'FROM HUNK TO DRUNK', read the headline. 'HOLLYWOOD STAR IN THE GUTTER'. The entire front page was a picture of Austin – flabby, drunken, and lying on a pavement. It had been taken at night, the flash catching his eyes and making him look deranged. He looked more like a hobo than a star, almost unrecognisable from the man from the billboards. He was wearing a tatty anorak and an ill-fitting shirt, a roll of hairy gut peeking out underneath. His mouth was open, his teeth looked dirty and something pale was matted in his beard.

Chelle gasped. 'My shoes!' she shrieked.

Everyone looked closely. And, sure enough, Chelle's orange peep-toes were in the edge of the shot – one shoe darker than the other.

'It's outside the Dog and Duck!' exclaimed Simon. 'It's the night Austin puked! We were all standing right next to him, working out how to get him in the back of the people carrier without smacking his head.'

'But how . . . ?' Terence was flummoxed. 'I mean, it was only us there. The street was empty.'

'I told you you pissed on my shoes!' Chelle poked Austin angrily. 'Three hundred quid, they cost me.'

Roxy frowned. 'But there wasn't a photographer; we'd have seen the flash. And besides, hadn't the paps all gone back to London that night?'

'They have their ways,' Holly said obliquely. 'The papers can do anything, if they want to.'

'*For the full story turn to pages 2, 3, 6, 7 and 13*', the paper instructed. Everyone flipped the page over.

'*EXCLUSIVE BY NICOLA BLUNT*', announced the headline. And there was the familiar silhouette.

'Can somebody read it out?' Sue asked weakly. 'I can't keep

the paper still. My hands are shaking.'

Woody started to read.

'"From Hollywood hero to urine-soaked zero, movie star Austin Jones was left seeing stars this week as he rolled around in a gutter outside his local boozer. Critics have hailed Jones, 37, the greatest actor of our generation. He was the plucky Brit who conquered Hollywood with his prodigious talent and dazzling smile. His movies broke box office records the world over. But just a few days ago, onlookers were dazed to see the *Puppy Love* star drunk and disorderly on a public street, ranting incoherently, and soaked in his own vomit and urine."'

Sue gasped. 'That's outrageous!' she declared loyally, touching Austin's arm in support.

'Actually, it's pretty accurate,' said Cressida. 'He *is* a Hollywood star; he *was* lying on the pavement; and he *had* just spent a penny on himself.'

Woody read on.

'"It's a sad decline for the actor whose recent movies were plagued by whispers of drinking and out-of-control womanising. Jones, who famously announced he was quitting movies to take "early retirement", returned to the UK in January. But with evidence like this, the question must be asked . . . was it his choice to leave Hollywood, or did Hollywood kick him out?"'

'See?' Terence whispered righteously.

Woody read silently for a moment. 'I'll skip this bit. It's just some shitty stuff about the studios wanting you to have Botox. And then there's the usual guff about you sleeping with your co-stars . . . OK, here we go . . . "Back in the UK, the extent of Austin's problems has become apparent. With no acting work to divert him, his alcoholism has been given free rein. He drinks anything he can get his hands on and, when the booze runs out, he drinks meths."'

'That was a joke!' Austin protested.

'But *when* did you say that?' Roxy puzzled. 'Was it at one of our houses, or in the Dog and Duck?'

'The landlord!' shrieked Chelle. 'The landlord's the grass!'

'Everyone knows pubs are in trouble,' added Terence. 'Doesn't one go out of business every second?'

'Dave wouldn't have sold the story,' Woody said calmly. 'He's a decent bloke. He's not the kind to go running to the papers.'

'Keep reading!' cried Chelle, excited. 'What else does it say?'

Woody scanned the article. 'Blah, blah . . . "Frequently drinks 'til he vomits . . . His good looks fading fast . . . Waistline bloated . . . Eyes bloodshot . . . Grown beard to hide double chin . . . Often speckled with own vomit . . . Rarely washes . . ."'

'I do wash!' Austin interrupted. 'A bit.'

'. . . "Spends his days holed up in his ten-million-pound mansion, drinking heavily and watching porn. The increasingly isolated star demands that his meals are brought to him on a motorised boat via the network of swimming-pool lanes he's had built into the rooms of his house . . ."'

'I've only done that a few times,' Austin protested. 'What's the point in being rich if you can't have a laugh?'

'"The only time he leaves his mansion is to go to a bizarre

self-help group of other washed-up celebs, where he has become 'showbiz mates' with a gruesome bunch of Z-listers . . .'"

'Z-listers?' Chelle echoed in outrage. 'How dare she? If my Dwayne ever got his hands on that Nicola Blunt cow—!'

'I thought you and Dwayne had split up?' Roxy asked, surprised.

'We have.' Chelle slumped, suddenly doleful.

'"One such showbiz mate, Sue 'Sugatits Suzi' Bunce, has become the subject of Jones' perverted obsession. Jones, who claims to be single despite living with fiery, Latino girlfriend Carmen Bonitta (twenty-five), makes routine unwanted sexual advances to women, and has a kinky appetite for virgins . . ."'

Holly gasped.

'I'm not a virgin! I'm not!'

'". . . but it's 'Sugatits Suzi' who Jones is really after. The *Love Games* and *Missing You* star has become obsessed with the big-breasted model, who shocked the nation with her sleazy affair with married MP, Rupert Hunt. Suzi, who made her first public appearance in twenty-eight years earlier this week, is rumoured to be making a comeback with a no-holds-barred kiss-and-tell autobiography . . ."'

'Oh my goodness, Austin – I didn't . . .' Sue had gone deathly pale. 'I mean, the way they've put it makes it look like I . . .'

Austin smiled. 'It's OK, Sue. I know you didn't go to the papers with this.'

'I would never . . .' she protested, appalled.

'The book was my idea,' Roxy stepped in. 'It's nothing to do with you, Austin, I promise.'

'But how do they know all this stuff?' Simon scratched his head. 'How do they know about the meths, and the dinner, and the swimming lanes? One of *us* must have told them and it *wasn't* me!'

'Or me!' Chelle snorted quickly.

'Nor me!' Holly declared.

'Do many people come to your house?' asked Woody.

Austin shrugged. 'The cooks, the cleaners, the gardeners, the housekeeper, the accountant, the woman who does the laundry, the guy who cleans the pool lanes, Carmen's mates . . .'

Woody flipped through the paper again, before suddenly stopping. 'There's more,' he announced grimly. And slowly he turned the paper to show them. Centre page was a photo of Sue with '*I JUST WANNA BE SUGATITS!*' in capitals.

Sue gasped.

'Oh my God! But how do they . . . ? I'd had a sherry, I was upset!'

'Disgusting!' Terry exploded. 'Utterly, despicable.'

'What are they saying about me?' Sue began to hyperventilate.

Woody took a deep breath and proceeded carefully. Everyone cringed as he read.

'"Neurotic, ageing sex bomb Sue 'Sugatits Suzi' Bunce may have been looking radiant on the red carpet at the premiere of *Fluffy Love Stuff* this week, but it was a far cry from her normal appearance. Sue, 53, has spent years hiding from the world in her luxury Lavender Heath home, stockpiling biscuits and bingeing on junk food. The former model – whose career was destroyed when lurid, confectionery-based details were revealed of her affair with former MP Rupert Hunt – has been piling on the pounds and losing her grip on reality. But recently, friends say that the chesty, scale-tipping scandal-survivor broke down entirely, insisting she'll regain her former sexy curves and show the world that she can 'be Sugatits Suzi again'."'

Sue's eyes filled with tears.

'It's not like that! I mean, I know I said it, but I didn't think—'

'*The fucking bastards!*' Austin exploded. 'They can say what they like about me – I can take it. But to go after my friends . . . ? I'm fucking livid!'

Simon frowned. 'Who is this Nicola Blunt, anyway?'

'She's dead, that's what she is,' Austin raged.

'I've never even met her,' wailed Sue.

'Nobody knows what she looks like,' Roxy told them. 'We only know her name and silhouette. She claims she mixes with celebs like a shadow, catching them when they think no one's looking. It's all just a con. It means she can write about everyone else's dirty laundry, but nobody can find out about her own. The truth is, she's a bitchy, conniving coward and if I ever met her in real life I'd—'

Chelle shrieked.

'Oh my God, Terry – you're in 'ere too!'

She pointed a nail into the newspaper.

'What the . . . ?' Terry spluttered.

'*WEATHERMAN OGLES WARM FRONT!*' And there was a photo

of him standing next to Sue on the red carpet, tongue out as he looked down her cleavage.

'"Terry 'Tornado' Leggett,"' read Chelle, '". . . obviously not a leg man!"'

'I wasn't . . .' Terence protested his innocence. 'I never . . . It's just the angle!

'". . . 'I'm a national joke' . . ."' Chelle continued, oblivious. '". . . 'Everybody hates me, but I don't care; I just want to get my hands on Sugatits' . . ."'

'I don't!' Terence insisted, red faced. 'I'm not a bloody pervert. Not that you would need to be a pervert to . . .' He looked at Sue. 'Oh, Christ! Are they allowed to print this rubbish? Can we sue?'

'Cressida,' Roxy said quietly, pointing to yet another article.

Cressida leant forward and put on her glasses. '"*FROM WEST-MINSTER VILLAGE TO VILLAGE IDIOT*",' she read. '"Former Secretary of State for Work and Pensions, Cressida Cunningham, may have dominated Westminster Village but, in her home village of Lavender Heath, she's fast gaining the reputation of village idiot. Since losing her seat in the last general election (plus its accompanying army of taxpayer-funded helpers) the former MP is said to be struggling with all aspects of everyday life, from making friends to mastering simple household items. Not only has the former minister confessed herself lonely and friendless, but she is also flum-moxed by ordinary, idiot-proof gadgets such as TV remotes, microwaves and coffee makers. 'If it's got a plug on it, or needs batteries, she's stumped,' a neighbour told me. 'She might have been a big cheese up in London, but round here she's little more than a laughing stock.'"'

Everyone was quiet for a moment.

'You OK?' Roxy asked in concern.

'Nobody's laughing,' Woody said gently.

Cressida took off her glasses and sat back.

'Oh, don't worry about me,' she said cheerfully. 'I don't give a fig what they put in the papers – never have, never will. Besides, it could have been worse.' She smiled mischievously. 'At least she didn't mention my gimp!'

'Your gimp?' Simon echoed.

'Oh, yes! Didn't he tell you? He's quite a treasure!'

'Didn't *who* tell me?' Simon frowned in alarm. '*Who's* quite a treasure?'

Roxy looked at Woody. 'Is that it?' she asked quietly. 'No stories about anyone else?'

Woody shook his head.

'Oh great!' Simon erupted. 'What about me? I'm part of the group too – or don't I count? This is just typical. I can't even get my character assassinated!'

Holly was looking at Roxy sharply. 'Why are you asking, Roxy? Do you *want* there to be a story about you?'

'God, no!'

Holly frowned. 'But you're the one with all the ideas about how to be famous. You're the one who actually *wants* to be in the papers.'

'Yes,' Roxy conceded, 'but no! Things are different now. *I'm* different now.'

'Oh. My. God, it's *you*, isn't it?' Chelle blurted. '*You're* the one who blabbed all the stuff to Nicola Blunt!'

'As if! Nicola Blunt never even takes my calls!'

'So you *did* ring her?' Holly pounced on her admission.

'No! Well, *yes*. But not for ages,' Roxy tried to explain, the weight of the group's eyes suddenly on her. I just used to phone to say which club I was going to, so she could send a photographer and I'd get in the paper. I never got through, though . . . just left messages. And, even then, none of my pictures ever made it on to her page.'

Chelle folded her arms. 'I don't believe her,' she declared frostily.

'I do,' Woody said simply.

'Me too,' agreed Sue. 'Roxy wouldn't do something like this.'

Roxy looked at them gratefully. And, despite all the horribleness and tension (not to mention the hung jury on his shagabout status), she looked into Woody's eyes and melted.

'What about you, Chelle?' Terence sniped. 'You're not in the paper, either. Who's to say it wasn't *you* who dished the dirt?'

'Oh, cock off!' Chelle replied with contempt.

'But *you're* the one with all the magazine exclusives.'

'Yeah, and they're *my exclusives*,' she snarled. 'Why would I want to give coverage to you lot? Besides, Simon's not in the paper, either, or Holly, or Woody – are you saying they did it too?'

Terence shut up.

'Look, fighting about it isn't going to help,' said Woody.

'We're friends, remember? The stories are in there, and that's that. We can't let this get to us.'

'This is my fault,' Austin suddenly burst out. 'They'd never have gone after you lot without me.'

'You musn't blame yourself,' said Sue. 'None of this is down to you.'

'Yes!' Holly agreed.

'Shit happens,' Roxy added sagely. 'This bollocks is nothing but chip paper. Most of it'll be in recycling by lunch time.'

Simon turned to Austin. 'You can stay here tonight, if you like. We've got a spare room. You can lie low.'

Austin shook his head.

'I've got to get back to Carmen; I can't leave her with the mob at the door. Besides, I'm used to this shit. The press have bugged me for years.'

'Well, do you want me to drive you back to your wall?'

Austin nodded. 'Cheers, Si; you're a mate.'

'What about you, Sue?' Roxy asked. 'Do you want to stay over at mine?'

'Yes, please,' Sue answered, relieved.

'Give me your keys and I'll nip back and pack you a bag.'

'But what about all the photographers?'

'They've managed to *not* recognise me for years.' Roxy smiled. 'I'm sure they'll manage again.'

Everyone returned to their bacon butties, chatting quietly. Despite all the bombshells, excitement hung in the air.

Instinctively, Roxy's eyes turned to Woody. He seemed paler today – deadly serious. She knew he'd be blaming himself for the papers, for being the one who'd brought them all together, for not thinking ahead and preparing for it. He looked miserable. Suddenly Roxy forgot all about Jennifer and Chelle. The urge to reach over and comfort him was so strong. She wanted to wrap him up with her body, to kiss the worry away from his forehead, to stop him beating himself up as he stared vacantly into the depths of the newspaper.

* * *

But Woody wasn't staring vacantly; he was staring hard. In the hubbub of all the exposures, nobody had seen what he'd seen – the tiny article tucked away on page eight. '*CHILD PRODIGY RETURNS*'. It was just a few lines announcing Holly's comeback novel, due in bookshops later that year. But it wasn't the article that Woody was staring at – it was the photograph pictured alongside: the old, familiar mugshot of Holly from her top-selling heyday; the grainy snap of the teenager her parents had been so careful to shelter; the unlikely romance queen, with glasses, plaits and a brace. And then Woody looked up at current-day Holly as she comforted Sue on the sofa.

3.31pm @foxyroxy

Papers AWFUL. These are good people that Nicola Blunt's hurt. Why did I ever want to be on her page? Feel sick at the very thought.

To: Roxy Squires
From: ITV Drama Department

Dear Ms Squires,

We hope you don't mind us emailing you directly, but we have a programme idea we'd like to propose.

For a few years now, we in the ITV Drama Department have been avid followers of your Twitter account. We have laughed, cried and revamped our wardrobes according to your brilliant #ROXYSAYS tweets. Some of your drunken posts have made us cringe in embarrassment, whilst your relentless positivity in the face of obvious defeat has frequently moved us to tears! But the one thing your tweets all have in common is that they *always* have us on the edge of our seats!

And so to our programme idea . . .

We think *all* single ladies of a certain age and in a certain state of professional frustration will fall in love with the #ROXYSAYS tweets, just like us. You have summed up the desperation of being an ageing former *somebody* just perfectly (what *does* a ladette do when the world's moved on and that hunky husband hasn't come a-knocking?). So we would like to turn #ROXYSAYS into a six-part comedy drama. And as a post-modern twist, we were wondering if you'd star as yourself?

What do you think? Are you interested?

ROXY

Roxy looked out of the window, wondering if the ITV email had brought even a fleeting flash of happiness. It hadn't. She still felt depressed. Lavender Heath's siege-like state was bringing her down. She watched bleakly as yet another news crew traipsed past the end of her drive, and wondered if the story would *ever* blow itself out.

The village had been crawling with press all week. It was as though the *Sunday Post* articles had been a starting gun, and they'd raced up from London within the hour. Everyone was desperate for more gossip on the Austin–Sue–Terry love triangle. But the Lavender Heath residents were a tight-lipped bunch, well used to being discreet. They'd retreated up their winding driveways and behind their sculpted topiary. The media discovered nothing. But there was nothing the press hate more than not winning, and no hack was going to be the first to withdraw. So they'd all stayed, endlessly pummelling the locals for gossip and scouring the streets for more dirt. And at the centre of it all, the scrum at Austin's gates was unmoving. Tents, cameras and satellite trucks had settled in on the pavement of Cherry Blossom Drive.

Roxy sighed.

This didn't rock.

Staying at home was pure torture. She was used to being a free spirit, rocketing wherever and whenever she liked. Being stuck in the eye of a news storm wasn't half as exciting as old Roxy would've imagined. It wasn't cool – it was boring, and frustrating, and crap. Like house arrest, with the added agony of not knowing what Woody was doing in her absence. Despite the opinions of Cressida and Sue, every time she thought about what Chelle and Woody might be up to, Roxy felt like she was going to hurl. Had Chelle taken shelter at Woody's house? What if Jennifer picked *now* to come back? Was she right, or wrong, about the affair? Did Woody love Jennifer, despite her absence? Did he ever miss Roxy at all? *Arrgghh!* It was driving her mad! Didn't the press realise that to be suspended in this state of not knowing – for her *not* to see Woody for so long – was a violation of her human rights, like being denied water, oxygen or satellite TV? And that, as a kindness to her soul, let alone her sanity, they should bugger off back to London forthwith?

Roxy sighed again. *Thank God for Sue*, she thought as she flicked on the kettle to make her house guest her umpteenth cup of tea of the day. Having Sue to stay had been the only saving grace – like flat-sharing with the sister she'd never had. Sue was great company, with an endless appetite for dissecting the *Sunday Post* scandals. They'd theorised over the source of the leak for days, like a never-ending game of Whodunnit. They'd followed the latest 'love triangle' stories on the internet, and Roxy had even persuaded Sue to laugh at their absurdity. They'd nattered, and baked, and drunk tea. They'd burnt Sue's plastic ransacking the high streets of cyberspace, and blown Roxy's mind with a crash course in crosswords. They'd watched Terry's old forecasts on YouTube. They'd even worked out to Roxy's exercise DVDs, feeling the burn with the curtains closed as they giggled at old-Roxy's Lycra. But best of all, Sue had talked about Woody. She'd sung his praises as a kind, thoughtful friend, without whom she'd still be stuck at home, too timid to look beyond her net curtains. Roxy nodded vigorously as she recounted tales of the first group meetings and hoped her friend couldn't hear how much louder her heart started beating every time she mentioned Woody's name. She'd even coerced Sue into watching his greatest hits on an old video – ostensibly for a time-filling laugh, but truthfully because gazing at vintage clips of him in a vest was the only way she could appease the pains of her withdrawal.

What was he doing without her?

Did he ever think of their *moment* up his ladder?

The kettle boiled to its crescendo. She filled up the teapot, cut two large slices of turnip-and-walnut cake and put them on a tray. But then her attention was caught by something at the end of her driveway. It was a lone photographer, separated from the pack. He was kneeling down, retying his shoelace, a cigarette wedged between his lips. Roxy's blood suddenly boiled like her kettle. Before she could stop herself, she opened the window, thrust her face angrily through and shouted with as much volume as she could muster, 'Bugger off back to London, you porky-pedalling, bloodsucking scumbag!'

The photographer jumped, startled at the rage that shattered the birdsong. His cigarette dropped from his lips. A moment later, he yelped as fag met skin through his trousers. Roxy cackled in manic delight.

'Mess with Lavender Heath at your peril, snapper boy!' she hollered, and lobbed a lump of turnip-and-walnut cake at him. She slammed her kitchen window and picked up her tea tray, victorious. That'd show them! There was nothing like a spot of cake-based violence to get the message across. Just because they were villagers, they weren't bumpkins. How *dare* they invade their home, insult their friends and deprive them of their God-given right to clean windows? Who the hell did they think they were? Well, Roxy had news for them . . . It would take more than a few cameras and microphones to break Lavender Heath. The media weren't dealing with a bunch of lily-livered city-dwellers here – oh, no! Mess with Austin, Terence and Sue, and you messed with the whole of Lavender Heath.

She carried the tea in to Sue with a smile.

SIMON

Simon dropped a packet of porcini mushrooms into the basket and tried to filter out the sound of Scarlet's droning. He felt a brief pang of guilt about not concentrating on the chat of his daughter – after all, *any* communication from Scarlet was better than *no* communication – but his brain was still too full with the *Sunday Post* exposés to concentrate on the latest twists and turns in the on-going soap opera of teenage life. Besides, it wasn't like Simon could *totally* turn off his daughter; she *was* reluctantly mooching beside him, after all. The price of him running the gauntlet of the photographers to ferry her to street dance was a quick but vital pit stop in Waitrose to get the ingredients for tonight's open-ravioli-with-squash-and-porcini dinner.

Scarlet's voice briefly filtered into his consciousness . . .

'. . . And then Jessica said deodorant gives you cancer, but I was like, *so?* I'd rather be dead than smell of BO. And besides, everyone knows lipgloss makes your teeth go black, so she's sooo gonna look like an old witch by the time she's nineteen, because you never, ever see her without jelly-baby pink . . .'

. . . and then it filtered straight out.

How *had* Nicola Blunt found out all their secrets? Simon wondered as he searched for the organic soya yoghurts. Had Austin *really* been as unsurprised as he seemed? Was having horrible stories in the papers just part and parcel of having fame? Simon had had quite a few nasty stories when he was Nick, but they'd stopped as soon as the jobs had dried up. But Austin had retired – and *still* the stories were being printed! Did it upset him? Did he care? Had he trained himself *not* to care?

Suddenly, Simon found his path blocked by an old lady.

He looked at her. She seemed inoffensive enough: about four and a half feet tall; wrapped in a hat, scarf and coat. But she had definitely wedged her trolley between him and his daughter – and she was definitely giving him 'the look'.

Simon stopped.

And then the old woman turned to Scarlet. 'Run away, little girl,' she told her in her wavery, old lady voice. '*Run away.*'

'*Excuse* me!' Scarlet answered with maximum sarcasm, cross at the interruption to her tooth-decaying-lipgloss diatribe. She looked the old lady up and down, as though she were not really a sweet-looking granny going about her weekly super-market shop, but actually a huge, giant turd in tights whose sole purpose of getting out of bed that morning had been to seek out Scarlet and waft its vile, turdy smell up her nostrils. 'Like, *we're talking*! Duh!' Scarlet spat.

But the old lady was unshaken. 'It always starts with the talking,' she said knowingly. 'He's trying to sweet-talk his way into your knickers.'

'Are you mental?' Scarlet recoiled from a fresh waft of turd. 'Are you *actually properly mental*?'

The woman nodded self-righteously. 'I've seen him, lurking in soft fruits. He preys on young girls. He *sniffs*!'

Scarlet turned to her father. 'Are you actually going to stand here and take this?' But before Simon could reply, Scarlet decided enough was enough. 'Fuck off, you retard!' she yelled with more venom than three years at RADA had ever helped Simon conjure. 'He's not a pervert; he's my *dad*! He's an actor – geddit – he *acts*! Christ!'

And she stomped angrily away from the turd's orbit.

Simon and the old lady were left togther. An awkward moment passed.

'Sorry, dear,' the old woman eventually muttered. And she slowly shuffled off to the spam.

But Simon was beaming ecstatically. He was smiling so hard his face nearly cracked. And suddenly he was welling up too. Scarlet's solidarity had moved him to tears. Technically 'he's not a pervert' hadn't been the most glowing of endorsements, but he didn't care. It was the closest thing to a compliment Scarlet had given him in years. His daughter had defended him! Scarlet Drennan had taken on the Sick Nick brigade and blown them clean out of the water. *And* she'd called him an *actor*. An actor!

Blinking back tears of pure happiness, he hurried off to the tills where his daughter was nose-deep in *Heat*.

ROXY

Roxy looked up from her book.

Normally she didn't read books; they were zero use as latest-It-people/hottest-nightclub research, and they took too long to finish. But today she'd found herself reaching for her bookshelf and perusing the dozens of free beach-reads she'd ripped off the covers of mags. She wasn't sure what had come over her. Was it boredom or 'new Roxy'? she wondered as she curled up in her armchair with her paperback. Whichever, her taste for the gossip mags had vanished. Maybe it was down to the *Sunday Post* scandals or down to her finished career – but suddenly she knew with absolute certainty that one of her addictions was finally broken. She'd gone cold turkey on *Heat*.

'I'm going out,' Sue declared.

Roxy looked at her friend. She cut a striking figure as she stood in the doorway. Several parcels of internet purchases had arrived that morning, and she was dressed to the nines like Audrey Hepburn. In her swing coat, headscarf and movie-star specs, Sue was the epitome of celeb incognito.

Roxy frowned.

'Are you sure? The paps are still out there.'

'I can't hide here forever,' Sue blustered nervously. 'Besides, I thought I'd drop in on Terence.'

Roxy studied her carefully. Sue shifted on her new kitten heels.

'Well, I think *someone* should see how he's doing,' she added. 'I mean, it's not nice being a prisoner in your own home. We're lucky being here together. He's probably going up the wall on his own.'

'OK,' Roxy replied lightly. She pretended to return to her book but inside she was ready to star jump.

'Ummm, Roxy?' Sue anxiously took off her sunglasses. 'Do you think the *Sunday Post* was right?'

Roxy kept her eyes locked on the page.

'About Austin being chucked out of Hollywood? Or about him being a sex addict alky with a gut?'

Sue fiddled with the buttons on her new coat.

'About Terence,' she managed to reply.

Roxy couldn't help herself. She looked at her friend. Sue was in a pickle; bound up like a contortionist by her embarrassment. But sometimes it was best to play thick.

'What about Terence?' she asked flatly.

'About him . . . *you know*! About him . . . maybe . . . possibly . . . just a little bit . . . *fancying* me.' Sue's cheeks were bubblegum pink.

Roxy put down her book.

'Sue, does Liz cleanse, tone and moisturise?'

'Eh?'

'Can Kate rock a party?'

'Um . . .'

'Do midi-skirts ming, maxi-skirts rock and nude shoes double your shaggability?'

'Well, I suppose so.'

'*Yes!*' Roxy sang out in reply. '*Yes, Terence fancies you.* He's fancied the bones off you since the moment you met. It's been as obvious as a newsreader's dye-job!'

'You really think so?'

'The *whole world* thinks so.'

'Oh!' Sue declared, blushing. And then she furrowed her brow. 'But why didn't he just come out and say so?'

'Short of getting the words tattooed across his forehead, he has! Haven't you noticed how he always sits next to you at meetings? How he's vamped up his wardrobe, restyled his hair and is a thousand times nicer to you than he is to anyone else?'

'Well, I suppose—'

'He asked you to the premiere, Sue. He blushed when he saw you in your dress.'

'But that wasn't a date. It was moral support.'

'He was trying to impress you.'

'He was?'

'I give up!' Roxy went back to her book.

There was a moment of silence. And then she could practically hear the smile crack across Sue's face.

'Right,' said her friend, trying to sound as though everything was still normal. 'Well, like I said, I'll pop round for a cup of tea. Just to see how he is.'

Roxy fixed her eyes on her book. But in her peripheral vision she could see Sue starting to bloom, a gorgeous radiance lighting her up from the inside, as though someone had finally found the plug to her fairy lights within.

'Yes, maybe you should,' Roxy agreed lightly, and bit her lip to keep her glee from bursting out. Who would ever have thought it? Who could have imagined that a middle-aged former TV weatherman, with skin the colour of skin, and teeth the colour of teeth, could have been the knight to kiss the sleeping beauty and wake her up to the rest of her life?

'Well, I'll be off then.' Sue tried to sound casual.

'I won't wait up,' Roxy replied.

But Sue didn't notice; she'd already departed, her feet floating over the gravel as she wafted dreamily in the direction of the Tornado.

WOODY

It had nearly killed him to wait until Friday. But nothing alarmed his older clients more than an unexpected ladder at their window, and Mrs Childs' windows weren't due until then. So Woody's patience had been stretched to its furthest limit as he'd watched the week crawl by. But Friday was here at last and he gave a last polishing sweep to Mrs Childs' final gleaming window.

He knocked on her door for his wages.

'How's Holly, Mrs Childs?' he asked casually, after he'd chatted about the weather and accepted a handful of warm coins.

The old lady blinked. 'Holly? Why, she's out, silly!'

'No, not that Holly.' He took a deep breath and tried out his theory. 'I mean Holly – your daughter, Mrs Childs.'

'Oh!' the old lady's face went tight. 'That Holly. I haven't spoken to Holly in years.'

Something in Woody sank. 'Years?'

Mrs Childs tutted crossly. 'You try and do right by your children, but she stopped listening the moment she went up to university. Took up with that Scottish hippy fellow. Peculiar, he was. Only ever ate cabbage. Of course, as soon as she finished she moved away with him.'

'Where to, Mrs Childs?' Woody tried to sound light.

'I keep forgetting. It starts with an *S*. Or is it a *P*?'

'And you've not seen her since?'

'What, Holly? Yes, she'll be back in a minute. It's chops for dinner tonight.'

'No, the other Holly. *Your* Holly, I mean.'

'She's not *my* Holly.' Mrs Childs pursed her lips. 'She's made that perfectly clear.'

'She's writing a new book, you know,' Woody told her, wondering if the old woman might relish news of her daughter.

'That's nice,' she replied flatly. But then she smiled. 'So are you a friend of Holly's, dear?'

'Lodger Holly?'

'Yes, lodger Holly. So much easier to talk to. Always cheerful. Should I give her a message?'

Woody smiled politely.

'No, thank you, Mrs Childs. No message.'

He walked back to the pavement, his ladder suddenly heavy on his shoulders.

To: Roxy; Terence; Woody; Chelle; Simon; Sue; Cressida; Austin;
From: Holly Childs

Hey everyone,

I've had an idea. Why don't we all meet up on Sunday to read the tabloids together? If there are no more stories about us this week, great – we can celebrate with some breakfast! But if there is more horrible coverage, then at least we can face it together.

How about meeting in the upstairs room at the Dog and Duck? Dave said he'll open up early, and he's even promised to lay on bacon butties!

Is 8.30am too early? I don't expect any of us will fancy a lie-in, and the paparazzi won't have got up by then!

Luv
Holly x

ROXY

Roxy stood on the Dog and Duck doorstep. She looked behind
her. It was 8.30am and Lavender Heath was eerily quiet. The
press pack hadn't woken up yet and, if the locals had already
ventured out for their Sunday papers, they'd left no evidence
to show it. Lavender Heath was a ghost village.

Hesitantly, Roxy knocked on the door. Dave peered cautiously
out.

'Just you?'

'Just me.'

'You followed?'

'I don't think so.'

He beckoned her in. As the door opened wider, the delicious scent of bacon sandwiches wafted under her nose. Bacon
sarnies were getting to be a theme of the week. Would she
ever be able to read the tabloids again without remembering
the smell of bacon? she wondered. Inhaling deeply, she stepped
inside.

'They're upstairs.' Dave nodded to the staircase.

Roxy headed up, trying to manage her nerves. Strangely,

the possibility of *more* scandal hadn't crossed her mind. Not until Holly's email, that was. Then, suddenly, the prospect of more exposés had been (almost) all she could think of. She didn't care if there was anything about her; her reputation couldn't be damaged. Once you'd shared your one-night stands with the nation and interrupted A-lister interviews with tales about fanny farts, a few lines in a newspaper couldn't touch you. It was the bullet-proof benefit of being Roxy Squires: nobody could expose anything about her that was worse than what she'd already exposed about herself. But the others . . . She didn't like to think how they could be hurt.

She pushed open the door to the upstairs room. The gang was already in there, coffee mugs and newspapers strewn around them. Hungrily, her eyes scanned the room like a laser. But Woody wasn't there.

'There's more terrible stuff about Austin,' Sue reported.

'Where's Woody?' Roxy's eyes now desperately hunted for Chelle. But, thankfully, she found her, over-dressed in the corner. She almost sighed with relief that she wasn't with Woody. But then panic gripped her again. Where *was* Woody? She ached to see him. And, if shit was going to happen, she wanted him with her.

'Woody's on his way,' Simon muttered from deep within the *Sunday Post* pages.

'And Hol texted she'll be here in ten,' added Chelle.

Distractedly, Roxy looked at Chelle. Even now, at 8.31 on a Sunday morning, she was dressed to kill. Her skirt was short, her lashes were long and she'd even glitter-creamed her cleavage. Her dedication to glamour was unstinting. But then Roxy was hit by a terrible thought. Did Chelle look so glam this morning because she was wearing the same outfit as last night? Had she glued on her eyelashes at 7am or 7pm? Had she come straight from the sticky sheets of a night of illicit Woody-love? She watched Chelle yawn without covering her mouth and suddenly felt a huge surge of anger. Did Chelle have no conscience about Jennifer *at all*? And, if she had no conscience about man-robbing Woody, *what else did she have no conscience about?* Could *she* be the *Sunday Post* leak? After all, she was always on magazine covers and she *did* have the best contacts with the press. Who was to say she wasn't best mates with Nicola Blunt? Her motives for joining the group had been dodgy from the start . . .

'You haven't exactly helped your cause,' Terence told Austin. 'What were you thinking, firing water pistols at them?'

'It was a subo-charged Flash Flood Super Soaker,' Austin grinned, 'and you should try it! There's nothing like drenching a few paps.'

Roxy looked at the *Sunday Post*s spread across the table like a blanket. '*IT'S A CHAMPAGNE STICK-UP, SAYS DRUNK-AS-SKUNK JONES.*'

Austin followed her eyeline.

'Inaccurate bollocks, as usual. I only shot champagne 'til Tuesday. And then Carmen pointed out that the buggers weren't worth the good stuff. That's when I started on the plonk. By Friday, I'd got down to Special Brew.'

'You drink Special Brew?' Chelle screwed up her nose.

'As if! I got the housekeeper to get it especially. If they think I'm an alky, I might as well act like one.'

Roxy turned back to the article and read.

'"The bizarre behaviour of fallen Hollywood megastar Austin Jones reached a new low this week. The reclusive actor, believed to be increasingly out of touch with real life, was seen waving a replica gun from the windows of his twelve-million-pound mansion, and using it to shoot passers-by . . . with champagne. Friends are said to be at their wits' end, concerned for the roly-poly star's mental health, which has taken a worrying downward turn since girlfriend Carmen Bonitta furiously called time on their relationship. Since learning of Jones' sex addiction, Carmen, nineteen, has bolted back to their home in LA, where she is being comforted by her personal trainer. Meanwhile, Jones continues to drink (and shoot) his wine cellar dry!"'

'Oh, mate,' Simon winced sympathetically.

'So I'm a freshly-dumped, sex-addicted, pistol-packing, alcoholic lard arse,' Austin shrugged. 'I've been worse.'

'Has Carmen really left you?'

'Has she bollocks! She's back at home, filling in job applications.'

'So why do they think she's in LA?' Chelle pouted.

'Why do the papers think anything?' Austin replied. And then he thew back his head and laughed.

'You don't seem very concerned.' Terence frowned.

'Why should I be?' Austin grinned manically. 'None of this

shit *matters!* If Mrs Moral Highground from petty middle-England decides *not* to unwedge her fat arse from her sofa and waddle down to the multiplex to catch my latest rom-com, *I don't care!* My career's over! I don't need to worry about whether the money men still think I'm "box office". I don't have to *pretend* to give a shit. As far as I'm concerned, the *Sunday Post* can print what they want – I couldn't give a rat's arse.'

Roxy turned away from Austin's euphoria and looked anxiously over at Sue. 'Is there any more about you?'

'I don't think so,' Sue replied with relief. And then she gave the tiniest of smiles. 'Well, just a little photograph from when I popped out.'

'Oh, yeah; cop a load of this.' Austin rifled through the paper to find the right page. He held it up. 'I told you our Suze was a stunner!'

Roxy looked. And, sure enough, the picture of Sue was phenomenal. She was hurrying down Honeysuckle Drive, Terry-bound, in headscarf and movie-star sunglasses, her figure, larger than average, but all woman, her cheekbones Grace Kelly statuesque.

'Fuck; that's never you!' snorted Chelle.

'What's a "bromance"?' Cressida interrupted.

There was a choking noise from Simon's direction. His face was as white as a sheet.

Roxy looked down at where Cressida was pointing. It was an old *Down Town* picture of Simon looking sweaty, greasy and haunted.

'*SICK NICK'S NEW CRUSH*', trumpeted the headline. 'Washed-up actor's one-sided bromance with Austin.'

Everyone leant forward and read.

'Sick Nick actor Simon Drennan may not have hit headlines for a while, but he's hoping his "friendship" with troubled movie star Austin Jones will catapult him back to fame. The failed TV actor, last seen in nylon tights, has struck up an unlikely friendship with vulnerable Jones, currently believed to be battling problems with alcohol, sex addiction and depression. Drennan, thirty-nine, who shot to fame playing dangerous paedophile "Sick Nick" Fletcher in TV soap *Down Town*, is said by friends to idolise the *Puppy Love* star with an affection that borders obsession. "Austin's one of the greats," he told friends. "Like Brando, only ten times more gorgeous!" "Simon worships the ground Austin walks on," added a source close to the former soap actor. "He's hoping Austin will take him under his wing and make him a star, but Austin doesn't have a clue who he is. Simon's walking around with his tongue hanging out and Austin's barely noticed he's there!"'

'Shit!' Roxy was stunned.

The room went peculiarly silent.

'It's not true.' Simon insisted. 'I mean, for God's sake, that's crazy – I'm *married*!'

'And they've set the dogs on Woody too,' Terence added gravely. Roxy gasped. 'Let me see!'

Austin flipped back a few pages of the newspaper and passed it to her. Heart pounding, Roxy started to read.

'No!' Her legs suddenly felt flimsy beneath her.

'What's up?' Woody was standing at the door, a small, blue holdall on his back. Roxy looked up. She wanted to run over to him, to throw her arms around him – to shelter him from the story ahead. But she couldn't. Woody put down his holdall and came over.

'*"WOODENISER" WOODY PREYS ON VILLAGE HOUSEWIVES*', he read. And beneath was a picture of Woody, carrying his ladder – grinning from ear to ear.

'Where have you been?' Sue wailed forlornly.

'Sorting something,' he replied.

'What?' Roxy demanded. *What on earth could need sorting at a moment like this?*

But Woody wasn't given time to answer.

'Want me to read it out?' Terence offered. The room went silent as he cleared his throat.

'"It's a fall from grace few could have predicted. In the nineties, babe-loving Woody 'The Wooodeniser' was the undisputed king of pop. Riding high in the charts he was everyone's favourite pop star, from schoolgirls, to footballers, to royalty. In just five years he earned untold riches, had a string of number ones, and left a stream of broken-hearted supermodels in his wake. Not a week would pass without another personal appearance being cancelled for dangerous overcrowding, or Woody being chased from nightclubs by lust-crazed fans. He had the world at his feet and the music industry at his beck and call. But then Woody went AWOL, declaring his music career over and his days as a guitar-toting lothario past.

'"Fast forward to the present, and Woody now works as a down-at-heel window cleaner, spongeing the windows of the rich and famous. He lives with beautiful girlfriend Jennifer in the posh country village of Lavender Heath – also home to Austin Jones and Suzi 'Sugatits' Bunce – where Woody tells anyone who'll listen that his womanising days are behind him, and lectures his celebrity clients on giving up their showbiz lifestyles and embracing a no-frills world of 'honest' manual labour. But it seems that leopards don't change their spots. Locals claim that Woody hasn't really reformed at all, and career-girl Jennifer is being cruelly duped. The showbiz trappings may have gone, but Woody's eye for the ladies remains, and he cynically uses his window-cleaning job as a cover for peeping-Tom thrills and easy sexual conquests." And then there's a quote from you, Woody . . . "I love my job. I'm always getting flashed at. Half the women in Lavender Heath have invited me in for nibbles – and they don't mean tea and biscuits."'

'That's monstrous!' cried Sue, disgusted.

'As if you'd say *nibble*!' snorted Austin.

Roxy stayed quiet. She looked over at Chelle, who was inspecting her nails with a yawn. How could she be so uncaring in this moment of crisis? Didn't she mind if her affair was exposed? Didn't she care that Jennifer would be devastated, or that her lover's reputation had just been torn to pieces? Roxy turned back to Woody. A muscle in his jaw had begun to flex. He looked angry but, strangely, not surprised.

'Where's Holly?' he asked the room lightly.

'Who cares about Holly?' ranted Terence. 'She's probably trapped at home by the press. What we need is a lawyer. This is defamation. This will seriously impede your ability to operate as a window cleaner. You'll have lost your round and your income by lunch!'

'Fuckin' hell!' Chelle shrieked loudly, making everyone start with fright. She was staring at the newspaper as though a ghost had just risen out of it. She grabbed it and frantically flicked to the centre page.

'*HE SHOOTS . . . HE DOESN'T SCORE!*' read the headline. 'Dwayne Blowers' infertility drove marriage apart.'

'Fuck! Fuck! Fuck!' Chelle dropped the paper as though scalded. Despite the orange, her face had turned deathly pale.

'Chelle?' someone asked kindly.

But Chelle was unable to speak. She was making a rasping noise, like an old banger trying to start. She motioned for someone to read. Hesitantly, Roxy picked up the paper.

'"Three months ago, the world of football was rocked when Dwayne Blowers split from his childhood sweetheart. Premiership star Dwayne, and Chelle, twenty-three, had been together since the age of eleven and had married in a lavish two-million-pound ceremony just nine months earlier. At the time, Chelle told numerous magazines that the marriage had broken down due to Dwayne's repeated infidelities, but the truth has emerged as less potent.

'"Blowers' estranged wife has now gone on the record to explain the real cause of the split . . . Dwayne's impotence. On learning of his zero sperm count, the footballer made a stark choice. He walked away from his wife, rather than condemn her to a life without children. 'We made out Dwayne had been playing away,' Chelle exclusively revealed to the *Sunday Post*. 'It's better than saying he's firing blanks. This way Dwayne looks like a man.'"'

'But I never went on the record with nobody!' cried Chelle, having rediscovered the power of speech. 'I mean, I know I do interviews and all that, but I'd never tell anyone *this* . . . Oh my God; *poor Dwayne!* His teammates are gonna slay him. He won't be able to play!'

'But you must have told someone,' Terence puzzled. '*Someone* knew for it to get in the paper. I can't imagine Dwayne would've told them himself.'

'But I swear I never blabbed!' Chelle protested wildly. 'Christ, he's going to *hate* me. I'm always really careful about what I say to journalists – *always*. That's why my agent gets copy approval – to make sure I don't put my stupid, big foot in it!'

'But think, Chelle; *think!*' Terence urged. 'Maybe it wasn't a journalist. Maybe it was someone else. A doctor? A hairdresser? A friend?'

'No.' Chelle shook her head. 'One hundred per cent definitely no one.'

Roxy cleared her throat. 'There *was* someone you told,' she said quietly. 'Remember . . . ? Our girly night out, downstairs . . . ?'

'But . . .' Chelle puffed up her cheeks as she tried to remember.

'*Me* . . .' Roxy admitted.

Sue gasped, her hand flying to her face in shock. In a nanosecond, the whole room seemed to fill with dismay. Six pairs of eyes bore into her with disgust at her betrayal. Even Woody looked seriously cheesed off. Roxy rushed to finish her sentence.

'. . . and you also told—'

'*Her!*' Chelle pointed at the doorway.

Everyone turned. And, outlined in the doorway, the early-morning sunlight radiating out behind her, was Holly. But she wasn't Holly. This Holly looked different: harder. The pastel woollies were gone, replaced by a pointy-shouldered jacket and heels. Her hair was darker, her lipstick bolder and her creamy cheeks had been sharpened with blusher. And flanking this Holly were two men in anoraks, one with a camera, one filming.

'Holly?' Sue asked in surprise.

'Nicola,' Woody corrected flatly.

And sure enough, the outline in the doorway was the same as the newspaper silhouette.

'Shit!' Roxy blurted. Could Holly *really* be Nicola Blunt? Impossible! Holly was a saintly mother-tending wallflower, who'd never even walked past a nightclub. Nicola Blunt was a hard-bitten showbiz journalist, a nocturnal scalp hunter, the torment of celebs across the land.

And then slowly, maliciously, Nicola–Holly grinned.

'Hello, gang. Everyone enjoying their breakfast?'

'But . . .' Simon looked lost. 'Are you Holly's . . . *sister*?'

The man with the camera snapped Simon's gormless expression. Nicola laughed – a brittle, tinkling sound, like shards being dropped in a champagne glass.

'So sweet!' she declared nastily. 'So naïve! It's been like taking candy off a baby, it really has! And how are *you*, Austin? An Irish coffee, I presume?'

'Burn in hell, witch,' Austin replied evenly, his hatred undisguised.

'But you're . . .' Sue faltered, brain lagging.

'Top of my game and heading for promotion?' Nicola grinned. 'Really, did none of you little flopsies suspect?' She looked around the room with satisfaction.

'Proud of yourself, are you?' Cressida asked tightly, ignoring the flash as the photographer as he recorded the group's betrayal.

'Yes, I am, as it happens!' She laughed. 'Really, Cressida, I expected *you* to be sharper. The others, no. But *you* . . .'

'You two-faced, lying—' Roxy hands balled into fists.

'I mean, Austin's off his tits half the time, Simon's too busy being bullied by his kids and there are more brain cells in Chelle's weave than her head.'

'I *should* have guessed!' Cressida self-flagellated. 'You looked so peculiar when I said you were writing again. I should have realised I'd just caught you out.'

'That's the problem with politicians,' Nicola smirked. 'They think they know everything, but when it comes down to it, they're actually one below window cleaners on the brightness scale.' And then she turned to Woody and smiled. 'Enjoying my handiwork?' she pointed at the newspaper. 'Pity you cottoned on to me two weeks too late.'

Roxy looked at Woody in surprise. 'You *knew*?'

'Suspected,' he replied, his eyes not moving a millimetre from Nicola, as though watching a cobra preparing to strike. 'I saw an old picture of Holly. The old one wore braces. But this one's got a gap in her teeth.'

'He's been phoning the office,' laughed Nicola, 'leaving messages, warning me off. Asking me, as a friend – as a fellow human being . . . *As if!* He even turned up at the office. Security wouldn't let him through, of course, and he still couldn't be one hundred per cent sure it was me. But he's not as dull as he looks. He got a lawyer to email my editor about your right to privacy. Not that my editor read it.'

'But why?' asked Sue, her face still rumpled in confusion. 'Why let us think you're our friend? Why pretend to be Holly?'

'Nobody's seen Holly for years,' Nicola replied crisply. 'Even when she was writing, there was only that one fuzzy photo. And I always believe if a story's worth doing, it's worth getting embedded for. Don't flatter yourselves – I wasn't after any of you no-lifes. The ins and outs of your little lives were so dull I could barely be bothered to type them up! No, it was the exclusive on Austin I wanted. I'd heard rumours Hollywood had had enough of him, and I wanted to make sure I was here when he scuttled back home. Woody unwittingly gave me a way in. He was so intent on helping you sad little nobodies, it was easy to pretend to be one of you and join.'

Austin stood up angrily.

'It's fair enough to go for me,' he thundered. 'I've played the game – I'm used to this bollocks. But why go for them?

You had enough muck on me to sell papers; why fuck up their lives too?'

Nicola shrugged. 'Why not?'

'I'm gonna deck her!' Roxy lunged, but Woody held her back.

'I'm gonna fucking kill her!' shrieked Chelle, flinging herself at Nicola, nails first. It took both Simon and Terence to hold her down.

'But you came to my house,' Sue insisted. 'We had tea and biscuits. We were friends.' She moved towards Nicola in confusion, but Nicola and her henchmen drew ranks. There was a panicky scuffle and the TV camera connected with Sue's face with a crack.

'Get your hands off her, you scum!' Terence roared.

Nicola paused, momentarily floored by his fury. But then she recovered herself. 'Go on, Terry – hit me,' she goaded. 'Teach me a lesson with the back of your hand. It'll give me a new angle: Tornado the woman-beating weatherman. Let's see how employable you are after that.'

Cressida whipped out her mobile. 'I've had enough of this nonsense. I'm calling the police.'

'To do what?' Nicola spat out a laugh. 'Have me arrested for crimes against egos?'

Terence helped Sue into a chair, her nose wrapped in his handkerchief. As she let out a whimper of pain, the photographer leant in and took her picture. Quick as a flash, Woody punched the camera away. The man cried out, reeling in shock, and the camera smashed on to the floor and into pieces. Roxy kicked the bits into the corner before the photographer could bend to retrieve them.

'You can't do that!' screeched Nicola. 'That's *Sunday Post* property!'

'Sue me,' Woody growled in reply.

'Right – that's it. Get out, you harpy!' yelled Austin. And he pushed Nicola, hard, in the chest.

'Austin, don't, she'll turn it into a story,' wailed Sue.

'It'll be worth it. Now, fuck off!' he roared at her henchmen.

'Stop,' Woody said calmly, but with an authority that brought the room to a halt.

'You're going to leave now,' he told Nicola evenly. He turned to the man who was filming. 'And *you* are going to give me that.' He held out his hand for the camera.

'In your dreams, SpongeBob!' Nicola laughed.

Woody turned back to her. '*You* are never going to print another story about any of us. You're going to print full apologies. And you're going to get the hell out of Lavender Heath.'

'Oh, yes?' Nicola smirked with pure venom. 'And how do you reckon on that? Because I don't see you holding any cards here, *window cleaner*.'

'That's your problem, Nicola. You're looking so hard for scandal, you can't see what's under your nose.'

Nicola looked down and, sure enough, right under her nose, Woody was brandishing his holdall. He slowly unzipped it and pulled out a netbook. He opened it up and a woman's face appeared on the screen.

'Woody?' said the woman on the computer. 'Are we on?'

'We're on,' he confirmed, and he held the netbook up to Nicola's face.

'Nicola Blunt?' the woman asked as Nicola frowned at the computer. The woman was in her mid-thirties. She was scruffy and wearing no make-up. Her features weren't strong, but they were determined and she was strangely, unconventionally pretty.

'Nicola Blunt who has recently been residing at fourteen Hawthorne Close as the lodger of Lavinia Childs?' the woman continued.

Nicola tried to look bored. 'And who the hell is this civilian?' she sneered.

'My name is Holly Childs,' the woman informed her. 'And this is a copy of a document my lawyer is about to serve on your editor.' She held a wadge of printed sheets up to the screen.

Nicola took a step back. And then she peered into the computer in shock.

'*You're* Holly Childs?' Her eyes moved frantically to Woody. 'But how did you . . . ? She's supposed to be up a tree on an island!'

'Just because I live in a tree house, doesn't mean it doesn't have a modem,' the woman on the computer replied. 'I'm very aware of what's going on in the world, and your reprehensible activities within it. When Woody contacted my publisher, I was only too happy to help.'

Nicola gave Woody a look of venomous hatred.

'Nicola Blunt,' Holly Childs continued, 'this document warns that, if you persist in stealing my identity, I will take immediate steps to prosecute you under the Data Protection Act of 1998. It also contains a copy of a letter of complaint, detailing your harassment of my mother, which will shortly be delivered to the police. And, finally, it contains a copy of an agreement I've signed with your rival paper, *The Bugle*. Unless you agree to my requests – in full, and within fifteen minutes – I will grant them an exclusive interview detailing your sinister deception of my family and my specific complaints about your personal conduct and methods. My words are bound to go global: I've never spoken publicly before.'

There was a long pause. Nicola eyed Holly.

'*The Bugle* will never name me personally,' she told her.

'On the contrary; they're only too glad to help.'

Nicola frowned. 'The public won't care about my methods.'

'"Hardened journalist harasses elderly, vulnerable lady"? Do you know my mother suffers from dementia? *The Bugle* have the medical reports that prove it.'

There was a pause. Nicola narrowed her eyes. 'Even *if* I agree to your requirements, *The Bugle*'ll never sit on the story. You've given them a scoop. No editor in the land wouldn't run it.

'I have complete confidence in *The Bugle*. Their exclusive extracts from my next novel are at stake.' Holly looked at her watch. 'And the documents are being delivered right about . . . now. You have until exactly 9am to comply.'

'Hi, Holly.' Austin peered into the computer. 'Great move – cheers for this. Hey, I *do* remember you!'

'Hello, Austin,' Holly Childs replied with a grin.

'You used to do your homework on set! You played with the puppies between takes!'

'I remember you were always very sweet to me.'

'Shhh!' Austin warned with a frown. 'This lot think I'm a bastard.'

Holly Childs laughed – and then she too frowned. 'Nicola – you're still there.'

'I . . .' Nicola floundered.

'Woody, Skype me in ten,' Holly instructed. 'Ding, dong, the witch is dead, and all that.'

'You're on,' Woody replied. He closed the computer and passed it to Roxy. And then he turned to the cameraman, who was still filming.

'Give that to me,' he commanded. For a split second the cameraman froze, but then he meekly offered it up. 'And now you're all going home.'

Nicola looked at Woody, her eyes boiling with poison. She looked set to scratch his eyes out. 'You're finished, you pathetic little sponge-carrier,' she spat, stabbing a long, spiky finger into his chest. 'Even *if* I don't write anything else, your life in your precious Lavender Heath is over. Nobody's going to want a sex pest peeping through their windows. Nobody's going to want to be friends with a scheming, cheating, two-faced, pussy-addict pervert.'

Woody sighed, rubbed his head and then, in a single movement, scooped Nicola into a fireman's lift and carried her
bottom-first towards the door.

'You're going to regret this, you dumb fucking bastard,'
Nicola screamed, upside down. 'I'm going to make *all* you
fuckers regret this.'

'Oh, for heaven's sake!' Cressida replied. 'It's words in a
paper; we'll survive.'

And then Woody carried Nicola downstairs.

For a few seconds, the room fell into stunned silence. And
then a telephone rang.

'*Barrington?*' Simon answered his mobile in a daze.

'Who's Barrington?' Austin asked mischievously.

'Yes; yes, I've seen the papers . . .' Simon said numbly. 'Yes,
I *do* know Austin Jones . . . No, I didn't see any reason to tell
you . . .' There was a squeal of excitement from the phone.
Simon began to look cross. 'Well, I don't really see how it's
relevant . . . I expect he *already has* an agent. Besides, don't
you *read* the papers? He's retired.'

'Put him on speakerphone,' Austin urged, as Woody re-
entered the room. Roxy quickly looked Woody over. He was
OK, she saw with relief. There were no nail marks gouged into
his face.

'But you're supposed to be representing *me*, Barrington . . .
Me!'

'Speakerphone!' Austin tugged Simon's arm. Simon looked
at him blankly, but then did as he was told. Barrington's voice
suddenly filled up the room.

'. . . if you could just put in a good word for me, I could get him the perfect comeback vehicle. A quality rom-com! In fact, I've got Richard Curtis' phone number right here. He's casting his new project next week.'

'Ballington?' Austin took the phone from Simon's hands.

'Ooo!' Barrington squeaked with delight. 'Is that Austin Jones? *The* Austin Jones?'

'Get your tongue out my arse and just listen. You've been a *shit* agent to Simon and he won't put up with it any more.'

'No, of course! Absolutely! But Mr Jones, whilst you're on the phone – Ooo, this is so exciting, I've got goose bumps! – I was just wondering if you fancied a coffee, you know, to mull over a few ideas abou—'

'I wouldn't piss on you, let alone drink with you. The only reason Simon's never sacked your substandard arse is because he's too bloody nice. But I'm not. So fuck off, Ballington; you're fired.'

And Austin tossed the phone back to Simon. Dazed, Simon slowly hung up.

'Someone call an ambulance!' cried Terence. 'We need to get Sue to casualty!'

'Honestly, Terence, I'm fine.'

'But that bitch might have broken your nose!'

'It's just a bit sore.'

'But it's *bleeding*!'

'That rancid, spiteful *slut*!' Chelle suddenly awoke from where she'd slumped in the corner. 'That lying, two-faced, devil-bitch whore. *I trusted her*!'

'Don't be hard on yourself, Chelle,' Cressida told her kindly. 'She fooled us all.'

'But Dwayne'll never take me back now!' she wailed. 'I don't want a stupid boyfriend. I don't care about kids. All I ever wanted was *Dwayne*. I was gonna hook up with Austin to make him jealous. I wanted him to remember how much he wanted me, so he'd come back home and everything'd be like it was. But now that evil witch Holly – Nicola – *whatever her name is* – has ruined everything with her bastard, cockin' lies!'

'But you and Woody . . . ?' the words escaped Roxy's mouth before she could stop them.

'Me and Woody *what*?' Chelle furiously snapped.

'But you answered his door . . . You said you were busy . . .'

Roxy looked from Chelle to Woody. And suddenly she felt very stupid.

'*Jesus Christ*, Roxy – he was giving me *advice*! I turned up at his house over the limit. I was crying my heart out about Dwayne! Woody let me stay over. He was just telling me to talk things through with Dwayne, to tell him that he mattered more to me than a baby, when you waltzed up the drive with flapjacks. And Dwayne's *never* going to talk to me now. Not after that evil Blunt bitch!'

Cressida comforted her, but the expletives continued to come.

Roxy turned to Woody. 'I'm so sorry! I've been such a muppet! I should never have thought—'

'It's OK.' Woody smiled at her kindly.

'No, it's not. I was stupid, and childish, and crap . . .'

'You weren't. You're not. It's OK.'

'But what about you?' She motioned towards Nicola's article. 'Are you going to be all right?'

'It's going to cost me a few clients.'

'But Jennifer! She'll be so upset!'

'Jennifer?' He smiled strangely. 'Look, Rox, there's something I've been trying to tell you about Jennifer. There is no Jennifer. There never was.'

Roxy's mouth opened. She made a weird noise; something that sounded like 'Mwhaa?'

But Woody kept speaking. 'When I first moved here and started my round, a lot of baggage came with me. Nicola was right. According to the papers I was Casanova on heat – real lock-up-your-womenfolk stuff! And you can imagine how well that went down around here. This place is full of women with time on their hands. I still get flashed at now, but back then I could barely pick up my bucket without some bored, under-appreciated housewife getting her kit off and trying it on. It wasn't personal. They didn't want *me*; they wanted Woody the pop star. Rejection's not nice, I know – Petra rejected me for Austin. So I had a choice. I could either become the most hated man in the village with a client base of none, or I could let them down gently by inventing a girlfriend. So that's what I did – with Jennifer. Jennifer's why I'm still here.'

'But the photo?'

'What photo?'

'The picture of the woman in your living room. The laughing woman with glossy brown hair . . .'

'JJ?' Woody replied with a frown.

Roxy took in a sharp breath. It had never occurred to her that Jennifer and JJ weren't the same woman. Suddenly, 'Hello, baby' and 'When are you coming home?' flooded depressingly back.

'But JJ's my baby sister.' Woody smiled.

'Oh!' Roxy's mouth hung open yet again.

'She's at uni in the States! My parents retired down under, so Baby stays with me for the holidays. She's back soon. Hopefully you'll meet her.'

'You call her Baby?'

'Always have. It's a stupid nickname, but it stuck.'

'So you're . . .' Roxy faltered numbly. She could barely believe she was going to utter the word. Forty seconds ago this had been the worst day of her life. But, suddenly, everything was changing. The room had started to glow, like someone had turned up the colour knob; and the air around her had started to fizz. And suddenly Woody was moving in close. 'So you're *single*?' She whispered the question.

'I'm single,' he confirmed with a smile.

And then all Roxy could see was the golden stubble on his jaw, the intoxicating deliciousness of his skin and the magical spark of something new in his eyes that – unless she was completely mistaken – were looking right at her lightly-glossed lips.

Voices floated in the background.

'If she's broken your nose, I'll press charges!'

'I'm going to find that sappy pink cardie and shove it up her cockin' arse!'

'You fired Barrington! You actually fired Barrington! I'm fucked! I'm totally and utterly fucked!'

And suddenly, in the middle of all the carnage, Roxy grinned. She grinned so hard she thought her face might never go back.

To: Roxy Squires
From: *This Morning*

Dear Roxy Squires,

We are urgently trying to book Sue 'Sugatits' Bunce and Terry 'Tornado' Leggett as studio guests for tomorrow morning's show, and we hear you might represent them?

Please can you call me, *urgently*, any time (day or night!)? We'd LOVE to have them on our sofa. Our viewers are big fans of this super-couple. Everyone loves a comeback story, *but when it doubles as a romance* . . . Well, let's just say, name your fee! Whatever it is – we'll double it!

Five days later . . .

10.46am @FoxyRoxy

Foxy Roxy RIP I think it's time I got a life. I'm hanging up my smart phone and signing out.

10.47am @FoxyRoxy

To all you younger, thinner, blonder blondes out there, GOOD LUCK! Go forth . . . bleach . . . have fun! #ROXYSAYS: over and out.

To: Roxy Squires

From: ITV Drama Department

Dear Roxy,

Really??? Is there *nothing* we can do to persuade you???

Obviously, it's GREAT that you're selling us the #ROXYSAYS tweets and it's fantastic that we can go ahead with the series. But we'd be lying if we said we weren't a teeny bit disappointed you don't want to star! You'd be fabulous! Is it the money? Because we can increase our offer . . . And are you *sure* you want us to change the '#ROXYSAYS' name . . . ?

Anyway, good luck with your new business. We're intrigued to know what it is! As promised, the money will be in your account by the morning.

ROXY

'Paradise fruit, anybody?'

Simon offered a plate of tropical-looking cakes. 'Or if you don't fancy those . . .' He delved into his shopper for some Tupperware. '. . . I've got millionaire's shortbread, strawberry tarts or lemon drizzle.'

Everyone looked surprised.

'What?' He shrugged. 'The twins are on a field trip. I've had a lot of time on my hands.'

They all took a cake as Woody filled their glasses. In the end they'd decided to meet at Woody's place. Lavender Heath was still crawling with journalists and they didn't want to cause Dave the hassle of descending en masse at the pub. When they'd tried to go for a quiet drink on Tuesday, the place had become overrun. So, tonight, Roxy, Simon, Sue, Terence and Cressida were all perched on high stools around Woody's kitchen island and had opened a bottle of red.

'That's a joke, right?' Terence frowned at Simon. 'You can't *really* have time on your hands? My phone barely stops ringing at night.'

'I've had to change my number,' Sue agreed mildly. 'It was non-stop heavy breathers on my old one.'

'But have you had work offers?' Simon asked strangely.

'Heavens! Tons of them!' Sue laughed in reply. 'It would take me a fortnight to read all the emails. Thank goodness I've got an agent now to do it all for me.'

'But isn't Roxy your agent?' asked Cressida. 'She *did* get you your book deal.'

'She turned me down. Nothing I said could persuade her.'

'Trust me; you're better off being looked after by a professional.' Roxy smiled.

'See? The only thing I can get her to do is pick out the outfits I'll need.'

'What kind of work have you been offered?' Simon asked stiffly.

'Ooo, well – where to start? *Graham Norton*, *Jonathan Ross*, *Loose Women* . . .'

Simon's face fell.

'. . . *Desert Island Discs*, *The One Show*, *Chatty Man* . . .'

'Don't forget our interview for *OK!*,' added Terence.

'What? "Terry and Sue welcome us into their love nest"?' Woody grinned.

Terence and Sue smiled coyly into their laps.

'What about you, Cressida?' Woody spared them their blushes.

'Me? Oh, I'm all right,' she replied. 'Roxy's got me an agony aunt column in the *Telegraph* and there are a few other offers on the table, too. Someone from Psycho keeps calling . . . He's got a big television show, apparently – although he's clearly lacking in rudimentary spelling because he thinks "psycho" starts with an *s*!'

'How about you, Woody?' Simon turned to his friend.

Woody laughed and rubbed his head. 'Oh, you know, the usual rubbish. It all went straight in the bin. I'm happy as I am, thanks – the wind in my hair, a rung at my feet . . . a cold, wet sponge in my hand!'

Suddenly Cressida seemed excited. 'Have you ever thought about going into politics?'

'With my skeletons? I wouldn't last a second.' Woody laughed.

'I don't mean *that* kind of politics. I mean local stuff – grass-roots. You know – motivating teenagers; getting everyone together for fetes. Communities *need* Woodys – just look what you did for us. We were all stagnating at home until you bucked us up. Lavender Heath's a different place, thanks to you. *We're* different, thanks to you.'

Woody shook his head.

'No, Lavender Heath's a different place thanks to Roxy!' And he turned to Roxy and smiled. 'Communities *need* Foxy Roxys. I may have got the group together, but Roxy made us a team. None of these new chances would have come about without her. I have to say it – she rocks!'

'Hear, hear,' Terence agreed and he straightened his Paul Smith shirt.

'How about *you* run for office and I'll be your campaign manager?' Roxy offered, delighted.

'What, you do the work and I get the glory?' Woody asked. 'That doesn't seem fair. No, politics is a nice idea, Cressida, but I can't see it working. Besides, half the village hates me right now. Thanks to me being "community-minded", everyone's had Fleet Street rifling through their bins.'

'Bollocks!' Roxy snorted. 'You *are* Lavender Heath.'

'Come again?'

Woody looked at her and she felt her breath get up and go somewhere else. There was no way she could tell him what she meant about him – not without spilling all the secrets of her heart. But it was too late now; the motormouth had spoken and everyone was waiting for more.

'How many clients have you lost since the Nicola Blunt piece?' she asked him.

'None.'

'And, when we tried to go to the pub, how many locals wanted to buy you a pint?'

'Quite a few,' he conceded with a nod.

'See? Nobody believed Nicola's rubbish. Face it, Woody – *people like you*.' She took a deep breath. They were only words, she told herself – nothing to be afraid of . . . Just a few important, extra little words after the millions and billions of rubbish ones she'd already spouted. 'They like the *real* you,' she told him truthfully. 'Not just the you in the vest.'

Woody looked at her, but differently this time. She could tell he was pleased, but there was something else too – something extra that flitted magically between them. For a moment she could barely breathe for its presence.

'All you'd need to do is what you're already doing,' Cressida continued. 'This village is too private. We've all spent too long hiding behind our leylandii. It's time we came together – got to know each other as neighbours.'

Woody nodded thoughtfully. And then he turned back to Roxy. 'I'll do it if Roxy does with it with me. What do you say, Rox? Fancy getting the village to party?'

'I do.' She smiled, and Cressida toasted them with her glass.

'I hear Chelle got back with Dwayne,' announced Sue.

'You're kidding?' Roxy blurted. 'Good for them!'

'And, thanks to her scoops on us, I read Nicola's up for promotion,' added Simon.

The room went quiet. It was Sue who finally broke the ice.

'What about Austin?' she asked cheerfully. 'I haven't seen him since that morning in the pub.'

'It's not the same without him,' admitted Terence. 'I actually miss the abuse.'

'He's back in LA,' Woody told them. 'Carmen's got a job interview.'

Terry snorted. 'Pull the other one. He's planning his comeback!'

'He's getting offers,' agreed Woody. 'And not just the usual rom-coms. Now the world's seen him with a belly, he's getting different stuff: cops, shell-shocked war vets, rack-and-ruin divorcees . . .'

'That'll suit him.' Simon nodded – a touch sadly. 'His talent needs to be stretched.'

'He's still adamant he won't go back to acting.'

'Shame,' mused Terence. And for once there wasn't a 'but'.

Roxy looked at Simon. He seemed down. 'No offers for you, then?' she asked gently.

He took a long sip of wine. 'It's the curse of Sick Nick. The twins are right: once a perv, always a perv.'

'Don't worry, mate.' Woody slapped his back. 'Something'll come along!'

'Yeah, shelf-stacking at Waitrose, probably. Mind you, I *do* know where everything goes.'

'There's nothing wrong with Waitrose,' said Roxy. 'I might join you there myself.'

Simon momentarily perked up. 'Didn't you get any offers either?'

Roxy laughed. 'I've had my fifteen minutes of fame and milked it for thirty. Now I'm just going to get on with my life.'

Woody turned to her and smiled. His hand touched her back, and he kept it there. Suddenly they were the only two people in the room. Roxy felt the heat of his touch surge through her, passing through her top, warming her skin – heating her down to her core.

And then Simon's phone rang. He pounced on it, as though he'd been waiting for its ring his whole life. 'Austin? Is everything OK?'

He listened intently for a minute and then hung up.

'That was Austin,' he announced in a daze. 'He's bought plane tickets for me and Linda. He needs us to visit him in LA, tonight. He says he's got an urgent proposition.'

And Simon's eyes began to glitter with excitement.

ROXY

Lit only by the light of her TV, Roxy sat in bed, drinking hot chocolate in her Wonder Woman pyjamas. She sighed. When would her mind stop its racing? She'd already put herself through the torture of *Newsnight* in an attempt to knock herself out – *and* that other politics show, with the man with the Shredded Wheat hair. She'd even endured *Camping Equipment Hour* on one of the shopping channels – all to no avail. It was nearly two in the morning and she was still nowhere near sleep.

Had she lost what was left of her marbles? she wondered as she took another slurp of hot chocolate, accidentally spilling a drop on Wonder Woman's head. She frowned and tried to blot it with her thumb. Had she spent so long chasing fantasy that she could no longer tell the difference between what she wanted and what *actually was*? Had she finally, completely lost the plot? Or had something *really* happened between her and Woody tonight? *And* up his ladder . . . ? *And* in the Dog and Duck. . . ? She could have sworn that it had! But then why was she sitting here – alone?

She sighed again, flicked the channel, and tried to be positive as she sat through the ads. There was plenty of happy stuff to think about. Right now, Simon and Linda were sitting in a first class departure lounge, bound for LA and whatever surprise Austin had got planned. Roxy grinned at the memory of Simon's face . . . If he'd been any more excited, he'd have burst. She mentally skipped the next bit, when Woody removed his hand from her back and offered to drive Simon to the airport. The evening was suddenly cut short so Simon could rush off to pack, and Roxy had scuttled home, cursing herself for ever imagining that Woody had been about to ask her to stay.

Happy stuff, Roxy reminded herself sternly.

And so she thought about Sue . . . Sue, who had the world queueing up. The job offers were coming in faster than lightning and her wardrobe was now every woman's dream. But it wasn't fame and fashion that was making Sue glow; Terry adored her – a blind man could see it. And Terry's life was turning around too.

And the good stuff didn't even end there, even Chelle was cause for a smile now. WAGs still weren't her favourite kind of people, but Roxy was chuffed that Dwayne had come home. Vile as she was, Nicola had exposed something good: Dwayne had left Chelle because he truly loved her – and it was as clear as Smirnoff that Chelle loved him back.

Roxy took another sip of hot chocolate, but then tried not to spit it out. The ad break was ending with a trailer for *This Morning*.

'*Join us on the sofa all next week for an exclusive heart-to-heart with the UK's hottest celebrity couple . . . Yes, Suzi-Sue Bunce and Tornado Terry will be our very special guests!*'

Roxy quickly swallowed before laughing out loud.

See? she thought to herself. *Life's good!*

And then she heard it: a little tap on her bedroom window. For a moment, she froze. What was it? A bird? A high-climbing cat that had got stuck? *A burglar?* And then it came again: more of a knock than a tap. Well, that ruled out the cat; cats didn't knock (no thumbs). And didn't birds sleep at night? *So that only left . . .* Without stopping to think, Roxy threw back her duvet and lunged over to the window. How ridiculous to burgle *her* house, she thought crossly in the nanosecond it took her to leap across the room. Of all the Lavender Heath houses, hers had to contain the least amount of high-value goodies (unless it was Top Shop the burglar was after, in which case he was definitely in luck). And why knock? What kind of burglar did that? It'd have to be the stupidest kind, her window was actually open, why not skip the pleasantries, jump in and get nicking? Roxy puffed out her chest and was about to give the burglar what for, when something stopped her dead in her tracks.

'Roxy,' whispered a voice. And then the knock again.

'Woody?' And she threw back the curtain and there he was – the man of her dreams, perched on a ladder at her window.

'Nice pyjamas!' He grinned.

Roxy was powerless to reply. It wasn't Woody's unexpected nocturnal appearance that was rendering her gormless – it could have been midnight New Year's Eve or midday in midsummer; she didn't care. No, it was his impossibly handsome face, his implausibly fanciable arms, his rescue-you-from-anything demeanour and his utterly irresistible pheromones that were robbing her of breath yet again. That, and the fact that, even in the dark, his eyes were still exquisitely, awesomely blue.

'I tried your phone and the door, but you didn't answer.'

'I've been watching telly,' she mumbled. Woody looked over her shoulder and smiled. She turned and and saw a middle-aged arse. *Swingers From Swindon* had started.

'What are you doing here?' she blurted. 'Where's your bucket?'

'I gave it the night off.'

'But you're supposed to be at the airport . . .'

'Been there, done that . . . I'm back.'

'But my windows aren't dirty. And it's not Thursday.'

Woody rubbed his head and looked at her in a way that made her insides turn to vodka jelly.

'You left really quickly. I was hoping you'd hang around.'

'You were?'

'I was going to ask if you'd come to the airport. We could have dropped them off and then chatted – alone.'

'We could?'

There was a moment of silence.

'Ahhh, you're not making this easy for me, Rox!' Woody laughed. 'Although, I remember you telling me you weren't.'

Roxy frowned. What was she not? *Easy?* That didn't sound

like her at all! But then she remembered her first night at Woody's, when she'd turned up expecting a date and had sassed him on his doorstep.

Woody rubbed his head again. 'Roxy, there's something I've been meaning to give you,' he said. 'Actually, I've been meaning to give it to you for a while.'

And he leant through the open window and put something into her hands. Numbly, Roxy looked down. Resting in her hands was an envelope – a card.

'But it's not my birthday.'

'I know. Just open it.'

And so she did.

Hands trembling at Woody's closeness, Roxy opened the envelope's seal and slowly slid out the card. Suddenly her heart went hyperactive.

'*It's a—*'

'Valentine's card,' he finished, with a smile.

'But it's—'

'Late?'

'. . . March!'

He grinned. 'I didn't think you'd be a stickler for the rules.'

'I'm not. I'm just . . .' Roxy looked at the card in wonder. It was the most perfect Valentine's card she could imagine: pink and funky, and with sparkles. She looked at Woody in confusion. 'But why?'

He cocked his head and looked right at her. 'Because I'm mad about you, Rox,' he said simply.

'You *are*?' Roxy could barely trust her own ears. All sorts of delicious feelings started whirling inside. 'But why now? Why give me a Valentine's card *now*?'

'I couldn't give it to you on Valentine's.' He smiled. 'You'd just yelled at me in the street for being a washed-up, hypocritical wuss!'

Roxy blushed at the memory of their argument.

'And besides,' he continued, 'I thought you and Austin were—'

'Knobbing?'

Woody nodded and laughed.

'So anyway . . .' He looked at her and something inside her ignited. 'I figured, why *shouldn't* I give you a Valentine's card in March? If you love someone, you tell them – right? You don't wait until February 14th.'

Their faces were suddenly very close and the proximity was too much to bear. He'd just said that he loved her, she told herself dizzily. *Woody had actually told her he loved her!* Suddenly she couldn't be *this* close to his skin, his lips, his amazing man-ness and not pass out. She felt literally drunk on Woody – like she'd just downed the world's most intoxicating cocktail. And then, firmly but gently, Woody put a hand around her waist and scooped the other through the back of her hair – and then he leant through the last bit of space in between them, and kissed her.

And it was *exactly* the kiss Roxy had dreamed he'd give her . . . only better – so very, very much better! As his lips fused with hers, she nearly groaned. She felt herself melt, dissolve. Suddenly she was glad he was holding her tightly. He might be the one balancing on top of a ladder, but it was she who felt like she'd fall.

'It's all right,' he whispered, as though sensing her buckle. 'I've got you.'

'I can be easy,' she told him between kisses. 'I can be very, *very* easy!'

And gently she pulled him over the sill and inside.

Fourteen months later . . .

SIMON

Simon gripped Linda's hand tightly. This was weird. Brilliant – fantastic – awesome – amazing . . . *but weird*!

He'd walked down red carpets before, but only as a minor oddity in his *Down Town* days. He'd only caused a ripple of interest at the time: a few boos from the crowd, a smattering of '*Give us a frown*'s from the paps. But this was different. The screams, the roars, the desperate begging for autographs almost made him laugh with joy. Not that he'd have heard himself do it . . . Whenever he answered a journalist's question, the cheers were so loud, he only knew he was talking because he could feel his mouth move.

Dressed in a brand new Tom Ford dinner jacket and black tie, Simon felt himself gently ushered forward. It had already taken thirty minutes and a fleet of headset-wearing PRs to get Simon just three-quarters of the way from his limo to the cinema door, and they were on a strict schedule. But, despite the ticking clock and officious PRs, Simon grinned absurdly. He, Simon Drennan, was being escorted by a public relations person. And not just one – a whole team! As much as he loved their attention, they really needn't have bothered. Their main purpose seemed to be to make sure he was charming and smiley. But, if it was up to him, he'd have personally hugged every man, woman and child in Leicester Square, before taking a note of their names and addresses and sending them all hand-written cards at Christmas.

Simon turned and looked at Linda. He'd been worried that the madness lurching just over the barrier might faze her. But his wife was smiling serenely, taking it all in her dignified stride. God, she looked beautiful tonight, he thought with a thump of emotion. Not a day had passed since they'd first met when Simon hadn't silently marvelled at his wife's gorgeousness and wondered how a hawk-nosed nobody like him had ever struck it so lucky. But Linda was beyond her normal levels of gorgeousness tonight . . . Tonight she was premiere-league dazzling. She easily outshone the Hollywood starlets posing bonily a few metres away.

And then Simon's eye was diverted.

On the other side of the barrier, a familiar-looking BBC newsreader was looking unfamiliarly frightened. Dressed in a smart suit and hard hair, the household name was overwhelmed by the animal crush. *What the hell am I doing here?* her face seemed to say. *Why couldn't they have left me behind the news desk, like normal?* But then she nervously cracked elbows with her TV-news-crew neighbour, as she did her best to stand her ground on a tiny patch of Leicester Square pavement.

'Mr Drennan!' she yelled. 'A few words for the BBC?'

She anxiously thrust forward her microphone, as much a

barrier to prevent him from passing, as a device to hear him speak. Simon could see her relief when he stopped.

'Mr Drennan, how does it feel to be Britain's hottest Hollywood export?' she asked quickly, as a dozen rival TV microphones muscled in.

Simon smiled. 'Well, I don't know that I'm that, exactly . . .'

'But critics are hailing this *the* hit movie of the summer,' she pushed. 'Did you ever expect you'd be starring in such a huge Hollywood hit?'

'It feels amazing to be starring in *any* movie – let alone one everyone's being so nice about. I keep waiting for someone to tell me it's all been a mistake – that they meant to book Colin Firth, and he's turned up now and I have to go home.'

'Could you tell us what first drew you to the role of the hero, Jake Love?'

'In two words – *Austin Jones!*' Simon smiled. 'When he told me he'd bought the rights to Holly Childs' new novel and that he was going to produce the movie, well . . . I just thought he was offering me a support role: second party-goer, third taxi-driver, or something like that. But when he offered me the lead, my wife had to scrape me up off the floor.'

'And what are your plans now? Are you going to stay in the UK, or is Hollywood calling?'

Simon started to answer, but the BBC's time was up. The PRs swept him along, away from the TV mics, to where the photographers were waiting. Simon looked at Linda, who beamed him a smile of encouragement before letting go of his hand and standing aside with Carmen.

Simon stepped up to his spot where Austin was already waiting, suited and booted in a dinner jacket.

'Downton!' Austin greeted him with a bear hug. Flashes popped like fireworks around them.

'Your stomach's gone!' Simon shouted over the noise as Austin finally released him.

'Man Spanx.' He grinned, slapping his stomach. 'Couldn't have my belly upstaging your big moment.'

The two men posed for the cameras, then Austin slapped him on the back.

'Milk it,' he said in Simon's ear.

'But this is absurd!' Simon laughed incredulously at the bank of flashlights that looked more Vegas than WC2.

'Milk this fame bitch to within an inch of her life,' Austin instructed. 'See you inside.'

And he left.

And Simon faced the photographers alone.

And, to his astonishment, the fireworks didn't diminish. If anything, the lights only grew brighter. Simon stood stock-still in amazement as wave after wave of flashbulb heat enveloped him, and the whole world dissolved into a haze of euphoric, loved-up white. This was it; fame at last! And *Christ*, it felt *INCREDIBLE*. He soaked it all up and breathed it all in, turning from left to right and back again, so the photographers could get the shots they craved. And still the clamouring continued. Simon posed and smiled, and smiled and posed. He posed until the flashes burned his retinas. He smiled until his muscles went stiff.

'Right, that's it, boys!' cut in one of the PRs. 'Mr Drennan has his premiere to go to.'

The photographers put down their cameras and became human.

'Good luck, mate!' a few of them called.

'Yeah, good on ya, Simon. Well done!'

'Thanks. Thanks a lot.' Simon was touched by their good will. But already the PRs had swept him away and suddenly the noise and mayhem of the red carpet dimmed, and Simon found himself in the harbour of the Odeon foyer.

'Here he is: the man of the moment!' Woody cheered, and his friends flocked around him with hugs. All of the Lavender Heath mob were there; even the twins were lurking by the confectionery, looking considerably more smiley than normal.

'You rocked!' cried Roxy, a ravishing brunette these days. She beamed at him happily, Woody's arm wrapped snugly around her waist.

'How would you know?' Simon laughed. 'You two sneaked in the back door.'

'We could hear the cheers from the pub.' Roxy grinned.

Austin looked cross. 'You've been to the pub?'

'To toast your success with tequila,' she protested.

'What can I say?' Woody shrugged. 'She's a bad influence on legs.'

'Fuck, tequila sounds good,' Austin lamented. 'I can't believe I wasn't invited.'

'You were busy.' Woody laughed. 'Sucking in your gut and doing executive-producer-type things.'

'Needs must,' Austin agreed, disappointed.

'Oh, I don't know,' countered Cressida. 'I quite enjoyed my turn on the red carpet.'

'You were brilliant, Cress,' squealed Chelle. 'Looked like you were born for stardom, didn't she, Dwayne?'

Dwayne obediently agreed.

'That's ridiculous,' Cressida protested. 'I merely put one foot before the other until I arrived at the destination. All I'm saying is, as experiences go, that one was more pleasant than expected.'

'Oh, shut up, Cress; you were lovin' it! You even bollocked the snappers for being too loud. 'Ere, did you get that bit?' Chelle turned to a film crew nearby. 'Me being friends with a politician? They're from Sky Living,' she explained. 'They're following me and Dwayne round for a new reality TV show. Mental, isn't it? Come on,' she instructed the crew. 'Wanna film us finding our seats?'

'Well done, Simon.' Sue gave him a hug as Chelle and her film crew disappeared into the stalls. 'We all knew you'd crack Hollywood one day.'

'You did?' Simon laughed in surprise. 'Well, you knew more than me.'

'It was obvious,' Woody agreed. 'You just needed a lucky break.'

'All good things come to those who wait,' added Cressida.

'Yeah, well, I could have done with a lot less waiting.'

'And miss out on meeting us lot?' Roxy asked. 'Rock off! I reckon fame found you at just the right time.'

'Yeah, Si,' Austin heckled. 'I mean, who'd want all those loose-knickered starlets cluttering up your twenties?'

'Mr Jones?' A PR lady hovered at his elbow.

'Uh-oh.' Austin rolled his eyes.

'Sorry to interrupt, but there's a woman outside, demanding to be let in. She says she's a journalist; a friend of yours—'

'Unlikely.'

'I don't think she's going to take no for an answer. She's being quite insistent with the security team. Actually, she's being quite threatening.'

'Nicola,' Cressida sighed.

'Nicola? Are you sure?' Sue asked in surprise. 'Surely she wouldn't dare.'

'Wanna bet?' Terence replied. 'The woman's shame-free.'

'Quite sure. I saw her when I was walking down the red carpet. She was kicking up a fuss because she didn't have the right pass. She was trying to pretend we were friends.'

'Shit!' For the first time in a year, Simon's smile faded. 'But doesn't she *have* to come in? I mean, she *is* from the *Sunday Post*, after all.'

'*Sunday Post*?' The PR paled like a ghost. 'Oh my God! We didn't realise . . . I mean, she's always just a silhouette. I'm so sorry, Mr Jones; I'll go and let her in immediately.'

'Leave her *exactly* where she is!'

'But . . . ?' The PR looked perplexed.

'But . . . ?' Simon looked scared.

'But what?' shrugged Austin with a grin. 'Fuck her; she can

stay outside with the tramps. You, Simon Drennan, are a movie star! You don't have to talk to shits like Nicola Blunt.'

Simon looked embarrassed. 'But I don't want to be rude—'

'I'll do it – I *love* being rude!'

'Gentlemen, *please!*' Roxy interrupted sternly. 'Before you get your kecks in a twist, here's a little something I prepared earlier.' And she dipped into her sparkly handbag and brought out an empty, scrunched-up beer can.

Everyone stared for a moment. And then Austin snorted a laugh.

'Is that Special Brew?' The PR wrinkled her nose. 'Did you actually drink that?'

'Only the best for our Nicola,' Roxy grinned, handing the can to Woody. And then she dipped into her handbag again and pulled out a ribbon strung through a card. She tied it around the can with a bow. And then she returned to her handbag once more, plucked out a red lipstick and flawlessly applied it to her lips.

'Amazeballs,' Cressida marvelled.

'You did that without using a mirror!' exclaimed Sue.

Roxy planted a huge, scarlet kiss on the card.

'Please give this to Miss Blunt as our answer.' And she passed the beer can to the PR. Everyone leant forward to read the inscription: 'To Nicola. Love from the bunch of no-lifes', and then Roxy's scarlet kiss mark.

'God, I love you, Rox.' Woody kissed her fiercely. 'As eloquent as an *Oxford English* – as straight to the point as *Viz*!'

Roxy beamed back at him with undisguised pride.

Austin turned to the dumbstruck PR.

'Go on; you heard her. Give it to Nicola.'

The PR looked nervous.

'But Mr Jones, are you sure? I mean, this *is* Nicola Blunt we're talking about.'

Austin turned to the group, his eyes twinkling with mischief. Something silent communicated between them. 'Absofucking-lutely,' he declared. 'Right, no-lifes?'

'Right!' everyone replied together.

And, giggling, they all turned – arm in arm – and disappeared into the auditorium for Simon's big moment; a disparate bunch of *used-to-be*s . . . an inseparable group of friends.

Simon Drennan and his family moved to LA, where he is currently filming a rom-com penned by the legendary Richard Curtis.

He remains a frequent professional collaborator and close personal friend of the movie-star-turned-executive-producer, Austin Jones.

Sue Bunce and Terence Leggett came second and fifth in the latest series of *I'm A Celebrity . . . Get Me Out Of Here!* and, upon leaving the jungle, were offered their own daytime TV chat show.

Sue's autobiography, *Suga-Coated*, reached number one in the *Sunday Times* best-seller chart.

Terence's new series, written by and co-starring Ricky Gervais and Stephen Merchant, premieres on BBC1 next week.

Sue and Terrence got married last May.

Chelle and Dwayne Blowers remain reunited.

They are the proud owners of a chinchilla, Chanel.

Cressida Cunningham refused Simon Cowell's offer to be a judge on *Britain's Got Talent*.

She runs an online advice service for youth enterprise and gives extra tuition to local school children, free of charge.

She remains the *Daily Telegraph*'s agony aunt.

After months of requests, Carmen Bonitta eventually agreed to marry Austin Jones. Simon and Woody are said to be organising the stag night, fitting it around Austin's numerous production commitments.

Austin still, on occasion, shoots paparazzi with beer.

Nicola Blunt's career continues to rise.

She is currently being headhunted by two major US news networks.

Woody and Roxy married in Lavender Heath in June.

It was a quiet ceremony, with only family and close friends in attendance. They did not sell their photographs to a high-profile magazine, but instead posed happily on the steps of the Dog and Duck pub. They are expecting their first child in the autumn – a girl.

Despite her growing bump, Roxy is often seen hurtling around the village, rushing to the aid of women facing a styling emergency or crisis in confidence. She has opened a tea shop, serving award-winning, vegetable-based cakes from behind the cleanest windows in Lavender Heath.

Woody continues to clean windows.

He hasn't been flashed at in a very long time.

THE END

From: Charlotte Van Wijk (Quercus Publishing)
To: Nicola Budd (Quercus Publishing)

Nicola

Roxy Squires has been in touch again (see below). Please can you let her down gently?

Thanks
C

——
————————-

From: Roxy Squires
To: Charlotte Van Wijk (Quercus Publishing)

Hey Quercus people

It's me again – Foxy Roxy Squires! Look, I know you said no to my book idea, *1001 Ways To Party (& Still Be At Work By 9)*, but I'm telling you – you're making a serious mistake. It's got stocking-filler written all over it. I'm talking an A–Z on living large and not getting fired – a handbook for the modern age!

Anyway, I thought I'd give you a second chance before another publisher snaps it up . . . so here are a few extracts to tempt you . . .

Rox x
☺

*If you fancy a Big Night Out the night before a big day in the office —
don't worry. You can have your party cake and eat it. Here are my tips
on how . . .*

Prepare, prepare, prepare

Before a big night on the sauce, you need to line your stomach.
Marathon runners prepare for a race with pasta, but I'd rather leg it 26
miles than self-carb. Common wisdom recommends milk, but I find
cream-based cocktails work just as well. White Russians do the trick . . .
two large ones, around 6 o'clock.

Think trotters

If you're already loved-up, or are in steady, civilian employment, you
might feel able to party without heels. Trainers are a clubber's best
friend and help avoid next-day 'broken feet'. But flatties aren't an option
for celebs. For anyone on the right side of the camera, don't even think
about less than 5 inches. Just remember to botox your trotters first.

Don't forget your toothbrush

You've got a lot to fit into that handbag, so pay attention. Sunglasses? Check. Toothbrush & gum? Check. Brand new supplies of make-up? Check. You'll need all this in the morning, so check again.

Put in the flirtatious groundwork

You never know when you'll be needing a favour from the office security guard, so make sure you give him a cheeky wink on your way out.

OK, so now you're partying. Don't forget to party hard!

No wimping

Worried about oversleeping for that big day in the office? The solution's easy – *don't sleep*! Sleep's for amateurs, and no excuse to cut short a top night. Just samba straight from the club to the office – some of my best work's been done pissed.

Office sleepover

If you *do* feel the need for a nap, go to bed in the office. Keep a duvet under your desk, just in case. Never mind the office mice (every office has them) — just smile at that nice security man again, flash him your pass (or anything else you think might work) and then head to your desk to power down. You can snooze safe in the knowledge that if you're already early, it's totally impossible to be late.

Pull

It's the ultimate win-win no brainer. Long way home to bed? Pull someone who lives close to the office, and catch a few zzz's at his place instead. It's office-promptness/stringless-intercourse double-bubble. And hey, you rock — *you deserve it!*

Pull a doctor

You get extra points for pulling a doctor (preferably one with a drip). After shagging him senseless, sweet-talk him into hooking you up to an IV. A couple of hours on the fluid bag, and you'll be perkier than a *Blue Peter* presenter.

Pull a fighter pilot

If no doctors are available, pull a fighter pilot and ask to have sex in his jet. Jets come with oxygen masks, and a few hits of oxygen have the same effect as a few hours on a drip. Plus, you get to indulge in a few *Top Gun* fantasies . . .

Reapply slap

So you've made it into the office — now your packing comes in handy. You need to bury your 40% sheen ahead of that big meeting. Open your make-up and apply with a trowel. Who cares if you look like a tranny? Think quantity rather than quality, and add an extra layer every hour.

Brush your teeth with Red Bull

As they say . . . *every little helps.* And your gums might absorb the caffeine.

Pop in gum

Not only does it mask beer breath, but the chewing action stops you nodding off.

Rearrange Cleavage

Make sure your friends are on show – they'll divert attention from your party eyes. Alternatively, an illegally short skirt will do fine.

Administer Coffee

I recommend a double Irish.

Switch on Tens Machine

OK, so these are normally used during childbirth, but did you know that Tens machines can be worn under clothing, and give small, but regular, electric shocks? Perfect for keeping you awake! Buy one, or rent one from Boots. I always book ahead and reserve one for the Christmas party season.

© Roxy Squires

You can follow Roxy on Twitter
@foxyroxysquires

THANK YOU!

Thank-you to Mum, Dad and Nige, for your sterling services to babysitting, and unstinting dedication to shamelessly plugging my books!

Thanks also to Jos, Nicky and Sevenoaks Bookshop – plus Charlotte, Nicola, Maggie, Sarah and all at Quercus and Ed Victor for the clever stuff.

Thank you to everyone who asks me how the writing is going, and gives me a thumbs-up of encouragement along the way. And thanks to Mr Pinot and his friend, Mr Grigio – plus Mrs Galaxy, Mary Landcookie and Miss Yorkshire Tea – without whom this book would never have got written.

Finally – thank you to all the 90s ladettes. You rock! I loved – and wanted to be – you all!

Alice Brown's Lessons in the Curious Art of Dating

Eleanor Prescott

Alice Brown is a matchmaker, and as far as she's concerned, she has the best job in the world. What could be better than helping others find love? Even if she herself remains single.

Her latest client is Kate. She's already five years behind in her life plan and she knows exactly what she wants, but that might be the problem. Will anyone measure up to her standards?

Then there's Audrey, Alice's misguided boss from hell, who has somehow managed to bag herself the perfect husband. But all is not as it seems. And when her love life and work life collide, will she be able to take her own advice?

Quercus

www.quercusbooks.co.uk